NOT REALLY

NOT REALLY

STEFAN EBERHARD

To everyone who tried to push me down.
Thank you.

1

IMAGINE YOU WERE GOD

IMAGINE YOU WERE GOD. Would you like your world to be perfect, or would you let it run totally on its own? Make no mistake: the consequences of your decision are difficult to grasp in their entirety. Let's assume you take the more obvious route and pour out endless love and well-being on your creation. It would be a peaceful existence, where everything was focused on the good. Science had all the answers, and uncertainty would be unheard of. The bad would exist, but only for contrast. People would use a standardized truth, and everybody had free food and do as they pleased. Love, peace, happiness, and freedom. Does that sound like paradise to you? Isn't that the perfect solution? But what might happen if you created the world on a less productive day, or if you experimented to change things up a bit? Maybe you could ask yourself what humans do on an empty stomach or how they react to desperation and turmoil. Will they be able to adapt and survive on their own? Although logical thinking and science are great, people would be drawn to other sources of information as well. When the world was hostile and uncertain, humans would look everywhere to find the truth, not just in one place. Magical thinking and searching for patterns could inform creative solutions and would be more productive. If everybody knows something and nobody has all the answers, there is no other way than inquiring until things work. This scenario wouldn't be as perfect, and people would have to figure stuff out all by themselves. Life would be chaotic and order a rare event. Some things would function—however, only in a raw and incomplete state. But why stop there? Universal uncertainty brings all kinds of issues with it. The truth would be malleable and people couldn't talk to each other in a congruent way, because every individual would have their own map of the world. And although they would likely get along somehow, it wouldn't be as productive as before. That would result in a uniquely creative lifestyle, but it also came with a price. These people would have to live in a strange world, full of odd and mysterious things, just to be able to look at paintings and listen to music. Art would quicken their souls; suffering would come with it, though. Have you made up your mind yet? Let's go back to the first one. How will they develop a culture and move forward in life? You showered them with the good stuff already, but now they won't move the slightest bit. Why? Because they have everything and live in complete peace and harmony. They are also omniscient, which is a little bit boring and would render you obsolete as a god, but this won't be such a big problem at first. Later, on the other hand, there will be no religion and spirituality, which is a major factor for connecting humanity through ritual and celebration. Perfection will break down often, and you will have to intervene frequently to keep them in the blissed-out state you originally made them to be in. Forcing more and more goodness into them to satisfy their ultra-high standards, which they had become so accustomed to. And after a while, you may decide for a totalitarian government with vast coercive machinery to make them happy no matter what. Or even better: you might sneak in through the back door and manipulate their entertainment. Administration would be easy and fun. But some people might still become judgmental toward others, since your world has only one truth, and all of them would perceive it differently. As a result, they'd try to force their truth on everybody else as well. If everyone thinks they know the truth and nobody would ever admit to being wrong, there would be a lot of disagreements. This might even cause a silly war on who's right. A miserable and self-destructing fight to defend the truth against everyone else. It would be all against all, but as a public-spirited god with highly magnanimous idealism, you would care for all of your creation equally, right? Seems like you're in trouble now. You don't want to love them to death, do you? But the answer may be simple. Since this is going nowhere without something to make them crave for a better future, we will make it happen by conducting the world in a less perfect way. We will invent a problem here and there to keep them moving. Demanding as little as possible but as much as needed, since they're still your creation and words cannot describe how much you love them. Or we leave them to their fate...

"What a stupid idea."

Gordon puts the book down and looks around anxiously. It's rather quiet in the bookstore, so safety first. The Japanese can't stand making a fuss in public, and foreigners always stand out. He's normally always switched on and mindful of his surroundings. Feeling a little embarrassed, but totally upset at the same time, he begins to think.

You can have it all. Why not? Guy is a jerk. If I would be god, I would make it happen. Everyone deserves a good life. Suffering is not how it's done. Forget all these shitty problems. Let's have a party. Endless beer, hammocks, and no work. I'm much more intelligent than all these amateurs.

Gordon makes an accomplished face at the store ceiling.

Don't overdo it, though. Maybe the guy is not as stupid as you think. Why move at all? Would you do something? Would you? Rather not. What if it's fun? What's fun anyway? Isn't it better to have success? Success is fun, but I also have to go for it. Work is definitely no fun. Being a CEO. That's it. Not doing much and getting all the cash. Damn. You know quite well that CEOs work their asses off.

He decides to call Steve a little later to ask him what he thinks of this mess. He's an expert with this complicated philosophical and spiritual stuff and most certainly knows how to dissolve the conflict.

Gordon leaves the bookstore and takes a walk to get something to eat at one of his favorite ramen shops. Tokyo is full of them, and he loves all different kinds of noodle soups and street food. There's just so much to discover and explore. It never gets boring. But a longer stroll will have to wait until next time. Today, it's Tonkatsu Ramen from the corner shop on the way home. Their broth is simply the best, and he's also very curious for Steve's take on the god problem.

■ ■ ■

He throws his keys into the bowl next to the little shoe cabinet. His small flat near Hiroo Station isn't famous for comfort, but the neighborhood is one of the most expensive in Tokyo. He lives in walking distance from his job at an international supermarket, and even though rent is hardly affordable for a middle manager like Gordon, he refuses to move. Instead, he's trying to negotiate with his boss for a higher wage for more than three months now. At least it's a paradise for food enthusiasts. He opens a beer and unpacks the food to devour it instantly. He sinks into the couch and starts to eat while TV and funny videos run in the background. The TV shows in Japan are ridiculous. Endless talking heads on every channel, telling audiences what to think and how to react. It's all totally positive, and it feels fake and obviously staged compared to American or European TV shows. Everything is incredible and delicious; awful sound effects populate the background, and superfluous text is plastered all over the screen. But Gordon got used to it over the years and even enjoys it from time to time. Three minutes later, he's rummaging through his fridge in the hopes of finding a custard pudding. They were perfect with a sip of beer and a nice movie. Especially after a bowl of ramen. He's surprised and delighted to find two of them in the vegetable compartment and inhales one instantly, while searching the fridge. As he sits down to eat the second, the phone rings.

"Hello."

"Hey, Gordo, how are you?"

"All right, I guess."

"Why? What happened? Are you still thinking about that girl?"

Mentioning Linda bothers him.

"Stop it, please."

Steve is smelling something.

"Calm down. Everything is okay. What is it?"

"Well, I just finished my dinner, and believe it or not, I wanted to call you right now."

He talks slowly as always.

"Great, I guess you need guidance from a friend?"

Gordon sighs audibly.

"How do you know?"

"Are you joking? You're always brewing something up in your head."

"Stop knowing me so well."

He starts explaining the god problem and tries to be as equitable as possible, because he wants to know what Steve makes of it, without him coloring the matter beforehand.

"So what do you think?"

"Looks like a great problem to discuss over a few beers."

Gordon slouches into the couch.

"Totally. Just tell me your first impression. I'm sure this is going to haunt me over the next days, so it would be great if you had a little clue for me."

Steve's eyes go into infinity mode. It seems like an interesting problem, but he primarily tries to find an answer to help his friend.

"Steve, are you still there?"

"Yes. Of course. Just let me think about it for a second."

Gordon plays with his empty beer can.

"Let's look at it from the side of the people. The perfect world had unlimited resources and certainty, but no diversity. The chaotic world had unlimited diversity, but total uncertainty. I have to say this is a no-brainer for me, and I'm truly disappointed you even thought about living in so-called heaven."

"Why are you saying that? I tried to be as neutral as possible."

Steve changes to a more serious voice.

"Of course you did. Of course. You. Did. Let me put it this way: I would want to live in hell any day, as long as it's full of color and creativity. Not to mention your heaven is inhabited by atheists. And even though I'm a Buddhist and god is not as important in our worldview, as compared to a more Christian-oriented belief system, I think the notion of something greater is needed to live a rich human life."

He tenses his slouching posture a bit. It baffles him that Steve was rigorous like that.

"There must be a way to have it both. I'm sure the guy was missing something. We can find solutions for heaven, if we think hard enough. I'm not saying it's perfect as it is, but it could be."

"Why are we doing this all the time? Don't you have more important problems?"

The discussion is canceled. He sinks back into the couch.

"Yeah, whatever. Maybe you're right, but this is not the end. Let's go for beer next Saturday. I'm not working on Sunday, and we could grab a few beers or even a few more and talk this through."

Steve gets more cheerful.

"Why not, sounds fun. Is Peter coming as well?"

"I don't know, but I'm going to ask him. I'll let you know."

"Great, looking forward to seeing you, Gordon. Now tell me about that girl."

"Man, would you leave me alone with her?"

"Of course not. Of. Course. Not. We both know you're desperate for a girlfriend. Don't be afraid."

Gordon twists his face.

"All right. I'm going to ask her for a date, but I'll need a drink to get in the mood first."

"Great. You should also wear that navy-blue shirt. Looks way better on you than these polos."

"What's wrong with my polos?"

"Nothing. Trust me, the shirt looks better. "

"All right. See you on Saturday."

"See you."

Gordon opens another beer and watches the cheerleading championship over satellite. Everything would be fine, if he didn't promise to ask her out. Steve will insist. The light of Tokyo illuminates his room as he stares at the ceiling with wide-open eyes.

Do I really want her? Enough? Is it right to ask her out? It's most likely a no anyway. I knew it. Fuck. I'm killing myself, if she says no. She is quirky and says stuff only I can understand. Maybe not, but it feels that way. It really feels that way. And those tits. If I do right, we might have a kid or something. But she won't be a good mother. I want kids. But freedom is also important. Your life will be hell for at least three years. Steve says it's the best thing that ever happened to him. But he's still drinking. Damn, what now? Calm down and make a plan. Or ask Peter. Yeah, Peter.

It is going to be a long night.

2
AN ORDINARY DAY

GORDON BARELY CLOSED HIS eyes, but the alarm clock screams louder and louder. He is late as usual and stuffs himself with a banana and some chocolate. His mouth is bursting with food as he leaves his flat to run with all he's got. Coming in late wasn't a good idea, since he wanted to fight for more money.

There was a time, when he was fitter, but now he is sweating and gasping for air. To his surprise, he arrives prompt, and his boss is nowhere to be seen. Slowly gaining back his breath, he passes Jade, who is shelving instant food in aisle three. His heart rate slows down as he gets to the office. A small table between toilet paper and a variety of dental products in the storeroom. He sits down and looks busy right away, since this is the gold standard to get a promotion. He opens the KPI file and is highly irritated, since someone must have changed it for the worse or, even more shitty, he made a mistake.

Not now. Temperature and BBD check. Where's Jade?

He gets up from his chair and heads to aisle three, but Jade was already done with the noodles.

Maybe outside?

He finally finds her at the hot food counter.

"Morning, Jade. How is it going?"

"Thanks, I already stuffed the noodle shelf, and now I'm preparing some more fried chicken. We had a shortage yesterday and a customer got very angry at me."

"Are you okay?"

"Mason popped like a balloon in a volcano."

"No good."

"He said you forgot to order and he wants to talk to you."

His head turns red.

"What, no. Is he free today by any chance?"

"He's in a meeting and might come in later. The chicken is sorted, by the way. Quite lucky for you, Mason managed to get some fresh stock for today."

Gordon's face relaxes.

"That's good. Please check the temperatures of the cooling and the BBDs. Do you still have the list?"

"Yes."

Gordon feels exhausted but tries to keep posture.

"One more thing. Did you change the KPI for some reason?"

"Why would I? What's wrong?"

"Never mind. Please get back to me, when you're done. Thank you."

"Done."

Going back to his table, he's playing back everything he can remember.

That's a lot. How can it be so totally wrong. Stupid idiot. You'll never be a top level manager. Shit.

Gordon's shoulders sink toward the computer. He opens the data files and tries to find the error. As he is about to cry after many hours of cluelessness, he finally realizes he looked at the wrong month.

Damn. The average transaction value is fine. I'm a failure.

The pressure slowly fades. Jade knocks on a box of toothpaste to get his attention.

"Tough day, Mr. Fitch?"

Piss off.

"Not at all, I just corrected the mistake and…"

"What was it?"

Gordon takes on his middle manager tone.

"Are you done with the dates?"

"Yes. Can I ask you something?"

He gets even more authoritative.

"Did you check all of the yogurt labels? They were from three different orders, and we really need to watch the BBDs. If you're not completely sure, please take another look."

Jade shakes her head.

"They're fine, and the temperatures are in the accepted range. I'm not going to check again."

"Well, better check twice. But it's all right. Thank you."

"No problem."

"What was the question?"

She changes to a more feminine demeanor and tilts her head slightly to the side.

"I'm a little bit worried about you. I mean, you look like you didn't sleep for days, and you gained a lot of weight over the last few months. Maybe you need to unwind a bit or something. I can't remember when you last took some time off."

He sees a spark of compassion in her eyes.

"What was the question again?"

"Gordon?"

"Okay, okay, I'm working a lot lately, but I need this promotion, and you know quite well that Mason never goes on vacation at all."

She prods his belly.

"I know, but it seems you're trying to make up for it by eating. Do you?"

He protects his belly fat with a windshield gesture.

"Well, I think this is my problem. Not yours. What do you want from me?"

"Can I tell you the truth? I want you to take better care of yourself. You will ruin your life if you don't stop. You're also hung over almost every day. Good thing your table is right next to the dental supply. It comes in handy to overturn the awful smell of stale beer you carry with you in the morning."

Gordon bends his arms to show both of his palms.

"Really? I didn't know that."

"Do you think it's a mystery, why he doesn't grant you the promotion? We both know drinking is the norm here and that we have to attend *nomikai* to avoid insulting the company. This is Japan after all. However, what you're pulling off is just crazy. I'm sorry to be frank like that, but I'm concerned about you, and we're working together for a long time, so I thought I'd bring it up."

What a shitty day.

"Maybe you're right and I should indeed take better care of myself, but I can assure you, everything we do at nomikai is forgotten the next day, as long as we come to work. Thank you for being honest with me, though. Please check the hot food counter. The first lunch customers will be here shortly."

"Done."

Jade turns around and quickly vanishes behind the potato chips.

At rush hour, Gordon helps Jade and makes sure to avoid shortages. After lunch, he is sitting at his desk as an email from Mason arrives. The annual metabo checkup is today. A doctor will carry out a general health check and measure waistlines. He just turned forty, so he had to attend.

Idiot, no calendar entry. Sloppy, truly sloppy, Gordon. This will cause problems.

The doctor arrives and swiftly unpacks his bag. He closes the door of the storage room and asks him to take off his shirt. Gordon is rather tall at 188 centimeters. He has short, parted blond hair.

His shoulders normally make up for a little excess weight and his legs never had an issue. But now, his middle part hangs all over his pants as he tries to suck in everything he can.

After examining him thoroughly, the doctor looks at his tape measure and is obviously disappointed.

"You have become a big face. I remember you from last year. I didn't measure you, but I thought you were in okay shape. Now what have you done? One hundred two centimeters is way too much. The waistline circumference limit is eighty-five centimeters. Can you see the problem, and more importantly, do you enjoy dancing?"

Gordon is shocked.

"What do you mean by dancing?"

The doctor looks at his belly and then in his eyes.

"Your employer is offering weekly dancing classes to meet the annual required company standards. As far as I know, they offer a dancing course and a gymnastics course. I suppose you'll be a dancer."

"What, no. Is that really necessary? I'm going to lose the weight. I promise."

He writes down the results and ticks a few boxes on a document.

"Ask your boss. I'm here to take measurements and make recommendations. What you'll have to do in the end is up to your employer."

Worst day ever.

"Okay, thanks."

"I'll be checking on you over the next three months. Your boss will give you the dates. Please be sure to work on these days and try to lose some weight. The ladies would be pleased as well."

"All right. Thank you for coming. I need to get some work done now."

"No worries."

Gordon puts his shirt back on. The doctor leaves to examine the other employees in the break room.

Fuck. This is torture. Move more. Eat less. No beer. I hate my life.

■ ■ ■

Later in the afternoon, he changes supermarkets to shop for groceries. At least a bottle of vodka and maybe some dry wine, since these are more acceptable on a low carb diet. Normally, he would buy everything from his market, but Jade left an impression on him, and he wanted to avoid her seeing all the alcohol. Hard liquor is also less expensive in Japanese stores, which is a plus. After a lengthy wait at the checkout line, he finally gets to pay and heads straight to the subway. Hiroo is only one stop ahead, and he thinks about carrying everything home by foot, but then he changes his mind.

As he arrives at his apartment building, Gordon is grasping for air again. Tired from a few steps.

Need wine.

He opens both, the vodka and the wine, and immediately pulls down his first shot. Pouring a glass of Riesling, TV and laptop come to life as usual. The oven is getting hot, and a lasagna is waiting for him.

Peter…vodka makes me tipsy.

Peter takes the call five seconds after he pushed the button.

"Hi, Peter. Long time no hear."

"Gordon! Glad to hear you now. What's up?"

He spits out a pointy laugh and takes a sip.

"I'm looking for a wing man on Saturday and you're my first pick. Are you excited?"

"Already drinking, huh? I can hear your greediness through the phone, mate. Anything special?"

He chuckles and takes an even bigger sip.

"I'm going to ask a girl out, and I need your help. I'm totally shit at this."

"I see. Sounds like the full Monty. Will Steve be there?"

"Yeah. He was asking for you as well. I'm also going to lose some weight in the coming weeks. Should we wait to increase my chances?"

Peter bounces up and down.

"Haha, what chances? The only reason she'll agree is because of me. Remember, your big face is not going to change that much."

"You're the second person saying this today. This must be a conspiracy."

"No, it's more like 'Welcome to Japan.' Where do we go?"

Gordon takes a second to imagine the subway map.

"Shibuya. She's working at…"

Peter interrupts him sharply.

"Maybe we can go to Roppongi first to get a few shots, eat a bite, and then visit the love of your life?"

"Slow there, Peter. Don't rush it. I'm just dipping my toes in, no more. Roppongi is great, though."

"Perfect, let's do Roppongi Station."

"Where exactly?"

"Your OCD isn't getting any better, is it?"

Asshole.

"Well, that's not fair. It's a big station."

"The exit right at the tower."

He is slurping his wine.

"Inside or outside the station?"

Peter bounces left and right.

"Outside. Write it down."

"Got it, outside then. Really excited. It's been a long time since I played the game."

"Don't worry, mate. I will personally drag you there and open your mouth with a forklift."

"I doubt it was a good idea to appoint you my wingman."

"Listen. Don't make it more complicated than it is. You will succeed like a boss. It'll be a doddle."

"All right. Roppongi Station at eight?"

"Fine, let's do eight."

"Cool."

Gordon throws the phone gently into a couch pillow, unmutes the TV, and proceeds to drink vodka. The lasagna tastes way below average but is very heavy and filling.

That's it. Okay, Saturday, but no more beer.

3

AT THE BAR

GORDON WAS WAITING AT the station exit for thirty minutes, but he was tempted to take a few more sips of vodka, and it could have ended in disaster, so he was content to look at his phone for now. Roppongi district offers a nice mix of expats, tourists, and Japanese alike. People drink, gamble, and indulge in all kinds of debauchery here. Gordon and his friends enjoy the spirit of the place, although they had some trouble with the Nigerian mafia once; however, it wasn't a big deal.

A perfectly groomed guy is jumping up the stairs like a stubby rubber ball to poke him. Gordon reacts with a microscare and quickly turns around. Peter aims for a false hug and gesticulates far and wide.

"Fuck me. You look like an absolute winner today. Are you ready, mate?"

He's still a little shocked but then salutes.

"Ready to attack, Captain."

"Fantastic, let's go to the Shotbar for a drink first. Have you eaten already?"

"No. I was thinking we could get something from a street vendor."

"Where's Steve?"

"He's coming a little later to the Shotbar."

"Perfect."

Peter throws his arm on Gordon's shoulder. The Shotbar is in walking distance. A rather small, but charming, place. The booze is reasonably priced for Roppongi standards, and it quickly became the go to. Despite some strange experiences and nights out nobody remembers, they managed to keep the right to drink there nonetheless. Approaching the entrance, they both get excited for the first hit, and Peter loosens his grip to jump in quick succession toward the door. Inside, they order beer and sake.

Nice and slow; you have to deliver tonight.

The small glasses clink loudly.

"Cheers, Captain."

"Cheers, mate."

Peter gets his voice back first.

"It's been a while. Care for an update?"

He never knows what to say at this point. Peter is as successful as a man can be. Comanaging a high class lawyer's firm and swimming in money. At least from the perspective of an assistant manager in a grocery store. Peter is also the only one fluent in Japanese, whereas most of Gordon's friends work at English-speaking companies. They almost exclusively drink at Roppongi, because foreigners are the norm here, and a lack of language skills is less of a problem. Gordon is able to express himself, but as a middle manager, he could be better at Japanese since he wouldn't last long in a serious discussion.

"Not sure. What do you want to know?"

"Matey, stop spreading low vibes. Get your act together and give me the facts."

Gordon pours half of his beer down.

"Well, I'm going to become the first foreign senior manager. Did I tell you about Mason? I'm talking to him for a promotion in the near future. That's also the reason I'm going to lose weight. I'll get my act together, and with a great job, I also need a proper woman. Right?"

"Wow. It seems the sake is already kicking in, mate. But cool, you're going for it. I'm all for working your way up from the bottom. I once started as a bouncer in Shibuya."

He looks at Peter in utter disbelief.

"Yeah, I think you told us this story only about a hundred times already. But go ahead. There might be a nuance somewhere I didn't fully appreciate up until now."

"Fine. I have another thing coming up anyway."

"What is it?"

"I'm going to open up my own business in a few weeks. The current company is great, but now is the time for my own thing. I'm getting tired of discussing with my partners. In other words, I'm ready to destroy the competition."

Gordon nods with a smile.

"Congrats; I might come to work with you, if you're interested. I'm great with numbers."

"Hell yeah. Why not. You could work as a receptionist or office assistant. That would be great."

His eyes are pinned onto the floor.

"What, no. I thought of something a little bit more interesting. I'm already managing my people at the grocery store, so…"

Peter heightens his voice.

"Whatever. We are not here to talk work. Let's party. What's the plan?"

Gordon is slightly irritated by the abrupt cutoff but takes a quick sip and switches quite easily.

"All right, I'm going for my woman tonight, and I'm motivated and ready to conquer the world."

Steve enters the bar. He's wearing a loose white shirt, black glasses, and a peaceful face.

"Looks like my timing is just right."

Peter jumps with excitement, and Gordon is expecting a hug.

"Pleasure to see you, mate."

Steve grants Gordon his hug.

"Same here."

Peter orders another beer and sake round. The bar reverberates as the shot glasses clink together.

Not too fast, keep it slow. No more sake.

Gordon shakes off the alcohol.

"Well, I was just telling Peter my plan for tonight."

Steve smiles.

"Great. So you're asking her out tonight?"

"I can see our date already. We will meet at a nice Italian restaurant and order pizza. Linda will wear a knee-long dress and pinned-up hair. She'll look irresistible, and I'll be the happiest man on earth."

Peter starts laughing.

"The law of attraction is working for you, is it? Don't be a dreamer. Be a man. You'll need to win her affection first, and then you can go eat pizza."

Steve nods.

"He's right. Stay in the now and the rest will sort itself out. At least you're wearing that shirt. Looks great, by the way."

"Thanks. Trust me, you guys know I'm a hopeless romantic, but I really thought it through this time."

Peter gets even more curious.

"Just tell us your plan already."

Gordon looks at the ceiling and immediately back at Peter.

"Easy. I'll order drinks and dial in some music in the jukebox. Then it's show time. I don't know how I'm going to start the conversation, but when she arrives with the booze, I'll be witty and quick."

Peter looks at Steve. Both giggle.

Steve turns to Gordon.

"Great. I have to say, it's not much, but the witty and quick part is interesting. Is this all you've got?"

An uncertain feeling is climbing up his chest.

"What do you mean? Did I miss something?"

Peter jumps in.

"Nah, you're good. Rigid plans are a bad idea. Just keep your head high and your expectations low."

Both laugh. Gordon tries to join them but can't.

"Are you guys with me, or what?"

Steve stops.

"Of course we are. You should learn to laugh at yourself. Just be who you truly are and don't try to force anything. If she's interested, it will work out great."

Peter points at Steve and taps on Gordon's shoulder.

"That's it. Just be yourself, mate. I mean. Not all at once. But in small doses, it should be fine."

Both are laughing again, but Steve holds back.

Oh my god, I'm going to fail miserably.

He gulps down his beer. The friends leave the Shotbar to get something to eat.

■ ■ ■

It's a two-station ride to Linda's workplace. A small izakaya called Tanotsuka on the fourth floor of an office building. They passed a lot of street stalls but couldn't agree on something. Gordon felt more and more excited as they got closer. His eyes look drowsy, but he walks upright anyhow.

It's on now. No big deal. Deep breath, then ask. Naturally. Casually. Easy.

Peter is jumping again.

"*Hara hetta*, guys. In other words, I'm starving. Gordon, how is the food there?"

Gordon abruptly leaves his head.

"I read the food is quite good, and they have international stuff too."

"Good."

It's rather crowded. They manage to get hold of the last free table. Gordon beholds Linda right away, but she is too busy to notice him.

Steve registers Gordon's stiffness.

"Everything is great. Just relax."

"Yeah, totally. I'm completely relaxed. Easy."

Peter looks around and points at Linda.

"Is that her?"

Gordon grabs his hand and whisper-screams.

"Shut up, Peter. Don't ruin it. Yes, this is Linda. And before you ask, Steve and I found this place a few weeks ago and I read her name on the nameplate. That's all."

"Haha. You didn't even talk to her?"

"Shut up and let me do my thing."

Peter smiles. Gordon's face is perfectly white.

Linda is coming to take their orders.

"Hi, guys, welcome to Tanotsuka. What can I get you?"

Steve answers first.

"Two beers, please. Gordon?"

He's paralyzed. She is too perfect. A few moments go by until Peter kicks him under the table.

"Yeah. Beer, please. I'm Gordon, by the way."

She throws a suspicious look at him.

"You got it. Anything else?"

Peter tries to save the situation.

"Could we also get the menu, please?"

Linda reaches out to a small cabinet and takes out three menus.

"Here you go."

"Thanks."

Peter and Steve laugh silently the second she leaves the table.

Gordon is whisper-screaming again.

"Please don't laugh at me."

The beverages arrive, and Gordon is still taken by her beauty. He is thanking her in unison with the table but keeps his head down. Peter takes a peek at the menu and asks her to come back later.

Go home. You already messed up. Loser. Fucking loser. Fuck.

Steve senses his fading hope.

"Look at me. Don't beat yourself up, yet. You are still in the game. We're here to support you. Take a swig and come down."

He empties his glass.

"All right. I'm doing my best."

Peter leans over to get closer to Gordon's face.

"Mate, this is ridiculous. Nothing happened. Maybe she even likes nerds like you."

Steve punches Peter's arm.

"Stop dissing him all the time. It's funny for a while, but it's not as easy for him as it is for you."

Peter defends his arm.

"Oh, here we go again. You laughed with me, didn't you? And now you're pissed, because I made a joke to comfort him?"

"Really? That wasn't comforting at all. You're a frigging bull-dozer, and you don't even notice it."

"Fine. I shut my mouth."

"Great."

Gordon lowers his arms to bring the energy down.

"Guys. We all need to calm down. Peter, would you get us another round of drinks, please?"

"I just wanted to go to the bathroom. Beers and sake?"

Both nod.

Peter is leaving the table, and Gordon squints at Steve's beer for relief. He points at the glass, while his face asks silently. Steve nods again.

Another empty glass.

"I'm sorry. You know Peter can be a hothead from time to time."

"No problem. I love him, but sometimes we disagree on things, and that's okay."

"Would you mind eating somewhere else?"

"Why? Are you going to chicken out? All this agitation for nothing?"

"I just can't."

"No problem with that. You'll need to persuade Peter, but it's quite sad, don't you think?"

Peter gets back to the table and grabs the menu.

"I'm totally starving."

Gordon cannot hide his buzz anymore.

"Guys, let's go get some Yakitori. The food isn't doing it for me."

Peter starts laughing.

"What about your attack plan?"

"I'm kind of serious about her, and I want to leave a good impression. I don't want to screw it up."

"That is a huge load of poppycock. You're just a little sissy, that's it. But fine. Let's get some Yakitori. I seriously need something to eat right now."

Linda arrives, and Peter pays for the drinks, while Gordon tries to keep his head down unobtrusively.

As she leaves the table, she turns to Gordon.

"It was nice meeting you. Enjoy your evening."

Gordon startles heavily.

"Thank you. Maybe we'll eat something next time."

Linda smiles.

"You should. Our pizza is one of the best."

He shows his teeth, but it doesn't even remotely resemble a smile.

"I guess I'll have to come back, then. I love pizza."

"Great. Until next time. Bye, guys."

The group leaves Tanotsuka, and as soon as they enter the street, Gordon starts dancing and hugs his friends enthusiastically.

"I knew it. I'm going to be number one. She loves me. Let's get fucked up."

Peter joins the party.

"You're the most badass loser ever."

Steve hugs Gordon into the air.

"I told you. Everything is great."

After a victorious battle, Gordon is leading his soldiers to celebration.

"All right. Let's Yakitori."

Peter is marching forward and plays the mouth trumpet.

♫ "I'm feeling…glad all over." ♫

It's only a three minute walk to the Yakitori place. Peter orders a huge amount of food. Gordon is relieved and drinks even more.

Steve mumbles in his shirt.

"Where do we go now? Back to the bar?"

Peter is still chewing.

"Perfect."

The Shotbar is crammed with people by now. Peter gets the finest liquors. It was totally pointless since the friends were already drunk, but he insisted.

Gordon gets ready to defend against the hardest of arguments.

"Steve, have you thought about the god problem in the meantime? I'm still working on it."

"I'm sure you will never let go, until we discussed this to death. So why don't you bring it on?"

He is delighted to hear that. His drunken mind comes back for a last gasp and tells Peter the story.

"What do you think?"

Peter shoots right away.

"Haha. What a load of bullshit. Think about it. Our world is a little bit like the place where everything is perfect. You just need to recognize how screwed up humans are. Then it's completely reasonable to push happiness and well-being into them. Just accept that people are selfish and fucked up, mate. If you want something, you figure out a way to get it, and then you don't let go. That's it. Who needs creativity, if you can have everything without doing anything. Who needs religion, if it's just baggage. I don't believe I wouldn't do anything, since I still very much want to fuck."

Steve has a different opinion.

"Fucking? The only thing you want is fucking? What a caveman you are. You reduce everything down to its elementary function, and then you talk people into believing it. This is a deluded way of looking at things. Life would be ultimately boring, if culture was conducted in such a way. You're mistaken to think our world is working like that. It's the opposite. Creation is full of diversity and challenges. You need to be imaginative to come up with solutions to problems before you get what you want."

Gordon tries to mediate and turns to Steve.

"Both worlds have their advantages. Why not have both? That's where I'm trying to get at. Why not have everything and eat the cake too?"

"Look. It's wrong to sentence people to a life of happiness and freedom, since you simply can't have one without the other. That's a fact. And if you can't see it, your vision for humanity is shortsighted, stupid, and boring."

Peter wildly gesticulates. Everybody in the room notices his arousal.

"Bullshit. To be happy, you need to get what you want. Listen, I'm happy, and I'm always getting what I want. That's a fact of life. You can discard everything else, as long as you get what you want. It's not hard to understand. Just accept the world as it is, and we can move on."

Steve gulps down his beer.

"Wow. You just can't see it. It's quite remarkable. The bigger picture seems to vanish from your field of perception the moment you get what you want. Are you even sure you know what you want? But you're the biggest and best. It's laughable. We wouldn't go anywhere, if there was no creativity, and everyone would just get what they already knew. It's what the guy in the book thought as well. Your world would simply stand still. No surprises. Just smartasses running around in circles, whining about a totalitarian government that won't make them happy enough to meet their ridiculous standards."

Gordon mobilizes all his strength.

"Stop it. Both of you. Sometimes, it's better to go for it, and other times, it's better to step back, think about the implications, and apply creativity to get there. Peter, why are you so stubborn? Steve, you'll need elements of the perfect world for your reality to function as well. So why can't we cater to both perspectives and come up with a better solution? I'm sure there's room for compromise."

Peter loses it.

"It's enough with your soft skills. Only outcasts come up with those hippie ideas. What are you going to do? Just wait for a better life? Brew a nice cup of tea and hope for fairness? Are you crazy? People are here for themselves, and if you say otherwise, you're lying. It's dangerous to be overly soft in this world. Sensitivity is nice and all, but it won't get you anywhere."

Steve is ready to engage in a fight at this point, but his friend is looking awful.

"Gordon, are you still with us?"

He is nearly floored by the last round of sake.

I don't know. Everything is so complicated. Why is nothing getting better, even if I push like crazy? I just want to be happy. What's so special about others? Why am I always losing?

Peter barks at Gordon.

"Are you okay?"

"I was successful, right?"

Steve and Peter look at each other and realize the unavoidable fact. Gordon is going down very soon. They need to come up with an escape route quick, unless they want to carry him to his apartment or even worse, deal with an ambulance and face the same tragedy as last year at his birthday party.

Steve tries to find words of encouragement.

"You made it. Trust me, it'll work out. It was a successful night, and you can be proud of yourself."

His answer sounds overly whiny.

"I need a win, Steve. A fucking win."

Peter grabs his arm.

"Time to go, mate."

"You will win someday. I promise."

Gordon's spirits leave instantly. He loses control over his body, and his voice is stumbling. Although he is still able to stand up by himself, he needs help to carry his weight out of the bar and into a taxi. During the ride home, he vomits out the window, shouts obscene things, and leaves an impression of undeniable defeat in the car. The friends open the door to his apartment and lay him down on his couch. Peter kisses him while he's fully knocked out and takes a ridiculous picture. Steve is concerned.

4

AFTERMATH

GORDON WOKE UP SEVERAL times to empty his stomach. His eyes were watering and his throat hurt, as he finally came to life early in the morning. He couldn't sleep any longer. The headache, muscle, and joint pain spread all over his body. He repeatedly tried to drink water, but it wouldn't stay in. Eating was out of the question, but he knew there would be lots of delivery food in the near future. He ate a few pills, which soothed his pain a little; the horrible feeling of guilt and shame persisted, however.

He always loved the sense of adventure and camaraderie when going out. They had so much fun, and the years flew by like nothing. Calamities happened all along, but they took it lightly. The acceptance of misery was oddly comforting, since nobody thought about the future, or if stuff would change any time soon. And then life happened, and the fact of getting older wasn't avoidable anymore. It started with thirty-two, and it got worse with every year of partying. Forty felt like the last opportunity to get himself in order, but his motivation was running out quickly. Back in the day, he would drink all week and didn't suffer at all, but the hangovers lasted longer and longer. He witnessed many crazy things, and nothing could shock him anymore; however, he paid with his youth for it. Gordon couldn't remember a lot of these nights out. But today, he was pleased to recall the whole evening including the taxi scene. He's accustomed to drink a lot of alcohol very fast, and he never stops until his mind and body shut down. Quite degrading, but still preferable over the nagging feeling of ultimate wrongness. Having an actual idea about what happened was infinitely better than drowning in an abyss of not knowing. Some of his friends loved to tell stories, which didn't happen and persuaded him into having a bad conscience.

The TV shouts overly positive nonsense at him. It's much too loud, but he doesn't want to turn it off or the volume down. He isn't yet ready to talk to anybody, but he needs to feel human in order to keep his crumbling sanity. This hangover isn't going away soon, so he tries to befriend it.

I'm hungry. But she smiled. Maybe you screwed up? Maybe she just did her job and you're deluding yourself? Shit. I should go for that pizza very soon. Please, universe, I want this woman. It's enough to vomit out of a taxi window. Peter will laugh at me forever. Just don't fucking post the pic, please.

He cries. Big tears are running down his cheeks. He is bewildered and unable to hold back any longer. The upboiling uncertainty and painful confusion of the last few months make themselves seen.

Alone this time. Sober. Frigging do it. Lose some weight, but don't wait too long. Food. Maybe I can invite her or something. It's a no. Don't fool yourself. She's too good for you. You have a shit job, shit home, shit life. You'll never make it. Fat and ugly. Loser.

The delivery driver knows him very well. He orders at least three times a week. Big portions of meat over rice and large bento boxes. Sometimes many dishes at once. That's his way of dealing with it all. He loves eating and food in general. Cooking was a big thing in his family, and sometimes he did even cook for the whole extended Fitch clan. The only problem: his lifestyle makes it impossible to prepare food for himself. He is exclusively lying down lately, and the fridge is always empty. There isn't a lot of energy left to gather motivation and shop for actual meals. Instead, he amasses big amounts of food containers in the kitchen. The flat looks like a garbage can, and going to sleep in it wouldn't be possible for most, but Gordon doesn't care.

Everything changes. No relief. I just can't push through. Nothing works. I need my share of success. Please. I want to feel proud of myself. Hope. Despair. Back and forth. It makes no sense. Why me?

■ ■ ■

It's a regular Monday, but he got up much earlier than usual. He fell into a food coma quite early and slept on the couch again. His head was still pulsating, and his hands were stiff and inflamed. The dreamless night was a dark hole of resurrection. He never dreams much and is quite thankful for it. Black is the color of forgiveness. No obligations and no judgment. If paradise is not an option, void is a great escape. He sat on the couch and watched the city slowly welcoming another day. A moment of silence. The quiet before the storm. It wasn't the first time and he would just deal with it and get through the day to come out on the other side somehow.

I'm screwed. Jade will notice. Whatever, this is not the end. If it was the end, it would be good. One day, I'll have a great home on top of the world. Fortieth floor and up. And Linda too. That is it. No more work, beautiful wife, and a great life. We'll see who is laughing last.

He takes a deep breath, practices a few winner poses in front of the mirror, and leaves his apartment, overpunctual. He walks slowly and tries to clear his head. Going through his checklist for the day, he plans every task meticulously. What to say and what to avoid. All the interactions he knows will take place and all the reactions he thinks are on point. By the time he arrives at the grocery store, he has a complete guide to survive and to keep any punishment at bay.

The staff entrance is open. Jade is smoking a cigarette.

"Good morning, Gordon. How are you?"

"I'm well, thanks. You?"

She's shaking her head.

"Pretty good. Mason is already here. He's waiting for you."

"Smells like trouble."

"You bet. The cologne is not helping."

"What, no. I only had a few beers yesterday."

"Are you kidding me? You're literally sweating liquor. It's coming out of every pore."

Gordon points at Jade.

"No way. I've only had a few beers and one or two shots. That was nothing. Stop interfering with my life. It's nice of you and all, but I have to draw a line somewhere. I'm your supervisor, and you simply can't talk to me like that."

She grabs his finger and pushes it down.

"You can't be serious. I thought we were friends. Don't you remember all the stuff we went through? I know you better than almost all your drinking buddies."

"Well, maybe you know me, but that doesn't give you the right to treat me like a teenager. We're at work here, and as long as I do my duties, there's no problem. Will you leave me alone with it now?"

"I can't believe it. You're incurable. This conversation is worthless. Get your act together, Fitch."

"All right, now go back to work or something."

Jade stubs out her cigarette, mutters a few unintelligible words, and storms off into the store.

Ridiculous. What friendship? You want to fuck me. That's all. You're not my mom. This is crazy.

He follows Jade into the building and goes straight to his table to update a few lists and to perform the usual checks. Gordon is still dedicated to make sure he doesn't get in trouble, and his calendar is thankfully filled with standard procedures and boring paperwork.

That's not the worst thing, if a drunkard needs to steam off. However, the main obstacle lies in front of him still. Mason will call soon, and he isn't sure about the outcome. He is a very conscientious manager. Everything is in perfect order at all times, but the sheer amount of fog is changing his formerly great work ethic into a defensive game of excuse-chess. He forgets to place orders often, and the cleaning frequency of the refrigerated areas could cause a huge problem. With all these recurring episodes of dizziness, he is lacking the resources to act in a proactive manner and is losing authority day after day. But he always appears to be busy, which is very important for his upcoming promotion. Mason is half Japanese/American, and he's well known for switching sides. When fully Japanese, he placed great value on honorifics. When American, he can be a lot more relaxed, but also quite cruel and demanding. In Japanese work settings, it's considered polite to add -san, preceded by the last name of the person. It's the same as referring to somebody by Mr. or Mrs. But since Gordon's performance is going down lately, Mason insists on being called Tanaka-san only by his middle manager. That would be totally unacceptable and very rude anywhere else. However, Tanaka-san couldn't care less. He keeps a firm humiliation agenda going to show him his place, while treating others as if they were friends since high school.

The phone rings. Gordon puts on his best Monday morning voice to show his willingness. He tries to do the right thing, although it's quite difficult. The alcohol is still influencing him, and it had become increasingly hard to hide his seething hate.

"Good morning, Tanaka-san."

"Morning, Fitch. How are we doing this month?"

"Nothing special. The numbers are slightly above average."

"Good. Are you done with all the checks yet?"

"Yes. I'm currently working on a better way to maximize store-room capacity. Remember, we talked about it last week?"

"I do, Fitch. Let me know, when you're done. Another thing: what is going on with our orders lately? We had a huge problem at the hot food counter, and two or three brands of toilet paper are almost gone as well. Do you want to tell me something?"

"Tanaka-san, I'm sorry, I forgot to order the chicken, but we already talked about it, so why are you bringing it up again?"

"You forget a lot lately, and I'm not going to tolerate it anymore. Do you understand?"

"Tanaka-san, I don't think this is appropriate. I apologized already, and I'm working hard to meet all the standards and to implement improvements."

"Fitch, don't try to fool me. I personally did spot checks regularly, during the last three months. Your results are getting worse. You even had the nerve to ask me about a promotion."

"Well, I've been an employee in this store for about five years. I always did great work, and you know that. I even got appointed assistant manager by you, and I'm asking myself why you're behaving like I've always been ineffective and lazy. It's not fair to force me into calling you Tanaka-san, while others are invited to refer to you as Mason. I think it's not right and you owe me an apology. I won't accept such treatment any longer, and I think I've earned another promotion."

Mason holds the phone away from his mouth and laughs into his office. Then the laughing stops. His voice sounds so close, he is almost inside of Gordon's head.

"Listen carefully, Fitch. You are not good enough to be a top-level manager, and you'll never be. Have I made myself clear?"

Gordon shrinks under the impact.

"Very clear, Tanaka-san. Is there something else you wanted to talk to me about?"

"Yes, do you remember the doctor who measured your waistline?"

"I remember him."

"He said you've become too fat according to Metabo law and recommended our dancing class to get you in shape again. I normally don't care about such nonsense, but we need to undercut the average employee limits. Otherwise, the company faces a huge fine. I'm afraid I'll need you to do it. The next course starts in about a week. Will you attend?"

Gordon's mouth and eyes open wide.

"No problem. I wanted to lose a few pounds anyway."

"I have a major meeting coming up. Let me know about your progress in the storage room."

"All right."

He hangs up the phone.

Stupid asshole. Fuck you. You're a fucking worm. A stupid fucking worm. I'll show you. I'll show you. One day, you'll stand in awe before me. I can't believe it. Shit.

He keeps his facade intact and goes on to finish the paperwork. There are a few minor issues, but it doesn't bother him. Jade left him alone for the day. Maybe she sensed something, but he didn't ask.

5

DANCING FOR LOVE

GORDON WAS MORE DEDICATED than ever to lose weight. After the catastrophe at work, he once more decided to eat healthier and get back into shape. In the past, he enjoyed lifting weights and going for runs. However, that was very long ago. Since then, he bounced back and forth between relatively healthy to downright shit. And although he feared the initial stage of getting back into the fitness world, he was determined to make it happen. What mattered was winning at love. Nothing else. He knew it wasn't a good idea to approach Linda right away. It was impossible to picture himself walking her into a restaurant or kissing her. When he tried to create a nice little fantasy, he always ended up being a fat donkey, walking with an Amazonian goddess. One of those friendships he became accustomed to during his school years, when he deliberately wanted to get a girlfriend. Girls would sometimes agree to go out with him, but it inevitably led to the friendzone. A place Gordon hated with passion, since he was a nice guy and he couldn't understand why it would be a problem. After years of experience in the field, he could even make out the exact moment she decided to keep him as a pet, just to call him in the middle of the night, because she went through a difficult time with another love interest. But it wasn't solely the fault of the girls. His insecurity was so severe, the thought of a good-looking woman seeing him naked was terrifying to him. The only thing that helped to overcome his insecurity was lifting weights. He wasn't terribly obese back then, but the baby fat was quite persistent throughout his life.

As a result, he lost twenty pounds and gained a healthy amount of muscle mass. He didn't look like a tank, but it helped produce sufficient self-confidence to actually try something on his dates. Starting at twenty-five, he had some success with the ladies, and a bunch of relationships followed. But the body image thing seemed to be only a minor issue, compared to what he later called the Walt Disney problem. Every girl he went out with was the love of his life. Some of whom hurt him badly. However, this time was going to be different. He had plenty of experience and didn't want to repeat the past. The training was about to begin, and despite him going back and forth all his life, he wouldn't end up as a failure. He monitored his food intake meticulously and stopped eating candy. The only treat he kept was Japanese ice-milk. It looked like astronauts' food, but he'd developed an addiction to sweets over the years and needed to soothe his urges. And even though it was only the first step, he already felt much better about himself. His friends tried to support him too, which was of great help to stay motivated. Peter told him to chin up and stop whining about five hundred times, and Steve always had an ear for depressive episodes and hardship. He ran, until he couldn't even walk anymore, and lifted weights, until he felt the pain. He gave it his all. That was the price he had to pay. He wanted to be a success in this world.

■ ■ ■

The day of the dancing arrives, and Gordon swims in anxiety. He was totally motivated to lose weight, but he wasn't at all inclined to attend. It was forced upon him by his boss, and dancing is a woman's thing. He gets there about two minutes late, but people seemed to be relaxed. The group consisted solely of men, ranging from forty to fifty years of age. It feels surprisingly secure in between all those fatties in the changing room. He can't help but smile a little, since he isn't the big guy in the room for once. Westerners greatly outnumber the Japanese. That means the teacher will most likely instruct in English, which is a relief for him. Working at an international company finally has an upside. Gordon isn't yet sure what he is getting into, but he calms down and even gets a bit curious about the actual dancing. A bell rings in the background and the attendees became quiet. The teacher is a small man in his fifties. Gaily dressed in what could be described as a colorful scarf. Unusually long hair and very tight yoga pants further embellish his body. He smiles and makes an inviting gesture. The group stands in front of him.

He bows.

"*Otsukare sama desu*. Welcome. My name Ikeda Kesseki. I'm teacher dancing class. Taking over for colleague. Got sick. You dance eight weeks with me. Great for belly."

What, no. Eight weeks? He looks like a narrow-eyed hippie in a rainbow scarf.

"We learning Kabuki. Lion dance. Is tradition in Japan. Please quick introduce."

After the rather boring group introduction, followed by a strange gymnastics warm-up, he puts down his scarf to round off his lofty appearance with a white women's tank top.

"Let me show you lion dance. We practice to make performance. Will be great for manager to honor them."

Ikeda-san takes out a massive white wig and puts it on. Age-old Japanese music plays on a nineties CD player. It starts slowly. His arms rotate around his body. He waves with the sound. Turning his head every half second. Jumping jerkily. Increasingly gaining momentum as the performance progresses. The music gets intense.

His former slow and controlled movements change to explosive running and frantic dancing. He screws himself deep into the floor, whirling round and round. His face is populated by unbridled emotion, and an untamed eruption of raw feeling leaves his body as he sways his long white mane from left to right. The music comes to a grand finale. Quivering. Shaking his whole being to finally release the unbearable tension from his face. Ending his unparalleled frenzy with a sense of restrained mastery. Standing still. Showing his proud face to a perplexed multicultural audience. The crowd is blown away. A huge applause fills the room. Ikeda-san acts modest and calm. He bows down deeply, gently wipes the sweat from his face, and quickly takes off the wig.

"Thank you. Now your turn."

The class bursts out into laughing.

He points at a formation of red markers on the floor.

"Please stand."

The group is stunned. There is a clearly palpable reluctance among them. It takes a minute for the dancers to position on the markers. However, Gordon doesn't move. He crosses his arms and makes a grumpy face.

Screw it, Tanaka. I quit.

The teacher notices and turns to Gordon. He points at the last available circle in the middle of the room.

"Your name Fitch-san, right? Here is marker for you."

No reaction.

"Fitch-san, please go to marker. We may begin now."

He crosses his arms more tightly.

"This isn't dancing at all. You just banged your head like a teenager in a mosh pit."

Ikeda-san looks confused.

"What is mosh pit? Please stand."

He is speechless and sulkily takes his place as the music starts again. The entry passage is playing in an endless loop, and they get to see the first move: a slow swinging arm motion.

"Wave arms. Please do soft."

I get it. Either we lose weight or they turn us around.

The men wave their arms and look at each other in disbelief. Gordon investigates: Who is ready to join his anger? Ikeda-san presses a button on the CD player. The next section starts looping.

"Now jump. Little jumping. One. Two. One. Two. Use head. Turn. See?"

Gordon is aghast. He's not sure if this is at one of those TV shows where people get humiliated, or if reality is self-destructing before his eyes. It feels real, but there is definitely something wrong here.

"Now practice. I help for questions."

The group is jumping. The teacher puts his scarf on and alternates between markers to help the dancers by correcting them with a trained eye. Gordon is next.

Ikeda-san takes a quick look at his jumping.

"You need practice more, Fitch-san. Will be star of show."

What is this shit?

"What do you mean? 'Will be star?'"

He points at his marker.

"You Onnagatta. Play both. Servant and lion."

"I don't understand. I'm here to lose weight."

He supports him with speedy hands and recalibrates his body.

"Don't worry, Fitch-san. I show you. Left to right. Bend one knee. Then other knee. Turn head. Jumping."

Part of the group is giggling. Gordon accepts his fate for the moment and follows the instructions.

"Very good, Fitch-san. Will be marvelous Onnagatta. Lots of heart. I can see already."

"Well, I don't know, what you want from me, but I'm pretty sure I'm the wrong person."

"I was Onnagatta thirty years. You perfect. Strong lion."
Ikeda-san turns the music off and bows at the group.
"Enough for today. Thank you for dancing. Please practice.
Come back next week. *Otsukare sama deshita.*"

The bell rings. The men head to the locker room, but nobody
says a word. They quietly change clothes and everyone goes their
way. Gordon takes the subway. He's dying to know what role he
will play. At home, he immediately searches the internet for Japanese
dancing performances. The facts are rather uncomfortable. Kabuki
is a traditional form of entertainment. An exaggerated performance
art that goes back to the seventeenth century. One of the most
cherished pieces is the Kabuki lion dance. A performance for two
actors who dance together as father and son. Supported by various
other roles. The lions wear giant wigs with chin strips and bang
their heads like metal fans in utter extasy. The music ranges from
fast and percussive to slow and very traditional. The father lion is
the lead and the most sought-after role of the whole play. He has
an additional duty though. He's miming a woman servant as well.
These actors are normally thin with female appearance and delicate
facial features. They wear enormous amounts of makeup and exag-
gerate for theatrical effect.

No way. I'm not the fucking lion king. They want to force me
to play a woman. This metabo thing is dogshit. Gay old man. I'm
not doing it.

He isn't in the position to quit his job or to fake a sickness,
and he will play the lion regardless. And to top it all off, they were
training for a show performance in front of Tanaka and the other
managers. There couldn't be anything more humiliating than playing a woman. A fat, ugly bitch with a ton of white makeup and a
supremely female appearance. Gordon thinks about suicide for a
while, but he's way too cowardly.

6
LINDA

GORDON HAD IT ROUGH. The training program was exhausting. His body was in constant pain. He even had to deal with a bunch of minor injuries. The will to keep up with it got tested every workout. This wasn't going to stop him, but it was stressful. He toiled on multiple front lines at the same time, while he had dragged himself to the gym for four weeks already. And day after day, he would lose some of his accumulated fat reservoirs.

He knew it was not the perfect moment, and he had to admit his body wasn't ready yet, but the suffering of the last weeks needed to yield a profit. Patience wasn't the right strategy anymore. The training was taxing every cell of his body and mind. It was time to reap what he sowed. He wanted to satisfy his appetite with something even more satiating. Love. Thus, he finally decided to attack Linda, but he also needed a plan. A bulletproof way to save the world and earn her love. He is her best bet. She simply doesn't know it already.

The only person who will truly make a difference in his game is Peter. He isn't a nice guy, but maybe this is the secret to his success. Woman like masculine bodies. They want to fuck bearded soldiers and athletic gym-rats. Prominent jawlines with lots of cash.

Heroes. Real men. Not sensitive losers like Gordon. He not only has to change his body and lose weight. He has to earn a lot of money and show his manliness.

Previous relationships prove that the woman he likes wouldn't be interested in a boy. There is yet a lot of work to do, but he couldn't wait any longer. Every day he isn't taking action feels like a mistake. She doesn't know he exists, and the more time goes by, the lesser his chances get in his mind. It isn't easy to reach Peter. The new business is consuming him totally. Gordon figured it would be better to talk without the presence of alcohol anyway. He couldn't really live without a vodka shot here and there, but he reduces it whenever possible. The diet has priority after all. After many attempts, Peter finally takes the call.

"Matey, how is it going?"

"Well, it's going well."

"Fine. I have a meeting in fifteen minutes. What is it?"

"Okay, straight to the point. As you know, I lost some weight in the last weeks. And that's great and all, but I can't wait any longer. I need to attack. I want my princess and I want her now."

"Man, that's some energy right there. Love it. What's your battle plan?"

Gordon power-poses in front of the mirror.

"That's why I'm calling. I need advice. You've known me for quite a while, and I don't have to tell you I'm not the toughest nut in the bowl. I need to show her the real me. The fucking machine hiding behind all this fat."

Peter's voice speeds up significantly.

"I already said it a million times. But now you're finally ready. Awesome, mate. What do you want to know?"

"Tell me what to do. How do I awaken the Fitch-machine? How do I kill the enemy and save the princess?"

"Your game console was your only friend as a kid, was it? But jokes aside. The first thing you have to do is to get comfortable with being uncomfortable. You're working out right now, correct? I bet you're training at an iffy little health spa with cozy air-conditioning and warm showers. Am I right?"

"Kind of. Yes."

"You can keep your membership, but you have to challenge yourself more. This isn't helping at all."

"What do you mean? I'm training my ass off. There's rarely a day where I'm able to move without pain. I'm running excessively on the treadmill, and I lift weights like a Greek god."

"Maybe a little much, but I believe you. You should go out and run in the burning sun. Tokyo has never been hotter. And when you're finally ready to quit, take an ice-cold shower. Machines don't cry, mate."

"Yeah, why not. I'm doing that tomorrow. Anything else?"

"Destroy your dumbbell game, do super high repetitions of dead lifts. Run with a twenty pound backpack. Sleep less and start fasting for long periods of time, just to fuck yourself up. Trust me, you'll build the resilience to crush whatever comes your way."

Gordon's posing comes to a sudden halt.

"Sounds merciless, but you know best for sure. I'll give it a try."

"Mate, you don't give it a try. You want to be successful. You fucking do it. You get that? Fucking do it. Start your engine. Don't pinch and go hard."

"All right, the Fitch-machine is about to take off. I'll show the world what I'm made of. You will be proud of me, I promise. I'll stop eating right now, and I'll end those fucking dumbbells."

"That's my boy. I'm off for the meeting now. Good luck with your princess."

"Thanks, Peter. You're a true friend. Bye."

"No worries. Bye."

■ ■ ■

Three weeks passed, and Gordon was doing everything he could. He slept for four hours a night, did ice-cold showers regularly, lifted heavy weights, and carried backpacks. His knees were screaming at him. His whole body felt inflamed. His soul was dying. But he persisted. There were things more important than fun. More important than drinking. A future worth working for. He wouldn't wait a single day longer. It was showtime. A new life was inviting him for a ride. It was a regular Thursday. The heat was intense. He finished work and went home to change clothes. The blue outfit with a short sleeve shirt, leather shoes, and a nice perfume. A few vodka shots to keep posture. Mouthwash to camouflage. He remembered something his mother would say: You're intelligent and you'll achieve everything you'll set your heart to. It was time to believe in himself.

Keep cool. You're sober and you look good. Maybe you know me from last time? No. Awful. Would you like to go out some time? I'm Gordon, nice to meet you. Would you like to go out? Don't panic. Improvise.

Two blocks before the izakaya, he takes a short detour to get some vodka and a packet of chewing gum from a convenience store. The fridge cools off his boiling body, and the cashier throws an encouraging look at him. Too much vodka could harm his act, but he needs it. The stairs appear to be steeper than last time. Not a lot of people. She is standing in front of the counter. The Linda of his dreams and the woman in front of him are quite similar; however, reality is more exciting. She's 174 centimeters tall. Blondish. Has straight, wavy hair and green eyes. Thin, sporty, small breasts and long legs.

"Welcome to Tanotsuka."

Gordon starts sweating.

"Thank you. I want a little something to eat."

She guides Gordon to his table.

"This way, please."

He sits down.

Don't get drunk. Damn it.

"I'll get a large beer."

"You got it."

She heads to the bar to order. He's watching every step. Normally, he likes bigger breasts and an overall chunkier appearance, but she can be excused of everything.

"One large beer."

"Thank you. Not much going on today. Is it getting more crowded later, or are you blessed with a nice job?"

She brushes some hair out of her face.

"It's crowded every day. We have way more customers in the evenings. Have you decided for food yet?"

Gordon has known for a week already.

"Yeah, I'll have the scallops, a small portion of rice, and an order of pickles."

"Excellent."

A drop of sweat rolls down his back, without being obstructed by his wide shirt.

"Do you remember me by any chance?"

There is something in her eyes.

"I don't know. Have you been here before?"

"Yeah. A few weeks ago. I was with two friends. We introduced each other."

She remembers.

"Not sure. I told you we have a lot of people."

Don't you lie.

"Uh, maybe I can refresh your memory. I'm Gordon."

She squints her eyes.

"Sorry, still nothing."

Shit.

"Well, you're Linda, right?"

"Yeah. Sorry, there's another table waiting. I'll be back in a sec."

The food takes a long time. Linda serves other customers and plays busy.

Dogshit. I didn't even start. Calm. You'll make it.

She finally arrives.

"Here you go."

"Thanks. Sorry, I didn't want to bother you."

"You didn't. Another beer?"

"Yes, please. Can I ask you a question?"

She strokes her hair. Her eyes wander from the table to his face.

"Of course."

Gordon's heart stands still.

"It may be a little direct, but I'm an honest guy. Would you like to grab a drink with me?"

Linda breathes audibly.

"Let me think about it, okay?"

His body feels shaky.

Oh god.

"Please do."

She goes hiding behind the bar. Gordon cannot see her. Five minutes pass. He's expecting the worst.

Done. I fucked up again.

The princess comes into view again. She walks straight to his table.

"I'm not sure. I'm normally not going out with customers."

"You know what I really admire in woman? Courageousness. And I hope you are. You see, I'm not doing stuff like this every day. To be frank, it took quite a while to gather my energy and be courageous myself. And now I'm here to ask you out, and I can assure you my intentions are good and I'm not one of those guys."

She seems torn.

"I don't know. Let me get your beer first."

He tries to radiate openness and positivity while chewing his last bite, but she doesn't look at him. Gordon is painfully tense; his stomach pulsates in unison with his raging heart.

"Here you go. Was the food to your liking?"

His behavior seems stiff.

"Thanks. The scallops were great. Please don't leave me hanging any longer. Will you go out with me?"

"What do you want from me? I don't have much to offer."

A spark of doubt colors his mind, but there is no going back now.

"That's on me to decide. Just say yes and we'll find out."

She rushes to another table. As she leaves the audible range, Gordon petrifies and presses out a sad sigh.

I'm going to kill myself.

Another awkward ten minutes. He waves. Ready to bath in self-disgust.

"Excuse me, I'd like to pay."

"Just a sec."

She returns with the bill. No more words. He pays, pockets his wallet, and gets up immediately. The door comes closer, and his head is sinking with every step.

The princess has mercy.

"Wait."

She takes out her pen and writes something down.

"Here is my number."

His eyes come back to life. He takes the piece of paper and smiles all over his face.

"I'll call you these days. You won't regret it. I promise."

"I hope so. Enjoy your day."

"You too."

Gordon leaves the izakaya. The pressure is falling away. His ravenous eagerness paid off. Finally a yes.

Who's the man? I'm the man. Fuck yeah!

He buys the most luxurious vodka and prances home to enjoy the rush. He is vibrating.

7

KING OF THE JUNGLE

GORDON HAS HATED THE weekly dancing classes. The exercises looked weird and didn't gain any results. He was the only one losing weight, but for different reasons. The actual stage performance was done by him and his partner, but during practice, they worked in duos. Playing the father needed synchronizing with his stage-son and memorizing mouth movements. It made him anxious. Gordon's singing voice wasn't going to cut it, and after a lot of discussion, Ikeda-san agreed to do it full playback. It got more laborious than he could have ever imagined. He tried to revolt several times, but Ikeda-san couldn't understand. It was supposed to be an honor for him to play the father lion. So he had no chance but to invest energy into it. Singing, banging, and his most hated part—miming the female servant—joined together into a comprehensive performance. It took him a long time to internalize everything, but he developed a strange work ethic toward it. He felt himself to be responsible somehow and wouldn't let his colleagues down. Japanese people hate to make mistakes in front of others. That's why they only spoke English when drunk. Over the weeks, a strong relationship with the son actor formed. His name was Chīsana Ishi. A small man nearing his fifties. Very sensible. They stayed longer many times to get everything right. It was the last chance to sort out the subtle points before the dress rehearsal. Gordon often thought about his own dad when he practiced with him. Meanwhile, Ikeda-san invited his former colleagues and their families to enjoy a new permutation of Kabuki with a Westerner as the main part. The managers would come as well, and when Gordon saw the actual theater, the pressure built up tremendously. Stage fright wasn't an issue, until he realized how enormous the whole thing was. Ikeda has created a monster. Twenty fat man support a family of headbangers in front of 150 people.

The dress rehearsal went surprisingly well. After everyone was gone, he sat with Ishi-san in the back of the theater to discuss the last points of concern. They were exhausted.

Gordon weighs the monstrous wig with his hands.

"Have you gotten used to it now?"

"Yes, I trained neck muscles."

"All right. We'll start shaking on the count of three. You need to come in a little earlier."

"You give cue, Gordon-san. I'll follow lead. Will be perfect."

Gordon nods. Ishi-san is drumming on his lap. He senses his nervousness.

"Are you excited yet?"

The drumming gets more intense.

"This my first time dancing for people. Big responsibility."

He lightly taps his shoulder.

"I feel the same, Ishi-san. It has grown to unbelievable heights and the audience is huge. It's insane. But we won't let the stress prevent us from giving our best."

"Are you excited, Gordon-san?"

The thought of setting foot on the stage alone frightens Gordon to death.

" I have to admit, it's a bizarre situation and I feel a little antsy. But again, we'll master the situation come what will. Remember, it's just head shaking for a bunch of managers."

Ichi-san's face brightens up.

"Understand. Good father, Gordon-san."

He grins, then pushes his chin up and his brows down.

"I actually thought about that during our training. My father wasn't really around, when I was little. He was an alcoholic."

The small man is mortified by so much Western openness.

"Sorry to hear you in so much pain."

"Maybe it was wrong telling you this. Sorry, I didn't want to shame you."

"No worry. I trust in you."

Gordon's eyes are glazing, but he holds back.

"I trust you too, my friend."

He smiles.

Let's go home, Gordon-san. Big day tomorrow."

"Yeah. Remember, it's on three, not three and."

"Will not forget."

■ ■ ■

Peter and Steve were exhilarated to see the show. The female servant thing was too good to be true. They made jokes about it all the time. Sissy boy was basically Gordon's new nickname, and he got very annoyed about it. Steve agreed to assist with the costumes. They arrived rather early at the theater. Gordon badly needed to acquaint himself with the atmosphere. Ishi-san was waiting at the entrance.

"Hello Ichi-san. This is Steve; he'll help us putting on the wigs."

"Konnichiwa, Steve-san. Nice meeting you."

Gordon strokes Ishi-san over the shoulder.

"Let's go in."

The theater is bright with lights already. It's the first time they have seen it from the audience perspective. Gordon senses a queasy feeling creeping up his spine.

Wow. Awesome lighting. I should come here more often.

Ishi-san disappears into his changing room. Steve follows Gordon to assist him first.

"Thank you for doing this. I don't know who else I could have asked."

"No problem. I had nothing better to do, and I'm happy to help. How do you feel? You trained quite hard for today."

"Not gonna lie: I felt devastated. However, yesterday I talked to Ichi-san and it's much better now."

Steve laughs.

"That's great. But how did he do it? Asking for a friend."

Gordon keeps a straight face.

"Not funny. He reminded me of my childhood. Didn't I tell you about it already?"

"Of course you did. But what has one to do with the other?"

"Well, I haven't had the best of times growing up in Scotland. My papa was an alcoholic as you know. We were dead poor and my mam was supporting the whole family. Dad stopped working to drink full-time, and he oftentimes beat mam when he got home from the bar. Sometimes, he also battered the shit out of me. I'll show you my back later. The scars are still there. Anyway, when they eventually got divorced, he left us for good and we've never heard from him again. There were no jobs, but I had to earn money somehow. I often begged for coins on the street, and mam would try to prevent me from doing it, but we needed the money to pay rent. She was very young at the time and helpless. Being a normal child wasn't an option. It was very tough. Having that said, Ishi-san is playing my actor son on the show, and I thought a lot about my past during practice. It's kind of peculiar, but when I saw him getting stressed out, I remembered how I felt growing up. All this uncertainty and pain we had to go through. I tried to comfort him like I did with mam, when she was crying from the nightly beatings. I would pretend to be strong and tell her the usual stuff. That we would make it and times change."

Steve tries to fit the servant wig on Gordon's head.

"Isn't it a bit late to talk to me about your childhood? You never told me the whole story."

"Don't forget the sticks for the bun. Yeah, what can I say. I suppose I needed the right moment."

"How did it turn out?"

Gordon laughs.

"Well, Ishi-san found some hope."

"Not funny. Come on, man."

"All right. I later moved to my mam-gu, and mam stayed with my stepdad. My grandparents had a lot of money, since her sister died early. She bought me everything I wanted. I had the best clothes and always the newest shoes. Having money was great, but I would have loved a real family growing up."

Steve nods repeatedly.

"Glad it got better down the road."

"It didn't. I'm a middle manager in a grocery store."

"But you always wanted a manager position."

"Yes and no. School was hell for me and my grades were, as my mam-gu would call it, a catastrophe before god. Later, I sometimes worked part-time at a store in Aberdeen. It fueled my hobbies, and it was okay, but it was not enough. I didn't have any idea what to do with my life, but I wanted more."

"So I decided to pursue a career in retail. I left school and started out as a grocery clerk in a big store in Cardiff, fronting stuff for eight hours a day. It was awful. But then a department manager granted me one promotion after another, until I became assistant manager. I did this job for a long time and hated it passionately. And as they let me go for no apparent reason, I was confused what to do next.

About five years ago, a fluke in the wind hit me and I moved to Japan. I thought I'd build a better life for myself and start over. Now I'm working as a manager again. Filling repetitive numbers into boring spreadsheets, while dealing with people's dramas and begging for more in front of my abusive boss. Middle managers, I came to realize, are the most useless people in any business. They're completely replaceable and don't have any right to decide the big stuff. Worst of all, being in the middle implies pressure from above and hate from below. I absolutely fucking loathe it. Life could have been a little friendlier to me. Don't you think?"

The wig fits, and Steve moves on to the costume. A traditional Japanese kimono.

"I think you have to ask yourself what you really want."

"I want to be happy, Steve."

"Great. What makes you happy?"

"If I knew, I would tell everyone. However, I need to focus on being a servant for now."

Gordon is almost ready to go. Only the makeup is missing. Steve leaves to take a look at Ishi-san.

"Right on. See you later, Sissy boy."

■ ■ ■

Music is playing during entrance. Steve is backstage to inspect the theater. Gordon tries to calm down Ishi-san but stays mostly in his changing room. The last thirty minutes before the performance is about to begin.

Gordon is working on his makeup.

Life is strange. You never know what happens next. Sitting here with a meter-long wig, waiting for a gig I've never wanted. What's it about? Is it a joke? Nobody could ever dream of this shit. Everything is so foreign. Is stuff just happening to me or am I responsible for it? Withdraw or fight? Push or pull? That's the question. Shit.

Streams of sweat are running down his body. The paint is hardly hiding his red face, and his hands are freezing cold. Ikeda-san enters the room.

"Fifteen minutes. How is feeling, Gordon-san?"

"I'm excited. Really excited."

"We worked hard for dancing. It was pleasure teaching, Gordon-san. Best actor. Always put effort."

"Thank you, Ikeda-san. There was no weight loss, but I have to admit, it was better than I thought. I didn't want to go there, but I may even miss the classes a little bit. It was an interesting experience to get to know the theater world. All the details we had to master and the challenges we faced."

"Glad hearing. All of group did great job. *O-shiawase ni*. Only few minutes left."

On the way to the stage, Gordon goes though the moves for the last time. The entry music stops. A moderator welcomes the crowd and tells about the great wonders they're about to see. The band starts playing. The lights go to position. The show begins.

A reluctant servant enters. Fiddly flutes accompany her. She is dancing for her master. In the center of the stage, she goes on her knees to bow deep down to the ground. Her intertwined arms flow left to right, presenting delicate offerings on open hands. Fragile eyes observe the master's benevolence. She leads the attention with humility and strength. Showing her complete sincerity. A hand fan opens up. And another. Whirling in grace. Hectic noises. There's imminent danger. Unknown forces begin to push her. She stumbles several times until she loses balance. She screams for help. He perceives her suffering but stays still. Pain penetrates her body as she falls down and crawls on the floor. She fights with her whole being and endures the attacks, but the enemy prepares for the last strike. The forces hit her directly in the heart. A final back bend marks her defeat. She's dead. Curtain. The audience is moved by her tragic departure. It takes a while to subside, but then an enthusiastic applause follows.

A smiling Peter welcomes Gordon in his changing room.

"Who is a Sissy boy? You are the fucking Sissy boy. That was the finest performance I've seen in a while. Congrats. You'll play the world stages in no time."

"Shut up, asshole. I know you secretly loved it, but your insecurity is hindering you from appreciating my fantastic playing. Where is Steve?"

"He's in the audience. I'm helping you with the lion costume instead."

"All right, but don't mess around."

Peter is surprisingly careful. The wig change goes quick and the costume looks great.

"Done. The bloody lion king is ready to go."

"Thanks. Five minutes until entrance. I'll go get my partner."

"Good luck, mate."

He finds his son in front of the toilet. Trembling. Gordon grabs him and looks straight into his eyes.

"We'll make it, Ishi-san. We're in this together. Let's go. "

Ishi-san tightens up.

"I'm ready, Gordon-san. *Anata ni shinjiru.*"

The curtain opens for the final act of the evening.

A big lion leads his offspring onto the stage. Sharp percussion sounds populate the back of the room. The father jumps dynamically. Left. Right. Bending knees. Turning head. The son joins his movement. Spreading arms. Dancing in circles. Releasing perfect bursts of energy. Feet are stomping. Four feet are stomping. Spreading arms. All of a sudden: a rattling from the back. The father lion gets ready to push his cub over a cliff. It's frightened, but there's no turning back. A forceful kick strikes him, and he falls into the abyss. As the screaming slowly fades, a wave crashes against the cliff. It's gone. Silence. The father protects his eyes from the sun. He is on the lookout. Dark clouds of grief overshadow his face. The tension is unbearable.

He sings at the top of his lungs.

♫ "What have I done?" ♫

A dot appears on the horizon. A small mane is making its way to the shore.

♫ "My son. My beloved son. You have become a man." ♫

A thunderstorm is approaching. Enormous waves hinder the cub's progress. Heaven wants to devour the little thing. Its father screams in utmost pain.

♫ "Have mercy. Have mercy, dear god." ♫

There is nothing he can do, but wait. The storm brings heavy rain and high winds. It rages all over the land. He's pinned to the ground. Loses sight. The murderous noises come to an end. Time is standing still. Auspicious winds deliver the cub safely to the shore. He is a man now. Father and son bang their heads in relief. Immersed in splendid circles of joy. Slowly building to ever new heights of speed. The celebration reaches the final stage. Crescendo. The animals of the jungle appear to dance with them. The father sings a song of redemption and joy until finally a bright beam of light joins the heads of the happily united family with a triumphant gong. Darkness. Curtain. Delighted cheering. Applause.

The actors reach the backstage area. Gordon is crying. He's completely overwhelmed by the energy.

Ichi-san passionately hugs his father.

"Success, Gordon-san. Success."

Gordon wipes the tears off his face.

"I told you, my friend."

Standing ovations. They have to get back onstage to bow repeatedly in all directions. People loved it. Everything went blazingly fast, and Gordon was totally consumed. There was nothing to think about.

8

LOVE AT FIRST SIGHT

GORDON HAD A RUN. The play was a success. Even Peter congratulated him. His general misery was alleviated by a sense of accomplishment. Helping Ichi-san was greatly rewarding. It gave him strength, and he felt good about himself. Now was the time to go full on with Linda. First, he postponed the phone call. Then he called between fake appointments to honor the game. Remaining mysterious by keeping it short. He planned the date meticulously and had second and third options in case something would go wrong. The table reserved. New clothes bought. Multiple chains of events were carefully considered and solutions crafted. Gordon was in top form. A skilled warrior. He would save the princess and may even start a family. It was an opportunity of a lifetime. A beautiful woman was interested in him. But he had to avoid mistakes whenever possible. His story ended with a kiss on the cheek. A romantic endeavor of monumental proportions. Epic dialogues, full of promises. Never-ending love. He bathed in lukewarm feelings. Hearts flew out of his chest. The love boat was finally anchoring. All these years of drowning in sorrow would come to an end. Linda agreed to go on a coffee date. He would pick her up at Hachikō Exit outside of

Shibuya Station. It was a very touristy area, but he thought it was a good idea. They had plenty of options there. After coffee, he would ask to go out to eat and their romance would begin. Gordon decided to walk to Shibuya Station. Two hours would be enough to stop a few times and get something to drink. The days of sweating were over, and he enjoyed the fading sun. Fall was about to end. His clothes looked mature; however, muscle-posing was for all ages. He left and went into his preferred store to get the first shot of the day. Vodka was his helper in all circumstances. He had emptied a whole bottle after the Kabuki show but also gulped down a great deal after his mam-gu died. Celebration and misery were basically the same. Today, he would settle for the sporadic shot to maintain posture. It was an important event after all. Linda would arrive in half an hour. He was sitting on a bench and observed his phone religiously. At the twenty-minute mark, he began to fidget. At five minutes, he put the phone down and tried to appear cool. One minute. His stomach felt like a washing machine. Zero. The weather didn't help.

Where is she? Damn. She's playing games. Don't forget she's a standard appointment. Relax. No, not her. No, that neither. Fuck, I need a shot.

He checks his phone. Five minutes over.

She'll come now. Lean back.

Fifteen minutes over.

This is it. More than fifteen minutes is a rule violation. Come on, girl.

Thirty minutes. Gordon is circling his bench.

All right. You want to fuck with me. You think I'm going home? I'm not.

He sends her a message: "I'm here. Where are you? :-)."

Eat this, bitch. Tell me you missed your train. Tell me your dog died.

Fifty minutes. The phone rings.

"Hello."

"Hi, Gordon, I'm very sorry. Something came up and I had to work longer. Should we go on another day?"

I knew it.

"Not a problem. Are you in the area? My next appointment got canceled and I have a little more time now."

"Amazing. I could be there in an hour. I need to go home first to change clothes."

Are you kidding me?

"Well, why don't you just come as you are?"

"I would prefer to shower first. Forty-five minutes?"

No.

"That would be great. I'll go grab a coffee. Call me when you're here."

"Perfect."

A nearby café catches his eye. Old-fashioned furniture plus modern coffee culture. He orders a vodka shot to ease the tension. The service is quick. Two shots and a small beer later, Gordon is about to leave. But there she is all of a sudden. Standing right in front of the table. Wearing a totally innocent face.

"I saw you through the window. I'm so sorry I let you wait for so long. Will you forgive me?"

"Not a problem. Since the meeting got canceled, I had nothing better to do."

She sits down at the opposite side of the table.

"Amazing."

A moment of awkward silence goes by. Gordon orders a large beer. She gets a fancy coffee.

He tries to speak.

"Are you often here in the area?"

"Yeah, I love to go shopping here. Shibuya 109 is one of my favorites."

A girly girl.

"Cool. Why?"

"I like the variety. They have a nice selection and it's very affordable."

Whatever.

"Yeah, Shibuya is rather popular for shopping."

"You seem to be very busy with all these appointments. What do you do for a living?"

"I'm the manager of a global grocery store in Hiroo.

"Sounds much better than my job."

"Not necessarily. We had a chicken shortage lately. The supplier didn't manage to come on time. So I had to jump in to make sure we had enough product. We're open twenty-four hours and work never ends, you know."

"So much responsibility. I like hardworking men."

God. She's beautiful.

"Well, there's a lot of room for improvement. I'm looking at my options for higher management now. Aiding the chicken supply is not really what I wanted."

She laughs.

"Right. Who wants to worry about chicken. Do you have a specific position in mind?"

Gordon signals a shot and another beer to the waiter.

"Not really, but I'm sure there's more to come."

"You surprise me. I like that."

A slight grin leaves his face.

"I even surprise myself sometimes. A few days ago, I was the main actor in a Kabuki performance."

She seems genuinely interested.

"What's Kabuki?"

"It's a traditional Japanese dance drama performance art."

"How did you come to it?"

"Long story. A colleague wanted me to take part. I didn't expect it to be so time intensive, but it was fun."

"Nice. What was your role?"

He empties the shot as soon as the waiter leaves the table, shakes it off and orders another.

"It's about lions. I was the father. It was fairly successful."

"Isn't it too early for so much alcohol?"

Gordon feels quite dizzy, and the masquerade is about to fall, but the machine demands more.

"Don't worry about it. I'm just missing my people. The play showed me how important family is."

"That's sweet. How long have you been abroad?"

The vodka is flowing.

"I didn't leave Tokyo for five years. My job is very stressful. I had no time to go back to Scotland yet."

"Pity. I think you should always make time for family. Maybe you could visit on your next vacation."

"I thought about that, but I can't take so many days off without upsetting my colleagues. In management, we're supposed to take only half of our days, if any."

"Understand. Why did you leave Scotland?"

He is about to depart from sobriety.

Fuck it.

"I didn't want to become like my mother. My dad left the family, when I was a young bloke. We were alone and had to overcome a lot of hardship. Mam did everything she could, but she was desperate and weak all of the time. When I later moved to my grandma's house, things got a lot better; however, I still came often to visit. Years later, I landed my first proper retail job, but I still lived with Grandma. At one point, I couldn't bear my mam's weakness any longer. She would lie in bed all day and complain about trivial stuff. I stopped visiting so much and left her alone with my stepdad. I'm sorry, telling this story on the first date is not okay."

She sounds curious.

"Don't worry. It's all right. Go on, please."

The waiter brings another set of drinks to the table. Gordon is drunk by now.

"Where was I? Yeah, so my mother was a weak piece of shit and still is."

She is horrified.

"Please don't talk about your mother like that. I'm sure she did her best."

He has lost control and runs on automatic.

"I don't care. I had no childhood and my family is shit. I had to leave the place. Otherwise the shitty life of a Scottish drunk was awaiting me. When I played at the theater, I noticed how much I miss my people, except they're all fucking losers and going back would be the worst thing I could do. I can still hear my mam's voice telling me nothing is possible and that I should face reality. However, the truth is she wanted me to face her reality. Her loser reality. The weak piece-of-shit reality I hated so much. Through some coincidence, I had an opportunity to go to Japan. Tokyo is a big city, and it seemed a dream came true. All these possibilities and a completely different culture. Leaving Scotland was the best thing that ever happened to me."

Linda covers her open mouth.

"I think you're very rude. You should be thankful to your mother. You wouldn't be here without her."

"I'm thankful. However, it's puzzling to me, how a person can be so delusional. It's like you only see one side of the coin and ignore everything else. You live in your own fucking world, no matter what. And if your world happens to be a shitty place without love, you're a prisoner there."

His loud voice upsets the nearby tables.

"Life is not worth it, if it's just a stupid masquerade. Why not end it? Where's god when you need him? The answer is there is no fucking god and life is hell, if you grow up in the wrong place with the wrong people."

Gordon is losing it. The whole room is listening.

"Nobody fucking cares. I hate my life. This is bullshit."

Linda is completely floored.

"I want you to calm down now. Please get the bill. I want to leave."

"What about you pay for yourself? I'm fucking sick of those games."

Linda gets up and takes her bag. She opens her purse and throws seven hundred yen at him.

"Don't ever call me again."

She storms out. A sigh of relief goes through the room. Gordon finally gets it. It's over. The most important thing right now is the vodka in his fridge. He pays for the drinks and heads to the subway station. It's just a few stops, but it seems like eternity. Back home, he puts the bottle on the table and grabs a water glass. He stares at the floor. It's moving in circles.

Boring bitch. Another fuck up. Not good enough. Never will be. Why do I always ruin everything. Alone. Alone forever. Just give up. It's worthless. And then you die. What a shitshow. Whatever. Nobody cares.

He finishes the bottle quickly and dozes off. Arms crossed on the table. Shortly after, he loses his grip and hits the ground, since he is too drunk to become conscious. The broken glass hurts his face, and the floor is full of blood. He eventually sleeps with his bloody face leaning against a cabinet. It's a dark and peaceful night.

9

THE END

GORDON COULDN'T MOVE HIS head. His neck was killing him. The battery of his phone was about to die, but the emergency music played very loudly. As he got his spine straight, he saw the blood on the floor and realized what happened. The mirror shocked him. Dried-up blood was scattered all over his face. A thorough washing revealed two scars. One small streak under the left eye and a bigger one over the right cheek. They were not very deep; however, he would be marked for a few weeks. Panic set in. He looked like he'd lost a fight and was already much too late. A massive headache and the immovable neck cared for the rest. Calling in sick wasn't conceivable, since his mind wasn't working properly and he didn't want to give up the promotion.

Fuck. Fuck. Fuck. What now? Fitch, you fucking idiot. Okay. Calm down. It's all right. Breathe.

He rifled through the first aid kit in the bathroom. The Band-Aids would support his story. There was no time to shower. He drank the whole mouthwash and used tons of perfume to lessen the smell, which evaporated from every pore of his body. Breakfast consisted of a half-burned, cold pizza and three energy drinks. He had an offender in his skull. A laughing demon. Hitting him with a mallet. The impacts reverberated in tantalizing repetition through all of his limbs. He called work.

Keep posture.

"Azubi Mart, how can I help you?"

"Jade, is that you?"

"Good morning, Gordon. How are you?"

"Is Mason in the store today?"

"Yes, he just asked for you."

Fuck.

"All right. I know I'm late, but I had an accident yesterday."

"Oh my god. What happened? Are you okay?"

"I'm fine. A bunch of friends and I went mountain biking and I crashed and flew over the han—"

"Do you need something? I can come over after work. Have you been to the doctor, yet?"

His voice sounds out of breath.

"I'm coming in later. I just slept over the alarm. Tell Mason, I'll be there in an hour."

"I was starting to worry. Please don't do that to me. You're the best manager I have."

"Nice of you. I'll be there soon. Tell Mason."

"Hurry up."

Gordon grabs his bag and jumps out the door. He crosses the street to the subway station and hastens to buy the usual chewing gum and another energy drink.

Wait. You've got an hour. Slow down and relax a little.

In the subway, he lives through the horrible afternoon again. Playing it back word for word. Every gesture. His bold remarks. Linda's dismay. From first to last drink. He should have called in sick.

You need help. But why? I'm fine. No, you're not. You bled all over the floor. Whatever. Things happen. Maybe a therapy. What. No. Idiot. No problem. I'll deal with it. I can deal with everything.

He opens the door to the staff entrance. Jade is waiting for him. She looks closely at his face.

"Mother Mary. What have you done?"

"I tried to tell you I flew over the handlebar of my bike. We went downhill and I didn't see the pointy stone in front of me. Then I fell to the ground. Hikers must have left glass on the trail and I slid over it face ahead."

"Will you see a doctor?"

"No. The cuts are shallow, and the Band-Aids should be sufficient."

She sniffs on his clothes.

"Disgusting. Did you get drunk after the crash?"

"Well, we didn't party or something. I was simply in shock and needed something to calm myself down. So we went to the pub to get a drink against the pain."

She shakes her head.

"Don't lie."

"Jade, can't you see I'm having a bad day? I've had a few beers. Where is the problem? Again. You're not my girlfriend. Please mind your own business. I'm done with your constant remarks."

She puts her hands on her hips.

"Look at you. I don't want to be your girlfriend. You're just too full of yourself."

"No. I'm not. You wanted to fuck me forever, and I'm sick of you acting dumb all the time. Admit it and we'll finally get over it. Fuck. Let me get this straight right away: I'm not interested in you or a further friendship. I'm your boss and that's it. Do you understand?"

She is close to crying, but she catches herself in the last second. Instead, she repeatedly points at him.

"You're a heartless, insensitive rock. And you will never make it, because you suck."

The tears are flowing. She pushes him away and runs out the door.

Finally.

Gordon takes a sip of his energy drink. The caffeine mitigates the headache to an extent. He's now ready to drag himself through the day. He suspects there's a huge pile of work waiting for him. Mason is about to go on his first vacation in years and ordered him to cover some of his tasks. People gossip he's depressed. The storage room table looks normal, but his new schedule reveals the reality. He must do a ton of overtime in the coming weeks. Even after Mason's return.

I already have 1500. Give me my money. I'm suing these gangsters.

He opens Mason's files and starts to look busy out of habit. Irritated from the night and pissed about Jade.

Not my type. Hate weak girls. What if something happens? You couldn't count on her. She would shirk and cry all day. But she's nice, piece of shit nice. Fuck.

A call is coming in.

"Good morning, Tanaka-san."

Mason is barking as usual.

"Fitch. Where were you today?"

"Tanaka-san, I had an accident yesterday. We went biking and I flew over the handlebar. I couldn't sleep. It was very painful. I'm sorry, it won't happen again."

"No reason to miss valuable work hours."

Pay me, asshole.

"I'm sorry, Tanaka-san. I just started with the work you sent me."

"Hurry up. I want the two spreadsheets and the presentation to be ready by tomorrow. Any questions?"

"Yes, I don't understand the bar graph. In line…"

"That's extremely easy stuff. We have training videos on the intranet. Watch them. You'll get it."

"Thanks for your help."

"No problem. I'll see you later to go over it once more. My off-time begins the day after tomorrow and you'll need to be able to deliver. Are we clear on that, Fitch?"

"Yes, Tanaka-san."

"Good."

Gordon's head is hammering again. He hangs up the phone and opens up the company server to look at the instruction videos. They're lengthy and boring. He seriously needs to go home. His body is inflamed and the scars are pulsating. Although his sight gets alarmingly blurry, he forces himself to persist. He feels dead inside as Mason resolutely opens the door to the storage room.

"Fitch. How are we doing?"

He talks into his screen.

"Tanaka-san. The spreadsheets are ready and the rest is in the making."

Mason scrolls over the documents.

"That's not ready by any measure. The equations you added are all wrong and the bar graph is a nightmare. I told you to watch the videos. Why haven't you done so?"

Asshole.

"I did. It's no wonder I'm making a lot of mistakes."

"Why? Is it because you're smelling like a magnum bottle of whiskey again?"

"No, it's because I haven't had any training."

"Enough, Fitch. I think we seriously need to talk about your performance."

"What do you mean? I'm doing my best here."

Mason pushes Gordon's chair to the side and looks him in the eyes.

"Are you sure you're doing your best?"

He backs off a little to keep distance.

"It's not okay to treat me like that. I have a question too. What's the hourly rate for the overtime worked over forty hours?"

"Why?"

Gordon grinds his teeth.

"I'm working an additional two hours every day. Always. On top of that, you just gave me your work without even considering compensation."

"Are you serious? You're a manager and your contract doesn't allow for compensation regarding overtime."

"I know. But you didn't even upgrade my salary when you promoted me. I'm underpaid and you don't give a shit. You didn't want to play fair in the first place and you keep piling up work on my desk."

Mason straightens his arms and screams with all his might.

"Fitch, enough is enough. Stop it now or bear the consequences. You've been late three or four times in the last month. You forget orders regularly. The yogurt is way over the BBDs and the cooling looks nauseating."

He hardly stays together.

"I never did anything major wrong. I'm having a hard time lately and you don't show any sympathy for it."

"This is business, Fitch. Suffering is normal here. It doesn't help to act like a weakling. Your performance is shitty enough. You need to face reality."

Gordon goes blind. He jumps up from his chair and screams back at him.

"I'm not your slave, Tanaka. I'm a human being. You know it's wrong to treat people like that, but you don't fucking care. The only thing you care about is for people to have an excruciating time so you can feel validated for your own suffering. You're an egotistic, abusive psychopath. And the truth is, you're a weakling yourself, but you don't allow yourself to be real, because you're addicted to success."

"You're fired, Fitch."

He shows him the finger.

"Take your spreadsheets and stick them up your ass."

"You're banned from entering the house again. Call HR to get your papers. Now piss off, asshole."

Gordon is seized by the most dreadful fear and is shaking all over his body. He takes his bag and sprints out of the store. Jade watches him run. Block after block, it dawns on him. He got fired and ruined a friendship, and his chances for Linda were virtually zero. The next store, however, is right around the corner.

10
ENOUGH

GORDON ENTERED HIS FLAT. His heart was still palpitating, and his soul demanded a big glass of Russian vodka. A tired avalanche of despair dropped into the couch. Multimedia was starting up and he searched his browser history. A small speaker played a chillout beat. He changed clothes, threw a pizza in the toaster oven, began to drink, and emptied glass after glass. Six beers and five vodkas. His belly was full and his eyes were glazing.

What's wrong with me? I always try to help. There's no justice.

He tried not to cry. Another beer poured down his throat. Japanese walls were paper thin, and he normally used headphones for porn, but he couldn't be bothered. Reading the title got him horny. He pushed down his pants, drank on the left and pumped on the right. Focused on plastic woman. Holding back the tears.

I'll show you, motherfucker.

A single tear ran down his cheek.

Come on, fuck her.

He came all over the couch table. His face changed from weird excitement to absolute sadness. He put his pants on and stumbled to the kitchen counter. The city was glowing. He reached the eye of the storm.

I love Tokyo. The lights are so alive. Like home. Connected and lonely at the same time. Used. Usable. Foreign to the world. Foreign to myself. Nobody. Nothing. Instantly forgotten. Where's the magic? Joy. Celebration. Together. So many odd stages. Young love. Microcosms behind the couch. Dancing on the streets. Big emotions. Philosophical debates. Intensity. Tons of drugs. It's a miracle you're not dead.

He sat down again and shut down the moaning.

What are they doing? What's the prize? They win at life and die inside. You want to hate these people, but they already hate themselves. They wronged you badly. Life is not fair. Tell them how low they are. All these horrible feelings. They tried their best. Never looks like it. That's what they've learned. Everything is fucked.

Conceptualized. Meaningless. Dead. What do you want? I want control. You have none. I know how it works. You don't. You're a doormat. I show them. Show them what? Why do you care so much? Money? It's doubt. Souldoubt. You cover it up. Fucking booze everywhere. It's fun until you can't move your head. Never stops. The depths of hell are the gate to freedom.

The pizza burned the roof of his mouth, but he was already drunk enough to bear it. He prepared a round of vodka and beer. Funny dinosaurs were jumping all over the screen. The city waved like air on the ground of a hot summer day.

Nothing ever changes. My tiny cage. All the useless shit you bought. Torn between apathy and longing. Work. Home. Food. Drink. Jerk off. Sleep. Lies and shitty pictures. What about people? Is it really about them? Why only food and trends? Connection is nice, but egotistic. Go on and change the me me me.

He fell back into the couch.

Tell the truth. Maybe you can help. With what? Stop it. Honor her legacy.

He fought the exhaustion, but his eyes kept closing. Conjuring up dreams. Half-asleep and half-alive. Caught between the worlds of right and wrong. Doubting the difference.

The suburbs are closer to life. My tree at home won't forget. It'll wait. Everything is forever until it's over.

11

A NEW LIFE FOR ME

FOUR WEEKS WENT BY. Gordon took a much-needed break. He started looking after himself. Ate a lot of healthy food and exercised regularly. His prescriptions for himself were plenty of rest and no alcohol. Healing wasn't really in his vocabulary, but he did to some extent. As the days got darker, he started thinking about a new job. The money he got from mam-gu's heritage wasn't sufficient to take much more time off, but he didn't want to work in retail ever again. Peter offered him the receptionist role at the lawyer's office; however, the thought of serving people in a formal setting in downtown Tokyo wasn't even remotely interesting to him. It needed to be something different. His experience wasn't very diverse, and he didn't have a degree; he tried his best to find something, though. As his mam-gu died, he'd promised her to be a good man and aspire to help other people, but he had no idea how. At one point, he stumbled across an article advertising resort jobs in Japan. He thought about the hotel industry at first, but his lacking language skills made it impossible to apply. Tour guide, ski instructor, or even lift operator came into more detailed considerations instead. There wasn't much availability, and in the end, he applied for all of them. He had a few brief interviews over the phone, until finally a resort in Nozawa accepted him as a kids' ski instructor. They provided training, and housing could be had over the employer as well. Pay was slightly below average. Although he wasn't sure if he'd stay in the countryside, gaining the opportunity to leave the city was exciting somehow. It was a great way to have a good time and make new friends, but it also worried him a bit. He felt his time was running out to try new things. Most people had their act together by forty, and he was starting over again. This wasn't exactly what he was dreaming up during all these drunken nights and wild parties, but it was the only job he could realistically see himself in. The issue wasn't his intelligence. Other people were a lot stupider than him; he had not much to show except a bunch of certificates from his former jobs, though. However, the preparations went perfectly smooth, and he could sublease his apartment to a young English teacher from the UK, who struggled for an affordable place. His beloved flat would be looked after, and if he wasn't inclined to stay in Nozawa, he could go back in a matter of months. He was quite excited. The training would begin in a few days, and calming mountains were awaiting him.

Nozawa was a small town. At first sight, it could be compared to any touristy place with a ski lift, but it had its qualities. Above all, it was scattered with thirty natural hot water springs. *Onsen* were popular all over the country. They possessed healing properties through an array of minerals, which helped the body recharge after a long day out on the ski trail, providing relief for all kinds of aches and pains. He already planned everything in perfect detail. The Shinkansen bullet train was followed by a local bus. The accommodation, as well as the means to get there, were crystal clear. The work seemed doable and the hours were comparable to a simple office job. Steve was rather sad to see him go; he would come to visit, however. Peter agreed as well. He was still very busy, but he said it would be a shame to miss Sissy boy teaching a bunch of kids on a hill in the middle of nowhere. The day of departure came quicker than he thought. His two friends couldn't let him go without a last beverage in their favorite bar, though. He accepted the invite, but only for a few drinks. The Shinkansen would leave early in the morning. Nobody was surprised he couldn't just have two or three, though. He was a dedicated drinker, after all. Still, he managed to stop after four beers and two sake. A great accomplishment and a good sign for the future. Gordon told the boys how much they meant to him and left the scene in dignity and grace. He was greatly looking forward to what the future had in store.

■ ■ ■

Shinkansen stands for perfectly timed, superfast travel across Japan. It only takes around two hours to get to the stopover in Liyama. He admires the snowy houses, and isolated patches of forest create a feeling of depth and tranquility. No traffic to speak of. Birds are flying high over the fields. A land of serene landscapes. A dreamy bus ride on the way to a new adventure. A new reality. The bus arrives in Nozawa. He gets out and takes a deep breath as a tall, dark-haired young man waves at him.

"Hello, are you Gordon?"

He smiles with best intentions.

"Yes."

The young man hugs him enthusiastically.

"Welcome in Nozawa Onsen. My name is Inuksuk, but my friends call me Suk. Glad to have you here. How was the journey?"

He is surprised to be welcomed this warmly but finds it rather pleasant.

"It was a great ride. I really enjoyed the scenery."

Gordon tries to take his luggage, but Suk is faster. In a brief moment of silence, he feels a weight is taken from him and realizes how taxing city life actually is.

" I'm your roommate, by the way. I'd love to show you around later, if you want."

"That'd be great."

"Right. Let's go home first."

Suk walks him to a modest building in the middle of a descent. Two stories with small encapsulated corners to frame the many windows. It's called Kegon. They enter the guesthouse and climb up the stairs to the first floor. Old tapestry and wooden statues decorate the staircase. The door is drenched in stickers and festival tickets.

"Come in, please. We have two rooms. One bedroom and a living room. No kitchen. I bought a water heater to make tea. The view goes out to the backyard. There's not much to look at, but we have our own beer-cooling system on the window back. It's a humble way to live, but I like it."

Gordon winks amused.

"No problem. I like it too. The Western style beds give it a touch of luxury."

"Haha, yeah. The newer one on the right is yours. Would you like to unwind from the journey now?"

He starts fitting the cabinet with his clothes.

"Let me throw my stuff in here first. I would be happy for you to show me around in a bit."

Suk nods.

We'll get along. Must be Canadian.

Five minutes later, the clothes are in their proper places. Gordon is dying to see everything.

Suk puts on his jacket.

"Are you hungry?"

"Yeah, I could use a little something."

"We could grab an *oyaki*. It's just a few steps away. Steamed buns with all kinds of different fillings. The most famous is called onsen manju with red bean jam. I prefer pumpkin though."

"Can't wait. Love street food."

As they arrive at the street vendor, it starts to snow. Both get a plump chestnut bun.

"It'll probably snow all night. We should go to Yuyu Café and do the touristy part tomorrow. To be honest, there's not a whole lot to see here."

Suk leads them to Yuyu Café. It takes no time at all. They order coffee and pastries.

Gordon takes a sip.

"Could you tell me, what's going on here? I thought it was bigger and there was more stuff to do."

"It always looks bigger on the websites and brochures. Marketing talk."

"Are you regularly working in ski resorts?"

"It's my first time in Japan, but I've worked a lot of resort jobs in the past. People are very friendly."

"You don't really come for the friendly people, do you?"

Suk laughs.

"No. I'm Canadian. If it was for the people, I would stay home. We'll have a lot of time to talk over the next few months. It's a long story."

"All right. I'm curious, how is work?"

"Being a seasonaire is always difficult in one way or the other, but I got used to it."

"What do you mean? Didn't you say you like to live here?"

"Kind of. Nozawa Onsen is rather quiet. If the trails are not filled with people, they give us other things to do. You cannot blame them, though. They pay you very punctual and want their due."

"Understand. They told me I'll be a kids' ski instructor."

"I know. Training will start tomorrow in the morning. An expert ski guy from the main trail is coming down to show you what you have to do. It's not rocket science, but you need to apply yourself fully."

"What are we doing during quieter times, if I may ask?"

Suk cracks all his fingers in one motion.

"Originally, I wanted to wait before I tell you. I didn't want to scare you off right from the start."

His former enthusiasm gets toned down.

"Well, hardship is my second name."

"You are my kind of guy. Most of the low season is cleaning work. We clean onsens and public restrooms around the resort. There is nothing written in the contract, but if you don't comply, they are allowed to let you go immediately."

"What. No. I mean, that's bullshit. Why don't you leave for another job?"

"I need to save money for the off-season. It's not easy to find something new right now."

"Shit. I was wondering why my job isn't more popular. I have no experience as an instructor and the guy was thrilled to have me."

"Now you know."

"All right. I want to go home now. Do you have a key for me?"

Suk reaches into his trousers and hands him a golden key.

"Here. Your key to our mansion. You can sign all the papers tomorrow at the resort office. I'll go for a round of sake or two. Will you find it?"

He gets up from his chair.

"No problem. Thanks."

"Right. You need to be at the resort office 7:30. It's right next to the bus station. You can't miss it."

Gordon leaves the café with a rebellious stomach. Cleaning toilets isn't going to be fun. He had high hopes for his new job, but the positive energy is already lost. At least it's a new adventure.

12

MODERN SLAVERY

IT WAS A SHORT night. Gordon couldn't sleep. The thought of being a cleaner felt very inferior, and he couldn't stop making escape plans. But since it was a new beginning and he had no idea what the job would be like, he tried to ignore these thoughts to some effect. The office was full of people in their twenties and thirties. One guy, he estimated, would likely be his age; however, the rest were a bunch of kids who were presumably here to party. Nobody was serious about anything. The young folks wanted an experience. The resort, on the other hand, needed cheap workers and replaced people on a regular basis. Gordon would likely be an outsider. A balding guy in his forties, working a low-paid resort job was mildly sad. A young boy, making his way through a shitty day to party and go after the girls at night, left a much better impression. The HR person executed a standardized check-in procedure. He had to sign his contract and some other documents. As the formalities were done, he had an appointment with the ski resort manager. They told him to wait in front of the room. About half an hour later, an unusually big Japanese man opened the door and asked him to come in.

"Have a seat, please."

He bows briefly and sits down.

"Thanks."

The man looks over a big pile of documents before him.

"Welcome to Nozawa Onsen. How was your journey?"

"It was great, thanks. Very quick too. I like the landscape here."

He nods.

"I'm Rokku, Joben."

Gordon bows again.

"Nice to meet you, Rokku-san."

"Don't be shy. We have a lot of work to do. I'm going to give you an introduction to our standards here. After that, you'll go see Jason. He's one of the best. Is this your first time standing on ski?"

"Yes."

"No problem. We are not yet full. There is enough time for you to learn."

"I'm sorry, can I ask you a question?"

"Go ahead."

"The guy on the phone promised me a single apartment. I was under the impression I would have at least my own room."

"Who promised you that? We're never offering single-apartments to seasonaires."

What a load of dogshit.

"Understand. What are my duties?"

"Working hours and duties are written in our detailed workers' manual. We here at Nozawa Onsen family are dedicated to deliver the best possible experience to all our customers. The majority of our rooms are newly renovated, and the food is phenomenal. Exceptional cleanliness, outstanding hospitality, and the joyful will to go the extra mile is our main concern. We're hard at work with all our hearts to provide service with utmost excellence. Our philosophy is simple: a world of fun for everyone."

Shit.

"Happy to be on board. I'm going to read the manual for sure. Could you give me a brief overview? Maybe I have some questions, and I don't want to waste your precious time, Rokku-san."

"Of course. You'll be an instructor at our kids park. Hikage Slope is perfect for beginners, and I'm sure you'll enjoy work. The lessons are one to four hours long depending on starting time and skill level. You'll have to adjust your break times according to the bookings. Food and accommodation isn't included and will be pulled off from your salary. Cooking in the rooms is not allowed. Finally, If you get tipped, you're required to give it back. The Nozawa Onsen family is not in need of assurance for our excellent customer service."

"I knew there would be no tip. I have lived in Tokyo for five years. Is it always busy, or do we also have slower days during the season?"

"High season is usually very stressful, but you can be sure to have a little time to breath in between as well."

Just say it.

"I was asking because my roommate said we're cleaning onsen and public bathrooms during low season."

"That's correct. Didn't HR tell you about it already? Normally we communicate this in our interviews. I guess I have to talk to my HR manager about this. Are you sure? It's written in our manual."

Fuck me.

"Well, yes, I'm sure. Nobody told me about the low season cleaning. I was a manager myself back in Tokyo. Is there another option?"

His answer appears rehearsed.

"That's what you signed up for, I'm afraid. However, you'll be surely proud of yourself. Remember, we always go the extra mile. You will guarantee perfect cleanliness for the parents and unforgettable times for the little ones. This is crucial to ensure customer satisfaction, and you are without a doubt an important colleague."

I'm a machine and you're my master.

"Customer satisfaction is my primary concern, Rokku-san. I'll take care. We had a saying at my last job: fulfill their needs at awesome speeds."

Rokku-san couldn't be more thrilled.

"That's great. I'm happy you will be a part of our exceptional team. You can go for lunch now. Jason will be at Hikage slope in about an hour. He's responsible for your training."

He gets up and bows deeply.

"Thank you, Rokku-san."

Gordon swiftly leaves the room. He isn't hungry at all, because he's about to throw up.

■ ■ ■

The hill is actually very tiny. Even for a beginner's slope. To his surprise, the expert instructor is the guy from the office. It's nice to recognize his face again. Especially since they're the same age. He stands in front of the magic carpet. Gordon has trouble walking over the snowy slope. His sneakers are too slippery. He falls in a wide arc into the snow and loses his shoe. Jason rushes to pick him up.

"Are you okay?"

Gordon takes his hand.

"Thank you. I'll have to buy new shoes, I guess."

"You should. Sneakers are worthless here. I've seen you in the office this morning."

"Yeah, I'm glad I have someone my age showing me around."

"I'm Jason."

"Gordon."

"Nice to meet you."

"Likewise. So what are our plans for today?"

"First, we'll get your equipment, and then we take a look at your skills at Uenotaira Slope. Rokku-san told me this is your first time?"

"Yes, I think I'm quite fit cardio-wise, but I need to practice. I went on a ski trip once with a group of friends and did a beginner's course, but I'm not sure if I'm good enough."

"That makes our life a lot easier. You most likely know everything already and we'll only need a refresher."

"Do we have a moment? I wanted to ask you something."

Jason grins.

"You can always count on me. We here at Nozawa Onsen family are dedicated to go the extra mile."

Gordon grins back.

"Exactly. Can you tell me what the ratio between courses and cleaning onsen is?"

"In high season, you most likely won't clean at all. That's about five to six weeks from mid-January until late February. In low season, you're basically a cleaner and you're also helping at the kids' day-care center."

"Are you kidding me? I'll be a kindergarten teacher too?"

"Yes. You look after the kids once a week, when the girls have their day off."

"What? No. Nobody told me. I have to share a room with another person and everything looks completely different from the pictures. I'm sorry, but this is not right."

"Welcome to Nozawa Onsen family. We're at work with all our hearts…"

"All right. I get it. Why are you still here?"

Jason takes a wide gaze over the mountains.

"I used to live in Seattle. Mainly for friends and family. They are great people. I've always felt a sense of self-sacrifice and wanted them to reciprocate that. But over the years, they slowly moved away or got married. I worked in IT for almost seventeen years. However, as I got older, I wanted to try something new and started as a ski instructor. Skiing was always a passion of mine. Teaching for a living is fun; I'm active all day, and my back got a lot better too. It just wasn't worth it to stay any longer, since there wasn't much money in tech anymore."

"Well, I don't think I'll have as much fun as you. I've never worked with children and the only thing I know is enslaving grocery clerks to benefit the company. I formerly managed a team in Tokyo. Now I'm again at the bottom of the food chain and there's bad news by the hour so far."

"That's nothing. Wait until you see the big picture. There's much more shit going on than you can imagine. Another reason I'm still here is they pay me very well. Someone needs to train all the newbies, you know."

Gordon has a bad case of suspicion making its way through his body.

"Well, what is the bigger picture then?"

"You seem to be a decent guy. I normally don't tell this story on the first day. You see, Nozawa Onsen really is a family operation. Basically the whole town is owned by the Nozawas. It all started with a bunch of beds in a barn about two hundred years ago. Over the years, the empire grew steadily. Naturally they wanted to keep the ownership within the family, but Nozawa senior only had a daughter. Fortunately, there's a tradition called *ie*. If there is no boy to inherit, they often adopt a stepson into the family to assure future ownership. The marriages are often planned to train the so called *mukoyōshi* in all matters beforehand and instill the right mindset in him. Rokku's legal name is actually Nozawa. He knew he was going to be the CEO very early on. Ie's purpose is to unite business and family to sustain operations forever. As the father retired about three years ago, he left everything to Rokku and his daughter. The senior was a genius and a perfect boss. People stayed for many years before they left. Work was enjoyable. However, it all changed as Rokku took over. The contracts, the scope of work, and the pay. As a result, the older employees gradually left, and I became head instructor. I'm also helping with the network and accounting. They wouldn't dare to touch my salary."

"Touch your salary? At the HR office, Rokku told me accommodation and food are pulled. From my research, this seems to be normal. Only prices and quality of the benefits vary a whole lot among resorts."

"Correct. This is common practice in almost all hospitality temples. However, please don't leave right away when I tell you this. Okay?"

"Do they have slaves in the basement? Is it like the 1800s, but they pay you?"

"Promise."

"I couldn't leave, even If I wanted to and I've seen it all. Go on, please."

"You will notice anyway. Better I tell you now. Turn around to the restaurant. Right in front of the entrance. Can you see the slimy little woman? The one with the lilac cat-cap? That's the daughter. She monitors every move of us. The resort is full of whistleblowers and wannabes whose main purpose is to control and spy.

"Although Rokku got trained in business matters, growing up in a small town in rural Japan wasn't adequate to prepare him for a multimillion-dollar operation. Nobody could foresee his paranoia. He only trusts his wife and carefully selected employee friends in his closest circle. I've heard he went to Tokyo once but got anxious over everything and came back the next day. I'm not a psychologist, but I would say it's severe OCD mixed with deeply instilled anxiety. Many pleaded the old Nozawa to get rid of him, but in ie tradition, the mukoyōshi gets it all after the senior retires, and everyone is expected to support him. We're stuck with a mentally unstable boss and…"

Gordon folds his arms.

"Wait a second. You're saying our CEO is a psycho and all he does is trying to control people?"

"Correct. Furthermore, he's treating people poorly. As you said, food and accommodation are not included. The problem, however, lies in the points system he introduced. It's very much against the law and nobody knows how it works. I think its main purpose is to keep people afraid of making mistakes."

"You get awarded points for your work?"

"Everyone is closely monitored. When you screw up or get a lot of complaints from guests, you lose a few points. When you've lost enough, they play around with your numbers. One guy paid double for the food. A girl from the kindergarten never saw a dime of her salary. She had three complaints in a month."

"Nobody tried suing them?"

"The seasonaires must leave after a year, because of the work visa, and the long term people just suck it up. Jobs are scarce around here, if you don't work for Nozawa. We have to go. She's already looking at me."

"All right."

They went to the Ski Rental Shop. The ski were old, but Jason said they would be satisfactory. The test run at Uenotaira slope revealed some issues with Gordon's technique; however, he still had plenty of time to work on it. His course started in three days, and Jason would meet him between his bookings to get him ready.

13

MY OLD FRIEND

SUK IS HOME. HE lies in bed and watches videos on his phone. Gordon is happy to see him.

"Hi, where were you last night?"

"We went to Lotus for sake. I saw you walking to the office this morning."

"Yeah, it turned out to be even more interesting than I thought."

Suk stops the video and looks at Gordon.

"Go on."

"I learned a lot about customs here and the weird ways the business is operated."

"Jason is such a blabbermouth sometimes."

"He's not. It was super nice of him to tell me about the points system and our psycho boss."

"Are you leaving?"

"I would, but I can't. I'll have to deal with it. Just like you."

Suk sits up in his bed.

"I'm glad you stay."

"I think I need a drink."

"Right answer. We could go to the staff lodge later."

"What's that?"

"We have a big common room above the canteen. All the instructors meet there to party."

"I don't know. Maybe I'm too old for that."

"Age is not important. Let's have a good time. We have some beautiful girls here."

"Now we're talking."

Suk gets up from the bed and takes off his clothes.

"Let me shower first."

He looks out the window, while Suk is heading to the bathroom.

No good. I cannot drink as if I was twenty anymore. Damn, alone is even more shitty. I don't want to party all the time. Why did I come here? Stupid, stupid Gordon. I want to chill and eat. They'll be playing drinking games for sure. No liquor. Don't fuck up.

■ ■ ■

The staff lodge is located in the middle of Nozawa. It's already full with people. They have an old TV, worn couches, and lots of different chairs and stools. Suk greets everyone with a big hug and kisses on the cheeks. Gordon shakes hands and follows him to a big round table. Some guy is halfway through building a pyramid out of empty beer cans. A girl opens the fridge and throws two shots at Suk, which he catches effortlessly. Before Gordon can say anything, he has a beer and a shot in his hand. The atmosphere is cozy and about to get drunk. Suk stands up and holds his beer in the air. He calls full circle.

"May I have your attention, please. We have a new family member. Stand up. Show yourself."

Gordon nods at his colleagues. The room applauds and whistles cheerfully. His face turns bright red.

Suk taps him on the back.

"This is Gordon. A great guy. He still has all his points."

All laugh.

His color fades a bit as he sits down.

"Why did you do that?"

"Fun. You know what fun is?"

A fake smile leaves his face.

"I need another shot."

The drinking goes into next gear. Gordon is paying close attention to his alcohol intake. His fitness is helping him a lot. He looks around to get a sense of the people. All this scintillating talk seems inane. Maybe there's a sympathetic person he could do his boring forties stuff with. A girl catches his eye. She appears reserved. Sensible. He observes her inconspicuously. Watching her gestures as she talks. She looks around. Their eyes meet. She lifts both her eyebrows. He smiles automatically but also freezes.

Suk notices and waves her over.

"Hey, Gemma, I want to introduce you to someone."

She gets up, finds her way across the room, and sits down on a small stool next to Gordon.

Suk points at him.

"This is Gordon. Gordon. Gemma."

"Hi."

He clears his throat. All the distress of late lends him a certain gravitas.

"Pleasure."

Suk jumps in again.

"Gemma is our resort saint. She's collecting money for the elderly to buy Christmas gifts."

Gordon looks into her eyes.

"That's very nice of you."

She plucks her dress right.

"There are way too many single old people living in Nozawa. It's great how many colleagues already agreed to give something."

Gordon eases into the conversation.

"I would like to take part too. What kind of gifts are you going to buy?"

"It's not easy to find something. The greatest gift I can think of would be a community gathering over the holidays. They don't need pots and pans. They're missing a good talk from what I've heard."

"Agreed. Before my mam-gu died, I talked to her daily on the phone."

"I'm sure she loved every second of it."

"I hope so."

Suk leaves for a fresh beer. Gemma straightens her posture.

"Would you like to organize something? I could use some help."

"Why are you doing this?"

"I don't know. Do you want to help or not?"

Gordon isn't quite happy with her answer.

"Sure."

"Fantastic. I'm off on Tuesday."

"Where are you working at, by the way?"

"I'm the revenue manager of the resort. And you?"

"I'm a kids' ski instructor. How about Monday night? We could meet at Yuyu Café?"

Her face lights up.

"Great. Just call me at work."

A hand is approaching from the side with a shot.

"Thanks, Suk. What the fuck is in there?"

"It's your welcome drink. Wasp sake."

"I'm not drinking that."

"Come on, don't think twice."

Gordon takes the drink in disgust. Three dead wasps are floating in the glass.

"All right."

Trying to impress Gemma turns out to be a bad idea. He instantly feels the venom on his tongue. His mouth goes numb. The wasps are crunchy and bitter.

She looks disgusted.

"Eww. Are you eating the wasps right now?"

He's still chewing.

"Cruspy."

Gemma laughs. A guy starts playing a strange-looking Japanese string instrument. The group divides the room with a screen. The pyramid guy is pouring sake.

She starts explaining.

"It's called Tora Tora Tora. Basically rock paper scissors with poses. Loser drinks. Watch."

It's fast. A little song. Showing poses. Laughing and drinking sake. It doesn't take long to understand.

Suk is pushing him toward the screen.

"Your turn."

The game is on. People are clapping to the music. Gordon is completely absorbed. He is losing a lot, but the family seems to be delighted to have him.

Where's Gemma? Thank god, she's gone.

"Throw me a beer, please."

The lights get dimmer. Letting go feels liberating. The movie stops. Darkness.

■ ■ ■

"Good morning."

Gordon's eyes are glued shut. His voice is croaking. He holds his breath.

"What time is it?"

Suk holds a tea in front of him.

"Open your eyes. You have all the time in the world."

He rubs his face.

"Thank you."

"Do you remember everything?"

He bites his teeth.

"No. I blacked out after the second bottle."

Suk laughs hysterically.

"Really?"

Fucking hell.

"What time is it?"

"It's 7:30. When is your meeting with Jason?"

His heart calms down.

"Ten thirty. What happened?"

Suk is kneeling in front of his bed.

"You were totally fucked up. At first, you fell down and took the screen with you. We thought you were sleeping, but then you started dancing all of a sudden. I've never seen anyone dance like that. You jumped from table to table and roared 'I am the lion king, I am the lion king.' It was epic."

"What? No. I didn't do that. You're fucking with me."

"You did. Ask anyone."

"Damn. How did I get home?"

"You held tight to the bottle. I was surprised you were still able to walk. I had to support you partially, but never mind. You're a freaking sake machine. Don't tell me you're too old again."

Gordon massages his neck.

"I am."

Suk's high-pitched laugh echoes in the room.

"If you're not the lion king, no one is."

"Whatever."

"I'm out now. I have a course at eight thirty"

"Thanks for bringing me home."

"No problem."

Gordon tries the lukewarm tea. His mind relaxes somewhat. He's looking forward to a nice shower and a steamed bun. The backyard ivies carry a fresh load of snow. He remembers a poem he wrote.

Cordate leaves, forgotten grieves. Heart shaped joy.

Bright with snow in colden winds. World is never done.
Enveloped by a shine of trust, the now is over soon.
The wheel is moving on and must meet the sun and moon.
Fleeting matter withering, a dream of butterflies.
Another cycle slithering, just sitting there is wise.
My eyes gaze wide for middle ground, the bluish breath of life.
Embrace the silence, follow sound, your love cuts like a knife.
I was very young back then. She must be the reason I'm here.
Hope it's not going to shit again.

14

MOTHERLY LOVE

JASON IS WAITING FOR him at Hikage Slope. Three oyaki and a big cup of coffee almost cure Gordon's dizziness. Gemma motivated him somehow. He is ready to learn the instructor craft.

"Morning, Gordon."

"Morning."

"I've heard you killed it yesterday."

"Did Suk tell you that?"

Jason laughs.

"No. But there's only one staff lodge."

"Things happen, I guess."

"We need to start. I don't have much time. In the afternoon, we're going to train over at Uenotaira again, but now, I'll tell you how it all works. You'll be doing the first timers and beginners. The kids are five to ten years old. We'll try to put them together by skill level. First timers need to be able to start and stop, change direction, and ride the lift. Beginners know the basic safety and the mountain rules. They're able to skate and turn both ways and can ski green runs. The courses start at 9:00 and last till 11:00. The afternoon lessons begin at 13:00 and end at 15:00. Any questions so far?"

"I was asking myself what I'll do when they cry all the time or if someone wets their pants."

"You'll be working closely with the kindergarten teachers. They'll come and help you or take the kid to the snuggery to warm up. Just call them."

"Understand."

"A few more things. The first lesson is normally at Hikage. The carpet gets you to learner's slope. On the second day, you change to Uenotaira Slope. Nagasaka only if they have talent. A word on safety: kids are almost never afraid, parents are. You have to get them to feel safe for their child. I had some particularly frightened parents in the past, and we can't afford complaints. Now the most crucial thing: try to connect with them. The success of a course depends a lot on how much they'll like you."

"Perfect. What now?"

"I suggest you go for lunch in the staff canteen. I'm going home to eat. My course ends at 15:00. Be at Uenotaira at 15:15. I'll meet you there."

"Done. Looking forward to the ride."

■ ■ ■

He was a great teacher. Within a few days, Gordon could confidently call himself a kids' instructor. He navigated the slopes well and knew all the pitfalls. There was room for improvement; however, his skills were proficient enough to teach a course. The parents will bring the young aspirants to the snuggery, where Gordon is waiting. His first course consists of a small group of three kids, who are about six years old. A brother and sister duo and a boy. It is quite a contrast. Upper-middle-class meets holey ski suit. The kindergarten teacher can't believe it when she sees him playing with the hole on the back of his trousers. She wants to talk to the mother, but she's left instantly. The parents of the siblings are upset about his appearance.

They're reluctant to leave. Gordon observes the situation. He can't risk a complaint and decides to settle the matter.

"Hello, my name is Gordon. I'm the ski instructor."

The mother points at the boy.

"Is he having his ski lesson together with our kids?"

"Yes. It's a small course. I can really take my time to care for their individual needs."

"That's good, but this boy can't go about in such rags."

"Why not?"

"Are you blind? Just look at him. He looks like a street bum."

"Ma'am, please don't refer to him in this way."

"I talk how it suits me. We've signed up for a ski course, not for a display of poverty. We paid good money and we're entitled to certain standards. My kids mustn't be in the presence of these people."

"We're holding very high standards for our courses. I'm sure the kids will enjoy it."

She takes on a hostile tone.

"Listen, we worked hard to provide our children with the life we've never had. I will not allow you to expose them to beggars. Who knows, maybe the little devil is aggressive as well."

"Ma'am, please calm down. It's just a minor issue with a ski suit."

"You can't treat us like that. I want to talk to your boss."

"I'm sorry, the head instructor is currently busy teaching a course himself."

"That is very bad. I'll have to leave my kids here now. We've scheduled a reunion with old friends at a restaurant. But let me tell you: this will not be the last word. Tomorrow, I'll be seeing your boss."

"I can assure you, we'll find a solution. I'll take good care of your kids."

"That's the least you can do."

She walks over and forbids her children to talk to the boy. Then she leaves. Gordon gathers the group together and starts his lesson in front of the carpet. The boy's name is Duncan. He's friendly and shy. The siblings are named Jasper and Amber. Both very lively. While Duncan waits patiently for Gordon to begin, Jasper is running around furiously and Amber rolls on the ground crying. Gordon attempted to get their attention, but they seem to be even more difficult than their mother. After thirty minutes of back-and-forth, he eventually calls his colleague.

"This is Gordon. Could you please come over? I need help."

"What happened?"

"Jasper constantly tries to steal stuff from other children, and Amber won't stop crying."

"I know, they're a nightmare. Give me five minutes."

The girl from the snuggery arrives. Jasper has his hands full with a variety of items. She empties his pockets and gives everything back to the rightful owners. He cries as if the toys are his own. Amber stands up and heads to the snuggery. As Jasper sees that, he breaks free and follows her. The girl has not much left to do beyond running after them. Duncan is still standing on his ski. Watching curiously.

He bends down.

"Duncan, are you not getting cold?"

"No, I want to ride down the mountain."

Gordon is delighted by the boy's straight and humble answer.

"You're right. Let me show you the basics. Tomorrow, you'll ride down the mountain. I promise."

The little boy claps his hands in excitement. He appears to be intelligent and eager to learn. The remaining time goes by quickly, as he follows Gordon's instructions to the letter. They have a lot of fun. Back in the snuggery, Duncan recounts his experience with glowing eyes as Gordon is leaving for lunch. He can't wait to see Duncan ride down Uenotaira Slope.

15
THE HEAT IS ON

IT WAS A SUCCESSFUL day. Duncan was very happy when he left. Gordon could even ignore the issues with the entitled mother of those badly mannered kids. He is preparing to meet Gemma. They'll have some coffee and talk about their charity project for the aging people of Nozawa. The meeting has a clear premise, so nothing could go seriously wrong. If the talk flows, he will go more into private terrain and find out how she operates. If not, he will simply go back to planning- and project-centered questions. It feels safe and not overly burdensome as many other first dates in his life have. Yuyu Café has been in operation since the seventies and, true to Japanese tradition, is led by one of the few families who managed to survive despite the meteoric ascend of the Nozawas. It has a strange nostalgia attached to it. Gordon is early as usual and thinking about love. He devours the great pastries and dreams out the window. Gemma is perfectly punctual. She wears a brown coat with a beige knit sweater. It is a wide, cozy fit. He thinks about how soft and cushiony it would feel to rest his head on her breasts. The tendency to sink into the soft clothing of a woman is irresistible to him. Her shoulder-long hair accompanies her kind face. His heart misses a beat as she comes in.

"Gordon, glad to see you."

He gets up for a brief hug.

"Likewise. Please have a seat."

She takes out a ring binder and orders a coffee and a chocolate brownie.

"I had some ideas we should talk about."

"Cool. Let's see what you got there."

"Yeah, the people here have known each other for a long time, but they don't seem to talk much. I wondered if we could just set up an afternoon coffee. Maybe with an all-around entertainer?"

"That hits the mark, I guess. Don't forget *taiyaki*. It's a favorite in Japan. A modest party decoration would round it off pretty well."

Gemma arranges the items on the table in perfectly aligned order. She is working on the relationship between the napkin holder and the menu.

"Let me write that down. I love painting and decorating."

Haha, what a freak. I love her.

"Do you have a specific entertainer in mind?"

"Yes, Jason knows a guitar player who worked a season for Nozawa. He said he had a great voice and could play whatever music they liked."

"Sounds great. Literally."

Her eyes move quickly.

"I'm afraid that's not completely correct."

"You like to be always on point, do you?"

"It's a bit of a habit."

Marry me.

"That's adorable."

"It's not. You don't know what I'm going through."

Gordon taps her hand. He smiles.

"I know exactly what you are going through."

She shies away from his touch.

"Maybe."

"All right. I'm in the mood for some fun."

"What do you mean? We are not finished."

"That's right, but in order to fix the date, you need to contact the entertainer first. The other stuff is worked out. We just need to make a few calls and put it together properly."

She's looking for something inside her purse.

"I didn't think about that."

"No need to rush. We have plenty of time. Are you up for a surprise?"

She holds a phone in her hand.

"What surprise?"

"I've made a reservation for a snowcat ride. I originally had planned to go with my roommate, but he prefers to soak in an onsen today. Would you like to go?"

"I'm not sure. How much is it?"

"Please accept my invitation. I already paid for the tickets."

She is weighing her head from left to right.

"Why not. I'm in."

"Terrific."

His heart is vibrating.

We're producing energy. This will work.

■ ■ ■

The snowcat tour is a forty-five minute ride over untouched mountain plateaus around Nozawa. Gordon has all kinds of romantic pictures emerging in his head as he finds out they are alone. Alone with her in the back cabin of this giant vehicle, cruising over the mountains is like a dream. Everything falls into place beautifully. He gently pushes her upward to get on board. The engine starts with an obligatory roar but calms down nicely. The weather is sunny with almost no clouds in sight.

Just be yourself.

"Have you been riding on the snowcat before?"

"Not this one."

"I hope we'll see some animals."

"Jason saw a deer family once."

They pass the first larger hill. A wide panorama opens up.

"I've read about the deer around here. They mostly live alone and come together only once a year during the rut. The Japanese think of them as a cross between a goat, a donkey, a cow, and a pig."

"Sounds like you have relatives in the mountains."

The cabin fills with laughter. Gordon winks at her.

"The locals call them *kamoshika*, and spotting one is supposed to bring luck."

She slightly lifts her chin.

"Do you think I'm lucky with you?"

He comes nearer.

"You could try."

She looks at his mouth. He bites his lips. The tension rises. She closes her eyes. He melts by the sight of her devotion. Their lips meet as her tongue enters his mouth. He caresses her back and a sensual kiss turns into a deep relaxing hug.

She eventually lowers her head to take refuge on his chest.

"I tried."

"Well, is this the first time you kissed a donkey-pig on a snowcat?"

She slaps his shoulder.

"Shut up."

The kissing and hugging feel more and more familiar. They enjoy the sun and the views over the mountains. Gordon is happy. Gemma is smiling.

16

YOUNG AT HEART

DAY TWO OF THE beginner's course is about to start, and Gordon is in a great mood. Duncan and his mother are sitting on a children's table in the snuggery. The boy wears the same clothes from the day before. Taking a good look at her, he realizes the family doesn't fit compared to other resort guests. He likes Duncan a lot and is highly committed to giving him the time of his life. However, he wants to talk to the mother first. How did they manage to go on an expensive vacation if at the same time, they couldn't pay for proper clothes?

"Hi, I'm Gordon. Duncan's ski instructor."

"Hello, Mr. Gordon. I'm Alison. Nice to meet you."

Mister?

"Same here. How do you like your hotel?"

"We're staying at a ryokan. It's beyond anything I have ever seen."

"Glad you like it. Your Duncan is a great boy. He is very dedicated and an avid learner."

"It was Duncan's biggest wish to learn skiing. He once saw the winter Olympics on telly and wouldn't stop talking about it. He even locked himself up inside his closet and didn't want to come out until I agreed to ride down the mountain with him."

"Where are you from?"

"We're from Aberdeen. Why?"

"I've worked at a grocery store in Aberdeen. Nice to have fellow countrymen here. Did Duncan want to learn skiing in Japan or is it a mere coincidence you're here in Nozawa?"

"It took a long time, before we had the chance to get to a ski resort. It's actually his birthday present. We couldn't afford it, and I was devastated we would never make it. But there was a competition in a magazine and we won first prize somehow."

"Congratulations. I'm very happy for you and Duncan."

The siblings enter the room. They instantly swarm out to bring harm over the snuggery. The mother walks over and interrupts their conversation.

"Gordon, right?"

"Yes."

"And you must be the mother of this little shit?"

"Did Duncan do something wrong?"

"Yes. The little street bum is a shame."

Gordon chimes in to clarify.

"Duncan has very good manners, and he's very intelligent. Your kids threw a spanner in the works."

The woman's tone changes to hostile again.

"What does that even mean? My kids are well behaved, because I keep them away from people like these. That's what's wrong with the world today. Losers everywhere. Lazy, offensive losers."

The siblings are hard at work by now. Jasper is destroying the fire truck of a child, and Amber throws building blocks across the room.

Gordon points at Jasper. His mother screams at him.

"Jasper. Put down that fire truck right now. Otherwise, you'll sit on your own when we get home."

Jasper shows no reaction. She is beyond upset and aggressively removes the toy from his hands.

"That's it. Give me that truck."

He cries.

"See what you did again. Your father will be very disappointed."

Fucking monster.

"I'm sorry, could we start the lesson now? Time is running out and we need to go."

"My kids won't take part in your shitty lesson. We're going to the hotel. Amber, come he—"

Gordon loudly claps his hands and the snuggery goes silent.

"That's it indeed. Do you know what your problem is? You are a weak, incompetent mother. You're not even capable of being with your own child for a second without emanating your encompassing uncertainty. You think it's about responsibility, but the truth is, it's about love. And to cover it all up, you burden your kids with your authoritarian ways. It's no surprise they resist. You are traumatizing your children, and they will struggle all their lives. And best of all, they will maybe never know what's wrong with them. Just like you. I don't want to teach your kids, because they're horrible. I want you to leave this place and never return. You're a shame. An entitled catastrophe of a parent. Fuck off."

Everybody looks at her. Gordon's heart is pumping. He can feel his blood rushing through his veins. No one dares to say a word. Amber and Jasper are speechless as well. The mother extends both her arms to takes the kids' hands. She leaves the snuggery with a hateful look on her face.

"I'll get you fired."

Alison cautiously turns to Gordon. She whispers.

"Sorry, Mr. Gordon. I promised my son a ride down the mountain."

He walks over to Duncan.

"Me too."

Gordon takes the boy outside and proceeds to Uenotaira Slope.

■ ■ ■

Duncan didn't say a word, while they were sitting in the lift. Gordon thought about ways to explain the incident. He wanted him to enjoy his great day and not worry about anything.

"Are you excited for the ride?"

He points downward.

"Do we ride here?"

"Yes, it's not very steep. It will be a lot of fun. Your mam told me how bad you wanted to come here. I'm so happy for you. How do you like it?"

"The food is weird."

"Why?"

"Breakfast at home is better."

"Yeah, English breakfast is the best. How do you feel about what just happened?"

Duncan curiously looks at Gordon.

"Is she a mean woman?"

"No. She just doesn't know how to love her kids."

"But you said she was bad."

"It's not really her fault. It's not easy to grasp, but people sometimes don't know who they are."

"Does my mam love me?"

"Your mam loves you more than anything."

"I had a dream last night. I was all alone and my mam wasn't there. I was very heavy. I couldn't move. Something held me back."

" I also dreamt a lot when I was your age. But it stopped somehow. What did you do?"

"I was afraid."

"There is nothing to be afraid about. I'll tell you something now that you must never forget. Maybe you're too young now, but it's very important. Will you remember when time comes? Promise."

"I promise."

"All right. First, when humans come to this world, they're all the same. Only later, when people grow up, they think they're somehow different. It makes them feel very sad and lonely. Always remember, you're not special. There can only be one Duncan, but you are just as everybody else. And second, if someone angers you, don't answer them right away. Have patience. Wait twenty-four hours, then come back and respond. Do you understand?"

He closes his eyes and nods.

The lift arrives at the station. Gordon takes his hand. He repeats his advice again. As the first meters on the way down are behind them, Duncan's face is brightly lit. It was all worth it.

17

FIRE

THE FIRE FESTIVAL IS Nozawa's greatest tourist magnet. Although it got rescheduled to an earlier date this year, the town was looking forward to it as usual. Gordon invited Peter and Steve to take part in the festivities. It wasn't easy to arrange for them to come though. Especially Peter was very short on time; however, he agreed to stay for a day. The happening centers around Japanese folk deities: the Dosojin. They were worshipped for bringing fertility to newly married couples and to protect travelers against calamities on and off the street. It's a cherished tradition to place stone statues at crossroads and local boundaries in order to secure people's transition. A selection of villagers in their *yakudoshi* years defended a wooden shrine against a mob of attackers, who tried to burn it down with torches. Yakudoshi takes place at twenty-five, forty-two, and sixty-one. It's considered an unlucky time in life, where one has to deal with the changes of a new period. The youngsters were positioned at the bottom, while the middle agers sat on the shrine itself. The old yakudoshi were spared. Accompanied by clamorous excitement and free sake, they fought for hours until the structure eventually burned down. His friends arrive relatively late in the day. Peter insisted to come by car and Steve was thrilled to be in the passenger seat. Gordon meets them at Yuyu Café. He can feel Peter's presence vividly. As he enters the street, the ground seems to shake under his repeated jumping. It seems he's getting ready to attack in the most destructive of ways. Ultimate party mode. Steve has trouble keeping up. The door bumps against the stopper and wide open arms are flying through the room. Gordon stands up and tries to catch them but makes sure to put one foot slightly forward to keep himself from falling.

"Matey, nice to see you. You look younger. Is it the cold or are you in love again?"

Steve joins the big hug.

"Hey, Gordon, great to see you my friend."

He's still digesting the impact.

"Haha. It's love, you idiot."

Peter orders beer and sake to celebrate the reunion.

"I knew it. Gordon is at it again. How's life up here?"

"Mixed. Pretty boring, but I had some great experiences."

"You better tell us now. There's a fire burning tonight."

"Well, I've met a nice girl, and I can't wait to see her again. We had a romantic ride with a snowcat over the mountains."

Steve chimes in to join the conversation.

"Let me guess, you found the girl of your life. Again."

"No, Gemma is different. She is trustworthy and a little bit like me. It's perfect."

"What makes you so sure of that?"

"Sometimes you just know."

Peter lifts his glass.

"Cheers, brothers. To a fabulous night."

"Thanks for coming, guys. We'll crush it."

The glasses clink once again. Steve is first to recover from the liquor.

"Go on and tell us a little bit about her. I'm curious."

"All right. Gemma is the revenue manager of the resort. She is punctual and has an inner need to do good. We're organizing a little charity event for the elderly of Nozawa. I love her laid-back clothing."

"Great. Are you planning to stay here, if it works out?"

"I don't know yet, but I know she loves me too. I'm going to do whatever is necessary to make her happy. I want to marry her and have kids."

Peter laughs.

"Wow, the little cub is about to enter manhood."

Steve pushes back.

"Shut your mouth, Peter. Again, what makes you so sure of her?"

"It's a feeling."

"You've had that feeling about every woman you've ever met. That is not enough."

Peter also has some concerns.

"Mate, did you fuck her already? Don't tell me you didn't fuck her already."

"No, I didn't. And yes, it's enough to have a feeling, if it's stronger than all else."

"You didn't? Man, you need to fuck her first. How will you know otherwise?"

Steve is disgusted by Peter's crudity.

"It's always the same with you. Fucking is not even ten percent of a relationship. Yet everybody talks about it all the time. A good relationship is based on love, trust, and believe it or not, letting go. You might marry a woman you absolutely love and she may be a goddess among girls. However, reality will kick in, and then you have to live with her. Marriage means to be there for the other person regardless, if they screwed up or if you're in a bad mood. That's the meaning of trust. Think of her as family. You'll hate her from time to time, but neither of you will leave. If you let go of your self-imposed conditions and prejudices, your love experience will take place in the real world, not on fantasy island. You may realize at some point that you both share a secret bond only time and dedication could create."

"Bullshit. There needs to be a thorough fucking."

"You know what? You're a pig. You suppress others out of calculation and you confuse freedom with egotism. People are mere tools for you and dignity is completely absent in your world."

"Listen, Steve. I've had enough of your repeated accusations. You're just weak. You please others out of calculation and you constantly suppress your deeply buried anger. That's why you always pull that hippie shit on us."

Gordon tries to appease them with a placatory gesture.

"Stop it. Both of you. The more I look at these things, the more I become clear at how similar it all is. Egotism and altruism are two sides of the same coin. Both are important in the right context."

"Except you need money for love. I'm just making sure I have enough instead of Gandhi here."

Steve loses it.

"Look, your whole career is just a means of showing your big dick to everyone. You want to be great, but in fact, you're nothing. When death knocks, you can't take anything with you. If you could realize this one thing only, you would finally be able to stop using other people."

"You're looking for trouble, are you?"

"Sorry, Peter, I cannot hear it anymore."

"Guys, please. One thing is certain: competition and love don't cancel each other out."

"Sissy boy."

■ ■ ■

After a few more rounds, the squabblers went to their hotel to change clothes and to prepare for the evening. The shrine was already in place and the fight would start at 8:30. Gordon was waiting at the tourist office. He ate an opulent meal and was ready for copious amounts of booze. From his intense appearance at Yuyu Café, he knew Peter would be merciless. He had so much energy, it seemed to be unreal. His friends were both equipped with a strong bottle of sake, and shot glasses hung from their necks. Steve brought one for Gordon too. They tried them out extensively and made their way to the festival. Peter documented everything with a myriad of pictures. The village stood around a group of men in white kimonos with conga drums. It could be heard all over Nozawa. Between the drumming, they sang songs to honor the Dosojin. The atmosphere was thrilling with anticipation. Another group in orange overalls appeared. They seemed determined to burn the wooden shrine with an enormous torch. It tumbled around without the slightest concerns for safety. The torchbearer presumably tried to light the street from left to right, while the spectators on the sidewalk tried to protect themselves. Team blue prepared for the first wave and built a circle. Gordon was anxious of the sparks and stayed away from the immediate battleground. Even Peter didn't want to risk burning himself. His sweater was made of cashmere, and he always used extensive amounts of hair spray. The torchbearer finally arrived at the shrine. Two team members supported his body during the first strike. Wave after wave hit the defense. A bonfire was lit to light a number of individual torches. It was ruthless. Peter made selfies, jumped as high as he could, and almost singlehandedly emptied his bottle. Steve and Gordon slowed down a little but kept a steady pace nevertheless. Gordon felt a lingering darkness inside of him. As their own supply died out, they switched to the free booze, which was available all over the place. Peter dragged them from spot to spot to get more photo opportunities. He has enough selfies to stick them all over his accounts. Steve hasn't digested the last discussion well and is waiting for his chance to express his bubbling resentment. As Peter grabs his arm to change to yet another place, he uses the opportunity to revive the debate.

"Why are you taking so many pictures?

"It's fun, Stevolo. It's fun."

"If it was fun, you would enjoy the festival instead of running around like a wild boar."

"Fine. You're still mad because I called you weak. Aren't you?"

"No, I'm just annoyed by your tremendous ego."

Peter pours himself a shot and gulps it down.

"Come on. My people appreciate the pics and I like to take them."

"Admit it. It's just another way of showing off your status in order to make your followers jealous."

"I'm just taking a few selfies, Steve. Fucking selfies."

"We're staying at the most expensive ryokan and you're taking pics nonstop since we got here. Food, booze, your Chelsea tractor, all accompanied with a fake smile. You're not really here with us. You're fishing for likes and shares."

"What the fuck is your problem?"

Steve holds his glass for Gordon to refill.

"You may have missed it, but you changed tremendously over the years. All that stupid money made you into a narcissist. A social media bitch. A show off. You're looking down on other people as if you were some sort of god and you firmly believe money can buy everything."

"You call me a bloody narcissist? Fuck you. I'm a lawyer and I help people with their issues. You know I came from being a bouncer. From nothing. And if someone doesn't like me or my pictures, they can fuck off."

He gulps down the shot.

"Don't try to hide your shitty attitude. I'm not saying I'm not drunk, but when you are, it's all downhill from there."

"Listen, people treat me differently since I have money in the bank. You know why? Because they are indeed jealous. They cannot contain their Robin Hood ideas and their hypersensitivity. If they would have their way, all my money would be transferred to the poor. But the problem is, if you're a fucking loser in your head, you'll always be one."

Gordon sighs extensively and blows a load of heavy air toward the ground.

"Guys, guys. We are at the fire festival. One villager just got hit by a torch over there. We shou—"

Gemma is watching the battle from the other side. She laughs and cheers at the passing yakudoshi. The adrenaline in Gordon's system peaks. His mind redirects his whole attention. Fire isn't the main attraction anymore. He thought about her body and face the whole day. She doesn't notice, but his magnification is set to maximum.

Truly a goddess.

The friends notice his open mouth. Steve signals him to stop dreaming.

"Gordo, what's up?"

"Gemma is here."

"Mate, where is she? We want to see her."

He points at her.

"Right over there."

"Are you kidding me? She's much too hot for you. Who's standing next to her?"

"His name is Jason. He's the head ski instructor. Basically my supervisor. Great guy."

Jason wraps his arms around her shoulder. She invites his touch with her hand.

Gordon's eyes are glued to the scene.

What the actual fuck?

Peter lifts the bottle.

"Give me your glasses. Let's drink."

Steve is first.

"Maybe they're just friends? I know a lot of woman who have cuddle friends like that."

Peter lifts the bottle again.

"This is fucked up. Are you going to confront her?"

He signals Peter to be silent.

"Let me watch a little more first. Maybe Steve is right."

The attackers get more aggressive. Sparks are flying everywhere. Team blue is defending with all they have. Flaming torches hit the wooden structure in rapid succession. The audience pulls back from all the burning bamboo bunches. Everyone has lost control. An especially rough wave of violence finally manages to ignite the bottom of the shrine. The middle ager's shout to reinforce their defense. Then it happens. Layer after layer, the fire devours the construction. Giant flames illuminate the night sky. Thick smoke indicates the unavoidable consequence. Team blue admits defeat and leaves the top as fast as they can. Circling winds turn the site into a foggy soup, and visibility goes down to almost zero.

Gordon tries to spot Gemma inside of the coughing crowd.

Motherfucker. Don't touch her again or you'll pay for it.

As the wind turns, the fire now has access to enough air to burn much more cleanly. It rushes to ever greater heights. Single buttresses burst under the heat. Team orange has accomplished their mission. The shrine is burning brightly.

The sight gets better. Gemma seems to be even closer to him.

This is not fucking happening.

The last cloud leaves. Jason turns his head. She does the same. Their lips meet for a passionate kiss.

You're gonna burn.

Peter hands him the bottle as a token of friendship.

"No need to cry. Here. Just go for it."

He grabs the liquor and takes a big sip.

"I'm not crying. My eyes are still tearing from the smoke."

"Whatever, mate. Fuck her. There's plenty of fish in the sea."

"Peter is right. We're here to support you. Always."

Posture is out of the question. The tears are flowing. Gordon's voice is surprisingly clear, however.

"Thanks, guys. I don't think I'm staying any longer. Would you mind, if I leave now?"

"No problem. Steve and I will have a few more drinks before we head back to the hotel. I want to take some more pics of the shrine."

Steve makes an understanding face.

"Not at all. The festival is finished either way."

"All right. Thanks for coming. Next time, I'll leave the woman out of the party. It's a shitshow anyway."

Gordon leaves the festival with the sake to provide refills for his leaking face. He's about to celebrate his misery in all its glory. Nobody is home. He's alone with the bottle and a window back full of beer. The jacket lands on the bed, and he sits with his neck erect to fill up his greedy mouth. He groans vigorously to thrust out the pain. The liquor runs down like water into a dried-up loveless wasteland.

Again and again. You fucking loser. Why should I keep hoping? It's all fucked up anyhow. It's a cycle. You hope, it's important, you push, you fail. Repeat. It makes me sick. Why do I feel relieved? Fuck.

He chokes due to his overflowing mouth. Silent tears run down his face as he watches the backyard.

Love hurts, and hope is damn risky. Stop hoping, Fitch. Just stop. It's frightening. Maybe I want too much? Maybe I don't want anything. No hope. No letdown.

Gordon's battery is in the red. The fire has burned his mind.

18
NO CONTROL

HARSH NOISES ECHO THROUGH the room. Occasional explosions and flashy music penetrate Gordon's ears. He has a hard time opening his eyes. The sake is still sticking all over his face. Suk is playing video games on an old TV.

"What the fuck. You've got to be joking."

Suk turns the volume down.

"Morning, Gordon. Sorry, I got carried away. Glad you're awake now."

"Why? It's my only free day of the week."

"You didn't answer the phone. Jason asked me to relay something."

Gordon brings himself into upright position.

"Jason? What did he want?"

"Rokku called him this morning. He wants to see you."

"Rokku wants to see me. Why?"

"I don't know."

"At what time?"

Suk looks at his phone.

"You're ninety minutes late."

"Fuck. Why didn't you wake me earlier?"

"Sorry, I tried the whole morning, but you didn't react."

Gordon gets out of the bed and tries to get his thoughts in order.

"It's my free day. Whatever."

He takes off the stinking clothes and jumps under the shower. After getting dressed, he buys an extra-large coffee and a pack of gum. Still somewhat hammered with a general disorientation and a severe headache, he sits in front of Rokku's office in expectancy of humiliation and pain. The Japanese giant opens the door and invites him in.

"I know it's your day off, so thank you for coming."

"No problem. We went to the festival, but I was home early. What can I do for you, Rokku-san?"

"We have to talk about the incident at the snuggery."

"What incident?"

"Let me make myself clear. We here at Nozawa Onsen family serve the customer to our best ability. However, we also stand together to support each other. Please keep that in mind."

"Thank you, Rokku-san. I appreciate the kind words."

Rooku-san opens a drawer and takes out a file with Gordon's name on it. He reads a few paragraphs, looks down, and deliberately shakes his head.

Gordon gets nervous.

"Is there a problem?"

"You just had your first lesson at Hikage, right?"

"Yes, Rokku-san."

"I read there was a problem. Would you tell me what happened?"

"Sure. The course consisted of three children. Two of them were very difficult to handle. They didn't listen to me or the kindergarten teacher. The boy tried to steal whatever he could, and the girl threw building blocks at other kids. We tried our best to work with them but had little to no success."

"Why didn't you ask Jason for help?"

"I falsely thought the kids would relax once the mother was gone; however, I was wrong."

"The mother filed a complaint at the reception, and I quote: 'The ski instructor deeply insulted me and threatened my kids. Nobody ever treated me like that, and we'll never come back. I'm going to write numerous reviews to let everybody know how terrible it was and I will sue this place for defamation, if said teacher won't get fired. I can't understand why he was even considered to be an instructor.'"

Gordon can't believe his ears, although he expected her to take revenge.

"Please let me explain. It all started with her being upset about the third kid on the course. The boy wore a holey ski suit, because the family couldn't afford a new one. She called him a street bum and wanted him to be excluded from the course. I tried…"

"What did you do to arbitrate the situation?"

"Well, she thought the boy would have a bad influence on her children. I told her it wasn't a big deal and it wouldn't have any significance. I wanted to treat them all the same."

"But that wasn't the reason for the harsh complaint."

"No. She complained because I told her how I felt about her entitled, hostile behavior."

"What behavior?"

"You told me we're standing together, right? So I'll be honest. I know my reaction wasn't perfect, but I couldn't let her continue to insult Duncan and his mother. They were very humble people, and they deserved a great vacation. Having said that, when I was young, we also didn't have a lot of money. In fact, we had a hard time surviving as my father left. There were no options other than hoping for the help of other people. That's why I understood the problems of Duncan and his mother straightaway. They won the vacation in a magazine and simply couldn't afford a proper ski suit for Duncan. People can't control the environment they're born into. The friends you're growing up with are most likely not a very diverse bunch, and the future we can perceive for our life often stems from surroundings. There are ways out, but it's more about luck or even fate than it is about hard work and dedication. You could ask yourself, for example, if it's really your doing that you're sitting in front of me as resort manager. And if you're honest with yourself, you might find out the circumstances were much more relevant than your intelligence or other factors. I don't want to be rude. Hard work is important, but nobody has control over the big things in life. We're only dealing with the consequences. Religion is helping us to make sense of the things we can't explain and everyone must decide for themselves, if they think this is a good idea, but being overly self-assured about the fairness of gifts is bad religion."

"Please get to the point; there's a lot of work waiting for me."

"All right. This woman could only see her prejudices. She had created a world where she was always right and everyone else was wrong. She thought Duncan was a threat to her children, but he couldn't possibly harm them. He was a threat to her worldview instead. She thought all that happened to her was her own making and she defended this misconception even if she hurt others in the process. Her kids will pick up her attitude, and this will cause later generations to act the same. Before we know it, there is a whole society of entitled people who have forgotten what love is and insist instead on talking to a manager. I got angry at her because I felt a connection to Duncan, and this woman was trying to destroy his only chance for a ride down the mountain. I'm not proud of it, but I think I was right to be honest with her, and if you want to punish me for it, that's okay."

Rokku looks into his folder. Gordon hopes for mitigating circumstances but doesn't believe in them.

"Listen, she wrote the baddest reviews everywhere. What will others say, if I let you go without any repercussions. Before I know it, the whole resort will do what they want. We here at Nozawa Onsen family don't treat our valued customers like that. We're at work with all our hearts to provide service with utmost excellence. A world of fun for everyone. You can't just go around and make people feel bad about themselves. You told her to fuck off and you'll clean onsen for it."

"What? No. Maybe it wasn't my best day, but…"

"I already talked to Jason, and we agreed you should join our cleaning staff for the rest of the season. Your replacement is on his way and will arrive soon. Our housekeeping manager expects you at 4:00 tomorrow morning at Furusotu Na-Yu Bathhouse."

"Understand. I'll be there."

19

MY RUSTY CAGE

THE STREETS WERE COVERED with freshly fallen snow. Nozawa Onsen was still sleeping. Gordon's alarm clock went off, but he silenced it instantly. He was awake all night and thought about his life. Onsen cleaner wasn't his dream job; the work didn't really bother him though. He cleaned vast amounts of stuff in his working life. However, he enjoyed being a ski instructor and sympathized with the idea of becoming a professional. But further dreams had to wait for now. He sneaked under the shower, got dressed, and left for the bathhouse. It was very cold outside. Icy air entered his body. The day isn't yet there, and the full moon illuminates the town beautifully. He is twenty minutes early and admires the dark light of the snow.

When does this torture finally end?

A person appears at the end of the road. Racy steps come closer quick. A middle-aged woman with a strict bun, big bags under her eyes, and razor-sharp wrinkles stands before him.

"Good morning, are you Gordon?"

"Yes, and you must be the housekeeping manager?"

"That's right. My name is Ruan Yu. I'm going to familiarize you with our high standards. Furthermore, Rokku-san told me you won't be responsible for the onsen alone. You'll be a full team member of the cleaning staff."

"What does that mean?"

"That means I'm happy to have you. We are chronically under-staffed, and you're a heaven sent. From 4:00 a.m., you'll be scrubbing this onsen. It has to be exceptionally clean at 6:00, when we open up to the public. After that, you'll have breakfast. During forenoon, you'll be cleaning and sanitizing toilets, countertops, and sinks. After lunch, you'll empty trash receptacles. I would offer you better work, but Rokku-san insisted you do what I just outlined. You must have lost a lot of points. Harsh complaints?"

I hope he dies early.

"I don't know about lost points, but I got fired from my ski instructor job for telling the truth."

"It isn't as bad as it sounds. As long as you follow our motto, you'll be fine."

"Our motto? A world of fun for everyone?"

"No, we have our own: Tidy, tidy all the things; customers will feel like kings."

Brainwashing 2000. What a joke.

The manager opens the door to the building. She shows Gordon the facilities and directs him to the important spots, which need the most attention. The onsen consists of three sections with water of different temperatures. Two inside pools and one outside. A huge shower, changing, and bathrooms.

"Never ever leave out any strand of hair on the floor, wall, or shower drain. Japanese people are very serious about onsen cleanli-ness, and hair is especially nasty for them. You should use a high-pressure water jet for most the surfaces; however, the green ones have to be scrubbed by hand."

"By hand? Why?"

"Nozawa's onsen are very old. Some of them date back to the eighth century. They have marbled floors and walls made of nephrite from the Japanese Alps. High pressure ruins the marble, and the only way to clean it is warm, soapy water. Sorry, there's no way around that. Rokku-san regularly sends people to check for impeccable work. He's totally obsessed with it."

"Wait a second. The whole room is green."

"That's why you're scrubbing it. Hurry up. It's half past four already."

"All right."

Ruan Yu leaves him to his work. He opens the cabinet with the cleaning utensils, prepares a bucket of soap water, and begins scrubbing. His body isn't used to this kind of work. Gordon's legs hurt, and his arms get tired. Especially his knees are killing him. The pain brings forth various bad feelings.

This is my reality. Hand-scrubbing the floor in a godforsaken place at five in the morning. For fuck's sake, what is wrong with me? I can't go back to the grocery store. Therapy didn't work. Anxiety and depression? No. It's fate! They throw pills into your throat to keep you arrested in this damned cage. You're waiting and waiting and waiting, but it never comes. Marble to die for. A rope for a noose and a shitty letter. The hangman's dance of death. Stop it, idiot. Goddamn weakling. I'll not go down like that. I'll break this rusty cage and run. No future. No past. Life is fucking now.

The floor is perfectly clean. He changes the water and goes on wiping the walls. Time seems to stand still. He needs to rush to be punctual, but the clock doesn't move. He wants to go home, but he can't stop before the job is finished. His conscientiousness keeps him from half assed attempts. Scrubbing is tedious and he's sweating profusely. The desperation causes occasional tears.

■ ■ ■

Breakfast never tasted so good. The canteen served leftovers from yesterday's guest buffet. Salmon, limp fries from the kids' section, and tons of rice. It was overdone from the lamps, but it provided lots of energy for a tormented cleaner. After his meal, Gordon continued with the toilets and sinks before putting even more calories in his system to bear the emptying of the trash cans. He finished his workday with a new appreciation for people in the cleaning business and headed to Rokku-san's office to talk to him. After a seemingly endless wait, the secretary condescendingly waved him inside.

Rokku-san's voice appears snootily.

"Come in."

"Rokku-san. Sorry to disturb you. I wanted to talk to you about my new work."

"Please refer to the housekeeping manager, if you have any questions."

"No. It's not about specifics, I wanted to talk about the work itself. I think it's by no means fair to give me only the worst of jobs. You said we're standing together, and I thought you were honest. And as I told you the truth, you rewarded me with punishment instead of understanding."

He changes from snooty to loud.

"What do you want? You're the latest addition to our housekeeping team. I already told you we care for cleanliness a lot. It's an honorable job, and someone has to do it. The end."

Honorable job. Asshole.

"If you care so much for your team, why are they so severely understaffed?"

"Are you telling me how I have to lead my company?"

Arrogant motherfucker.

"I wanted to point out that you massively care for cleanliness, but not for the people. Human beings are capable of great things, if you let them. Everyone has something uniquely creative in them, but if you treat employees like machines, you rob them of their dignity. The reason why people don't think they are creative is because they have never practiced to use their imagination. There is no honor in cleaning toilets all day. It's simply a way of surviving in a shitty world without chances."

"Are you complaining because you worked in housekeeping for a day? What about better education? If you're stupid and lazy, you might be in the right place after all."

"As I told you before, it's tough to be born into a wealthy family, because you have no control over it. Think about gay people, for instance. Or what about being disabled? What I'm trying to say is, if you have no money for your education or your life, while being educated, you only have a slim chance to pull yourself out of the mud, without accumulating massive debt. And sometimes not even amassing debt is an option. I was poor all my life, and it's depressing to realize my limitations. Especially as I am getting older. Being a worker with no connections or a supportive family makes it virtually impossible to attain future professional credentials."

Rokku-san loses his patience.

"You're wasting my time."

"Is it too much to ask for, to simply think about the people your company is relying on so much? You take them for granted and don't acknowledge who they really are. You put up this facade of family and cohesion, but you don't care about anybody, as long as they don't screw up. However, if a single hair is left in the sink, there's trouble ahead."

"You better take good care of what you're saying. Just ask around. Many of my workers are perfectly content. There will always be a few depressed people, but that's normal. Besides, I have real work to do. You must leave now."

"No one would ever admit they're depressed. Even to themselves. These days, people must appear happy; otherwise they're not part of society. In fact, people are considered a failure, if they are not happy all the time. If you take a look under the mask, you'll see they're angry, irritated, and anxious. We're molded into being workhorses all our life and we lose the ability to love ourselves and others, just to serve a system, which doesn't give a shit about us. But one day we'll understand that we are the system, and the moment we stop believing the lies served to us, we will be free for the first time."

"Technological advance at all costs is not how you make people happy. It didn't work, and it never will. It's great, but it's no substitute for love. Capitalism is held together by made-up arguments, instead of actual benefits. The flip side of consumerism is that we get all this great stuff but suffer like crazy to justify it. And if people sacrifice themself for others and actually get something out of their work, they get paid less. The sickest are actually the most healthy, and the symptom presents itself to tell you something is wrong. But if you're severely disconnected from yourself and resemble more of a robot instead of a human being, you have lost all possibility for change. You have adapted to being completely numb, and you'll lead a life of quiet desperation and suffering, only concluded by a shitty death. All right, I don't want to steal any more of your time. Please accept my resignation. I'll support the housekeeping staff until the end of the season, and then I'm going to leave this place for good."

"I wanted to let you go anyhow. It's good we agree on one thing at least. If there's something else you want to discuss, please refer to your supervisor."

Self-righteous piece of shit.

"Thank you for your time."

Being suppressed and looked down upon was a painful experience. It was a great feeling to finally find the right words to express his disappointment. Gordon lost a lot of weight on the way home.

20

DEAD DEVOTION

New Year's Eve was coming up. The cleaner days didn't get any shorter, but Gordon developed a somewhat positive outlook. The end of the year always marked a new beginning for him. But there still was something he had to sort out before the new year could begin. He thought Gemma was different, only to find yet again that things didn't turn out the way he wanted. In order to clear his head, he took a walk through the winter landscape outside of Nozawa and tried to feel himself into what he could do to handle the situation.

I guess Jason didn't even know. Cannot blame her. Wouldn't do it though. Why so selfish? How stupid you are. You think it's love you're missing out on. Right. The love in yourself. Does it even exist? Fucking love. I want to fuck you, another love story? Like animals? Procreation machines?

He passes a group of trees. They're heavy with snow. The twigs overlap into a spiderweb, and the sun shines through the branches. Beautiful structures unfold themselves with every step. A kaleidoscope of warm light.

I love *komorebi*. Japanese is beautiful. No word, no existence. Words are perspectives. I don't know. People say I love you every day. But what's love? Is it a locked-up bird? Open up the cage and fly? Nobody owns it. It can be everything, and maybe it is. Don't snap into place. Knowing is different.

Gordon arrives at an old Japanese shrine. The entry is followed by a long staircase. Several layers of snow cover the path, but he cautiously finds his way around the outbuildings. The main structure looks majestic.

Right or wrong, whatever. Does it work? Being human? Not just a dick punani? Fucking culture. Judgment needs two. Yes-No. Good-Bad. Love-Hate. But there's only one. No want. No snap. No pain.

Ornately carved timber decorates the exterior walls. Old and tall trees secure the serenity of the sight. Some birds fly by and greet with their call. Gordon discovers an inscription on a stone in front of the shrine's entry. A small sign, which could be a translation, sticks underneath.

Attention is love. Below and above. How beautiful. That's what I want. I want you to understand me. I want you to know me. I want to be accepted. I want to feel whole. Everybody wants that. Show yourself. Don't be afraid to escape. But all they do is fucking. Money fucking. Fame fucking. Punani fucking. It's stupid. And it's never enough. Make a decision for god's sake.

He sits down on a bench behind the main building. The view over Nozawa, enveloped by the mountains and caressed by the sun, inspires his body to let go. His gut relaxes and connects to the brain to utter the truth.

I've had it. Just follow your heart. Get a handsel. A chance for love. Be patient. Sincerely felt is always true. True love creates freedom. Accept the tidal flow. Everything is on the table. I'm not alone and I'll never be.

■ ■ ■

Gordon hadn't seen Gemma since the fire festival. He was wondering if she had organized the event and how it had turned out. He couldn't bring himself to come forward after he saw the kiss. However, all this uncertainty and careful inquiry brought him to a better understanding of what he wanted. He would very frankly talk to her and find out what the kiss was all about. Does she love him back? Or was it just another story she would tell her friends at some upscale manager meeting? He thought about calling her, then quickly departed from the idea. A personal conversation would be better. He would try to win her over, but he wouldn't accept any more lies. Gordon could imagine staying in Nozawa, although it's hard to find a job outside of Rokku's reach.

He knew there would be a party on New Year's Eve. The staff lodge was already preparing for the event. Suk told him not to buy any booze, since they were equipped with everything needed to annihilate a Quebecian soccer team for three weeks straight. Gordon also learned that Jason never missed a party and Gemma would be there as well. Direct confrontation made him nervous, but according to his newly crafted rules, there was no reason to shy away from a proper conversation. It was essential instead. The last day of the year arrived. Gordon finished work and went home to change and shower. He was about to leave town to get his present. Later in the day, he played video games with Suk. They had a few beers, and he enjoyed the nostalgic feeling. Around eight, they set out to the lodge and ate a ton of buns to prepare for the night. The atmosphere was mostly relaxed, but he could feel the anticipation of the steady stream of incoming people. As the evening progressed, he got more and more anxious if she would come; however, he managed to keep the sake under control and felt quite good about himself. At ten, he considered calling her, but Suk calmed him down. Jason would normally arrive at eleven and stay all night. He stopped drinking and circled the lodge to sober up. As he wanted to get back in, he saw them coming arm in arm. They didn't see him, and he ducked down behind a small truck to avoid talking to her right away. The fear of rejection numbed him and he also wanted to talk without the presence of Jason. He waited a few minutes for them to get comfortable and sneaked in with a bunch of ski instructors. The lodge was filled with people, but he spotted her in an instant. Jason must have taken a trip to the bathroom. She didn't smile back. The present in hand and his fate on the line, he fought himself through the crowd.

He hugs her gently.

"So nice to see you."

She doesn't move her arms or her torso.

"Yeah. Where have you been? I canceled the event."

"Why?"

"Because everyone wanted to help, but nobody did."

"I'm sorry, I was busy with my new job. I got fired as a ski instructor."

"I've heard. Cleaning is hard work. Must have felt like a massive downgrade. I thought you would leave."

"Can we have a real conversation? Unpretentious and truthful?"

She straightens out the collar of her shirt.

"I don't know. Yes."

He hands his present over.

"I have something for you. A gift for a new beginning. Back in Scotland, we called that a handsel. It's an old tradition on the first Monday after New Year's Eve, but I thought it would fit perfectly today."

The gratefulness seems fake.

"Thank you."

"You said you liked painting and decorating. It's a selection of arts and crafts supplies. They're for you to beautify, stick, tear, or cut to your heart's content. Hope you like it."

"Thanks. I appreciate your thoughtfulness."

Gordon gets nervous.

"I saw you at the fire festival."

"I saw you too."

His heart flutters.

"I didn't think you noticed."

"But I did."

"I know nothing was fixed between us; however, I thought we had something going on."

"I agree. The snowcat ride was beautiful."

"So why are you dating both of us at the same time? Am I not good enough?"

"I don't know."

"Is it because he is better looking than me?"

"No, I don't care for muscles that much. I found most of those superhot model guys are too much in love with themselves, instead of with me."

"Well, what is it then?"

"I cannot say."

"You cannot say? What the fuck? I did everything I could, and you don't know why you're cheating on me?"

"It's not cheating if there's no relationship, Gordon."

"Not yet, but I thought we were on our way. I'm like a bowerbird. I dance and sing for the woman in my life to make her happy and to express my admiration. The only difference is, the women simply don't get why I'm doing it. Either they have bad self-esteem themselves and don't understand why anyone would admire them or they're not mature enough to accept it. Do you know how terrifying it is for a man to gather all his courage and ask a girl out? The more we like you, the more anxious we are. You're judging our performance with a simple yes or no, and it can be terrorizing to be rejected again and again. Exposing your vulnerability is not an easy task, and it's no wonder why men loose interest."

"You seem to think all woman are selfish bitches who don't consider how men feel; however, we care a lot about you. To be honest, I've known Jason for a long time, and it just recently happened somehow. I don't know if I should be sorry about it, but maybe it's just the way it ought to be."

"All right. I have a question. This is something I thought about for a long time. Do you believe you might have avoided me, since we're rather similar to each other and you don't want to be constantly reminded of your own problems and imperfections?"

"I don't think we're very similar, Gordon."

"I disagree, but let's keep it that way. What do we do now? Jason will come back soon, and I want to know if there's a chance for us. I love you, and I'm dreaming about a future with you."

"How do you know you love me? We've only met a few times and it seems unreasonable. You may confuse sex drive with love. It's a problem for most men."

"Testosterone can be a sneaky drug, but love is more than just sex drive. I might not know you very well, but do we know anyone, really? Do we plan to fall in love? You would have dumped me in the first place, if there wasn't something inside of you answering a certain resonance."

"Listen, I can't go on with this. We had a nice afternoon together and you're making a complicated mess out of it. Can we be friends, please?"

A tiny needle pierces his heart.

"Friends? That's the worst thing you could ever say to me. I'm idealizing woman. Fine. However, putting my heart on the hot plate for later is degrading and horrible."

"I can't give you what you want. It's the best offer I have."

"It's the worst offer you have. The best offer is a compassionate no and an explanation. Just because you're afraid of speaking the truth, you're making everything worse. Whatever, these things will come to haunt you anyway."

She makes a fist behind her back and breathes in deeply.

"You want to know the truth? My heart says yes to Jason and no to Gordon. I wish you all the best and hope you'll find Mrs. right, but I'm not. You have no future here, and you shouldn't throw your potential out of the window because you met a lady on a mountain."

The sadness comes in waves. He fights it off, but he doesn't know how long he'll be able to withstand.

"See, it wasn't that hard. Was it? I hate everything about what you just said, but thank you for saying it."

He turns around. The first tear runs down his cheek. He grabs a bottle of sake and gulps down a big sip. He ignores the protesting voices, takes a second bottle, and pushes himself sideways through the crowd. Jason is coming back from the toilet with a smile on his face. Gordon holds up the liquor to say goodbye. He steps out of the staff lodge. His eyes pointed to the ground, taking another sip. To his surprise, there's no turmoil. No affective forces tell him what to do. Only a dark silence is watching the tears slowly rolling down. He has no words to describe his emotion. The wind is ruthless. It churns up the water of a hotel pool to turn it into frazil, pointy droplets of ice. He jumps over the fence and sits down.

Why are you doing this to me? This is your plan? Billions of flawed people. Crawling around, only to find a nagging needle piercing our hearts? Again and again? This is love? This is the way humanity works? You're a sadistic, fucked up god. Omnipotent and omniscient? No. If you cared, it would be bearable, but it's hell.

The humid air from the pool and the breezy wind freeze his face, but the sake creates an illusion of warmth.

Now I know why Steve is still drinking. No freedom. No time. No life. Fuck god. Fuck marriage. Fuck love.

He throws the empty bottle in the pool and opens the other. End it already.

Bells start ringing. It comes from the shrine. People step out of their houses. Merry voices pervade Nozawa. Rockets appear on the night sky. Gordon is facilitated. He doesn't need to hug anyone or play happy. He just sits there. Sipping his bottle. Freezing. The hotel's site fence guards him against the outer world. Howling streams explode above the valley. Loud lighting in the silence of the night. Coming from nowhere to fade into nothingness. Born to vanish.

21
DEEP BLUE SEA

THE FIRST UME TREES carried blossoms. A sure sign of spring in Japan. Weak sunrays came through the clouds. Dark and light slowly made way for a new cycle to begin. Small bridges over lakes connected parts of a newly awakened ecosystem amid the big city. The trees were mirrored in the still waters. An old man sat on the edge fishing. All the hectic activity of the ever-moving forces were kept out of Arisugawa-no-miya Memorial Park. Gordon was about to meet Steve. He touched a tree to marvel at the treetop and to feel the connection with the earth underneath him. A flock of birds included him into the process of life. He arrived at a statue of a boy who was carrying a newspaper. While he was leaning at the base of the figure, the sun was shining in his face. He took a deep breath and let go.

"I'm so happy you're back. I missed you my friend."

Gordon turns around to hug Steve like a long-lost family member.

"I missed you too. I'm glad to be back in Tokyo. It was a rough ride."

"Yeah, we didn't talk since the festival. What happened?"

"Well, Gemma decided Jason was the better fit. I tried to fight a little, but it was fairly obvious."

"Jason was your boss, right? I thought so already."

"It turned out to be a bad idea to stay in Nozawa to marry her. In hindsight, it also feels a bit stupid."

"Indeed, but you did your best. Don't beat yourself up about it."

They slowly walk to a nearby park bench. Gordon sits down first.

"Thank you for saying that."

Steve sits down next to him and crosses his legs.

"What else? How was New Year's in Nozawa? Must have been a great party up there."

Gordon presses his lips together and pushes a compressed burst of air out of his nostrils.

"I'm a little hesitant to tell."

Steve smiles.

"Why, what happened? Did you swim in booze and perform your Sissy boy thing once more?"

"Yes, I swam, but not in booze. We had a party at the staff lodge. It was the first time I saw Gemma after the festival. I confronted her, and she surprisingly told me the truth. I mean, I asked her to be honest, but I didn't really expect her to do it. It was hard, and I completely lost it afterward."

"What happened?"

"When our conversation was finished, I left the lodge and took two bottles of sake with me. It was the coldest night of the season, but I was completely numb at this point."

"Let me guess. You killed those bottles and made a complete fool of yourself."

"No. Let me finish. I sat alone beside a hotel pool, which was under construction. The whole building got renovated, and I thought it was the right place to escape from the crowd. I wasn't upset anymore. I had no more tears left. I switched off into a perfect darkness. No obligations. No feelings. No pain."

"Slowly there, Gordon. What did you do?"

"I can't remember exactly, but I somehow drank both bottles, lost consciousness, and jumped in the pool. I told them I fell into it; however, I can't tell if it was on purpose. I blacked out once again."

Steve laughs.

"Shit. One thing is for sure, you didn't kill yourself or we wouldn't sit here. Why did you do that?"

"I thought a lot about it in the hospital. Something inside of me just gave up."

"But that's not the whole story. Tell me why you jumped into the pool?"

"I don't know, Steve. I only have the picture of the guy pulling me out of the water. He screamed at me to grab the golden chain, where the life buoy was fixed on."

He holds his finger under Gordon's nose.

"Don't lie. You tell me right now why you wanted to kill yourself."

"Fine. Fuck. I think I reached the final still point. I couldn't imagine how to come out of this horrible situation. I had to work as an onsen cleaner, only because I told a customer how illusionary she was, and I lost my girl to a much more attractive guy. I'm a depressed, poor, unlovable piece of shit."

Steve laughs heartily. He enthusiastically taps on Gordon's thigh.

"Your imagination is the best I've seen."

"What? No. Are you serious? I wanted to kill myself and you laugh at me like it's a joke?"

"Look, Gordon. Do you know why you're such a loser?"

He folds his arms.

"Tell me."

"It's because you want to be a winner so bad."

"Pardon?"

"You're missing the bigger picture, and you're not able to deal with the consequences. You just don't recognize when you're happy and you make yourself miserable for no reason. Assume you would be a businessman or an acclaimed actor. You had the most beautiful woman and you would live in a big mansion with a garage full of cars. Would you be happy?"

"Of course. Who wouldn't? I would finally be on top of the food chain instead of under it."

"Of course not. Of. Course. Not. Do you think your mind would just let you be happy? No. It would find new ways of telling you what a loser you are, because there's always something better. That's capitalism 101. They tell you to always buy new shit, be better, do more, and aim for the stars. But what they don't tell you is that if you reach the top, you're not any happier than you are now. Think of it as a relationship in phase two, when you begin to think of other woman again after the initial blast of dopamine has gone."

"So you're telling me the satisfaction doesn't last at all? What about the money? I hate to be poor."

"Granted. Money makes a difference to a certain point. To be safe from money problems is a good thing. However, that doesn't mean you're more happy. Rich people often don't know why they're not happy, although they ought to be according to everybody else. It gets old quickly."

Gordon folds his arms even tighter.

"All right, Mr. Sage. What makes us happy, if it's not a comfortable life with everything we wish for?"

"See, your definition of a great life is completely crooked. Having beautiful surroundings and lovely things is great, but these marketing people destroyed our lives to keep the wheel turning. I just saw an ad for permanent hair removal. Thirty percent off for the first three sessions. Or a stop smoking app. It was based on behavioral therapy, which is good, but it's a subscription service. Do you understand? They told us we all deserve to eat what they sell as the best food and to have magnificent stuff for cheap prices. That we'll be happy and fulfilled, if we own that fucking sports car, but it'll never be enough. The truth is, nobody needs that shit and their food makes us sick.

You might say that's nothing new; however, we're all still trapped in a world of lies, and we've heard it so often that it's ingrained in our culture at this point. A big flood of misinformation killed our common sense. The system, as it plays out now, states we're all completely selfish. That capitalism and therefore the world is in a state of all against all and that cooperation doesn't play a role. It supports ruthlessness as the foundation for our prosperity. We supposedly look only for our own self-interest with a complete disregard for others. The people adapted to this insane idea over the last hundred years, and we're all suffering because of it. Most might know they're being ripped off, but very few recognize the overall place they're in. It has become the norm to make us an object of their desires and wants. As a result, we think it's okay to do that to everyone. There is no room for dignity in this equation. The goal of life has to be greater production and consumption, not the real needs of a person. In order to be free, we should not aim to own everything and to be on top of the world, we should try to eliminate our desires instead. Our culture is all about having and not becoming. If money equals happiness, happiness is lost. If people don't get the successful life culture pictures for us, they feel alone, lost, and angry. They develop an inner hatred for the world and want to destroy everything because they got cheated on. They wake up and in their thirties, forties, or fifties and are afraid that life continues to be empty of meaning. It manifests as addictions, anxiety, and depression, and they want to show the world how badly they've been hurt. The disease stands as a memorial for their desperation and rage. Not everyone can win the game."

Gordon relaxes his arms a bit.

"Understand—so depression, anxiety, and addiction share all the same cause. Don't you think you're a bit exaggerating here?"

"No. Do you know what they all share? They're either a way to suppress or a way to avoid the realization of something. There are genetic influences, but we don't know if it isn't just a result of

epigenetics. This means you could have learned it from your surroundings, or that it's an effect of your prior behavior. I think it's
epigenetics. We came here with a need for love, not fucked up with
a hunger for stuff. The reason why people are sick of everything is
the suppression or avoidance of the answer to a simple question:
Who am I. We're afraid of growing up. To find out who's behind
the mask we're so used to wearing all the time. Culture has made
us blind to who we are, and we are terrified or too deluded to face
reality. That causes much stress, sadness, and fear, and we don't
know where it comes from until a catastrophe or an illness cures us
from our false hope and illusionary entitlement."

"Well, what should I do, in your opinion?"

"It might sound comical, but stand in front of the mirror, stare
in your own eyes, and ask yourself the most important question of
your life: Who am I? You may see strange things, but be courageous
and don't look away. I call it recognize yourself. An easy technique
to get a glimpse of the other side. It's great to get yourself back and
to inquire into a world of wisdom, peace, and fulfillment. Just be
quiet, and if you truly want it, a door will open and you will finally
realize there's nothing wrong with you."

"You sound like one of those TV priests."

"Haha, great. Let me give you my blessing, son."

"Very funny, Steve."

"What are you planning to do now?"

"I don't know. I like Japan, but there may be better opportunities
elsewhere. I saved a bit of money."

Steve shakes his head.

"Are you going to run away again?"

"What do you mean?"

"Gordon, you have the tendency to leave a country in order to
solve your problems. But you'll come to the same conclusion wherever you go. You're still the same."

"Bullshit. Different cultures widen my horizon and open up new job opportunities."

"That's right. However, you forgot as long as you don't change, there will be no improvement in your outer world. You'll take your misery with you wherever you go until you learned your lesson."

"I don't like to hear that, but you may be right."

Steve laughs.

"I'm proud of you. It only took you forty years to get out of your comfort zone."

"Serious or irony?"

"Both."

Gordon thanks Steve for his advice and leaves to go home. He has to think about his future.

22
A MIRACLE

IT'S ALL MINIMALISTIC. A small chair. A table. The rather tiny oven. Magazines of different sizes sit on the shelves, sandwiched by a humble selection of books. Life happens mostly on the floor in Japan. The futon has to be put away for the day in order to move around in the flat. Two windows care for an overview of the city. Basic commodities of living are present; the feeling of emptiness caused by a lack of alcohol as well as stimulation is alien and scary to Gordon, however. Slow down and listen to your mind. That's the advice he picked up from Steve's quite religious speech. He wanted to know what was going on with him. Being alone wasn't his problem, but being alone with no distraction feels dreadful. The constant impulses to turn on the TV or to grab a beer are annoying. He didn't know it was so terribly demanding to just be. To sit in a room and simply do nothing whatsoever.

Don't be lazy, stupid idiot.

"Why are you saying that?"

Why are you talking to yourself? Make a sandwich.

"No."

Gordon inspects his room. It seems quiet at first, but all of a sudden a knot appears in his stomach.

I've not eaten. Maybe I'm indeed hungry.

The feeling gets more intense. It pulsates with his heartbeat.

That hurts. Lay down a bit.

His breath accelerates, and his lungs start pumping in bursts.

Make some tea and lay down to relax your belly.

His upper body is swaying forward and backward.

What's happening? Stop it.

His heart is racing.

This is a fucking heart attack. Get up and call for help.

Sweat runs down his forehead.

You will die if you don't do something.

A dreadful fear crawls up from his stomach. His whole body is shaking.

Do something. Are you crazy?

"No."

I need help. I'm going to die. Move, motherfucker. Time is scarce.

He holds his belly to alleviate the pain.

"No. I will not move."

The voice in his head is in a furious panic.

For god's sake. Move. I'm dying. Move now.

He throws his arms in the air and screams with all his might.

"I will not move. I will not move. I will not move."

You're losing your mind.

His belly expands and contracts rapidly. He's panting like a dog. Holding up his arms to make way for the bellows. The fear reaches an unbearable level.

"I will not move. I will not move."

He loses more and more energy, but the shock keeps him erect. His voice softens.

"I will not move."

Silence. The shaking subsides. His heart slows down and his arms lose tension. From the back of his head, deep down in the abyss of not knowing, a gentle whisper emerges.

~I love you.~

The panting stops. He closes his eyes. A relieved sigh leaves his mouth.

~You are innocent. You are beautiful. You are everything.~

Gordon is perfectly still. After a much-needed calming down period, he gets up, opens the door to the bathroom, and stares into the mirror.

"Who am I?"

Don't be silly.

"Who am I?"

Are you kidding me?

"Who am I?"

His gaze focuses on the spot behind his eyeballs. The whisper becomes clearer.

~You are the actor and the act. A dot in the story of life. A witness, who woke up to the truth.~

The tears are rolling.

"What did I do to deserve this?"

~You did nothing wrong. Everything happens for you. Black and white is all the same.~

"Will the suffering finally stop?"

~What interests you is the door to your freedom.~

His sight sharpens and reveals a tired pair of eyes. He washes his face and goes back in the living room. For the rest of the day, he sits on the couch. No TV. No distraction. He doesn't understand, what had happened to him, but he is grateful for the peace.

23

WHERE DO WE GO

STREET FOOD IN JAPAN has a long tradition. The Japanese make everything into a ritual with a carefully staged order. It all has to be mastered. They pride themselves on spending their life to develop and perfect their procedures, ingredients, and taste combinations. Long hours are invested in extracting the most intense flavors. Japanese work is about community value, not the individual. But there are always some obsessed people, who do it for the passion of taste and the contented customers.

Gordon loves the dedication and the precisely orchestrated processes. Since he came back from the mountain, he has abstained from ordering out a lot and started cooking for himself again. It's cheaper and a lot more fun. He tries exotic new recipes, works on his techniques, and develops an array of spice compilations. Health and taste were not easy to unite at first; however, keeping processed food out and sugar at bay does the trick most of the time. His weight stays off and his body is energetic.

The experience in front of the mirror showed him a different side of himself. He tried to make sense of the event, but he ultimately needed more time to process the actual implications of it. One direct change was immediately palpable though. His mind became somewhat more curious for the reason of a thought. He followed long and tiresome paths in order to find the root of a habit, but he wasn't always satisfied with the result. A number of questions persistently came up to be worked on: Where do I go from here? Who can I trust? What do I do? Other people always caused issues somehow. To tolerate all these unavoidable disagreements would be rather stupid. The goal was to find a solution, not going to war, however. How can one be able to find authenticity, when thinking is leveled by the same mind people use all their life already? Childhood seems to be a challenging period, and we all bring our accumulated pain with us. Some human beings appear to be more capable of evil, but we forgot we're all ripe to become an adult at some point. The reality of the individual is not really in his hands, and the opinions that arise from living life are always in tune with the conditions. It's unavoidable and cannot be any other way. The situation gets recounted after the fact to make sense of the world according to the circumstances. Right and wrong is equally accurate, since the observer is the judge of the matter. Children are highly creative, but fantasy and an inherent understanding for love are not very useful in our environment. Some people even think it's a fact of life. This has mainly to do with our conditioning and the delusions we hold in order to shield us from emotional harm. Most secretly wish to go back to being a child, when life was a fantastical adventure on a ship to nowhere. Where beauty was everywhere, love a given, and magic the norm. We long for the playful energy of extended rainy afternoons in a world full of building blocks, just to embrace the immense freedom of creative expression and self-forgotten thought. Where it came together just like that. Being an adult, as a result, means to lose all connection with this natural joy and to exchange it for difficult relationships and economic uncertainty. The adapted is the most insane, and the sane is a lunatic. Going further into this darkness is stupid; running away a postponement and fighting against it is dividing us. So what is the right thing to do? Life often feels haphazard. Without order or logic. Every moment is indefinite and soaked in randomness. Actions seem understandable in context, but seen separately, they lead to sad paths of disappointment. It was time to look at the big picture and recognize life's patterns to develop a better understanding of the world. It needed to be enjoyable. A source of fulfillment and delight in spite of all the difficulties and entitled people. Money will always be important, but it can't be the main player. If it isn't the reason for a happy life, why not become a musician or a painter? Gordon was walking in the city. His mind was a lot quieter when it wasn't hopping on every incoming thought train. He watched the trains pass the station to disappear in the distance. His new routine required him to do so every day. It consisted of an easy walking meditation to calm his mind and a slowly progressing fitness routine to keep his body engaged and happy. He passed all kinds of shops and food vendors on his way through the narrow back streets. Manifold store windows caught his attention, but as interesting as they were, he always came back to his peaceful concentration. Not to be affected by the outer world was one of the most valuable skills to have. He gained many benefits from his practice because he knew how to control his reactions. It would not always work, since stress can be overwhelming, but he finally felt free to go his own way.

A guy on a bike. A convenience store. A bunch of construction workers. Some vegetables. *Ohuzim. Daifukumochi.* Traditional preparation. Not too sweet. Yeah, why not.

The storefront is not very informative. A humble wooden door with the inscription "Ohuzim," only embellished by a short curtain. He walks inside to take a look at the confections.

An older woman welcomes him and asks if he's looking for anything in particular.

"*Irasshaimase. Nanika osagashi desuka?*"

Gordon feels lazy and tries his luck.

"Konnichiwa. Do you speak English?"

"Yes, I do. How can I help you?"

"I can't believe it. How come?"

"I've lived in New York for many years."

"Great. I'm interested in some of your mochi cakes."

"Our specialty is *mame daifuku*. A sweet rice cake with a red bean filling."

He is delighted.

"Daifuku mochi are the best. The anko paste is made from adzuki beans, right? Their unique taste is very popular. Chewy, tender, and delicious. Do you have the sweet or the unsweetened version?"

"You're quite the expert. We have both, shio and mame daifuku. But we like to use traditional recipe. Not as sweet as elsewhere."

"Perfect. I'm trying to avoid these blood-sugar roller coasters lately. They're messing with my mind."

"So you're looking for shio? How many would you like?"

"Let me get two shio and one mame. I'll have to try the sweet one as well. The traditional recipe part made me curious."

She grabs a box of three cakes, exchanges one and hands it over.

"Here you go. That's 777 yen."

Gordon reaches into his pocket and pays.

"Thank you. Have a good one."

"You too."

He is about to leave the shop but turns around in the last moment.

"Excuse me, It may sound weird, but are you looking for help right now? I'd love to learn the mochi-making process. It's one of my favorite foods."

The woman pauses for a second. She lays her head slightly to the left and narrows her eyes.

"I thought you were a tourist."

"No, I've been living in Tokyo for over five years. I'm always trying, but Japanese is very hard to learn. You happen to speak English and I love mochi, so I thought maybe that's a good sign."

She lays her head to the other side.

"I'm indeed looking for someone. My son just left to live with his father in New York."

"Well, maybe I'm coming just at the right time."

Her eyes open fully again.

"I don't know. We're starting very early in the morning, and it's strenuous work to pound the rice."

"No problem, I know how it's made. I'm in the shape of my life. It shouldn't be an issue."

"Have you made mochi before?

"I recently tried a recipe with *shiratamako* flour. It came out great."

"Okay, we'll try for a day or two. I'll show you how we make it and we'll see how you manage."

He smiles all over his face.

"Thank you so much for giving me a chance. You'll not regret it."

"I'm usually here at 6:00 a.m. What's your name?"

"I'm Gordon."

"I'm Kazuko. Tomorrow morning at 6:30 a.m.?"

He turns around and heads to the door.

"I'll be punctual."

■ ■ ■

Gordon's first day as a mochi maker began with a bowl of millet and his last shio. The cake was great overall, but the filling missed finesse somehow. With the last bite in hand, he went on his commute. It took only fifteen minutes, and he was grateful for the fresh air. The lights of the store were on already. He knocked on the doorframe and tried to look through the windows. Kazuko opened the door and showed him around. The bags of glutinous mochigome rice, the big mallet to pound the dough, and the giant mortar-like bowl in the middle of the kitchen gave him a good clue of what he was getting into. First, the rice was washed and soaked for two days, then steamed to a soft consistency. Once it was done, it would be transferred into the *usu*, kneaded together, and finally pounded with the *kine*.

To make it in the traditional way, two people were needed for the pounding process. In the past, she had done it together with her son; however, since he was gone, she had to do it all on her own. One person hit the dough; the other folded it between the poundings. Any cooling changed the taste and texture for the worse. The dough had to be creamy and airy, and they needed to be quick. It required a deep trust in one another to get the timing right and not to hurt the other person. She was right in saying it would be a tough job, Gordon liked the work, however. Kazuko was positively surprised by his decent beginner skills and agreed to take him on another week. If he would keep up the quality of his work, she promised to show him how to make the other sweets they were selling and to give him a fixed job. Gordon knew he had to work hard to please her demands, but they seemed to get along nicely. He appreciated her plainness, and she thought he might be a good replacement for her son, although she still grieved for him since he'd moved to New York. On the last day of Gordon's probation, they sit together to talk about his performance and if he will get the job. He wants to have it, but he also knows he cannot deal with any more slave labor. The first few weeks of a job always feel somewhat interesting, because everything is new and exciting. Then later, when the employers showed their real face and the issues become obvious, it's already too late to run away. The contract they are about to negotiate is of utmost importance. The next few minutes will define the whole tone of the collaboration and his ability to intervene with the unavoidable wrongdoings and idiotic behavior.

It's not about showing his strength but to oversee the conditions, the hours, pay, and amount of shit he has to tolerate in order to make the relationship happen and the work enjoyable for both of them. Although he avoids coming over as negative, he also wants to negotiate thoroughly and intelligently. What will happen in this little shop is neither of their doings, however, but a mixture of economic, personal, professional, and psychological factors. There is no one to blame. It's about the allowance of the truth. An honest relationship will be more satisfactory. Everyone is able to notice a lie subconsciously, and some people are even fit enough to be called a walking lie detector.

They're sitting at the table in the kitchen over a cup of coffee. Gordon is prepared, Kazuko relaxed.

"What do you think of my performance?"

She nods at the floor, weighing up with her fingers on the chin.

"I'm satisfied with your skills, I must say. You're the first person who did well during the first week."

"Thanks. I can see why the cakes are so popular. You're a master at your craft, and it was hard work to meet your expectations. I'm glad you're satisfied with my efforts."

She takes a break, then looks directly into his eyes.

"Would you like to work for me? I think we're a good team. The pounding needs more attention, but I'm sure we'll be able to make it work."

"I think the same, and I would love to work with you."

"Excellent. Your salary will be 1000 yen per hour. Everything else stays the same."

"I researched a little bit, and the average pay is slightly above that. I have a lot of experience in sales."

"You're quite good for a beginner, but I can't offer you more."

"Well, but my flat is quite expensive. It's not easy to survive in this neighborhood."

"You can take it or leave it. Your decision."

"Okay, I accept, but there's one more thing I wanted to talk about."

"What is it?"

"I want to be able to bring in my own ideas. I think we could improve on the shio, and I have an idea for a mochi of my own."

"We're doing the shio in this way for over eight hundred years. I have accounts of my family dating back to the Heian period, and we've never changed the recipe."

"I hope we can be honest with each other, because I think it's about time we do that. It's bland and frankly a little bit boring."

"It's not as popular as the *mame*, but that's to be expected. I'm not comfortable changing it. It's my family's recipe, and we used it for centuries."

"All right. What about a mochi machine? We could produce faster and use the freed time to be more creative with the fillings instead."

"No machines. Traditional method is fine. There's no need to change."

"Look, we could make mochi with all kinds of fillings. Ice cream or a mixture of dried fruits and nuts. Maybe even candied fruits or chocolate in some way. I'm sure customers would love more diversity, and we could spare ourselves the tiring pounding."

"I can see what you're saying; however, I don't want to miss it. It's work, but I already told you so."

Gordon nods understandingly.

"I have no problem with hard work. People love tradition because of the memories and the heritage, and I respect that. Maybe you could try and view it from my perspective. I want to show my skills by being creative and feed people exciting new stuff. I have a lot of ideas, and I'm fantasizing all the time about new taste variations and toppings. We could modernize our product range."

Her face shows a steady dislike in changing anything.

"I'm not sure if I like your ideas."

"Please, let's try a bunch of new varieties on the side. The only way we will succeed in the future is by being ready to experiment and incorporate the results. If we don't react to the outside world and the demands of the people, we won't have a chance in the long term. Times change."

Her answer is very reluctant.

"Okay, I will agree to your request and we'll get the machine, but only one new flavor at a time."

"Fantastic. The machine will be of good use for my idea."

"Do you have anything specific in mind?"

"We should consider wheat gluten. Even better would be to use older wheat varieties to avoid all the pesticides. It's easier to swallow, and we won't have to worry about old people taking a trip to the hospital because the rice mochi got stuck in their throats."

"Not bad. What about the flavor?"

Gordon is very excited.

"I thought we could try *Mehalabya*. It's a traditional Arabic milk pudding made from just milk, cream, sugar, and flour for thickening. We could also add some Japanese rose pedal syrup for a nice touch."

"Sounds interesting. Do you have a name for it?"

"I'd like to call it cornucopia. That's our link to tradition. The name comes from ancient Greece. It was connected to the harvest as a symbol for abundance."

"You'll have to convince me of the taste, but you sold it nicely to me. Good job."

Finally someone with courage.

"Thanks. I'm looking forward to start experimenting."

She stands up from her chair. Gordon follows her lead. He offers his hand.

"We don't normally do that here."

"I know, but it would make me happy."

She grabs his hand and shakes it softly.

"To good collaboration and great new products."

"Thank you for your trust."

24
FULL OF ENERGY

OVER THE WEEKS, OHUZIM's kitchen saw a gradual makeover. The mochi machine performed well, and the mortar got a new spot in the corner. A new table took its place instead. Tradition was held up by the mallets, which were hanging on the wall as a symbol for craftsmanship. Customers appreciated the new mochi varieties and enjoyed the weekly special. After a lot of trial and error with the fillings and corresponding techniques, it became very clear that Gordon's first idea was the most desirable.

Cornucopias slowly develop into a favorite. Even among the regulars. This is very surprising to Kazuko. The older customers love the wheat base, since it's easier to swallow, and the younger ones are very curious for the new taste. Ohuzim's reviews explode, and the pictures of the mochi-eating faces are scattered all over the place. Gordon realizes it's time to get a website. Kazuko shuts the entrance door to end another successful day. The mochis sold out quickly, and they've had to close way before the advertised time. They can't produce enough to keep up with the demand, and Gordon figures it's the perfect moment to ask about the next step.

"Kazuko, please come over. I want to ask you something."

She enters the kitchen and they sit down at the new table.

"I'm all ears?"

"I'm very pleased with the cornucopias. They sell out even before the mame."

"I noticed it too. Thank you for convincing me. I would have never thought they turn out so well."

"Welcome. Thank you for saying that. I have another idea I would like to propose to you. We're not present on the internet, but our mochis are everywhere. Therefore I would say we need a website."

"We just bought a table and the machine. Business is going well, but I can't afford to hire people for building a website right now. Also, why having a website, if we're doing perfectly fine without one?"

Possibilities, baby.

"Money is not an issue. There are many options these days to set up a business website for close to nothing. We don't need to hire designers and whatnot. It's more professional; however, to start off, I could write the texts and make a basic layout with one of those building blocks systems, where you can pick the elements and create a site in no time at all. Then later, we could opt for a unique design, if we want to expand further in the future."

"What do we need it for?"

"Well, if we don't have a website in the age of technology, no-body will notice us. Customers may be abundant for our current output, but if we plan to grow, we'll need it. People are looking at reviews and blogs to find the next big thing, and a website is helpful to introduce them to our philosophy."

Kazuko is incredulous as usual.

"A friend of mine did the same thing, and she says the numbers are not worth it."

"I believe you, but let me put it this way: when new technology arrives, the people who're not able or willing to adapt to the new circumstances go extinct. That might seem to be a harsh comparison; however, that's the way it works in nature, and since we're not outside of nature, but a part of it, we can't sleep through the evolution of anything. In the beginning, the argument with the numbers may be valid, but a website is a virtual business card and an easy way to get information and directions. It builds trust, because we are serious about what we do and we can present the shop and ourselves in a beautiful-looking format. We're basically telling our story to celebrate the craft of mochi making."

She laughs.

"So, you're a mochi maker by heart already?"

"I'm going to be a *shokunin*. I feel right at home here, and you remind me of the mother I never had."

She turns slightly red.

"A shokunin? There's a lot more to be done before you will be able to call yourself that. A shokunin is about doing the best you can to work for the general welfare of the people. To exercise an attitude of social consciousness and to maintain the obligation to improve your skills until the day you die."

"I love this collective spirit, and I'm going to fulfill my obligation at all costs."

She smiles.

"Now you remind me of a son I would like to have. Except try to be a little more humble next time. I see your struggle, but serving as an example is only possible through humbleness and dedication. It's a long-term agreement and therefore a daily incremental routine with no deviation. It is the supreme way to grow and reach perfection, although we all know that true perfection is impossible for us."

He nods slightly.

"I will keep that in mind."

"How much is it?"

"What?"

"The website?"

"Just a small monthly hosting fee. I'll set it up in my free time."

"Agreed. Let me know when you're done. I want to see it first."

"Will do."

■ ■ ■

Gordon worked hard to make the website look beautiful and blazingly fast. He even created his own code snippets to extend the site's functionality. It was very simple, yet inviting. The mochi offerings appeared stylish, and the bios communicated their passionate quest to create the perfect daifuku. After about a week of testing and polish, the site was ready and he brought his computer to present it.

"Here it is. Take a look and tell me what you think."

As she clicks through the menus, Gordon is surprised to learn that she's rather quick to comprehend the concept and the overall vibe of the layout.

"I like the colors. What's the logo all about?"

"A friend of mine made it for free. It features our mallets in a kanji-like style."

"Looks great. It's interesting how the computer is able to do all this. When I was younger, we didn't have such powerful technology. I'm wondering what will happen, when they're able to take over all our jobs. Some of my school friends already retired, because they got replaced by a robot."

"I'm sure robots could do our job with no problem. And on a larger scale, they do it already in mochi factories around Japan. However, you don't need to worry, since you're my boss, and our operation is probably way too small to be automated profitably. Otherwise, I would be the first in trouble."

"I'm not concerned about me. What will my grandchildren do, when the robots take over? There will be no jobs left, and people will lose their livelihood."

"I understand your concerns, but I assure you, we've always adapted to changes in our environment, and this will be no different. It may be a shock at first, but they'll never be able to fully replace us. Computer programs are just ideas that execute either once or in loops. So to assume a program is able to replace a human brain is only possible if you believe that an idea for a software can create a conscious being, which it thankfully can't. Computers will always be our servants. They will be a lot smarter than us, but they're here to do what we want, and they'll never possess a creative soul."

25

WHAT IS THE TRUTH?

EVERYBODY WANTS THE TRUTH these days. It is one of the most important things in our modern world. We not only want to know the truth, we want to know it now, and we desire to extract as many benefits out of it as possible. But the problem is, we're looking so hard for it, it has become impossible to find. There's always a nagging feeling of doubt—if our truth is really the last truth and if it holds up against the world. Some people close down quickly. They're not interested in wrestling with it, since it can be tiresome. Others aggressively look for it and, when they think they've found it, defend it passionately. The third group falls somewhere in between. These people are interested in the truth and they will look excessively sometimes, but if they get tired or something gets in the way, they will do that. What we all should do, however, is take a closer look at the soil the truth is growing on. Where it comes from and how we discern we have it. If we investigate it thoroughly, we'll find it's our perception of reality, and reality consists of words. These words are concepts to describe the world and to make sense of it. The main characteristics of a table should be clear to everyone. But if you ask ten people to imagine a table and explain it to you, the results would be wildly different. Now the question is, How do we know the tables are identical to the ones we have imagined out of explanations? The answer is simple: we don't. As long as we don't have the exact same picture, we will never understand how they looked and what shapes and colors they had. That means, we don't live in the same reality as other people, and we wing it by trying to make ourselves as clear as possible. For tables, that may not be a problem, but it makes it hard for us to understand each other, and when it comes to even more significant things, it can cause us to get upset and angry. The picture we project onto the screen of our shared reality inevitably opens up a myriad of different perspectives. During that early time in life, when connections are built inside, when we try to create a map of the world and how to function in it, we cannot help but being strongly affected by our caregivers due to our helplessness.

Most of us don't remember being five years old, but our brain records everything, and we can't escape the consequences of these early modes of relating to the world. They deeply affect our behavior and color our perceptions according to former experiences and eventually become the templates of our reality. Later, we continually form and maintain these structures to function and interact with our families, friends, and strangers. But as soon as we speak, we are immediately misunderstood by the listener, since we all attach our own meaning to the words we use. Furthermore, and that makes it even more ridiculous, we pick our words in order to affirm a developmental self-image onto the other person, believing they'll interpret it the same way we do. In other words, we try to profit from a self-image we create depending on our mental state and the environment to get the reflection we like. It's essentially lying in order to feel good. Combine this with our reality template and the possibilities for failed communication and wildly incongruent images are unavoidable. Words define who we are, and we're totally unable to control the outcome of our projections. Needless to say our template also dictates our opinions about other people and the things they are doing to us. If we think someone is trying to harm us, it might not always be the case, because through the changing view of our reality, a friend may turn into an enemy and vice versa pretty quickly. We often defend these wrongly held notions in fear of our reality to collapse, and the older we get, the harder it is to change these beliefs. At some point, we've mapped the world so clearly and thoroughly that the habit to search for threats with a certain attitude is almost inevitable and deeply written into the cavities of our brains. We cannot control our surroundings and want to recline into known behaviors to alleviate anxious feelings and to deal with the constant danger of change. The expected emotional pain is so severe, we disregard our own good to take refuge in a reality, which is neither helping nor serving us.

Although all of this needn't be bad, depending on our experiences, it can be very bad if we try to suppress and avoid the reality of our personal life journey. We end up in a job we hate, form bonds we don't want, and live life like a person we don't know. Developing diseases and addictions in the process, just to guard us against the imagined burden of reaching maturity and being alive. The only possible solution to this is being honest with ourselves. To be open to other perspectives and not live in angst about what people think. Is it worth it to suffer like crazy, just to appear interesting and cool? Is it worth it to play this game to the end? Is it worth it to remain hurt forever, just to be able to hate someone instead of letting it go to learn from it? We ought to be brave enough to ask these questions. Even if we're afraid of the outcome. The truth might actually bring temporary chaos into our world and may disrupt our universe. It can be very scary, and the result will likely not immediately please us. However, it unlocks a path to a better future. We all need to understand our destiny is tied up to everybody else's destiny. Thus, we'll only be successful if we accept this connection and work to gradually uncover our true self and the calling we have. Finding our passion is hard work; however, shying away from it is a bad strategy to tackle this responsibility and a surefire way to never be satisfied with our life. There was once a singer performing in front of a stiff audience, mostly consisting of members of academia. It was a famous folk song, and she did a good job in the beginning, but the pressure crawled up her mind and she started making mistakes. It built up more and more until she capitulated and eventually stopped. It was embarrassing, and she must have felt completely naked in front of all these people. She apologized and told the audience about her nervousness. The guitar player, however, was dedicated to finish the job and encouraged her by playing a few gentle intro bars over and over to bring her back into the song. It worked. She began singing again, and even though the lyrics weren't on point, she was able to reach the end. Her struggle was obvious and palpable to everyone. A bunch of woman had tears in their eyes.

She allowed herself to be seen, and the room could relate. They sensed the stress she had gone through. During the song, the faces cheered her up, and after, the hands congratulated her. In the end, she found relief in a passionate applause. The audience could have gossiped about her mistake or judged her as unprofessional, and some of them did, but the majority had their heart onstage. Cheering for her success. This is a fantastic example of the courage to speak your truth and the consequences of it. Some people will always find ways to mislead us by pushing us down or suppressing our truth, but the majority will always understand as long as we are honest. It creates compassion. It helps us succeed, and it brings us together. The more we tell the truth, the more we will be aligned with what we ultimately want in life. It's the most power we'll ever have. But how can we honor our truth and, at the same time, live in a society with other people, who might have a very different truth? When concepts become words and words are imbued by manifold meanings, the truth must be our perception of the combined meaning of all the words we are exchanging. If that's true, then it becomes very clear that reality consists of stories. The stories of our life are a collection of words, assembled into meaningful narratives. Everyone has a personal story, which is connected to their truth, and our society also has a story, which consists of the accumulated truth of the people who are living in it. What moves our world is therefore perceptions of the truth. All our individual stories generate and change the bigger story. The bigger story reflects these narratives back to us as our societal reality. A constant balance of reflections and input governs our life to an unbelievable extent. People rely on their peer group for a lot of decisions in their life. Every peer group most certainly has its own narrative. Every person belongs to multiple collectives of shared attributes, interests, or tastes. In other words, once the ball is rolling, nobody is able to stop it. This nudges development of the individual as well as society as a whole.

It might seem we don't learn much from history, because we repeat the same mistakes over and over again, but the lessons learned usually enter our collective consciousness, or else we would still be sitting at the fire in our cave. Politicians are surprisingly not the people to blame. The word "inaugurate" stems from Latin "inaugurāre" and means to observe the flight of the birds. They may be bad, but they're just avatars for the most pressing issues of our culture. When the problems add up to an unbearable amount or the next step of the story needs another direction to come to fruition, the appropriate person is usually on their way to govern the country. In times of prompt change or confrontation of large interest groups, this can mean that one hell of a person is suddenly sitting in the chair. If a change in government is not possible, people usually opt for other outlets like trends. Whatever may be the case, politicians are not the problem, they're an image coming back from the mirror. Otherwise nobody would vote for them. Elections are popularity contests, and politics are perceived as unfunny entertainment. Some kind of perverted TV series with villains and heroes included. If one side strikes against the other, the injustice reflex gets triggered and discontent arises. A while later, the tables turn and the cycle begins anew. Politicians are observers, not doers. But if they're only puppets of the truth, what narrative is governing our story driven world? The dual reflection remains the most important thing; however, to know the influencing factors, we first need to look at stories in general. A bare-bones story is usually a want, an obstacle and conflict as a result. This scaffold is then turned and repeated until the goal is reached or the mission has failed. Every story has one element that is most important for the course of the whole narrative. A premise. A premise is a base theory or idea to describe the setting and sums up the experience. It's the framework of reality and narrows it down to an understandable chunk of information. If we know the premise, we can pretend how it ends. So which are the powers? The two important players in our world are, without a doubt, capitalism and science. Capitalism because it delivered the premise, science because it added the rigidity nobody is able to handle anymore.

The message is as easy as devastating, but it is everywhere, and we can't possibly escape it. The pergola narrative reads: humans are selfish by nature. It is the all-encompassing premise of our culture. It means we're doing everything just for ourselves, and if someone is messing with our right to be selfish, we are allowed to treat them like shit. We're entitled to undermine people's dignity to feed our greediness and the endless desire for stuff we don't need, because we suffer so much from the work we don't like. Some of us secretly doubt it, but it's so universally accepted that nobody ever brings it up. It influences the way we try to motivate people. It turns out modern motivation is a mixture of reward, fear, and conviction. Without a reward, people wouldn't do anything. And if they do something, we need to hold them in an anxious state to keep their behavior under control. A controlled consumer is an exceptional worker. But surveillance is not needed, because we do it ourselves. The narrative is so strong that we want to climb to the top with utmost aggressiveness, just to be totally disappointed when we arrive. We might be acting in a way that nobody can touch us, parading our strength to show that nobody can hurt us, but that's just a sign of how lost we are and how desperately we want to escape. It's a perfectly normalized state of affairs. Accepted and understood by all. It's the reason for the suffering of our world. People are encircled by an accepted unshakeable truth and all they're trying to do is survive. If we're members of the system, the deepest premise is almost impossible to recognize. Our whole being automatically adapts to the circumstances and our opinions get aligned with it. We're primed to the point we are unable not to believe in it. We have become the masks we put up. The information given to us is reinforcing itself into infinity. There is absolutely no chance of something else. The original state got compromised by the character we have made ourselves to be, and the only way out seems undetectable from inside our construct.

And if an outlier dares to ask the question of why we can't readjust, we tell them Darwinian selection is the justification for our behavior. If we don't push others down, we'll not succeed. This is the natural order of things, and it can't be otherwise. Tribalism is a gamble of rivaling groups, and the corresponding individuals on top of the distribution are fighting mercilessly. They're representatives of our belief that only one truth exists. The truth of the group we are in. Our truth. We enter these tribes by birth or other measures we don't have control over, and they're usually not very diverse. They shape smaller narratives inside our society and provide support to plan new attacks or recover from fights. On the personal level, they're predictors for life success, and it's very tough or completely impossible to escape them. Only if conditions are right, the talent is there, and luck is on our side. Suppose Darwin was right, which he was not; are we really just animals on a mission to survive? Is it our purpose to compete ourselves to death? Is peace only kept by everyone being equally lethal? The problem remains the premise. It insists on selfishness. What Darwin refused to acknowledge was the relational character of the world. The cyclic nature of necessity and joined survival. Lichen is an organism consisting of a mutual relationship between algae and fungi. Algae are responsible for photosynthesis, and fungi in turn contribute protection from UV light and access to nutrients. However, it's not as easy as it seems. Nobody could recreate this organism, since the number of members in this relationship is far greater and more multifaceted than we thought. These joint ventures are not only found on a micro level; they can easily be seen in far more common places. They're found all across the natural world in the form of complex systems, which use feedback loops and emergent properties to grow and adapt to an ever-changing outside world. They self-organize and expand or shrink depending on the requirements, grow more complex or simplify themselves.

Growth, in this context, means specialization of community members and tighter integration into the system. Each part cares for their own self-preservation and at the same time provides resources to other entities. The whole is therefore stronger than its parts. Stability and efficiency is mainly derived from give and take. Thus, selfishness and selflessness are equally important in that equation. The difficulty in seeing these relationships lies in the communication aspect of the system. As they're getting more specialized, some of the members might stop talking to each other, but the system is dependent on all of them. A successful system needs as much diversity as possible to widen resources and stabilize or expand adaptability. Its members follow the requirements of the whole, and coherence secures flexibility in times of crisis. In this network of talents and attitudes, disruptors are needed to push development, if it has come to a halt for whatever reason. The disruption is done when the forces who were out of balance return to a state of homeostasis, where growth and retreat were in optimal proportion to each other. A state of mere equilibrium would lead to standstill and is therefore not desirable. In other words, there's always something, and there always will be. Systems are connected on differing levels of magnification. The zoom level gives us small insights into relationships, but to fathom the whole network, we necessarily need to have an overview of the parts, since change on one level may influence entities of a completely different node. This process of influencing is called emergence, and it gives rise to ever new levels of organization. System networks have no central entity to govern or regulate forces inside of it. Instead, the natural interaction of forces cares for development on its own. They are self-regulating and self-organizing structures of life. A simple example to illustrate how such a system works would be a small fish called golden shiner. These little fish exclusively participate in schools, because it helps to reduce the friction of the water and makes them appear like one big organism. The single fish are advised to swim slower when they're in a more dark area and to speed up if they're in lighter regions.

Every fish is also looking for their direct neighbors, since darker areas are better to hide from predators. This helps to diminish the chance of being eaten. They don't just look like a big fish, they act as one. Cooperation is the most important survival factor for the golden shiners, and competition is not as important in their relationship. The idea of competition in natural systems, however, is dependent on its energy consumption. The species that needs the least energy is the most successful, because it is able to support more specimens on lesser resources. If they're less efficient, they'll lose influence and go extinct.

And since energy can be used more productively, namely to build a nest or hive, they change behavior until a win-win situation emerges, where competition is not needed. Examples for this are nighttime and daytime hunters, foraging in different places, or differentiation in food. As a result, diversity strengthens, duties in the ecosystem are widely distributed across differing species, and resilience of the whole system climbs up. Thus, to benefit systems and to keep them resilient, specialization is needed in order to stabilize network activity. While we cannot get away with saying we're all good, we can start to accept our animal nature the way it is. We can't be completely on one side of the spectrum, since it stuns development and it's harmful to us. The attitude of delusional self-righteousness feeds our misconceptions by assuring an unending correctness, and the easily offended egos are fighting each other as a result. But our limitations are possibilities for creativity, not hurtful facts of life. We are pieces of innumerable systems we either created or changed depending on our needs. These systems aren't competitive by nature, but by design. However, we humans are better than that. We're expressing ourselves in a multitude of ways, and we're capable of feeling compassion and love. The facts are not the problem. They are ultimately just means of development and interaction.

A certain friction will always be necessary in order to move on to the next level of evolution, but the next stage is reached by progressively subtler confrontations, not smarter ones. It's the perception of things and the perspectives we take that will guide us forward or make everything worse by regressing to a former section. What would our life be if we stopped making it difficult? We might judge things by zoom level, emotional involvement, complexity, or any other metric. The often feared cognitive dissonance is not as bad as it seems, because it forces us to implement or at least consider the option of another truth. The more we zoom out and look at our collective issues from a bird's-eye view, the more we will be able to understand other people and their truth. In fact, if we fly to the moon, the earth looks like a giant blue ball of life, not a collection of thoughts, perceptions, feelings, and misunderstandings. Depending on our level of honesty and dedication to explore other chunks of reality, we will be able to recognize the dissolution of apparently opposing truths to finally express a higher state of consciousness. However, it will only be possible by overcoming our filter systems, which we generated to protect us from emotional harm and to make sense of the world. When we look at an optical illusion, two dots might appear the same size, because they're surrounded by other circles with different sizes. The context might distort our reality and makes the exact same thing look utterly different. We often come up with narratives of causality and try our best in describing the phenomenon to predict the future. Oftentimes we use averages for that, but these are not at all sufficient to map reality in a clear and concise way. Quantum physics tells us that the reflection of light is not predictable with logic, and it all has to be viewed individually. There are too many averages and probabilities to be exact. Reality is famous for behaving in a nonlinear way, and what is implied on one side might not even touch the matter at hand and can lead to wrong assumptions. A chili pepper is not really hot in temperature, it just feels hot. When we're aware of our inability to look at a problem from all angles at the same time and start to respect our differences, which derive from this idea, the full picture will provide us with a more compassionate take to other people's opinions.

What was formerly considered stupid and deluded becomes a discussion, where opposing actors are not seen as a threat, but as a necessity to find the truth. The desire to please loses its appeal in favor of meaningful competition. The will to win should therefore not be oppressed; it should be embraced instead. Only the way we look at competition has to change. The conduct is as important as the perspective to find a satisfactory answer to an issue. It surrounds the conversation like the two dots in the optical illusion. The identity we built for our opponents, the opponents' imagined identity, and the one we created ourselves make it impossible to completely understand. Next are the thoughts about what they have done and why: whence they came to a conclusion, how they'll use this knowledge, and what their next steps might be, according to the information we've collected. Before Sicilian fishermen go out, they say something in Greek to confuse the fish. This makes perfect sense, since Sicilians believe Greek fishers aren't very good. The goal to survive is identical with the goal to understand each other. A discussion between parties where both of them agree on most of the points is rather boring, but comfortable and self-assuring. It feels good. A discussion between parties where both are violently opposed can be interesting, but also quite challenging. It drains people of their energy and patience. However, the challenging discussion will be more fruitful than the easy one, if the parties overcome their fish tactics. Opening up and accepting the chance of being wrong or having our narrative changed is hard. Our ego will always find a way to insert difficulties, since its purpose is to create and maintain a stable self-image and a causal reality. It uses everything including memories, real-time input, and imagined prospects of the future to do so, regardless if the prejudices, ideas, notions, stories, and truths are wrong, deluded, based on false assumptions, or derived from fantasy. The way to cut through all the problematic story telling is not to agree to disagree, nor to tolerate the other party.

What we want is to come to a conclusion or to learn something in the process by always reminding us that it's possible to be friends with everyone, independent of their opinions. Our differences drive the world forward, and goodwill is our motor. Being honest means being open to having our truths changed and avoiding silent competitions, where nobody listens and people just wait for their turn. Everyone should be allowed to say everything and also feel everything. Every wound we have from someone else is merely used as a function of our own self-importance. People must be given the same chances. Multiple expressions of the same thing are desirable. Physical harm is forbidden as usual. Is smiling at the hateful neighbor not the most satisfying answer we can give in the long run? Unacknowledged hatred is the cause of violence, not acknowledged. Giving ourselves the opportunity to speak our truth is the most freeing act we can accomplish in our life, and living according to it is the equivalence of fulfillment. But what about hate speech? People suffer tremendously from words other people tell them over a cable from a faraway culture. We have to divide so-called hate speech from a witch hunt first, and then we need to find out what hate speech is and how we can prevent it. However, who is deciding what it is and what's destined to be censored and what's not? Everybody has their own concepts, and someone will always disagree with the decision any individual will make. Also, would it be that much of a problem, if platforms weren't interested in maximum engagement from the user side? We could assume it might not be a big deal, if it would just slide down our feeds with no reaction, but we could also be wrong. It's important to participate and interact prohibition and manipulation often results in disaster though. Witch hunts, on the other hand, where people come together in mobs and try to find individuals or groups to hold them responsible for a certain injustice are almost always based on a difference in narrative. The mob is not willing to accept other perspectives and makes everything worse by fighting an entity instead of a narrative.

If someone took part in a crime, the person has the right to get a fair trial and nobody should be allowed to condemn them further. If they're only holding a different opinion, the whole operation should be seen as an offense against the entity who stated it. We don't get to choose which opinions are allowed and which are not. The trick is to be mature enough to abstain from using the platforms as an outlet for frustrations and go for a climate of acceptance and understanding instead. An even better idea is to limit exposure to stressors. Video games, social media, and news sites are demanding and cause emotional spikes. Sugar and processed foods trigger insulin rushes, which, in turn, are responsible for mood swings and obesity. Keeping ourselves sane by accepting the uncontrollable and only trying to change the controllable is a proven mindset and a responsible way of looking at the world. Making peace with oneself and giving up entitlement to the truth might be unbeatable, however. People should be allowed to make mistakes. We should be accepted despite our failures. We should encourage experimentation, and we should celebrate when we achieve a superior level of understanding. It'll take time to get there, but the willingness to approach advanced modalities of conduct is enough to be able to reach them. However, errors happen, and given the advantage of allowance, we need to think about ways to forgive. Sometimes we may have wronged somebody or we feel guilty and want to make amends, but we don't know how to do it. If it's simple, we're generous and enjoy it, but if it's hard, reconciliation might be too far away. Forgiving can be a somewhat impossible task. But if we regard it as a process of getting to a point of mutual understanding, we open up to a solution. Irony might enable us to laugh about our shortcomings, but only if we're laughing together. Scars are unavoidable on either side; the ability to learn from confrontations and the will to move forward are superior, though. Understanding is another difficult thing.

Often, arguments are based on so many false assumptions, the whole conversation becomes a kind of dance, where one is avoiding exactness to appear a certain way and the other is trying to decipher the message in order to understand what was said. Punctuation, symbols with seriously limited capacity to transport meaning, or the art of omission are equally disastrous. Whatever the sender meant is almost definitely not the same thing the receiver creates on the other side. By committing to be exact in the first place, we make it easier for everyone and might eventually arrive at mutual understanding. There may always be people though who don't even get what we're saying and think we must be crazy to think what we're thinking. Confirmation bias, for instance, shows us that we want to believe what we already believe. Every fact or idea counteracting our prejudices gets dismissed the moment it arrives in our minds. Sometimes we are so confident in our truth, we're only seeing the info we want to see and we find ways to use rivaling information to fortify it even more. Invaders have no chance of changing our truth, and we have a hard time changing our reality. Hindsight bias is a false confidence of our knowledge of why stuff happens. We always "knew" it would rain today. The halo effect is based on assumptions we make using our ideas of previous incidents or perceptions. If our impression of something or someone meets our reality, we tend to make judgments using metrics we made up to be connected with it. Is a knife good if it looks neat or if it's sharp? Recency bias favors recent findings over older ones. It might seem wrong to believe the most recent scientific narrative over a huge body of empirical evidence, but some people do just that. Implicit bias is the expectation of a behavior, based on attitudes, beliefs, or stereotypes. If we think other people are an enemy, we will perceive everything they do as offensive or hostile. We're assuming how they will harm us. It's often combined with confirmation bias to perfect the illusion of the world being against us. Framing is evaluating a subject through made-up assumptions. "All is good at all times" might be a nice overall worldview, but if one really believes it through and through, nothing will ever change.

It can be hard to detect all these biases, but we should check ourselves regularly, if we're overlooking something. Sometimes, we're more imprisoned by our surroundings than by ourselves. Family and friends may prevent us from rising out of the bleak universe we are getting a whiff of during moments of clarity. Every person in a system fulfills a role to keep the status quo of the structure alive. Like a baby mobile, where balance is necessary to keep the figures from bouncing up and down. If one individual dies or leaves, others need to fill in the missing elements the person used to provide. Assuming they hold up the notion of being losers with no future or chances in life, even if it's barely noticeable, we'll have a difficult time changing until we recognize the influence over us. To grow intellectually as well as holistically, we need to know how the powers in our lives affect the way we think and the means by which we use our productivity to benefit the whole. Capitalism is our life. The proud flag we raise in spite of all the problems. It brought us all this great stuff. Technology is contributing to a lazy lifestyle, and things get better all the time. Easy communication, fast travel, and modern medicine provide us with convenience and safety. For our society to survive, we must grow, consume, and suffer infinitely. Trying to avoid this argument is ignorant. The story needs to change; otherwise the future of the human race may be more difficult, than it needs to be. Nobody denies the notion of selfishness, because we have become it. If somebody tells their children they're working hard and they're doing it all for them, given the family leads a wealthy life, it always appears a bit off. The purpose of such a statement is the upholding of the story and the individually created identity. Capitalism is envy, not egotism. The premise is especially harmful if the environment is competitive and hostile against losers. We have so much stuff, we need external storage houses to keep our own homes from overflowing. We buy everything we can to relieve the pain of not being enough.

Our soul wants peace, but our life is missing connection. The design is grand, but the mirror only shows a selfish face. We're getting tons of discounts, and we're constantly pushed to act. We eat as much as we can, because we don't want to miss out on our right to enjoy life. We party until we've forgotten half of our lives. We take drugs to slow us down, help us sleep, make us smarter, faster, healthier, and stronger. This never-ending cycle of compulsions and painful withdrawal symptoms carves the path through our days. And when we're sick and destroyed, we ask everyone else why they let it happen and why these idiotic things are available and encouraged, when in reality they do nothing for us. The truth is, we're not always able to recognize or resist these feedback loops from amplifying the impact of said premise on society and ourselves. We ignored our precious parts in favor of crude and uncivilized ideas. It's so surprising that nothing helps, some get ready for an appointment with a psychotherapist. These wizards have a reputation for restoring our sanity and preventing suicides after all. It is tempting to whine about reality and find relief for our pain and suffering. However, as useful as they can be at times, what they try to do is help us function inside of the narrative, not escape it. They're not telling us to quit our jobs and aim for a better life; they'll work with us so we enjoy the grind instead. But that's not what we want. What we want is to be loved, happy, and useful, but the way we were shown is dividing us. It starts in school, where we're primed to follow instructions, with the threat of becoming a loser no one ever cares for. The pressure is felt from a young age. Our parents, if they are fit enough to take action, push us to ever new heights to obey the education system, in fear of parenting a coming street bum. We want to make them proud and perform well, although we're only partly conscious of the consequences of screwing up our grades. Later, the patterns we inherited from our parents become ingrained in our worldview.

The pressure to win hinders our development and the real reason for school, namely getting a hint of what the future has in store for us, turns into a competition to outdo everyone who gets in the way, and to impress all, who may come to join our team in the war against ourselves. It's not important what our real talents are or what our heart wants. We have to become a winner. Earning as much money as we can to win a game nobody asked us to participate in. It's just assumed that we'll come to love it, since the propaganda inside our systems and branched out subsystems encourages us to enjoy the pain and to kick down, if needed. We invest our energy in appearing superior, but we feel a fraud at best and want to kill ourselves at worst. The people who cannot make it are predominantly average and not stupid. They are mostly sensible and/or haunted by a subsystem instead. But isn't it great to be on top? If we enjoy the up spiral of nagging fraudulency paired with constant fear of not being enough, then the top is the place to be. As soon as the admiration and envy of our people fade, the individual gets the feeling of not living up to the unreachable and omnipotent fantasies they have become so accustomed to dreaming of. The notion of all the CEOs being psychopaths is hardly true, but the system itself encourages people to be firm, to have no mercy, to grow infinitely. And if it works, they become addicted to success and money. It's a mean adaptation process. People want to count. People want to leave a legacy. People want to be leaders. But the narrative prohibits humaneness, and if the ones who pushed up recognize weaknesses, they'll increase pressure until the person crumbles and another even more merciless individual gets the job. There is simply no space for soft skills. The other side of the coin is the new breed of friendly bosses who try to be human by talking about private affairs. They attempt to be friends with people, and it seems they care. "It's all fine and dandy" appears to be the message; the underlying parole, however, is to persuade employees into doing free overtime and working harder in the spirit of community service. It's exploitation via friendship. It teaches us that an improvement on the surface level can and will be used as a tool to extract value from our dignity.

Regardless of the rank on the fraud versus loser scale, all share the same feelings in the end. We're plagued by shame, guilt, and sadness, and we need solutions to issues we honestly can't find the source of. The tactics are many: alcohol, drugs, prescription drugs, sex, consumerism, activism, nihilism, hedonism, sadism, masochism, baptism, antagonism, despotism, extremism, ageism, atheism, and pejorism. Simply to avoid or suppress the reality we have created with our supposedly best interest in mind. Some of these solutions become permanent frustration valves; they never deliver in the long run, however. When it comes to money in general, most people say they are happy if they have reached a worry-free life. Others say happiness increases, as long as their bank account grows. This discrepancy can be explained. The former group reflects on the past. They're influenced by their overall life. The latter looks at the future; they anticipate happiness through bank account growth, because they have been told it works. The main issue is the unfortunate fact that it all works sometimes. And when it does, it counts as reassurance and verification in the realm of the winners and beneficiaries. The reason they have no interest in changing the world is due to the hard work they've invested and, even more, to the luck they've had. If people are winners in a hostile universe of competition and they think they did it all by themselves, why would they stop and risk losing the luxury life in order to give other people a chance? The gamble is just too dangerous from their point of view. And even if a small group of philanthropists would be ready, they will not easily convince the others. Complex relationships between people and manifold attitudes regarding societal issues can be terrible hindrances in the pursuit of changing the world for the better. It's disappointing to hear that nothing really moves and that we're trapped in the rat race. However, there are ways out. What we can do today is to stop believing in the media.

While it's true that politicians are puppets to the truth and we're voting to further our story, it's also true that big parts of the narrative gets made by the media we consume on a daily basis. The owners of the media control it and try to shape our reality. They're regularly concealing unwanted facts or overemphasize things that benefit them. It's basically a bunch of billionaires who own and manipulate every news item through the lens of their interests. And since they're the winners of the game, they're actively shaping and molding our reality to generate money from our naivety. People are shamed or praised depending on their usefulness. Almost all media outlets are bought or threatened to obey the status quo. The Western world is organized as an oligarchy, where a group of corporations and their owners are responsible for the policies and laws. They think they're the only ones intelligent enough to handle money correctly. Others think that people should rule. But there's no question of who's ruling. It's us. We're ruling if we stand together as one and stop to believe in confusing lies, which are solely made to divide and control the power we have. If we keep in mind that no matter who is ruling, they're just there to implement and push the narratives they're given, then we have a chance to see behind the charade and get a hint of the underlying truth. We may not be able to prevent all this narcissist behavior at once, but we can start with the things we read, watch, think, and talk about. We should consider the opposite of what we hear, ask if the news item is trying to divide us or if it's trying to cleanly inform us of the facts. Who gains from the reporting? Who loses? Why is the item appearing now? Who owns the company that is putting out those news items? If that seems all too exhausting, we can default to turn the news off altogether and look for better things to spend our time with. This might even be our best option, given the system is not changing by voting, but from us expressing our values and boycotting lies. All the important things reach us anyway, and the remainder is not in our hands. Some may say these are conspiracy theories, but if we imagine a manager who kicked down and pushed up like mad to arrive at the top, would it be so offbeat for us to please shareholders at all costs?

Wouldn't we be ready to sell our mothers to remain in the chair and earn big? Wouldn't we try to threaten everyone who stands in the way of shareholder value? Would we buy ads to control the press? What they do is controlling what topics are reported on, what content is emphasized or played down, what information is allowed, in what context information is presented, and how it's talked about. All to serve the interests of shareholders, to design a brand identity and to create a story. However, it unfortunately doesn't stop there. Our favorite celebrities are mainly brand ambassadors these days. They're there to uphold an envious mood among us and to sell products and promote services nobody needs. The separation between companies, product ads, and news are hardly recognizable anymore, and the narrative that results out of this mush is messing with our minds and ultimately our souls. Life is not easy sometimes, and we welcome every possibility to distract us from our busy schedules, but even the most innocent representatives of fun and leisure may mess with our ability to see the truth. We cannot change anything before the collective believe the market economy in its current state will finally be revealed as ineffective and dangerous to the planet, our dignity, and life in general. Not only nature is taking a big hit from these dangerous notions of the almighty market; it is a huge factor in keeping selfishness alive, because it depends on it. People worship it as if it were a religious leader of some sort. The market has to be untouchable, and the rules and laws trying to regulate its behavior have to be minimized or stopped altogether. They think of it as a mirror of nature, since it allegedly emerged out of necessity and no single entity formed it to their standard. But it's painfully obvious that the interests of the rich and the wish for an omnipotent parent who shows us a means to a marvelous future, where growth is infinite and recourses never end, are just delusional self-deceptions.

It's a scam to distract us from the real issues by trying to comfort our anxiety and telling us the market will make everything okay somehow. What they want is a government that is run like a business, and they're succeeding. The problem is that humans cannot be governed by greed, envy, and selfishness, because the consequences are killing us. However, let's say we are one of the people with the all the power. Capitalism seems to be working great for us, and we're making so much money, our pockets are overflowing and our shareholders are cheering in the background. Let's assume further we're competitive, but not stupid. We might recognize that the world is suffering from our efforts, and we might already try to amend some of it, but we can't change anything, because we're just a somewhat bigger wheel in the machine, and it will grind us up if we revealed our true attitude. It's not like these people don't know what they're doing; they are also witnesses themselves. They just happen to sit on the other side of the table. Another much bigger problem is the fear of a system collapse. Nobody knows an alternative, and the rich are afraid of losing their wealth. We desperately need ideas for a better world and a new premise, one which is congruent with human nature. If we look at the current system and how it handles its participants, we can only ask ourselves how bad it needs to get until the people in power can't ignore reality anymore. Is it worth it to build gated habitats for the super rich in a destroyed environment? Is it worth it to suffer endlessly, because we wrongly believe there is no way out? Corporate narratives exclusively generate separation. It's the age-old story of us against them. If something goes wrong, there needs to be a scapegoat of some sort to narrow our perception as to who is responsible for the issue. Our side has to win for stuff to go well, and we have to prevent others from telling their truth in order maintain our idea. LGBT and especially transgender rights, man versus woman, racism, fascism, politics, science, and religion are topics with diverse perceptions. While it is true that some of these problems will not be easily eliminated, it's also obvious the media has an interest in maintaining conflict and confusion.

Politics seem to be an especially difficult one lately. The right has gained a lot of power back since WWII. They've actually perfected the "them against us" game, and the established parties are afraid of losing power all over the world. They're a great example of the losers of a system. They have been marginalized for many years now, and they survived in tiny groups until their comeback was due. People vote for them because they've been heavily cheated on, and they're expressing their truth by making a fist and punching in everyone's face. They seem to be so divorced from the truth, nobody can understand how they could even come to such outrageous narratives. If it wasn't so brutal and unnecessary, it would be funny. They're connected to their imagination like no one else, and they believe in magic, myths, and stories of gods and superheroes. These people are divided within their own circles; however, what unites them are not individualities. What unites them is the hate for everyone and the wish to destroy the world, because it is hostile, bad, and hell to live in. Conspiracy theories are the absolute norm and encouraged. Every reason to bash others is welcome. Society has to burn to ease the pain and the deep-seated sadness of loneliness. These feelings are not immediately obvious, but a closer inspection reveals the reality of them being highly sensible and confused. They're creating echo chambers on their platforms to guard their stories by curating comments. They always try to prove their ideas, not to falsify them. They live inside a spiral of apophenia, where they perceive meaningful connections between unrelated things. A common manifestation of that is seeing faces in trees or pigs in clouds, but it can also mean that "they" are trying to kill "us" and we have to arm ourselves for war. Sensible individuals are also more prone to fear. They might seem dumb to some, but they're fulfilling an important role in society. All the wrong information that's been circulating to confuse us will not touch them one bit. They can detect lies, because they believe nothing but their own theories. They revolt for reasons no one else can understand, but they're not wrong, only much too immersed in fantasies.

The far right and their often magical ideas and inhuman behaviors are a sign of our collective shadow. We're not acknowledging the fact that we could be doing the same thing, if we were in their shoes. We collectively regard them as nonexistent if they hide in the dark and as outrageous if they come forward to show us our aggressive side. We don't accept their magic and their fantasies, since we think rational thinking is superior. And through our habit of abandoning them and downplaying their existence, they're deeply hurt and sad as a result. We could actually accept their way of seeing the world. It might connect us to a realm of wonder and awe, but we only reduce them to be of inferior intellect. Fascism would not be necessary, if we would try to connect with them. We would learn about ourselves and prevent a lot of misinformation and violence. If we feel cornered and there's no way out, wouldn't we look for others to be on our side? Wouldn't we trust and support them no matter what? Even if one of us turns out to be a monster? The answer seems obvious, since they've got no alternatives and nowhere to go. When they say they did it because someone told them so, we should believe them, because they simply tried to hold on to the only thing that brought connection to their lives. Consequences are as always necessary, but it's not so apparent what they have to be. The reason for the occurrence of this negativity was a long, slow buildup nobody noticed. We were too occupied with our own affairs, which always took priority over the courage to look at these people. It's not weak, if we would try to understand. We'd show our strength by facing our demons and could create an opportunity for change. Many scientific findings of today were already a reality in the mind of an insane person many years from their actual appearance. If we refrain from judgment and ask them who they are and what they want, we may be surprised to find a human being who is anxious of being judged. If we accept the challenges and listen, instead of telling them how stupid they are, they may have a chance to see actual reality and built up confidence in themselves to better deal with the world. If we're already judging ourselves, do we need more judgment from outside?

Would it help us, if we were told nobody wants us? Is violence the right answer for violence? If we want to help people to get well, to change their opinion or to be part of society, we need to meet them with compassion and try to see society through their eyes. Another almost almighty narrative is the fight between men and woman. It took a long time to arrive at our current situation. Equality seems to be far away. What currently happens is a fight for the prestige positions in society. Women want their share by pushing up and fighting for their claim to sit in chairs with power. At least in the Western world. In other countries, there are more pressing problems. But men also have very serious issues women don't share. So who is right? We don't know. What we can say, however, is that we all have to adapt to our environment and make the best of our life. Men and woman are different. There's no doubt about it. However, equality is not the problem, fairness is. The most equal societies with the tightest regulations have shown that woman will do whatever they like, if they're free to choose. It seems unreasonable, why woman want to face their own problems and shoulder all of men's problems on top of it. It looks like the narrative succeeded in its function to divide us once again. If the way to success is the pursuit of power and money, women would be stupid if they would let men have it all. But if money and power cost a lifetime of dedication to career advancement and thus a sacrifice of the joy of having a family, is it really worth it to try and equal everything out? It might even be possible to have it all, but wouldn't it lead to a major cut in time spent with important parenting? If men already suffer from not taking part in the development of their children, should woman do the same by spending more time on the job? If money and power are not the answer, why play the crooked game at all? If the child needs both parents equally, why put it away so it can have the best toys instead of the best care? If there's no desire for a child, is it smart to neglect who we are just to exceed at the unwinnable rat race? Is career success more important than love? Is it worth it to fight a war for equality and destroy our families in the process?

There are many narratives; both sides have become rather rigid about in their storytelling. We should try to celebrate our differences instead. People frequently use different ways to define themselves. It depends on the situation and our mission how we perceive our daily life. Challenges arise out of who we are and what we have to do to get where we need to be. One of the most influential factors of our destiny is still the color of our skin and the country we were born in. It's one of those stories that runs deep inside of us. An archetypal example of discrimination against minorities and the consequences are the Garifuna people. The Garifuna are a mix of African and indigenous peoples, who came to Saint Vincent through slave trade and built families with the Caribe and Arawak people. They mostly live in coastal Central America and have developed a unique culture with a distinct language and traditional rituals. After many fights and wars with the goal of protecting their culture and heritage, the biggest chunk of the Garifuna population lives in Honduras today. However, their fight is not over. Although they were given part of the land from the Honduran government, corruption and greed forced them to live in ever-smaller areas, because of a big coup against the president in 2009. President Jose Manuel Zelaya got overthrown and was put to exile in Costa Rica. As a result, crime and violence took over, and poverty, as well as unemployment, skyrocketed. The new conservative rulers of Honduras had no interest in the Garifuna or their culture. Instead, they illegally sold the land of the Garifuna to foreign developers, who built five star resorts in midst of harshly impoverished villages. The impeccable beaches and fully intact eco-systems slowly made way for tourists coming with cruise ships. To worsen the quality of life for the Garifuna and to put them under pressure, basic services like garbage collection have been stopped, the traditional way of fishing got prohibited, and a lot of homes were sold in expectation of eviction through the government.

But tourism is not the only issue the Garifuna are facing. A number of big corporations are buying the land to use it for palm oil plantages, and a drug epidemic is shaking the country. As a result, the Garifuna lose their traditional way of life and slide more and more into poverty. In order to survive, they accept jobs in the resorts and on the palm oil plantages. The owners of these establishments see themselves as Samaritans, because they're "rescuing" them from poverty. People who decline to work for the capitalists enter a life of drug usage and gang crime, while younger Garifuna are forbidden to speak their language in school. However, they are trying to fight back by building their own schools to teach their kids who they are. Although the UNESCO has inscribed the language, dance, and music on the representative list of the intangible cultural heritage of humanity, it is uncertain how long the culture can be held up. A lot of Garifunas have already left for the big American cities in the hope for a better life. Most of them fled to New York, where the expected opportunities were endless and the dream of money and fame was still real. In actuality though, a lot of them got deported; others became criminals or addicts. When they eventually came back home to Honduras, they brought the American way of life and all their problems with them. The culture is under attack from all sides, but the Garifuna remain a very tough people. They are con-necting on social platforms and share music, learn their language, and communicate with each other. It's admirable to see them endure in spite of all the challenges. The Garifuna teach us resiliency, and their example shows us that if we lose our personality to corrupted capitalists and fall prey to their tactics, the future is uncertain at best and deadly at worst. "Developing" a country means to exploit resources, enslave the locals, and destroy their culture to maximize profits, while trying to sell it as an act of improvement to the people they assault. Their only chance is to fight for their rights, preserve their culture at all costs, and never forget who they are.

Immigration has become a huge issue all over the world. The Garifuna flee mainly due to poverty, but other reasons like racism, beliefs, political affiliation, climate change, sexual orientation, or war play an even bigger role. In Germany, people from all over the world celebrated New Year's Eve around the Cologne Cathedral. In the last night of 2015, a group of refugees sexually assaulted a local woman. Some said they were not used to the customs in Germany and did it because of alcohol. The majority of people, though, were simply shocked to learn what happened. A huge discussion arose, and the right gained a lot of new members as a result. The women's movement made cultural differences responsible and thought it was about driving the women out of the public sphere and using sexual violence to harm the women of Germany. But it was not their culture or their alcohol consumption. These people were frustrated, because they had no work permit and couldn't get one. They were waiting for their deportation although their countries wouldn't take them back. Trapped in a dead zone, they expressed their hatred for a system they weren't allowed to take part in. Most refugees in Germany are Syrians, though. The Syrian war remains the biggest contributor to their displacement. It has become a harsh conflict between rebels, activist groups, and Western backers, who pay for weapons and aid to fuel the ongoing fights. The capitalist agenda, which centered on exploiting the people and stealing their oil, benefited investors worldwide. As a result, the Syrians had to deal with higher living costs and inflation. Demonstrations escalated quickly and the first bullets were fired. A lot of the land got destroyed due to the war that ensued. The capitalists plan to develop the region to build up the framework for a profit maximized economy and to strengthen their political power, while from the outside, it seems like they're trying to fight the rebels and discipline them. Meanwhile, the media created a climate of fear against Islamic countries to manufacture consent and to justify the necessity of the war in the East.

They're mainly spreading a common story, where the West is in danger of being attacked, and the enemy is waiting for a chance to harm innocent people. They're animals with a fiendish culture and an even worse religion with the only goal of blowing up our cities. We're under threat and must defend our high moral values against the barbaric terrorists. The war is hard on the Syrians. A lot of them got killed, and floods of refugees try to flee from the war often to one of the countries coresponsible for the issues in the first place. Oftentimes, they have to leave their families behind in order to get a chance for the future. The people from Italy, for example, got very upset at the foreigners for disturbing their communities. In a right-wing-controlled part of the country, they opened up camps for refugees to force cultural inclusion and obedience among them. This military drill causes fear and uncertainty, although refugees try hard to fit the standards no average Italian would accept. They have no freedom and have to work with little to no compensation. If they pass the so-called "academy," they're awarded with a temp work permit and low-paying jobs in order to extract as much cheap labor from them as possible. These "educational" institutions can be found in different configurations and intensity in many countries. They might appear helpful to us, and some might even think they're crucial to ensure the refugees learn the customs to navigate our culture, but their main purpose is to extract labor and to instill conformity inside of the system. This is also true for all of the Westerners. The capitalists want us just smart enough to fulfill the duties we're given. Creativity is not welcome, as long as the work isn't requiring it. Measurement and constant testing for rapidly inhaled facts keeps critical thinking at bay. Young children are forced to sit for hours to learn things they don't need, and if they don't conform, they're pathologized and medicated. In the States, student debt keeps people from finding themselves in favor of a work life with hardly a chance for change.

Furthermore, it's troubling that colleges are funded by China, Russia, Saudi Arabia, and Qatar to an extent. Why would they do that and why isn't it paid by tax money? If a tree grows round a supportive stake, the form is fixed. Economic refugees are seldomly accepted in the United States in the first place, but if they get a chance to live in the country, a resettlement organization usually takes care of their needs. However, this help has limits. The financial aid is a fixed amount per person and ends if the money is gone. Until then, the refugees have to have a job to provide for their families. The jobs usually consist of low-level work, because the refugees can't speak the language and are still shocked by the vastly different culture. The woman want to nurture their children, but they have to work to be able to pay rent and avoid being displaced once again. The refugee life is tough; staying in their countries is often impossible, though. This results in opens doors for human traffickers and people smugglers, who arrange sham marriages to avoid deportation. Business likes to confuse human beings with human capital, a grim misconception millions of people pay for. Roosevelt once said to the US Congress: "The first truth is that the liberty of a democracy is not safe if the people tolerate the growth of private power to a point where it becomes stronger than their democratic state itself. That, in its essence, is fascism, ownership of the government by an individual, by a group, or by any other controlling private power." Regardless of him being a good president back then, he had a strong truth. From all this, one might think that the religion Islam is not as bad as it seems, and the main responsibility is only found within the war-mongering capitalists. However, the Islamists and especially the Muslim Brotherhood caused issues as well. They've proved to be very rigid in their beliefs and can be understood as the fascists of the East. They mix religion and politics to influence the narrative and recruit young people at an early age to indoctrinate them with their violent views on the scriptures of Islam and to infiltrate society to spread Islam as the only allowed religion in the world.

And since many of them grew up in a harsh reality of war against the West and they've been told that the enemy is trying to kill their families and is actively blowing up their country, there was no doubt it would lead to a merciless terrorist organization. People who try to oppose their narrative or start a discussion with them will fail. They regularly dehumanize others in the name of their understanding of the will of god and do everything to maintain their hate. Even the most kind and friendly people are not safe from their extreme judgments. But we should keep in mind, and that is hard to fathom, they're doing it to bring more human kindness into the world. In the famous Stanford prison experiment, researchers did want to find out if the guards were violent because of their environment or if it was due to their personality. Volunteers were brought into a simulated prison, and the experiment was supposed to last two weeks, but the scientists had to stop it within six days, because the guards treated the prisoners with utmost brutality, although they'd never possessed these traits. The Muslim Brotherhood can be seen in a similar light. Their shared faith causes people within the group to lose their personal sense of self. This leads to grim behavior, which gets normalized to get the job done. The challenge is to stop our hate reflexes in favor of a long and tough discussion wherever possible. It will not be successful, and a few generations will have to pass before the center moves, but it will be worth it in the end. Many say Islamism and Christian beliefs will never agree with each other and the constant war is unavoidable. However, although France is not the best example, it shows a coexistence is possible. At 3.7 million people, France has the largest Muslim minority in the world. There are tensions we're not going to dissolve in the next few months, but if everyone is steering toward a celebration of the many truths our life can have, we should be able to create multicultural societies without all the unnecessary violence. There is a small town in Syria called Maaloula, where people are still speaking Aramaic. It's half-Muslim and half-Christian. All of them live in peace, though, and they refer to each other as brothers.

Everyone knows that family is important. These people will always love us, even if it's in the most crooked way. There isn't much a child can do to lose the affection of their parents. However, sometimes the child develops in unusual ways, and conservative caregivers may be flabbergasted to find out their offspring is homosexual, bisexual, transgender, or intersex. The variety in these communities is absolutely staggering. While gay, lesbian, and bisexual people are more common than others, they're still struggling to find their voice in the world. As discrimination decreases, the numbers increase. Why are we having problems accepting the richness and diversity of the natural world? Why is it weird to us, that some people have another anatomy? Why do we care so much that love has to happen between man and woman? Why do we need drawers for everything, only to pigeonhole everyone we meet? Intersex people are an example of humans who are still hiding in society. Nobody really knows how many actually exist in the world. And we may never find out, if we continue to stigmatize otherness. Intersex people are born with variations in sex characteristics such as chromosomes, gonads, sex hormones, or genitals. They deviate from the usual anatomy, and while some of them get the message at birth, others might never find out, because their genitalia are not ambiguous and the differences only show inside the body. Doctors often react by inviting colleagues to a medical freakshow. Parents are normally advised to give their child into hormonal treatment or surgery called "normalizing" to enable doctors to be comfortable again. They try to invent medical reasons for treatment; however, intersex people are usually as healthy as everybody else regardless of their anatomical makeup. Transgender differs from intersex in so far as it describes a different gender expression, oftentimes opposite to the sex that was assigned at birth, but not necessarily so. There're a lot of people who don't conform by the usual categories and use many different terms to describe themselves. Nonbinary, gender-queer, or fluid are among the most used. To make it even more complex, some of them also want to be addressed with gender neutral pronouns like singular "they" and lesser known "xe."

Several reject pronouns on the whole. While a lot of transgender people hide, others actively fight for their place in society. The many pronouns might be quite confusing and seem like an entitlement, they're often just a means to keep the discussion alive. People experience gender dysphoria as a result of a mismatch between their preferred gender and their sex assigned at birth, which causes severe distress. Being transgender is stigmatized in a lot of cultures. They're often persecuted and physically hurt. Some get imprisoned for no reason other than being alive. Many of us don't know that we're all somewhat gender fluid over the course of our life. Sexual fluidity is not a rare phenomenon. Some people experience a temporal or complete shift in sexual affection; however, if they are able to confess it is questionable. Social pressures and fear to be different is hindering them from accepting it and trying to be someone else, instead of who they have become, can be painful. Especially if it's lurking in the unconscious and comes occasionally forward. Another group of people are not interested in sexual endeavors at all and call themselves asexual. They can be interested in a partner, but just for companionship. Demissexuals, on the other hand, only feel sexual attraction if an emotional connection has been formed before the actual act takes place. Any change in sexual belonging can influence our truth in both directions and should therefore not be regarded as an issue, but as a chapter in our life. In 1874, a German called Carl

Hagenbeck invented a kind of human zoo. He called it a zoological exhibition. Different peoples were exposed to crowds of visitors, who were thrilled to watch some savages in cliché reproductions of their home countries. Eskimos, Samoans, and Sinhalese were in his repertoire. They had to dance, sing, and perform traditional rituals. A few of them were even touted as human freaks for their height or other noticeable body traits. It was highly stressful, and once a group stayed in their hut to avoid being exposed to the crowd, fences were pushed down and things got destroyed because the visitors wanted to watch the "retarded freaks" jump in circles.

It's a strange kind of curiosity humans carry out when they look at others just to satisfy their own sensation mongering. We want to fit in at all costs, since we don't want to be exposed to judgment. People hate when others make fun of them because of some condition they have. The exaggerations and stereotypes may be funny at times, but it's no fun to see people being humiliated for who they are. A division between pain and entitled behavior is hard to pull off, although both of these cases deserve attention, albeit in different forms. A balance of taking ourselves seriously and loosening up at the same time is necessary to deal with the often hilarious relational situations full of misunderstandings. The ways in which we treat our fear of judgment are many. Some of us hide in plain sight, others get tired and decide to become fake introverts. A third group becomes narcissistic and overemphasizes their self-importance to avoid rejection. What they all do is creating a false identity for themselves, which has to be put forward whenever they interact. However, trying to fit the perception of other people in order to avoid living life according to who we are is unnecessary. If a certain amount people have an attribute, it should be accepted as real and they shouldn't be regarded as freaks or locked out of society. There are an infinite number of perspectives we can take. The concept of gender and sexual orientation is a fluid expression of life. We should encourage people to tell the truth in every moment, but to expect others to know our uniqueness, without allowing them to ask questions, is not a successful strategy. If we're feeling not enough to be part of the community, we need to embrace life's complexity. Telling our story is crucial for an authentic relationship with the world. We should tell it to anybody who is willing to listen. Some want to fix us to feel better for themselves, but if we tell them how it makes us feel, they will make an effort to change. Sometimes we will need to leave to find our people, and that's okay, because it shows our dedication.

Being vulnerable isn't a flaw, it guides us through life and allows us to celebrate humanity. However, transgender people are not the only ones who're treated badly because of rigid views of reality. Racism, the belief that different races possess distinct characteristics or abilities, is prevalent across cultures around the globe. It's used to define people and categorize them, mostly to alleviate the anxiety of learning about the otherness of people and the need for safety in our own truth. It's just another "us against them" story, which derived from the wish for superiority and to normalize improper treatment. It still indicates an important part of the sense of self for many. The division causes people to accept stereotypes based on culture and deep-seated prejudices. While it's true that different countries have differing expressions of life, all of them can be traced back to cultural backgrounds. Growing up among white people, for instance, will result in a black individual with identical behavior to their peer group, given acceptance and care was the same. These people will very likely experience the same racial discrimination as everyone else with a contrasting skin color, but they can't understand why they're supposed to act as their stereotype. It unavoidably leads to failed attempts to fit in and in an inner division between the identity they're expected to have and their actual identity. In the end, they mostly turn back to the community that is regarded as racially correct and learn customs and a new sense of belonging, where the picture of us against them is just again. The implicit biases many people have stem from information we gather from a mixture of cultural divisions we notice in society and the resulting prejudices, which generate positive feedback loops via consumption of modern media. The notion of Asians being good at math creates more mathematicians among them but triggers the resentment in people with other skin colors. Depending on where we're at the spectrum, this can cause superior or inferior feelings. If someone looks different from us and we were previously primed to regard them as a threat, we perceive them as an enemy. If a stereotype is reversed because of the status as a famous celebrity, these perceptions can quickly change.

If we spend time with people we formerly thought of as dangerous, we'll eventually learn they're human beings like us, only the created identity is different. We don't have to pretend colorblindness in order to solve the problem, we could just acknowledge that race is a human construct and that it has no footing in reality. DNA sequencing helped us understand the source of our origins. 99.9 percent of our genes are the same. Only the expression of the remaining 0.1 percent is different. Homo sapiens originated in Africa, and we populated earth from there. Groups of people divided from clans and got isolated over time to generate new tribes with different genetic mutations. Adaptation to environmental factors was responsible for many of them. Most notable the adaptation to the burning sun, which inspired the skin of our early ancestors to become dark or sometimes black. Dark skin was a blessing for hotter regions, not a curse to endure never-ending unconscious biases. The highly variable colors of today correlate mainly with latitude. Closer to the equator and people have darker skin, more toward the poles and it gets increasingly lighter. Tiny variations are making up all of our distinct features, even if it doesn't look like that. There are no discrete biological borders. Differences stem more from the adaptation to our environment than from genetic factors. Since migration is unstoppable, geographical groups have always mixed to create an increasingly diverse people. There is a rare occurrence happening in twin births, where fraternal twins from differently colored parents can develop opposing skin tones. One can in fact be dark brown while the other is white. In the future, we might laugh and look at it as shades of gray, but we'll need more time until the prejudices erode. We should be thankful for the infinite variety, but the more we grow, the more we should protect our cultural legacy.

Twenty-five languages are lost every year, though people seem to be more concerned with others speaking a certain dialect, since they impose prejudices of stupidity over them, although they're vital to preserve our heritage. Intelligence has nothing to do with "race" and varies through life. Spoken word can sound rhythmic, musical even, and interesting to hear.

The varied sounds and grammar in languages teach us who we are and where we came from. The language we use to describe ourselves defines our life. Most people in our world today try to use logic to find answers, but linear reductionism doesn't really work for us. Logic has become an alibi for decision-making. To justify our deeds, we need numbers and hard facts to back them up, and if we don't find a causal explanation for our successes and failures, we're lost in uncertainty. But logic is still our primary way of seeing the world, since we suppress any other explanation. Cause and effect might be useful sometimes; the reason it doesn't always work is the fact that for logic to be sound, there must be an assumption of an absolute truth. If the speed of light is variable, does that make all following deductions true? The logician must have something to hold on to; otherwise we had all the answers already. What logic cannot grasp is the infinite expression of existence, because the perspectives of any theory are necessarily narrowed down to generate a congruent picture. While it's true that a narrowing is needed for creativity to shine, the last answer cannot be given due to the finite character of the variables. That means we cannot describe reality to the fullest, because nobody has the needed capacity to process it. If we categorize the world in cardinal directions, aren't there infinite possibilities in between? If our reality is dependent on the frameworks we use, can we really know it? A pair of shoes is two shoes, but one pair. To stretch a particular framework or science to account for the whole of life is virtually impossible. The truth that men are mortal is not a logical rule; it's an existential fact. A judgment can only be true if it affirms what actually is and denies what is not. The purpose of language is to express reality in a way that creates a truth and enables us to incorporate all possible options. Although grammar constructs rules of the application of a language, it cannot account for the richness of its content. This is where the fun of perspective comes in. To turn things around and try to see the other side helps us to localize blind spots in our truth and enables symbiotic coexistence instead of aggressive wars in the conviction to be right.

How we relate to existence is more important than our way of seeing the world, because it's unavoidably flawed. In the endless quest of mapping the world to theories based on previously agreed on truths, the logicians and grammarians try to compress infinity into a frame of thought. Formal correctness and accuracy may be the main pillars for the thinker, but intelligence is not thought. It's the perception of the truth. Every thought is creating conditions to further a story of illusionary progress. The content gets constricted by being in the world of the thinker. Thought tries to make sense of reality, but it fails miserably. Language cannot account for the whole of reality either; however, it holds the possibility for all understanding. Fragments of sentences arise in our mind to form the picture we're about to express. The concepts serve as name givers to words, which can't be broken down further. The smallest unit cannot be understood, and if no language holds a concept for the desired manifestation, it can't be voiced. What happens behind conscious experience remains unknown, and the emergence of the fabric of our reality is the secret of being. Thought is not useful since it's just a measurement. It's based on knowledge and memory, but knowledge is limited. Science has its merits, and we owe it a lot of progress in terms of technology and convenience, but there are a number of things we have to keep in mind when working with its principles. To make sure it uses the right assumptions, a great number of different alternative truths get discarded in favor of endless mantras of its own making. Academia loves to create echo chambers of authority to keep everything else out. Allowed sources are inside of the established thinking framework and will therefore never be challenged. It's postulating clean facts due to fear of external agenda, but it doesn't zoom out far enough to see its own. The ability to take risks is essential to find truths; the current scientific environment is hindering people to take them though. The pursuit of recognition and looking smart became a superior factor in the idea of research, instead of a much-needed curiosity about the world. Disproving theories is always more essential than proving them.

The credo reads, If we can't make it wrong, it doesn't exist. But is this really true? There has to be one explanation that accounts for everything, and it needs to take all the previous ideas into account as well as all the imagined consequences. But can we really foresee the future? Equations and mathematical gymnastics are the only way to accurately describe nature according to science. But isn't the world more variable than that? Gravity for example, is not a fixed constant. And even if we suppose mathematics can be right. In actual application, there is no way of storing infinite values in a single variable, because the binary system is preventing it. Only quantum computing solves this by having continuous variables to handle infinite dimensions. A field where people are actually encouraged to use their imagination. The reason why science was always slow seems to be the ego of the scientists and the system they have established to place reputation before truth. The tree of life with its taxonomy to describe plants, animals, and microorganisms is one of those systems that was put at work to list all species in hierarchical structures. It classifies organisms and describes evolutionary relationships via morphologic, behavioral, genetic, and biochemical observations. But it has significant problems with the infinite interrelationships of the organisms. It consists of eight levels, starting from broad to specific. Each level was organized by shared characteristics, regulated by international codes. The problem is the generalization of all groups as monophyletic, which means every species has only one ancestor. However, birds and crocodiles are paraphyletic; they both have the same ancestor, dinosaurs, but different classes. As a result, birds can't be listed under reptiles, because there can't be a class within a class. This causes a lot of issues, because the whole structure is compromised and doesn't fulfill its purpose. Nature can't simply be put in a framework like that, and the ideas about possible changes to make it better go nowhere. The complexity and richness gets lost in confusing definitions and classifications. Taxonomy is treated as reality by many people and thus distorts our picture of the truth.

However, we can see the world and our place in it through the lens of ecology. Ecology is the relationship of organisms in their environment. Truffles, the expensive mushrooms from France, are a great example. They grow in close proximity to the root systems of trees and exchange nutrients to support each other's growth. Scientists tried to grow them in a controlled setting, since their habitat is dwindling due to deforestation and climate change, but it takes multiple years and it's not always successful. The reason, why it's so hard is that truffles need very specific conditions to grow. They attract animals like rabbits and meerkats with their unique aroma and spread their spores in nearby areas via the animal feces. The spores find their way to a new host tree and the process begins anew. In this way, the growing truffle stays connected to the network in the ground, which is made up of roots, microorganisms, and mycelium. If the truffles are refusing to grow, the soil conditions in the new location are not optimal. Although the functioning of this mycorrhizal system might be somewhat known, a myriad of other systems are completely mysterious to us. Here comes permaculture in, an organic farming system that has been around since 1978.

Its principles consist of rules for observing, caring for, and creating gardens. Farming is seen as a systemic way of looking at small ecosystems and their players, instead of using modern agricultural methods. It respects the system as a whole and tries to integrate everyone around to yield the best results with the least amount of energy. It needs patience to find solutions, and it accounts for patterns as they arise. Creativity is a must if someone wants to start such a farm, but knowledge of the elements and their requirements is crucial as well. It takes a lot of time for the beginner to internalize; however, it guides the practitioner to a better understanding of nature and how systems work. One of the major principles is cooperation before competition. For any system to work effortlessly, the members are required to use their energy for the important things, instead of meager yields due to fighting and competing for food, space, or other resources.

Everything is designed to be long term, and sustainability is emphasized for the systems to be self-sufficient. It uses the least amount of space possible with minimal impact on land and settlements. Placed correctly, all the elements will perform their functions, while benefiting the rest of the system. As long as the energy expenditure is higher than the energy usage, the system is functioning well. Otherwise it needs help until it's in order again. A good design is usually very diverse, and forcing conditions is seen as a bad strategy. The farmers will need to work with what they have and carefully influence the system for the desired results. Although it became somewhat reductionistic in approach over the years, it is still trying to work with nature, not against it. Our modern methods, on the other hand, require a lot of resources and chemicals to work. To start designing a permaculture farm, people often use preconfigured assemblies of plants or animals that were successful in other places. These assemblies are called guilds, and the truffle system is an example of one. Even the old Maya used similar techniques to add to their yields. They grew beans, corn, and pumpkin on their fields. The corn was helping the beans grow by providing a climbing aid, the beans provided nitrogen for the corn to feed on, and the pumpkin protected the soil from too much sun and rain. This combination was also called three sisters and can be understood as the holy trinity of some indigenous cultures. The Mayans also used a method named slash and burn to cultivate their crops and fed approximately two million people with it during their peak. Milpa fields and forest gardens are unplowed operations with high biodiversity and accompanying animal habitats. They were fertilized with composted, organic material (dead weeds), manure from humans and animals, and ashes from burned trees or kitchen fires. Chemical fertilizers weren't yet invented, and the Mayans never used monoculture methods, where one crop alone is growing on an agricultural field, like we do today. One milpa cycle lasts approximately ten years and goes through different stages. It rotates annual crops, short-term perennial shrubs, and different trees, culminating in the regrowth of the once-burned trees to get to the beginning of a new cycle.

It needs two years of cultivation and eight years of natural regeneration. If these time frames are respected, the cycle can be upheld infinitely without lasting consequences to the soil. What we might learn from these methods for cultivation is respect for the cycles of life and the wonders of the world. The current agricultural practices destroy soil health, rob the soil of nutrients, facilitate pests as well as erosion, and lead to poor fertility and low yields. Farmers, like doctors, only treat the symptoms instead of the causes. With the attitude of using extensive chemical warfare to fend off pests, weeds, and fungi, they're exterminating the whole system and prevent it from getting healthy again. Monoculture is not able to provide for a functioning system, because the players are mostly dead or nonexistent. Nutrient cycling can only occur when the soil and the networks are alive. The CO_2 is taken in and converted via photosynthesis to be distributed into the soil. A majority of it gets consumed by microbes and a small part is converted to carbonic acid, which breaks down rocks and other matter to extract nutrients. Fungal networks are a critical factor in the process, because they produce biotic glues. These glues create new soil by sticking matter together. Without them, the soil and everything in it cannot live properly. Tilling destroys the units of soil, although they recreate themselves approximately every four weeks. By letting the field lay dormant and keeping plants from growing, the cycle cannot work. After harvest, the plants are removed from the fields, and thus, all the carbon is lost. The subsequent tilling finally releases all the carbon that has been added to the soil from the last growing crops, and the result is a sad field of dead soil. If we would stop with the tilling and the chemicals, the systems could complete their cycles, which would result in healthier soils. High diversity, livestock, and an initial understanding of what the individual soil can produce rounds it all off. The secret to healthy soils is microorganisms, though.

Bacteria, fungi, and animals such as earthworms and nematodes have a lot of influence over the performance of the crops. The plants affect the microorganisms and the other way around. Some can be responsible for better yields and others impede them. Especially nematodes. Not visible to the human eye, these little critters are everywhere, and people say four out of five animals on earth are nematodes. They can be male, female, and hermaphrodite, lay millions of eggs within a few days, and can live in the toughest conditions. Some of them are parasites, specializing in only one specific animal. Humans have around sixty, dependent on our nutrition. To get rid of their waste products, they excrete nitrogen directly through their body walls. Nematodes also share some of the same tissues with humans. They have skin cells, neurons, and muscles, which were passed down from a common ancestor, and they live for the duration of a few weeks. Every plant generates its own specific community surrounding its roots, and the different kinds of nematode species result in a positive or negative plant-soil feedback. The balance of detrimental versus useful nematodes indicates the performance and the overall chance of a successful multiyear existence. For example, drought may cause the predatory nematodes to die, which, in turn, supports the growth of grass roots nematodes, and this eventually leads to the death of the plants. When monocultures are used, the plant-soil feedback takes exactly this course, and potato yields, for instance, decrease. To make sure microbial communities are diverse, taxonomy must be ignored in favor of the root traits. Damage can be avoided by rotating crops over the years, and the fields' edges should be surrounded by trees to support the network of mycorrhizal fungi, to temper winds and floods and restore water supplies through retention. There are various forms of collaboration in nature. Everything is somehow alive and a part of the system. To understand the players and their roles, we have to zoom out to distinguish different kinds of collaborations. A form of loose cooperation are coalitions. They're formed for single issues and require no coordination.

The actions are performed independently from each other but help achieve a common goal. An example for such coalitions are sailfish. They hunt in groups and attack shoals of sardines in a chaotic manner. There's no sight of coordination, but the cumulated injuries the single sailfish achieve lead to better hunting success for all. Then we have alliances, where the group's actions aren't coordinated either, but the individuals respond to outer stimuli and their peers. This behavior can be observed in golden shiners, which swim slower if single fish reach darker areas and faster if the light increases. By mirroring the neighbors response, they're able to protect themselves and the whole school effectively. Next are partners; they have a basic understanding of what a partnership is and wait for the actions from others. Pistol shrimp are vulnerable to predators because of their bad eyesight. They usually partner with gobies, whose eyes are much better. The antennas of the shrimp stay in contact with the fish so they can alarm the shrimp in case predators arrive. The gobies profit from this partnership by being allowed to hide inside the burrows of the shrimp. The last direct relationships are teams. Here, individuals are able to monitor and respond to others with a common goal in mind. Vampire bats ensure survival by sharing food with each other. They sometimes fail to find food for themselves, and if that happens, other members of the community share. If they go two nights without a meal, they die, so it's a crucial strategy for a long life. But it only works if every individual is following the rules by returning the favor. Cheaters do exist within the bat community; however, when word goes around others stop sharing with them. Quid pro quo at all times. Collaborations can be single or multi-issue, temporary or permanent, and dependent on location. Participants might change or stay for longer. It depends on the job at hand, the skills of the individual, and the energy output of the system. Members may contribute recourses, expertise, or connections to generate a broader range of options. Systems are almost never in perfect balance, because there's always a favor open or an action to take. There are no leaders of the systems, and the whole operation is completely decentralized.

Collaborations come together naturally as things become necessary. New parts are welcomed as long as they participate successfully. Everyone is fully accepted, and the consequent diversity keeps the systems resilient and corporations alive. The secret of our whole ecosystem is all about negotiation and an initial trust in the other. Conflicts are sometimes needed to push the systems forward, but the members are dedicated to resolve the problems, not perpetuate them. Darwin's theory of natural selection was wrong. Heritable variation doesn't come from random mutations or sequential steps. The reason for new traits lies in the adaptation of participants to a system. They emerge by necessity, depending on location, the species involved, and the performance of the system. This leads to rich complexity. The interplay of the parts determinates the required change and which species needs to act. It's not survival of the fittest; it's survival of the best adapted. The adjustments might happen relatively fast and in direct response to an issue. If the issue persists and the adaptation is successful, the trait gets passed on. Cliff swallows, for example, used to build nests on cliffs, but now they're building them under bridges. Many people tried to prevent this development, but the bridges appeared to be better suited for their needs. As a result, the birds had more and more collisions with passing cars. However, the cliff swallows adapted during the last thirty years and the accidents declined, although the number of birds had increased. The secret to this adaptation was shorter wings with which they could maneuver faster to avoid collisions more effectively. The rabbit populations of Australia, Britain, and France had to deal with the deadly myxoma virus in the 1950s and onward. The European rabbit got introduced to Australia in the 1850s by an English settler. It has produced hundreds of millions of descendants. Then the virus got unleashed and killed ninety-nine percent of infected animals. Later, the rabbits adapted to the virus and fatality rates dropped significantly.

What's puzzling is the fact that all of the many small effects across the genome were exactly the same in all three countries. How probable was it for this to happen, given it was not the often observed change in one single gene? Canada geese adapted to urban environments such as parks and took on the role as the dominating species due to changed migration patterns. American geese normally bred in the Arctic and flew south in the winter, but the new environment provided protection from predators like foxes and wolves, so the geese began to stay all year long. Thus, the populations exploded to an unmanageable extent. The increased occurrence of invasive species is an effect of moving them to other locations. Sometimes this is caused by human distribution, or the species travel alone to participate in a new system. The habitat of a species may be occasionally characterized by large gaps. This is called range fragmentation, and a good example is screaming hairy armadillos, which reside in Argentina, Bolivia, and Paraguay. They are split in two distinct areas, mainly due to climatic changes starting at around twelve thousand years ago. Range splitting explains why some species may have evolved on one continent, while they have descendants on another on the opposite side of the globe. Marsupials evolved in North America and went south after due to tectonic shifts, which separated South America, Antarctica, and Australia about 180 million years ago. As a result, about 330 distinct species evolved, and about 250 of them reside in Australia today. Many trees got distributed across the earth's coastlines by their buoyant seeds, which were able to float long distances. Hurricanes displace species across many different habitats in record time, not only due to wind but also due to the resultant flooding. After arriving in their new homes, these plants and animals restructure food webs or create new habitats. The great plague of London occurred in 1665 and lasted for one year. It killed approximately one hundred thousand people and was caused by bacteria called Yersinia Pestis. Humans were infected by a parasitic flea called Oriental rat flea, which normally infests rodents like the brown rat but also feasts on humans and drinks their blood.

Although the plague was concentrated in London, there was also an occurrence in Eyam in Derbyshire. People said that it was brought there by a tailor, who got a parcel from London. A box of cloth. As he opened the box and shook the cloth, the fleas must have gotten out with it. The tailor died two days later, and the disease spread over the little village of Eyam. How can a species multiply so rapidly and take over whole ecosystems with just a few individuals? Isn't the genetical diversity too sparse for that to happen without complications? Inbreeding greatly decreases the ability to deal with diseases and may cause deformities. Thus, it can affect adaptation to new environments for the worse. Yet, a lot of species overcome these hurdles somehow. How do they do it? The answer: epigenetic alterations allow changes in traits without changing DNA sequences. The marbled crayfish emerged about twenty-five years ago in German aquariums. They were freed across Europe and are currently invading Madagascar. They reproduce by laying eggs, which don't need to be fertilized by a sperm (parthenogenesis). This is very rare. The descendants are low in genetic changes, and thus all the observable characteristics (phenotypes) are epigenetic alterations made possible by environmental adaptations. Gene expression variability stems from reduced levels of gene body methylation. Genes are turned on or off depending on outer factors such as temperature, pollution, or immune response. To simplify it even more: nature and nurture work together, but nurture is able to overcome everything. Good news. However, what about us? How did we manage to dominate the earth and adapt to manifold circumstances? Is it a slowly progressing path to perfection? Did the first Homo sapiens gave birth and the rest is history? No, it was a lot more complicated than that. We've evolved alongside the Neanderthals, the Denisovans, and many other similar human species. Right now, we know of about twelve of them. For hundreds of years, people thought humans evolved in a treelike manner. But the tree of life is not the proper way of looking at it. We constantly interbred with others. This hybridization resulted in a lot of diversity because of migrations back to Africa.

About forty-one percent of Neanderthal DNA and ten percent of Denisovan DNA can be found in modern humans. During these trips around the globe, our species picked up adaptative changes to better deal with new environments. Homo sapiens around Tibet adapted to high altitudes with the help of Denisovans, and humans in hotter environments adapted by changing skin color. However, the most important factor for adaptive changes was to fight off pathogens. These discoveries led to increased complexity of our ancestry model. It's now agreed upon that we evolved more in an entangled braided stream than in a tree structure. We're the result of an extraordinary development throughout the millennia, and we evolved with other species to adapt to our environments. Humans are intertwined with the evolution of all other species, and we are a part of nature. There are so many things we thought are unique to us, but over time, we discovered that animals are able to do a lot more than we assumed. Chimpanzees use sticks to fish for termites; lyrebirds pick up songs from other birds in their habitats and arrange them into unique performances. Elephants regularly grieve over their dead. Even a formerly explicit human behavior like disposal of the dead is not so sure anymore. A new species of humans that was recently found, called Homo Naledi, may have buried their dead in a cave. It had DNA from humans and prehuman species alike. Apes didn't descend to better apes, which then evolved into humans. We are simply another species and we adapted and evolved within a network. In the early evolution of earth, life happened mostly inside of water. Before fungi began with the creation of soils, animals mostly ate bacteria, and their bodies were limp. Later in the Cambrian, photosynthesis took off, and a lot more oxygen was produced. This led to the emergence of the predator-prey relationship. Predators need a lot more energy to search for food and chase after it than peaceful bacteria feeders, but it was worth it, since even though they needed much more oxygen, the prey adapted as well, and an explosion of species diversity followed.

Prey hid under bacteria carpets on the ocean floor and produced stronger tissue to avoid being eaten. Along with additional adaptations, like changes of mineral compositions and flooding, which created shallow habitats, life could flourish at an astonishing rate. Many animals started their evolution in this time, and nature gave rise to vertebrates such as chordates and eventually humans. Good and bad seem to be two sides of the same coin, since nature needed both parts to flourish and evolve. The relationship between early animals was simple, but millions of years later, humans lived together in ever growing communities and managed to build complex cultural rituals and a myriad of different truths through music, art, and writing. Our creative abilities, inner worlds, and advanced storytelling guide us to increasingly subtler levels of emotional diversification and growth. The world of art appears to be beautiful, but some think it isn't the answer to our problems, because we have to deal with war and hate first. In 1974, a war of epic proportions took place in Gombe National Park in Tanzania. It was a chimpanzee war. It lasted for over four years, and a lot of apes died. It began with the death of Leakey, the former alpha animal. The tribe needed a new leader, and after Humphrey, a rather aggressive fellow, took over, the issue seemed to be resolved. But Humphrey wasn't able to keep his seat. The brothers Charlie and Hugh wanted to rule by themselves. The tribe divided into the Kahama group and the Kasakela group. It was a surprising incident, because people thought chimpanzees were a peaceful species, and some considered them to be better than humans. However, a part of Humphrey's Kasakela group attacked a single Kahama while feeding on a tree. It didn't take long to pull him down and beat him with a rock, but he somehow managed to flee. He wouldn't come back. After the victory, the Kasakela celebrated savagely, and during the next four years, they would carry out merciless assaults with the same cowardly strategy.

Most chimpanzees prefer to eat alone so that the Kahama were constantly watching their backs. Goliath, the eldest of the tribe and also a Kahama, wanted to make peace, but he was killed as well. One by one, the Kasakela eliminated the Kahama until only two were left. One of which fled. The other, a young fellow, died as the last chimp standing. People were shocked to see the sheer brutality of the attacks. The chimps were beaten to death by multiple attackers. Limbs were detached; the flesh was eaten and the blood drunk. After the males succeeded, the females were partly killed; one ran away, and three were kidnapped. Later, the Kasakela declared victory, and the war ended with the Kasakela infiltrating the whole territory, until another tribe came in and gained back the Kahama side again. That all these attacks were planned and strategically executed was a major find. We formerly thought only humans were able to pull off such atrocities, just to find out chimpanzees seem to be warmongers in the pursuit of power and recourses. This is especially interesting since they share about ninety-nine percent of their DNA with us. People argued animals are designed by evolution to respond to change in environments and that adaptation is not the right way to think in this context. Darwin called it "war of nature," from which the production of higher animals follows. However, it was the only appearance of a chimpanzee war anywhere. If humans are only different from animals by a small degree, couldn't it be we're also at war by nature? We are proven to have repeatedly fought against each other for oftentimes neglectable reasons. To understand this issue better, we can reach out to the cognitive development of humans. In the first stage, we're learning about the world and are very curious. We want to know everything and begin to sit, walk, and run. This lasts until we're two. Then we enter the next stage, where we're able to understand and categorize thoughts. We act intuitively and explore the meaning of words as concepts for symbolic functions and doings. Pretending to experience something is our catalyst to learn about the real world. When we turn four, asking questions is our preferred way of acquiring knowledge, but we haven't yet developed empathy.

Apes, on the other hand, never reach the capacity of a four-year-old. Communication, social learning, and mind theory are exclusively human domains. Although some animals are seriously smart in certain areas, our sophisticated intellect, the ability to create advanced technologies, and the innate desire to participate are unmatched. Our triumphant advance was made possible through shared intention and collaboration, not childish power struggles. And if it wasn't the ability for benevolent empathy toward others, it was nature's call to maximize energy output. What we can learn from people who went to war is the horror it creates in us. The feeling of being torn and the overwhelming guilt paired with shame forces them to reexperience the killing over and over. Some push it down by justifying it, but it doesn't really help. War terror seldom leaves the body memory on its own. It's hard work to address the ingrained patterns of constant alert. To avoid or suppress the consequences and to sustain function, people opt to take drugs or slide into depression and other mental disorders. The constant stressors in daily life become too much to bear. If we have to run from our truth, because we are constantly afraid of what may be hiding under the pain, the chances to lead a dignified life are slim to nonexistent. To find energy to forgive oneself and the enemy can be an impossible task. It feels like an injury to them, even if they successfully managed to come home in one piece. Suicide is often on the table as the last solution to alleviate the suffering for good, but the only way to go on living is to be brave and openly talk about it. In a situation where people need to kill each other to survive, the psychological outfit will adapt in some form. People do this by disassociating from the task, which means viewing the enemy as a bunch of targets, or by disassociating from themselves during combat, often described as out-of-body experiences. We can't deal with war, even if we wanted to. Our humanity doesn't allow it, since there'll always be consequences.

The reason why we go to fight is because the enemy wants to harm us and our family, and we'll do anything to prevent that from happening. But in today's times, the reasoning behind the war is not danger, but money. Someone has to give us the power to kill another human being; otherwise we wouldn't understand. Why is it even possible we allow someone to do so? Is serving our country's financial interests worth the horrors of war? Is it appropriate to generalize our perception toward other people to endure killing? Are psychopaths so widespread in our society that killing is socially acceptable? Is the intoxication of power and the thrill of victory over a helpless enemy the satisfaction we need, until we wake up from our illusion of grandiosity? Is it worth it to numb people emotionally and let them wake up amid never ending panic attacks, to watch them suffer from PTSD for the rest of their lives so we can maintain our parasitic lifestyles? Can we afford to uphold the illusion of selfishness while keeping a straight face? Is this who we are? Is this our truth? The first instinct of human beings is to be cooperative, but if we've the time to craft a story of some kind, we're often deciding to give less in order to have more for ourselves. Cooperation between groups is often predicted by how similar we believe we are. The more similar, the more we cooperate. It appears all the us-against-them stories we tell ourselves are not working to our advantage but are destroying our relationships and hinder effective cooperation. It's not all bad of course; we're able to communicate with total strangers in a civilized manner, and we can use public transport without killing somebody. But when it comes to the hard decisions, a lot of us are still believing in selfishness; although it's not only wrong, it's stupid in the long run. If we'd be indeed selfish, the longer a relationship would last, and the more energy we'd put into it to extract the most for ourselves. The shorter a relationship would last, the less effort we would be willing to invest, because there is less to gain from it. But what if our prediction is wrong? The chance to encounter people again in another context or on another occasion may seem impossible at first, given how broad our world is, but many of us have experienced it.

If we take a closer look, long-term selfishness and cooperation are equal. If we want to maximize our chances for success, we have to adjust our decisions to fit a long term paradigm, instead of a short-term gain at the expense of others. Short-term selfishness is a bad strategy, since it's indistinguishable from conflict. It prevents us from acquiring important knowledge and keeps us isolated. Our natural instinct to cooperate is not only deeply ingrained in us, it's the smartest approach to success. A seemingly unimportant transaction has the power to change a relationship, and the table will turn someday. If we push ourselves to break culturally imposed thinking patterns and allow effective communication and mutual trust to arise, our life will be much more harmonious, and we'll open ourselves up to love. Aggressive individuals, unwilling to share and cooperate, always died out at some point. Language and culture develop through collective effort, knowledge about our truth, and ritual celebration of forces in the natural world. The important interactions that make our life possible are cyclic in nature. Sun and moon create the cycles of day and night. A solar eclipse arises when the new moon blocks the sun. A lunar eclipse turns the moon red because the earth gets aligned with the full moon and the sun. Tides are cyclic movements of the moon and are influenced by the gravitational pull of the earth. A tipping point is always followed by a turnaround. All these systems work in perfect harmony to make existence possible. There is nothing we can identify that is not permanently in relationship with another thing, and if we have patience, we're able to use it to thrive. The pyramids weren't built by slave laborers, as it was believed for a long time; they were built by workers who got paid for their efforts and respected for their work. If someone died during construction, they got buried in tombs near the pyramids of their beloved pharaohs, and time off wasn't unheard of either. One of the biggest structures was indeed a cooperative effort, not an oppressive death sentence.

Stonehenge was also built by a whole lot of people. It took them an estimated 1500 years and probably many generations of descendants to do so. It's a great structure, and it proves what humans can achieve if they work together. It was used as a ceremonial place, a burial site, and a memorial to stay in contact with the ancestors. Death can be hard on us, and it is a phenomenon many people try to play down. But when death knocks and we begin to feel our mortality, we think about our achievements and if our time was spent well. Some get excited and buy a motorcycle or get a divorce. Others start a new life in another country. Adventure is a major factor. Did I live enough? Is there something I want to experience before I die? Is there enough time left to start a family? Questions like these are oscillating in our mind, and it may be too late to do the things we neglected over the years. Mechanical everyday existence, laziness, and fear are reasons we didn't have the courage to try and carry out our ideal. Immediate comfort seems to be more important than meaning. Too much short-term pleasure leads to long term self-pity. As long as the story is held up, the more time we waste in order to live our life without feeling at home in it. The Vikings, for example, had none of these problems. They were paganists, believed in many gods, and had a rich collection of stories, which got handed over from generation to generation with organic alterations to accommodate for changing times. Nature was respected and a major driving force in their life. Contrary to popular belief, they weren't just barbarians who drank out of skulls and wore horned helmets. A closer look reveals that they had much more to offer. Although they were decidedly brutal and ambushed churches, they also had a mystical side and were immersed in all kinds of spiritual endeavors. At the end of their life, they went to Hel, which is only related to the Christian hell by having the same word origin, not by how it was. The underworld of the Vikings was just another life.

They would eat, drink, sleep, and simply go on learning. There was no notion of damnation or anything. It was even considered pleasant. Death was not seen as the final end, just as a passage to another world. There is a lot of confusion regarding their customs, mainly since scholars had a shining fantasy and a tendency to perceive history through the lens of Christian beliefs and the then propaganda by the church. This can also be said about the Aztecs, who seem cruel and bloodthirsty, while in fact, the storytelling was done by European Christian writers and got supported by the elite. Oppressing the people and keeping them in fear was profitable for the state religion, which was forced onto the regular folks to morally control them and for the possibility to silence critics. The hunger for power is not new, but in the Middle Ages, the church was the means to enforce obedience. They had many sacrifice rituals and displayed skulls on racks to intimidate rulers from neighboring cities and to prevent social unrest. From the eighth until the tenth century, the church expanded all over Scandinavia and forced the kings to join them in their pursuit of pushing Christian beliefs and destroying folk religions. The greater it got, the more crimes it would commit.

The Vikings tried to push back, but the power hierarchies were too seducing for the rulers, and all the beautiful stories slowly faded out of the communities. It's a pity; paganism was a lot more mystical and interesting than Christianity. The center of their belief system is a tree called Yggdrasil. It pervaded all their many fantastic worlds rich of darkness and light. It's a part of everything. It's nature itself. Three maidens live beneath it. They're called past, present, and future. Despite the many gods they worship, Vikings seldom had contact with them. Daily life was full of other beings instead. Trolls, landspirits, giants, and especially elves accompanied them in their houses and during any other activity. They regularly talked to these beings and asked for better times or abundant harvests. It wasn't a matter of belief, it was a matter of knowledge what all these mythical creatures meant. There was no doubt in any of their beliefs. They knew exactly who they were and where they came from.

Ginnungagap was the bottomless abyss, which brought two worlds into existence. A cold world named Niflheimr and a hot world called Muspellsheimr. The chaos that arose gave birth to the first being: a giant named Ymir. As the ice in Niflheimr melted from the flames, the cow Audhumla emerged to nourish Ymir with its milk. She licked the ice to set free Buri, grandfather of Odin and chief of the gods. Odin and his brothers Vili and Ve slew Ymir to create the world from his corpse, the oceans from his blood, the soil from his skin, and the sky from his skull. The four cardinal directions were indicated by dwarves, who held Ymir's skull above the earth. Then the gods created the first humans from two tree trunks and fenced their place from the dangerous giants. Ginnungagap is a synonym for "nothing," out of which the chaotic powers emerged. Limitless potential is the myth behind all of creation, and it needs two opposing forces to make the world happen. Ymir is an asexual hermaphrodite, who could bring his own into the world without reproducing, since genders weren't possible yet. The giant also brought all the things with him. Ymir translates as *screamer*, and as the gods tore him apart, they created words out of his scream, which was the wordless sound of concepts. Paganists not only believe in some kind of afterlife, they also support the idea of a simple karma concept. Although it's not a form of punishment or reward for certain actions, it's regarded as an inherent natural process, describing a systemic causation in nature. The heathens think of nature as a sacred cycle of birth, growth, and death, where we are equal to other animals, plants, trees, and everything else. They unite in diversity by worshipping countless gods, living within a network of agents of all varieties, and existing in an eternal continuity. Their gods weren't perfect and served more as a mirror of themselves to impart wisdom with the many stories and legends. The ritual places and ceremonial sites were closely linked to community festivities. They celebrated huge feasts and honored their ancestors by drinking large amounts of beer and mead. Alcohol was a way to feel closely connected with the heroes of the past and the manifold gods in the mythical realms outside of everyday life.

General medicine and giving birth also took place in these holy buildings. Midwifes applied runes on the woman's wrists, grabbed them, and performed prayers to ask for healthy offspring. The Vikings were not very literate but could write few runes. History was passed on by poets, who were highly valued for their work. To this day, there are many customs to be found in Scandinavia dating back to the tradition of the Vikings. In Sweden, a tree is planted to reflect the connection with the ancestors and to bring fertility. The Christian cross, which was equilateral before it got its gothic form, was called sun cross, and people were often confused by the differing meanings. The church had much difficulty to teach them that Christ wasn't the sun, and later in the thirteenth century, it was changed to how we know it today. Interestingly, Odin hanged himself on Yggdrasil to gain knowledge and wisdom in an act of self-restraint. He pierced himself with a spear and stared into the Well of Urd, next to the three maidens who had the power of constructing fate. His hunger for knowledge was so strong, he endured for nine days and nine nights, without accepting any aid from his fellow gods. As the runes gave in and presented themselves, he got initiated and could perform magical deeds. He could heal wounds, render the weapons of his enemies worthless, and wake up from the dead. Odin was willing to accept any hardship in his quest to understanding. He sacrificed his lower self for his higher self to attain his goals. Some of the most powerful stories in human history center on similar myths, and they will never die. In fact, we are highly trained to talk with invisible entities, we just don't perceive it that way. Gods can serve as friends to discuss fate or future. Some are terrifying; others fight with us or trigger sadness. Many people are talking to deceased family members as if they were still there. A suitable example are children and their imaginary friends. They can be quite complex beings with a variety of opinions, and they're used to explain events and encourage dreaming.

Great narratives not only catch us, they engage every part of our brain. The creation of meaning often happens through wonder and fantasy, by letting go of preconceived notions and ourselves. In all of human history, the occurrence of atheism was pretty minor, and indifference for god or a divine entity mostly happened during times of oppression through, or conflict with, religion. The problem with atheism is that the sensemaking mechanism, which derived from centuries of interactions with the gods, passed on by a long line of ancestors through the teaching of concepts and myths, is lost in favor of rational thinking. The former ability to explain the world and pinpoint agents who are responsible for the effects we observe is not available anymore, and the new sensemaking possibilities are highly inconvenient and narrowed down to a framework of infinite uncertainty, while at the same time failing to deliver explanations for its emergence. It's almost impossible to find satisfying answers, if cultural pressures prevent us from dealing with the world in a coherent manner. The result is a loss of meaning, which led us to depression, anxiety, and addiction. But our love for stories also comes with a number of problems. The indoctrination through fundamentalists and religious groups is both sneaky and effective. They tempt us with their claims of a universal truth and the notion of pureness, spiritual freedom, and various powers over the physical world. A lot of their material is laughable, and it seems impossible to ever get caught up in their delusional lies, but people who're already inside these organizations were not any different from us. They may be recruited during vulnerable times in their lives or by family members with no way of knowing anything else. People normally believe they're able to think clearly and perceive reality as it is, but we all have blind spots. Cognitive dissonances can help with seeing more of reality, but they're also able to bring us into situations we can't control. And before we know it, we bought a book or agreed to a meeting.

Soon, gods get stronger and more powerful than ever before, but not in a good way. Religious groups extract money, resources, and time from their victims. Captivated in their story world, we slowly start to indoctrinate others to gain recognition and love from our new peers. Us and them is the primary game, and we get caught up in their deceptions. Asking questions is not welcome, since the answers are already there. All other options of relief are taken from us by modifying our impulse responses in favor of the group's methods. Fear is unlikely to ever arise again, since we're protected by a supernatural force, which will guide us to peace. Life can be difficult, and even the most stable person may fall for some of these promises. It might take years before we're able to see through the lies and try to leave the group. But by then, we already invested a lot of time and built up a circle of friends or even family bonds inside the organization. The longer we stay with them, the harder it is to begin anew without our carefully sculpted believer identity. Human beings are not rational, and so it happens that any attempted escape fails due to the person we have become. A split between what we want to believe or believed over many years and the actual truth is often indicated by a double-down effect, where we can't admit we were wrong. The transition of "I know," to an honest "I don't know" often takes years or even worse, decades, of combat with the lies we became so accustomed to. Another issue is the ongoing moral oppression by the church and the obnoxious covering up of their crimes. Begging for forgiveness is sometimes not even a necessity. Priests with a track record of child abuse are not properly disciplined, they're simply transferred to another place. The reason for their disgusting behavior is in most cases a violently suppressed sexuality. When they decide to give their life for the church and remain in celibacy, their sexuality often isn't fully developed. The early twenties are not an appropriate time to go for a sexless life. It appears obvious to everybody, but the church is still living in denial.

If people are forbidden to follow a natural human instinct, the consequences seem clear. Religious ideas and Bible-subordinated living are simply not feasible, if they cause oppression, lies, and abuse in the name of collective delusions, made possible by a tradition of time-adapted mythical literature. Spiritual truths don't change through adherents' reading the Bible; they only change if we confuse a collection of stories with laws, although they developed over more than two millennia. Why do we have to take this book so seriously or even literally? People have to suffer all their lives, and some harm children in the process, just to uphold the illusion of what's morally acceptable and what's not. Is it okay to abuse in the name of love? Some believers appear to be blinded soldiers, who not only follow every idea to the letter but constantly add more fantasy-derived material to an already deeply confusing pool of opposing truths. And if we refuse to play their games, they become hostile and repressive to protect their rigid illusions. Isn't it sad that otherwise decent people cause so much pain? To make it clear, there is no need to be religious in order to lead a morally sound life. Morality is in fact not needed at all, if we dedicate our energy to finding the truth and dare to live with it. Spirituality enriches our life by expressing the need for connection, and religion can provide the community to do so; however, it is perfectly fine to watch the stars and wonder how it all works. People commit crimes because they feel alone inside. By thinking they're different and by believing nobody will ever care for them. To soothe that pain is to talk about what it means to be human and to help them in accepting themselves. We are not in need of a system of reward and punishment to keep our lower selves in check; we need the courage to tell the truth and an insatiable urge to know ourselves. The search for the truth has many pitfalls and dangers, but it's possible to find it. The atheist movement gained a lot of interest over the years, and some people claim it's closer to the truth than most other belief systems.

It originated mainly out of three different stories. The first are deadly terror attacks from fundamentalists, the second is neglect and hatred for people who don't believe in god, and the third is the impossible idea of demanding evidence for the existence of god and trying to understand the universe in the conviction it's possible. The question is if we should rely on scientific evidence to explain such matters. A "three sigma threshold," as scientists call it, describes a 0.3 percent chance of deviation from the truth. That means 1 in 370 occurrences can be wrong for it to be regarded as evidence. For a truth to be valid enough to call it a full-blown discovery, they demand an even greater number. For a truth to be absolutely true, they fixated an accepted deviation from the norm of 1 in 3.5 million. This "five sigma threshold" is what they've declared for the Higgs Boson, or as some people call it, the god particle. This particle could be proof that the Higgs field exists, an energy field we are not able to see although we can detect it with sophisticated machinery. It probably exists in every region of the universe, and it gives particles their mass. To accomplish this task, it needs the Higgs Boson. While particles move through the Higgs field, they generate excitation and add energy. That means a particle creates chaos by moving through the field, and this very chaos is called the Higgs Boson. Basically

all particles are the result of excitations of fields. But scientists are still not sure if this is the last answer. In fact, scientific progressions are made by testing an existing model and coming up with even better models to incorporate the data, which accumulated during the process of trying to prove the current theory wrong. One in 3.5 million might seem like a huge number, but it also means there is still room for skepticism and questioning. Everything possible will happen at some point. Scientific proof is a term used by many media outlets, but it is ultimately misleading. There is no definite answer, and there never will be. The current framework of thinking isn't allowing it, and scientists will forever be looking for a better fit. It doesn't matter how much data is there, it's never enough.

In the famous thought experiment Schrodinger's cat, a cat sits in a closed box with a radioactive atom and a detector. A hammer is connected to the device, and below the hammer sits a glass filled with poison. If the atom decays, the hammer falls, and the cat is dead. If the atom does not decay, the cat lives. The probability of decay is fifty percent, so if the observer is not looking inside the box, the cat is dead and alive at the same time. A look inside the box will reveal the result though. The measurement done by the observer is sealing the deal for the cat, so to speak. Being in two states at the same time is called superposition. A particle that is not measured yet can be in both conditions unless it is. Let's assume god would exist in a superposition and we try to make the discovery of a lifetime; does our belief change the outcome? In other words: Are we able to find god if we believe in it? Are we able to lie to ourselves? Let's try another thought experiment. According to the Viking creation myth, nature is everything, and all is created out of it. If we break that down, we could say there is only one huge thing. Thus, we're all part of it as well. If that's true, how can we ever observe the thing in its entirety and find out what it's made of and if it's actually a being or not? Everyone can measure a table, but if we're the table, how can we measure it? To say something isn't science because it

doesn't fit the current paradigm is exactly what's wrong with it. An openness to ideas seems to be at the heart of scientific thought, but it doesn't appear to be the case. There are people, who would be excited to do research in the field of extrasensory perception (ESP), but they're ridiculed by the science community, although there's a lot of statistically relevant evidence. Is it really necessary to destroy careers, just to stay in the current paradigm forever? The issue seems to be the scientific landscape of oppression against everything that doesn't fit the beliefs of people who would like to keep believing what they already know. Why do they prevent scientists from exploring alternatives?

Is it fear of being wrong or is it pride? The fact that all contradictory evidence is dismissed right from the start by assuming that any investigation will turn out to be false is not the right way to explore the truth. It's a means to hide it. People are manipulated to accept deceptions, and scientists who complain about inconsistencies get silenced on the accusation that their methods are not good enough and their numbers are wrong. A perfect means to protect lies only accepts its own truths. Critical thought would encourage scientists to look into the unknown, since this is precisely the place where progress can be found. For many of us, this is all confusing talk anyway. What most people want is a good life, not the answer to the question of god. Science has brought us fantastic technologies, and we are hungry for more conveniences all the time. Medicine is advancing rapidly, and it seems we can really trust it to be on our side. There are a lot of studies done to find cures for diseases and improve therapies. This is where evidence is actually affecting our lives. But is blindly accepting everything that is coming out of a laboratory a good idea? In an attempt to replicate studies in critical care research, more than half of clinical practices couldn't be reproduced. Not 1 in 370, more than half. What became known as the replication crisis is happening across many disciplines from medicine to psychology, though people are still parading their grandiose all-knowing egos.

The reasons are many. Career pressures and stakeholder interests seem to be the most important next to actual human errors. Science is a tool like anything else. A hammer can be used to build a family home, but it can also be used to hit holes in people's heads. The most suspicious company in modern agriculture doesn't need to be mentioned. We all know who is providing the farmers in the United States with the controversial herbicide everyone hates so much. And they're right. Healthy food is more important than money, and when people get sick and die from working with it, it can't be fit for human consumption.

The suppliers work almost exclusively with it though. Why do they do that? Is it out of habit? Don't they know other ways of dealing with such problems? Is it because it's perfect to work with genetically modified crops like corn, wheat, or soybeans? Why are they using poisonous stuff to grow our food at all? If they are so concerned with the health and well-being of the consumer, why aren't they looking for alternatives? Could it be a combination of laziness, greed, fear, habit, and carelessness? Have they gone too far inside the rabbit hole, where there is no escape? Many questions nobody knows the answer for. If the system would be concerned with us, there wouldn't be a debate about if chemical fertilizers, GMOs, and other substances with the probability for disease were fit for consumption. They just wouldn't be used. There are hundreds of studies, but we have still no final verdict on how harmful the said herbicide actually is. Is science responsible for this? Are they not smart enough? Everybody should know by now that science is buyable. If a company needs a study to support a claim to make money, they'll get it. They kicked down and pushed up, and now they want to be rich, regardless if people die or not. That's all. It's possible to nourish the world without slowly killing everyone, but farmers and food suppliers have to be interested in a solution in order to stop the negative health consequences. There will be some losses, and it will cost money. The technology is there, but there's no shortcut to healthy soils. Nature needs support to recover from decades of chemical warfare. Killing important entities in an ecosystem, which developed over billions of years to incorporate every organism in the process, just to be able to fulfill fantasies of power over the natural world is laughable. The universe can't be known. We manipulate everything and everyone to our liking, and our will towers over any other living being on earth. We pass policy decisions for nature. We have zoos, because we think children like to watch imprisoned animals.

We kill, poison, oppress, hate, and despise people to amass more money and power than everyone else. We have no respect. It's okay to be a slave, if we can have a big TV to watch ridiculous commercials all day. We have no life skills, since our lazy lifestyles remove us from the only thing that could provide any meaning. People are measured by output, not valued by birth. Stupid people are good enough to vote but laughed at for everything else. People hide from their shadows and wonder why they follow them everywhere. Nobody knows, but everybody is right. Why does everything appear to be so complicated? Why do we do all that shit? We do it for love. We do it for a better future and for our families. We do it to contribute. We do it for recognition, to fit into our environment, and to adapt to our circumstances. To avoid bad feelings and to survive in a system informed by oppression and fear. We do it for success, to provide for others, to support them. To find meaning and the truth. We do it to be known, loved, and understood. Some people cannot take it any longer. That's why they become activists. They believe peace is possible and try to live their ideals. The church is not completely bad after all. Charity projects depend on particularly vigorous individuals, who passionately fight to feed, heal, provide, and care for others. The problem with NGOs is the bigger they get, the more they have to conform to the rules of the elite. And they do, because they wouldn't be able to continue otherwise. Activists believe we will be able to get along with each other, if we only can see the truth. They like to think they're different. That the more people they convince, the more the general public will understand, and if society would take them seriously, they would leave a mark and change the world for the better. They're admirable, really. Nothing will ever stop them from following their hearts. They're not convinced by propaganda and value people sometimes even more than themselves. Living for the truth is their job, not bending over. Striving for an intellectual humanism and using all the options at their disposal is of more importance than everything else. They are fighting for the good with all their might. However, by pushing so intensively for peace, they often create a state of war within their surroundings.

They try to dominate the storytelling and push for control. Longing for change is their justification for conflict. Spiraling themselves into power grabbing dynamics and self-righteousness in the pursuit of self-importance and the immanent wish for leaving a legacy. They actually have begun to play the same games as the people they would like to annihilate. But any form of violence is wrong, not only the brutality of the others. Sometimes, "they" don't even exist, and it's fighting for war's sake. To kill an enemy, who can't be found, because they're invisible. The reason why roughly two thirds of the educated world is not terribly interested in believing in god is partly due to the evidence craze and also since the advocates of the system were very convincing. Atheists are indeed activists in a way, although they avoid violence at all costs. Any attempt to label them gets rejected, because they know it would make them vulnerable to attacks. But disbelief is still a belief, regardless of how one looks at it. If we can trust science, there's no evidence, and we might never have proof. Faith gives us meaning. It helps in everyday life, and it empowers people. The belief to be right in a matter, where the odds are likely on "our" side according to an adopted thinking framework, is a false claim for the truth. Fighting against injustice is great; however, trying to demolish a belief system is not encouraging peace. Rationality doesn't always lead to freedom; it might lead into self-centeredness too. True freedom is the acceptance of all truths in the absence of story. Real answers can only arise if the judge capitulates, and understanding can only be gained when we're eventually wise enough to accept our limits. Religion was originally never about truth. It was about love. While loving god is optional, most people might regard romantic love as necessary to live a happy and fulfilled life. Our culture is aligned with it. We are told that we have to have a plan for our life, and marriage is part of that plan. After school, we get a job, fight for money, marry someone, and live in a big house with three floors, since we're successful and happy.

It seems obvious, however, that this equation doesn't work very well. Marriage was a useful construct to survive in rough times. It was never meant to make people happy. Scholars and translators used the scriptures in their favor to oppress the natural condition of the human being, just to impress their notion of morals. Do we still have to make more kids to survive and accomplish stuff? Are we still living in a place of scarcity? Why is everyone so obsessed with conforming to age-old customs? We're not realizing how much trouble we cause to ourselves unless we're drowning in pain and loneliness. It should be a personal decision to take the need for a partner seriously, not an uncomfortable feeling of robbing society of precious children. If the reward is the option to pass on our genes, why are more and more children born outside of marriage? About forty percent of kids in Europe and the United States could be regarded as "bastards" if we take the medieval law of England and Wales into account, where children weren't allowed to inherit until 1926, when post hoc legitimization was introduced. Why do we still marry? Is it because we want to do the right thing by conforming to morally correct living standards? Are we afraid to be alone, or do we want to share a story with someone and enjoy to get to know the other? Marriage rates are fortunately constantly falling in the Western world. More and more people live alone, and the use of dating platforms has become the norm. However, the falling rates are not responsible for an ever more lonely world. It has more to do with our lifestyles and how technology changed communication. When we are young, we often have high hopes and even higher standards for a possible mate. After school, a lot of people want to experiment and find out what life has to offer. The sexual marketplace is huge, and finding an interesting person is not all that hard anymore. Technology gave us thousands of options, and the new game is to find the right one. Not anyone. The right one. Expectation has gone through the roof. If there's so much mating material to choose from, it's easy to expect no less than perfection.

The best we can ever hope is for the search to deliver exactly what we wanted. Everything else must be a disappointment. There is no excuse for failure, because it's on us to decide, and if were wrong, we alone are responsible for our misery. People who grew up in earlier decades had hopes for a nice home, children, and maybe a possibility for them to go to a good school. These rather low expectations had obviously much more winning potential in contrast to a society of nonperfect people looking for perfect relationships. Sex for sex's sake can be had within hours or sometimes even less. This changes the perception of the whole dating universe. Profile tuning and lying has become a popular sport around satisfying sexual needs. But having sex without emotion is like eating lunch without nutrition. It might be possible, but it does nothing for us in the long run. It's more like an obsession. There's always the danger of feeling something, and some sexual experiences can be so strong that we can't erase them from our memory. Rape is a rather cruel example for this, but extremely fitting nonetheless. The body seems to be acting like memory foam, where especially intense feelings may be saved until the day we die. Something that truly moved us can't be let go of. It defines all future experiences for the worse instead, and it resembles the image of a responsible drug user. A professional who likes to have sex for the kick of it. Some people bond faster; others don't. Fact is, testosterone and estrogen are driving our lust. Dopamine and oxytocin are fostering attraction and attachment. If we're feeling horny, sex hormones are starting us up, but what leads us to go over or signal interest is dopamine, which is responsible for our emotions toward mates. Norepinephrine comes with dopamine and makes us giddy to prevent rational behavior from happening. As we experience a deep attraction toward our conquest, feelings can be overwhelming and consuming. It's a constant emergency state, where the danger is longing and lust coupled with some kind of love.

We start to crave the other person, and we're happy to do the stupidest things to be with them. Dopamine affects more if the other person is not there. Missing them is a much stronger feeling than holding them in our arms. The anticipation of sex or seeing the other person is much more intense. This explains a lot of pain and suffering and also why longing is love. If a relationship suddenly gets real, the intensity fades away, and we have to be with a person, instead of a dream. This often causes massive problems and disillusionments. Unfulfilled love seems to be the most exciting, but it costs intense suffering and severe pain. There is no way to suppress this or otherwise affect its workings. If we're having sex with someone, feelings are rather unavoidable. The only way to minimize them is robotic sex without talking. However, if we're honest, we're looking for connection and love, not mechanical juice exchanges. Sex can be pretty dangerous, but it doesn't have to be this way. It doesn't matter if we are straight, gay, intersex, or transgender. Love follows the same routes for all of us. We just need to find out on which role we're acting out. The blindness of men is the beauty of woman. They are often so mesmerizing, men forget everything they've ever learned and sell their possessions to buy jewelry. Men usually don't notice what's going on until it's too late. They get horny before they can think of anything else. Immediately testing strategies in their heads to start a conversation and to get closer to the woman. An enormous amount of them have aggressive representations of intercourse and also an intense drive to win a mate through competition. These mechanisms are not their fault, since they're hormonal consequences of being a man. The illusion of control over what they're doing complicates the situation even further, and their perception narrows a sane mind down to a unitasker. A man will often not get how stupid or manipulative a woman might be as long as she's able to seduce him with her appeal. The narrative sounds simple: I want to fuck you, another love story. It might get so far the man marries the woman for this reason, and this leads to all kinds of suffering as a result. An aggressive man will fight with all he has against other men or everything that's holding him back from a successful sexual intercourse, and a lot of females will greatly encourage that.

Although aggressiveness is the most prevalent trait in men competing for a mate, it is not the only one. Men try lots of different things to win over a woman they fancy. If they're too weak to compete aggressively, the next best thing is to act nice. Nice guys are doing everything to get a woman's attention and affection. Their narrative is much more painful, since many like to exploit their kindness. A lot of frustrations come their way, and if it keeps happening, they might stop looking altogether. From a woman's perspective, exploitation may be a successful strategy in the short run, since she's gaining from the situation and may be able to recognize her previously learned misaligned love language, but womanhood as a whole has lost when all the nice guys are gone at some point. A third strategy is faking it. Some men use their creative mind to win a woman over. They're funny, interesting, artsy, or different in some way. Good talkers and smart flirters have good chances but will often lose against the aggressive type. If all else fails and they are lost inside their fantasies, while at the same time don't have any success with woman, men may become rapists at worst or, more likely, regular clients of professionals at best. Women, on the other hand, also have their strategies and blind spots. Nature makes the aggressive male attractive for them, and they may lose themselves in rough sexual fantasies. They like a strong man who is promising them the world. In some cases, men are worshipped for their dedication and competitiveness. A common feedback loop consists of a proud man and a weak woman. She is sensible and useless; he is working his ass off to please her, but it's never enough. Some men use this for payback by exploiting her sensibility, which in turn is a major factor for prolonged suffering in women. Sometimes, he is acting nice and cooperative; other times, he seems to have lost all respect and just does what he wants. An emotional roller coaster and a myriad of puzzling interactions follow. This is where women are lost and quite similar to nice men who have to learn when to agree and when to defect.

Assuming we have found what we think is our perfect fit and the first few dates went well, a relationship may form. As we settle into prolonged sexual adventures and high hopes for the future, our dopamine supply is at its peak and we'll feel happy and fulfilled. The male seduces the woman with his masculine smell; the woman triggers secretion of oxytocin to increase trust and familiarity. Further trust also develops if woman appear reluctant in the initial encounter, because it increases the man's readiness to let his guard down. After the honeymoon phase, the perspective may change and the all-consuming excitement makes way for a lot of questions. The ones we haven't asked since we knew this love would last forever. Here, the roads are parting. Some people try to uphold whatever illusion they've created; others are dealing with the issue by actually trying to get to know the other person. The prize for all the struggle is a comfortable relationship with someone we might even like. When the drugs stop working, we feel empathy for each other and ease into being together. A sure sign for a successful long-term relationship is if the other person is able to love us the way we want to be loved. Childhood plays a big role in creating our love preferences. If Daddy was an obese guy with aggressive traits, his girl might look for similar features in her love interests. If Mommy was reluctant and sensible, her boy will prefer to see that in his relationship. Our parents teach us how we like to be loved, and we act it out in mostly unconscious ways. There are exceptions to every rule, but this is the general pattern. Another property of relationships is their execution. Meaning how love style plays itself out between partners. The fully dependent love is marked by long-term attachment. If it goes wrong, people love others superficially and by habit. *I love you* becomes an empty phrase, because nobody really believes it. If love is independent and fails, there is no real connection between partners, and one or both are much more concerned with freedom than with loving a person.

If an interdependent relationship is reached, lovers often forget about themselves, and a heart synchronization is established, where the other becomes more important than themself. It has a beautiful narrative: as long as you're cared for, I'll be cared for. Hugging this person will quickly synchronize heart activity. Much like a child lying on one's lab in the process of slowly going to sleep. The frequency often calms down and synchronizes. This isn't a sure indicator for love, since systems synchronize all the time, but making the same music helps. From all the variations of love, selfish love is without a doubt one of the most exercised. Our culture around sex and marriage dictates it to some extent. The love style we inherited by observing our parents supports its claims, and talking to our peers cements the story as completely real and valid. In times of profile surfing and content forgery, the idea of loving people for their qualities, instead of who they are, is the standard of dating. We're so obsessed by breasts, booties, crotches and abs, our main activity is to compare numbers, as if we would decide for a good washing machine. The narrative reads, I love you for my own good, not yours. These lovers like to feel selfish pleasure by enjoying what they receive, while at the same time giving only to satisfy their own needs. They cannot love causelessly, and being with them might be very draining. However, people can usually feel that, and although they may choose acceptance because of an ongoing marriage, any respect for the relationship gets lost. Regardless if it's a case of constant resentment or a long-lived nagging feeling of anxiety, we should leave these people whenever possible and make ourselves available for honesty. Love might be the most misunderstood thing in the universe, and it's an impossible task to incorporate every aspect of it into a congruent whole. It's dependent on so many factors at the same time; a rational approach is of no use, since feelings are constantly changing and developing. Facts are hard to gather, although there are thousands of statistics. If we want to be with someone and we're sure they're right for us, we may want to go the next step and marry. Our culture sees it as a fluke to find a partner, and many are primed to regard marriage as required for success.

Reasons for marriage include beauty, financial benefits, social rankings, and rules or even love and affection. Women judge a man's wealth and social status to validate a marriage. Men are more concerned with the look and feel of a woman. It's not wrong to consider those, but they should be looked at with love in mind, not personal gain. If people get married, they're promising to spend all their life with each other, come what may. Thus, many of them are not successful, especially as they usually come to an end within ten to fifteen years. The idea that marriage should last forever and ever, that it will render us fulfilled and sexually satisfied at the same time is a delusional one. In Japan, it's tradition to gift the freshly married couple with the skeleton of a sponge called Venus flower basket. It usually accommodates a bunch of mated shrimp inside its cavity. The Spongicala Japonica shrimps swim inside when the skeleton is still in its building stages. They mate within its walls and feed off the particles, which stick to the sponge. In return, the sponge lives off the shrimps' waste. It's a nice story and an example for a symbiotic relationship, but it comes with a price. As the cavity develops, the shrimp are not able to escape any longer. Even worse, during thousands of years of adaptation, they lost many features that enabled them to live independently. Their gills shrunk to save energy and their spiny carcass became smoother, since the sponge protected them from predators. As a result, they're forever damned to live together with the sponge and die within the home it provides. Only the shrimp descendants are able to leave the nest, because they are small enough and will inevitably search for their own little prisons. The cure for a failing marriage is regularly to get a dog or make a child. Some try exotic sex variations; others simply buy more stuff. Either people start a project or they look for experiences, but after many years of trying, the magic is often gone and the partner turns into a comfortable, but boring, armchair.

Lots of misunderstandings arise, and communication is one of the first things to fail. We want to be understood on the deepest level; however, not knowing what to say is pretty common. The barrier between two people can get unbelievably high, and they may consider a therapist or fantasize about leaving. A person becomes unbearable if we're stuck with superficial talk instead of getting to their core. An intrinsic need to get to know the other and ourselves is existent in all of us, but every good story comes to an end. The suffering intensifies if we cannot accept the loneliness of being with our partner and refuse to leave at the same time. Then the stepmother enters the room. She had many tragic relationships herself and life wasn't always nice to her, so she tries to live through her daughter. If things go bad with the marriage, she knows what to do. A good spy is always prepared to process information and tell a horrible story around it. The wife becomes her secret agent and reduces the partner down to behaviors and motivations, often accompanied by illusionary daydreams of villains and heroes. She has to find out what this creature is and what it wants, thus she begins to act like a scientist. However, zooming in on the parts to understand the workings of the machine is not an intelligent strategy to know people. Reducing a human being to a bundle of selfish practices in the hopes of understanding them is what causes people to get a gun and shoot for the fun of it. The husband usually gets angry, agitated, and might go out to seek revenge. They're open for an affair and try to bring themselves into situations where contact is possible. The natural tendency for men to always look for better or newer mates can't be ignored anyway. Especially if the Coolidge effect is taken into account. It describes the urge to mate with multiple partners in animals, even if mating just took place. Bulls breed up to eight cows a day, and rats are ready for another round almost immediately, as long as there are fresh mates available. A naturally occurring diversity-enhancing tactic build up over millions of years. Humans are not free from it, as we all can imagine, and religion as well as politics has always tried to limit it by allowing multiple wives or even child marriage.

Although it's not acceptable at all to let children take part in such cruel customs, it shows that this issue was always known and tried to be taken care of, so society is able to flourish by producing stable families. Many men today live in monogamous relationships and wonder where all this sexual energy comes from. It never subsides; it only temporarily transforms in the face of oxytocin. If men want to stay with their spouses while they're young and hormone levels are still high, they usually consume porn to relief the constant horniness. Some singles make it into a hobby. Older men might have less interest in sex, since their hormone levels are down; the home became a prison, and morals get in the way, or they experience a general distrust. The Coolidge effect is often responsible for people's porn addiction. If new partners are immediately available, it's very likely to lose control over consumption. Women might have greater interest in bonding over longer periods, but they naturally seek variety as well. One reason is the need for another partner in case the current one is infertile. The other is better-fitting immune systems. Attractive men are frequently preferred, but the average guy is a better candidate to start a family. Monogamy isn't natural for human beings. However, the fact that a mere agreement has the power to override biology in order to raise children, secure finances, and increase social stability is proof we can will ourselves out of substance addiction and that intention is able to overcome the unavoidable urge for sex at least for a while. Why sex is such an important factor in people's lives is obvious. Why we take it so seriously, not so much. A lot of priming and false moral claims have produced much pain in the past. Why isn't it possible for people to accept diversity as the rule, not the exception? We need to talk about sexuality and what we'd like to experience in bed; otherwise we'll never be satisfied with our sex life. To learn about anatomy and to calm down while discussing such things can be easy, if we allow ourselves to forget all the culturally inspired moral stories. A satisfying sex life can be had in monogamous, polyamorous, or open relationships. It's not wrong to try new things, and as long as people feel safe and communication is up, there is a lot of fun involved too.

We may develop a game plan with our partner or specific rules to make it work. It's about who we are and about our experiences. It's about our upbringing, children, and health. It's about many things; however, it may be difficult to deal with the arising feelings, and the best fun turns into a broken heart. Finding a balance can be very tricky, and complicated arrangements with many partners often fail. Having the courage to tell the truth and the flexibility to communicate effectively is absolutely essential. When looking at different sexual orientations in nature, the question arises of why a species would have a few exclusively homosexual exemplars? Just for fun? Bisexuals are fine, since children are at least possible with them, but gays? People did find brain differences between homosexual and straight individuals but couldn't decide if it's a good thing or not. Some say the findings normalize being gay; others argue for a deformity in the brain and think about curing it. When people find out, they are sometimes not very happy with it due to family issues, but they remain totally gay nonetheless. However, it cannot exclusively be a biological thing. A mixture of nature and nurture seems reasonable, since identical twins both don't always turn out to be gay. Homosexual people are allowed to marry in many countries now; the only issue is they'll soon face the same problems as everybody else. Many gays and lesbians view sexual relationships as friendships, and people are equally valued, since they celebrate differences and promote a more inclusive love. Couples form easily and simply part when the relationship is over. Substance abuse and health issues remain a problem with people of varying sexual and biological distinctions. The approach of these scenes to welcome all while condemning nobody has a lot of truth in it though. It's a natural way of handling sexuality, and a combination of close and far is key to create a loving society we can all enjoy, without playing games and holding onto outdated moral notions.

Many are afraid of change, but every journey begins with a first step. Relationships will end at some point. The idea of saving an already dead marriage is wrong. A majority of today's love stories can't deliver a lifetime of happiness. People can't be made responsible for their mistakes, if requirements are impossible to fulfill. To project an ideal onto a person, only to find out they aren't that, is a consequence of misconceptions and cultural conditioning. The promises cannot be true, but they hurt tremendously when the bubble finally bursts. What follows is often a phase of self-loathing and misery. Some try to suppress the pain, while others avoid it altogether and bury it deep inside themselves, where it waits for an unavoidable revival. When the meaning of life has become to love another human being, expectations are most likely set too high. The more people insist on superficial love, the more they will be in trouble. If we really see a chance of a successful long term relationship, we have to do a daring thing. By putting in a lot of effort and patience, we'll need to constantly try and get to know each other. To accommodate for changing circumstances and ongoing development, we have to be willing to fall in love with the same looks, although the person is different. Discussions are best if we understand that attacking is ultimately leading to the end. The ability to step back and view the situation from different perspectives is what eventually brings relief.

A story that unfolds itself over a long period of time is very valuable and should continue if ever possible. Sharing our lives can be great, and a narrative with fluctuations and bumpy passages as well as successes connects us within experience. To run is therefore not always the answer, but negotiations can be so complicated, it may be better to leave and try again. However, ending a marriage with children not only prolongs the whole process, it may additionally ruin the life of both people involved. It often leads to financial loss and a lesser standard of living. Many years of continual tiring confrontations are depressing and completely unnecessary. The children might prevent the new relationship from blooming, and involuntary stepparents hate to be alone.

As a last resort, many go to therapy to revive communication and, as a result, find out it could have been much easier for them. If there are mental issues, it's best to research options for that particular thing and change the therapist until it fits. It can be beneficial to have someone guiding negotiations and mediating in tough situations. However, if we are at our worst, it unavoidably gets better. For serious diseases, the therapy is a must, but if we're just running from the truth and insist on our conditioning, the money might be better spend living the life we always wanted. Humans are masters of adaptation, and if we get the possibility to change our future, we should have the courage to abandon the past. Forever is just too long sometimes, and sacrificing money is probably better than wasting time. As a rule of thumb, we can say as long as we don't lose ourselves inside the marriage or relationship, we are safe to love another person with every cell of our body. If we abstain from masking ourselves to rescue our love lives and keep the freedom to develop with another person, instead of becoming a shrimp in a sponge, we can accept other ideas and form stronger bonds as a result. Does detachment make unconditional love a possibility? We don't know, but it takes the power of truthfulness and a strong mind. The balance of letting go and holding on is an art. Love is acceptance in change, but true love is changing acceptance. By letting go of control, we enter a world of uncertainty. However, the best things in life often happen without a plan, and although we might feel scared, we'll inevitably let go of a lot of weight too. It's much easier to unburden the mind from conditioning to experience life as it is and explore its possibilities, instead of preconceived notions and story scripts to prevent it from happening. Competing against the person we were yesterday is the only way to know if we actually made progress. Mental issues might go away, and we awake with more energy to explore with greater trust than ever before.

Trust is the currency of all relationships, but we're only wealthy if we give more than we can bear. Many see trust as counting on people, but it is so much more. We cannot demand happiness from others, but we can gift them the opportunity to make us happy. Trusting blindly is a mistake; doing it intelligently without prejudices and expectations makes true love possible. Building trust in relationships takes effort. To keep it going during times of stress can be a burden on our mental resources as well as our energy. If things go wrong, it might be tough to develop empathy for the other and see the issue from their perspective while at the same time trying to work through it. When we're lost and need help, we should reach out for support from our friends. However, our highly connected environment had a big impact on us, since we're able to instantly talk to everyone, but many find themselves to be alone in their world. At certain stages in our life, we will realize that we are indeed alone in our head, regardless of the people living with us. The recent loneliness epidemic is problematic, not because we're alone but because we have never learned how to be with ourselves. We often get nervous when there is no one around and we have nothing to do. In order to avoid unpleasant feelings, we look for activities to keep us engaged and ease our minds. An enduring fear of sitting without stimulation is making us anxious. All kinds of worries pop up, and we escape them by falling into long established patterns. Being with ourselves is often reminding us of who we want to be and how far away we are from reaching this goal. We dream of advancement and appreciation but cannot find it. However, if we constantly indulge in distractions, we might never find meaning. Accepting ourselves not only makes a lot of things easier, it results in others being more comfortable with us as well. But aren't there people who want to be alone? In Japan, they are called *Hikikomori*, and their numbers are rising drastically in recent years. The social isolation they put themselves in is a way of coping with the outside world. They are not taking part in society, since they're circling around themselves. Afraid of the projection of people and their judgment, they withdraw from the world.

What they need is a friend who is mirroring them, but they avoid perceiving themselves. They're sick of competing and gave up completely. They don't fit in, because they're not equipped with the required dedication. They've removed themself from everyday life, and it has become impossible to picture themselves as part of it. Maybe it's the realization that working is producing no reward other than the activity itself, since they've no clue who they actually are. If we reject our needs just to be at peace, we're not accepting responsibility for ourselves and eventually become hostile and jealous. Meditation can be a good way to practice being alone; however, stopping distractions may also help. If we desire to be a better person, we have to start there. It might lead to the reemergence of old traumas and tough memories, but the task is to overcome them with compassion and patience. The most challenging things are oftentimes the most rewarding. Being alone is the absolute best tool to find out who we actually are. Conditioning and the influence of social systems in our lives increasingly fade away with every hour we spend alone. Our tribe often overwhelmed the capacity to make sense of the world, and all our heart wants is to find the truth. The more we suppress our truth, the more we will suffer. The more we avoid it, the harder our lives will become. Our hearts invite us to become conscious of our freedom. To release pain and suffering and to find meaning in a confusing jungle of voices. If we have the courage to stand tall in the face of our demons, we open up to get answers for all our biggest questions. Only by embracing the light within are we able to know the world. Asking "Who am I" can have the most profound implications in our lives. To learn about blind spots in stories we sometimes told ourselves for a long time can be as freeing as it is challenging at first. Asking difficult and open-ended questions will inevitably bring up previously unknown information, and if we're not truthful with ourselves, we may end up with an old wound freshly exposed.

Taking time to reflect can help in dealing with the new and exciting feelings we may encounter. Therapy may be useful too, but the oftentimes prescribed antidepressants have many side effects and the overall results are not worth it. They inhibit daydreams and self-reflection, interfere with sleep, and cause emotional numbness by suppressing empathy. They prevent the ability to deal with the negative resting state of the brain, which established itself over years of suppression and trauma. REM sleep gets disrupted and as a result, negative emotions and depression can't be processed properly. Negative fluctuations cannot be resolved if a person is taking medications to prevent amplifying a problematic experience in order to deal with its consequences. The chaotic syncopated patterns of thought emerge from a stream of noise. Their goal is to become conscious, but the patterns can't arrive in our mind if the stream gets inhibited by antidepressants, which are hindering the water supply of certain brain areas. If depression kicks in, the smiling faces of everyday life become stale. The person often can't sleep, is unable to feel joy, and a disconnection from the self separates the being from becoming. Dread arises to make itself seen, while sometimes rebounding far back into mania. When the condition is more established, the person often desires to end the misery by all means possible, because the existential terror gets so intense that an immediate solution is less frightening than a steady lingering in despair. The process sustains itself and cuts itself off from the people experiencing it. They often can't even cry, since the pills dried up all fluids to do it. All means of pleasure are completely lost, and as time goes by, humor, awe and love vanish as well. They get replaced by grief and guilt instead. All these mechanisms not only lead to severe problems, they also have a strange ability to obstruct the story-world in favor of much more solid observations of reality. If we suppress these realizations and try to ignore the implications of them, the symptoms get unavoidably worse. The fear to be alone inside and the angst for helplessness in freedom kills the opportunity for liberation. Hope is evil, because it prevents us from accepting the truth.

Amassing stuff is only one way to keep the false hope from destroying itself by preventing all honesty. When success becomes the only road to happiness and love, the automatic optimism we insist on leads to ineffective and debilitating results. The hope to manage death by suppressing life is what destroys the chance for dignity and peace while we become absent from ourselves. However, hope as a process of being, not suppression or avoidance of who we are, will stop our urges from arising. Being what we are is infinitely more important than the fear of uncovering the truth. If the story of yesterday is dead and the future is free to unfold, we gain the power to go out and live. If all constraints fall away and we allow these intense feelings, we will realize that all we ever wanted to overcome was the fear of separation and the emotion of being alone. Living from this instant, to embrace the emergent properties of life, is the awakening of health and freedom. Depression is an isolating pain; it cannot be communicated. When we are at odds with nature, we can't concentrate, our memory is impaired, and we're not able to love. How one is able to deal with life's challenges is usually much more powerful than taking a myriad of useless pills, but sometimes it's unavoidable, especially when it comes to manic depression, which is frequently tied to substance abuse and other addictions. People often don't realize that they are going to die if they're not taking medication and try to alleviate their condition with alcohol. Mania can feel ecstatic and cosmic with a strong sense of self-importance, leading to agitation and distraction. It can also cause hallucinations, illogical thinking, sleeplessness, euphoria, and racing thoughts. A hospital can be crucial, but picking the right doctors for diagnosing is important as well. People regularly overemphasize their ability to deal with their issues, and although friends can be helpful to talk, professionals are able to intervene, if treatment is much needed. It is very important to show love for ourselves by taking care whenever possible, but there's another side to it as well: medications can not only be expensive, they're often not as safe as pharma companies want us to think they are.

Chemists say there's nothing to be afraid about, since all they do has its roots in nature, but mixing natural ingredients to create completely new compounds, which were previously unknown, isn't the same as selling tap water in bottles. Toxicologists are testing if the new medicine is safe for human consumption and they can be surprisingly generous if their expertise is affecting the profit of pharma companies. The objective seems to be clear, if business is dependent on medication addicts, who don't even need it. A lot of naturally occurring substances are toxic and should not be consumed, but lab-synthesized medicaments, which cannot be found in nature, mixed with a myriad of other stuff and tested by bribed individuals, can never be trusted, even if they have a few positive effects. A solid example are synthetic drugs, where labs try to mimic a drug's effect by recreating it. The resulting compounds are sold as "not fit for human consumption" and labelled as bath salts or jewelry cleaners to avoid regulation. They change in composition as soon as regulators prohibit them, and even though modifications are small, they're creating different effects. Users cannot be sure what they consume, and health risks are manifold. Some drugs even caused death in the past. Modern medicine has a lot more regulations, but the full extent of effects often show themselves only after the drug has been used by a number of patients, who are involuntarily testing the constantly changing formulas. The clinical trials are too short to evaluate long term effects, because they only account for efficacy, not for usage duration. If study sizes are too small and length not sufficient, new products enter the market although they're not safe. Some might say why bother, if the modifications are so small. The regulations are in place and actual studies are done to meet the requirements of legislators. That is true, but very low doses are sometimes even more dangerous than greater doses. BPA was invented in 1891. It's been used for producing plastics since the 1950s. An innumerable amount of food containers and water bottles contain it to this day. Around ninety percent of people have it in their system on a regular basis.

Alternatives are increasingly common, but it took regulators many years to consider limiting exposure, and even the new compounds aren't proven to be safe. What toxicologists are still trying to fight is the fact that as exposure decreased over the years, the situation wasn't under control. A large number of findings show harmful effects on the endocrine system in small doses, but their truth only allows bigger effects by increasing the dose. The human body is not a machine; it undergoes a lot of change over the years. In puberty, when tissues are still growing, hormone receptors are sensitive, and very low amounts may trigger significant effects. If a system is awaiting a certain amount to start a reaction, there is no reason why it wouldn't ignore higher doses. If the influx of disrupting compounds constantly messes up levels, otherwise healthy individuals might get sick or develop dysfunctional tissues. BPA may affect fertility, and it's linked to prostate and breast cancers, miscarriages, birth defects, and premature delivery. Exposing mothers to high levels of BPA during pregnancy results in hyperactive and depressed kids. Why is a harmful compound like BPA still used, if people get sick from it? Lobbying and spreading of false information due to fake studies resulted in over twenty years of court rulings, which led to confused scientists, unsatisfactory bans, and minor regulations in the United States and Europe. All the plastic produced since 1950 weighs approximately 8.3 billion tons, and the estimated amount by 2050 is 12 billion. Preventing sickness and a world drowning in plastics is only feasible if we avoid using it and start by protecting nature instead of industry interests. When we finally wake up to the damage we have done, nobody will be responsible, but we might change from the cheapest product with the highest price to the healthy and sustainable one, which helps the people and the world. If medication gets tied to selfish interests, while it's often not even needed or working as advertised, what can we do to heal? Nobody is safe from having a depressive episode, and when it happens, we should look for a stable mind by eating a healthy diet, doing regular exercise, and maintaining strong connections to other people.

However, if things go south, psilocybin is a great alternative to other drugs. It gets extracted from mushrooms, and it gains more and more reputation. Some people prefer microdosing, but larger doses in controlled environments are advisable too. The experience itself may be exacting, but it works. Psilocybin has little to no side effects, although beginners should have professional support, and the mentally ill have to talk to an informed therapist. Psilocybin disrupts circling thoughts by shaking fluctuations in the brain like a snow globe. Bad thinking patterns can loosen up, and changing habits becomes much easier. Getting enough healthy sleep without influence of alcohol or cannabis is helping as well. Walks in nature might lower stress. Depression and PTSD are caused by adaptations to adversity and false ideas of who we are. Many people try to forget misfortune by losing themselves in hedonistic behavior, but it's much better to see it as a means to study and gain knowledge about our interests. Letting go of anger, fear, disgust, and frustration is possible, if we dare to give up control. Medication will make us numb, and by inhibiting suffering, it constrains creativity. Life feels stale, and emotions, energy, and enthusiasm fade away. Creative work is the antidote for depression, and depressed minds can create wonderful things. The myth that most people are not creative is a culturally impressed story to generate obedient workers, but we all have ideas, and we spent sizable chunks of our day fantasizing about something. In 1968, George Land tested 1,600 children between three to five years old. He gave them a creativity test he developed for NASA to help recruit innovative people. The results of the test were very meaningful, because he repeated it with the same children at age ten and again at fifteen years of age. While ninety-eight percent of five year olds were found to be creative, this number fell to thirty percent at ten years old and twelve percent at fifteen years old. When the test was given to 280,000 adults, only two percent of them turned out to be creative. Is it really true we get less creative as we age, or are we just adapting to boring jobs and the rat race?

Mr. Land concluded that noncreative behavior is learned, and if we are not completely lost in a false story, we should believe him. A vivid imagination is not always helpful, since many people have nightmares at daytime, but if we're able to conjure up all these horrors, why can't we dream about the good stuff too? Researching inner worlds is the science of the heart, and development never stops. Everyone expressed their creativity at some point, and if we quit practicing a skill, it's often in a sleeping state instead of gone. To bring a new concept to life, we first need to ask ourselves what issues we want to solve. Then we should feel ourselves into all aspects of the problem and collect as many perspectives as possible to come up with a potential solution. We might apply systems thinking, pattern recognition, abstraction, or we could just play around to have fun and bring a smile to our face. The content is dependent on the story it represents, and a good narrative helps to reframe information in new ways. Nobody is able to imagine anything that wasn't already there in some form. True innovation is therefore to tell an utterly new story with familiar concepts. Starting small and slowly building new connections is what eventually leads to complexity and sophistication. Intelligence is not as important, since imagination is the real predictor for performance. Repetitive thinking patterns not only lead to boring ideas, they're also an enemy of imagination and a sure way to lose ourselves in false stories. Creativity is about being as special as we can be, while at the same time knowing we are all the same. Switching from having to becoming is not done by conforming to fit in; it's done by accepting the truth and moving with joy. We can't compare ourselves to others, since we're not them. We won't stay as we are, since we are constantly changing in our quest for the truth. We cannot keep lying to ourselves, if we intend to live a meaningful life. What we can do though is to turn our gaze and find out who we are. Standing on the shoulders of all the people who came before us, we will work through rejection and fear in order to survive in a technologically driven world, where obedient workers will soon be a tale of the past.

The projections we produce to create meaning in a world we can't fully understand will come back to us like throwing a movie onto an invisible wall. We need to be independent, but not stubborn. We need to be humble, but not weak. We need to be knowledgeable, but not haughty. The interesting stuff happens on the verge, and the most beautiful place in a room is where dark and light meet. Becoming our own person and supporting our interests to attract the future, is essential to free the truth-seeking mechanism by which we will discover our place in the world and receive fairness from life. To begin the process of becoming, we have to look at our environment, our story, and the type of change we have to carry out. Only when we look closely and honestly will the next step present itself to us. Before starting, we need to make sure we're prepared. The more comfortable our life is right now, the harder it is to give up. Rich people have an advantage, because they don't have to earn money, but the reason why many of them will never escape the suffering of the story world is the pleasant life they are living right now. Money itself is not the enemy, since we all need it to live inside of society. Having beautiful things is not the problem, since the issues only arise as soon as we become attached to them. We cannot know where we'll end up, and the moment we move toward our interests, the world will respond. We cannot control our lives, but we do our best to live with dignity. The meaning of life is not upon us to give. It is a given. The isolation we have to opt for is the only way to know the truth and since it's not permanent, we should try to learn from it in all the different ways it presents itself to us. At first, we are only able to sense dark and light. Later, when we acquired richer vision, we're able to incorporate more and more aspects until we finally gain the capacity to zoom in and out seamlessly. If we've come this far, we attained a much clearer perspective of the world, and the path will lay itself out. Other people have other eyes. They have different brains, different stories, and different destinies. We can't project our wishes and hopes onto them, and we will never be able to see their truth through their eyes.

Some might sense more colors than others. Some can't tell the difference between green and red, and a few of them see no colors at all. People adapt to their circumstances, and by overcoming handicaps, we're able to find to our truth. Empathy is great to get to know people, to know what they may be up to. While it's helpful to feel with others, it also creates many problems. If one of "them" becomes a part of "us," we've applied empathy and accepted them by denying the "them" trait and projecting "us" onto them. They stop to be gay, black, or transgender, because they belong to "us," but we've ultimately fooled ourselves and the false story keeps going. Poor people on the street appeal to our empathy; however, even if we decide to give, we could have extended our circle of care by developing compassion instead. Rational thinking is often suppressed by empathy, and compassion should always be preferred. By being compassionate, we're accepting humans for what they are. We see their pain and act in accordance with our humanity. We often try to use our truth as a universal guideline we're applying to everything; however, this narrows its richness and its value. What others are telling us about it is often wrong, and to take on someone else's truth must require careful consideration. Therefore, it's best to distance ourselves. Inside of us is a world full of possibilities. A wealth of concepts, pictures, words, and emotions. We're full of ideas and dreams. This is our reality. But abandoning the story is frightening and risky. If we're obsessed with what people think, it's no wonder why so many will never see themselves. Without natural people, there cannot be a loving society. Do we have to live this way? Equality is the motor of the future, but only for a capitalist system, where people only work because someone is forcing them to. Diversity is the heart of the truth, and creativity is its mind. People want to make their own opportunities or at least control what they're doing by themselves. Nobody wants to rent themselves out to slavery, only to be controlled by a particularly sneaky breed of capitalists, who wear big smiles in order to distract from their real agendas.

We must treat people differently, because they are, but we have to understand the difference is not hierarchy, else we would create the same problems all over again. When society is divided by the idea of equality, the goal of peace is far away. The world got superficially better and more secure, but the terrors happen increasingly inside our heads, and with every country that's oppressed and robbed in order to bring about "progress," another culture will vanish in the pursuit of pushing prosperity for a limited few. There is no question people face hardship in poorer countries, but enslaving them is not the solution. If the rich try to make everything right, they'll always fight for themselves, because that's what they've learned. Nobody has the intelligence and the power to change the world for the better. It's like playing the lottery, hoping it will not only satisfy their hunger for big, megalomaniac games, but also that everybody will win in the end. To be our own person and live our own life, we have to be our own boss. That means we are responsible for the work we do and why we do it. It's so easy to fall into a bearable routine with lots of TV, a little vacation, and ready-made delivery food. As a result, health suffers, energy gets low, and the will to live a meaningful life goes away. The longer we do something, the harder it is to get rid of it. Freedom is not that. Freedom is the excitement for work. The excitement for a truth, which can only be experienced with an open mind. Making it happen means digging in. Every day. Taking cold showers, eating healthy food, moving regularly, breathing deeply... no complaining, just hard work. Only discipline turns an obedient worker into an agent of the truth. When in doubt, we should push to go only a small step further. Wherever we are, whatever we do, isolation is the gift of having the day to ourselves with no distractions. It is our decision to be alone as long as it takes to find the truth. People who love us will understand. Keeping connection is great; falling into stale routines is not. Taking good care of ourselves is key to become the person we are. Overly crushing ourselves to rush the process is not. Exercising good judgment at all times helps to find the middle way. Not talking to anyone for a while turns our perception around.

Experiences are more direct; they lack narrative other than the one we impart on them. As a result, we will start to understand what's inside. It needs a strong mind to pull it off. As the days go by, it will get easier though. When the issues come up, utter honesty is imperative. The universe exists inside our mind, the place where we'll find answers. There is no need to lie, because we would only fool ourselves. We are on our own, and we will not only learn to appreciate it, we will love it. The dissolution of perception is the beginning of art. When science is always in doubt, art knows. Our feelings will guide us. When answers arrive, we have to test them, apply them to our imagination. The goal is to have clear truths, not sloppy new concepts. It always takes longer than one thinks, and it can hurt badly. When conditioning is leaving and old memories come up, we have to stand tall. Thoughts come and go but only the truth persists. What we are missing in the Western world are initiations. A lot of indigenous cultures have initiation rites to transition to a new time in life. The education systems can't provide them, and people get steadily fooled by con artists, who deliver on the feeling of progress and the innate desire to reach the next level. If we're ripe to mature, challenges usually come up naturally, but the intensity is often not sufficient to provide the right questions, and as a result, don't lead to the truth. Instead, people follow assumptions about themselves and suffer from being wrong about who they are. It's a guessing game with good intentions and poor outcomes. Refining our strengths and working on weaknesses is much easier, if the misaligned, well-meaning voices are no longer a threat to our integrity. By learning to cope with discomfort, sorrow, and anger, we develop ways to deal with times of trouble and uncertainty. It's not about pretending to be a tough person, who is able to push their feelings down, it is about allowing these feelings and learning to handle them. They're guiding us to our blind spots and showing us the means to overcome them.

The notion that purpose is something we can invent is not only wrong, it cares for a freedom nobody enjoys having. If we allow people to tell us what we need, the answer in a capitalist system is always what they want. The truth changes throughout our life, but if we keep it close, we'll learn in dignity and gain a chance to understand a tiny fraction of its true meaning. Starting with our environment, we evaluate the current situation and look for cues. What is history telling us about our decisions of the past? How have they influenced our lives? Could we control the outcomes? What deemed to be helpful? Are there things that were bad in the beginning and turned out to be beneficial in later phases? Were there enemies who change their role after looking truthfully at what they did? Could we unfold our potential given the circumstances? Could we apply our skills to benefit the whole? Was our life a lie? Did we lie to ourselves or have we been lied to? Can we forgive, since we're all trapped inside a story to some extent? Are our friends real? What liabilities do we have? How does a long term-routine look, if we want to be able to follow it? How reliable was our word in the past, and what is needed to strengthen it? What was the story we told ourselves? These questions are tough to answer, but absolute ruthlessness with ourselves is important to extract the needed insight to change our story and to avoid falling for lies ever again. The working world will change drastically in the next decades, and physical labor will be replaced by creative and caring occupations. But since all humans want to creatively express themselves in one way or the other, there will be much more joy, if we're prepared and know who we are. To be wary of exploitation and stories, which are solely crafted to support selfish interests, while at the same time acknowledging our connection is crucial to keep the truth alive and to pass it on to coming generations. Having the courage to start as soon as possible, regardless of our current situation, protects us from thinking it's too late. Some may fear change or that they've already invested too much into their job to start all over again; however, postponing or avoiding action will become more and more painful as time goes by.

Is it all right to live the life of someone else? Can we be so lost in our story that any approach to escape is futile? Is it better to go easy and die asking what if? When seniors get asked what they regret the most, it's always the things they didn't do, not their failures. If the road obviously leads to the wrong place, is it smart to take it anyway? We have always the option to free up time to take a small step forward. Assessing the situation and looking for gaps will work, if we're honest. Let's imagine we are an outsider who is looking at our life. Zooming out as far as we can and then leaving the structure to observe it from a cold and rational point of view. If we weren't invested in any of the things, we think are important to us, the solutions to the issues frequently show themselves so easily, we'll be amazed at how blind we were. Being part of a system prevents us from recognizing obvious problems and finding all the options available to us. Only the outside shows us the levers with which we're able to act effectively and save energy and time. If our story-world is a structure with many floors, which one should we manipulate to get the best effect? In other words, we must pick our fights wisely to avoid the mistake of wasting resources. However, ruthlessness and aggressively pinning down issues is not enough to uncover our potential. A much more important aspect is vulnerability. A trusting woman cannot change her attitude toward life, only to be equally gruesome as her environment. She has to be authentic and only when she is humbly showing her humanity will a strong acceptance form and things change in her favor. The fear of judgment must not stand in her way toward finding herself. She will be treated differently, because she is, but that is a blessing, not a fault. She must be exceptionally honest, but if people don't accept her for what she is, it's time to leave. By hiding our truth, we fight against ourselves, and the angst of being treated differently cripples us by prohibiting the emergence of connection and belonging. Natural people can be awkward; however, they're also adored for their courage and followed by many. Being odd is often a gift, if we eventually allow ourselves to be seen.

The issue appears to be the canyon between ourselves and the group we want to belong to. Going back to human beginnings, it was a catastrophe to be ostracized from the group, because it meant to fight all alone, and the possibility for starvation and death was much higher. That's the reason why we're afraid of standing alone. Loyalty and trust were essential to remain inside the group, since the outer world was too dangerous to face on our own. Fitting in was essential to our survival. Thus, it has become human nature to maintain a healthy bond with others to avoid isolation. Therefore, being alone makes us nervous, and we feel the urge to do something about it. Some introverts have learned to go alone for a long time, but if they don't get feedback, they're losing the opportunity to get better. An introverted person is also not completely alone. They usually have at least some friends and stay in contact with a few other people. They prefer time for themselves not because they love solitude, although this might be true for some, but because they generally need space to process their experiences. It drains them to be around people, but they don't despise it. Most humans are somewhere in the middle of the introvert extrovert spectrum. For people who truly love solitude and being on their own, all of this seems to be very easy. Some may even think they don't need to practice solitude, since they've already figured it out. However, stories weren't as powerful as they are, if people could escape them so easily. Introverts do many things right in terms of finding the truth. They tend to turn inward and focus on thoughts and feelings, and by avoiding external stimuli, they create the rare opportunity to find out who they are, but they're also the most prone to self-deception. Through an increased frailty for stress, they often misinterpret things and twist them in order to align with their story. What shapes our narrative is authenticity and connection. If we want to go on the adventure of finding the truth, this conflict is one of the most important. Our parents not only teach us how we like to be loved, they also impress us with the conditions under which we're accepting of something or if we're pushing it away.

We're fully authentic when we come to this world, but if love and affection is not an accepted way of expression in our environment, we'll suppress them in order to fit into our parents' world. Every family has a story, which is usually passed on to the next generation via subconscious or even conscious behavior. The result is often a child who is bound to a story it never subscribed to. Trusting natural abilities is discouraged throughout childhood, and the fear of isolation makes it too risky to try. The later adult will oftentimes avoid having their beliefs changed. This prevents them from recognizing important information about themself, since feedback cannot occur from lies. The urge to retreat to safety, where these challenges don't exist, is a symptom of the fear of truth. Controlling information consumption hinders development, and in some cases, the traumatized person tries to save society by fighting "wrong" information to help the world become a better place. While this is a great goal, the means only create confusion, instead of reaching it. By exposing ourselves to different beliefs, cultures, and new experiences, we learn to be flexible and open up to growth. This happens through informal conversation and freely given trust. Balancing fear and trust is critical; especially beginners need to practice in order to deal with the stress of cognitive dissonance and to learn arguing with themself to make sense of the world. We're happier if we want what we already have, but we are weaker if we close our mind and refuse to become more. The best predictions are made by people who are capable of having their mind changed. Compassion stems from Latin *misericordia*: "miser" means misery or poor, and "cor" means heart. If we are willing to listen to people compassionately, without losing ourselves, we might win friends who surprise us. What we all share is the air we breathe. It connects us to each other, and it gives us life. By cutting others off, we take their breath away to protect our false story. However, the inability to listen isn't the only preventing factor when it comes to knowing ourselves. Morally correct behavior on the societal level is important as well. If a certain attitude toward a topic is morally right, but factually wrong, we'll often opt to bend the truth to strengthen what we think is accepted.

This is often the case with very intelligent people, who can't believe they could be biased. When cultures seem to be wrong with what they're doing, the narrative is almost certainly shaded by comfortable righteousness. That's why humility is important. An open mind is nothing if people think they know more than others. We simply have to live with different moral concepts, and as long as they aren't harming people, there is no reason to condemn them. Everyone hates to be judged from a moral high ground, even if the judgment is sound. To win people over, all we can do is to listen and use our arguments to bring more perspectives to the issue. Rendering black-and-white thinking useless by approaching diversity honestly is the best way to reach an agreement. Placing positive outcome before story is hard, but worth it. Coming to a conclusion is not always what people want though. In this case, they often call for fake news to dismiss contrasting information. Their reasoning is not hard to understand. First, they'll always protect their interests, especially if they're financial. Second, their opinions might stem from group beliefs, and third, they're lost inside a story and too afraid to let it go. Objective information will not produce any results for these people, and what they want us to believe is what they already believe, even if there's compelling info against it. Saying facts don't exist, since it comes in handy, stops people from creating their own opinions. While reality is indeed multifaceted and drowning in conflicting ideas, there's still a satisfying answer to many things. We don't know much, but we might smell if a study is bought or the truth is purposefully concealed by following the money, evaluating the source, and looking for specific interests. Making sense of a multitude of information gets easier by talking to other people to develop solutions. Picking the right ideas is challenging at first; however, experience will build up. A good mindset is marked by strong foundational ideas and an interest in the truth.

After we opened our mind to incorporate the wisdom of the heart, we can abstain from chasing money and power to free ourselves from desires, which hinder our progress. Since we cannot find freedom and love in these things, they can't be above all else in our life. Although money is needed, it's not the end of the path. It may be hard to understand, but it either comes with our truth or not. Not everyone becomes a superstar, but everyone will be fulfilled with their life, if they're honest. It can appear hypocritical, if a rich person says money is not the answer, but we all have our challenges, and the richest are often the most depressed. To be poor in this world is tough and stressful. We can only wish that one day, it becomes irrelevant in our society. If we're trapped in a meaningless job with no perspective for the future, we don't have the option to say no. Many retreat in alcohol or other addictions to deal with the soul-crushing requirements of the workplace. A turning point is only in sight if the mental pressure becomes unbearable. The solution is to calm down and prepare ourselves in order to overcome this hardship. If we're not believing in our ability and can't find the energy to act, our lives may never get any better. We're all overwhelmed at some point, but confidence is a habit. If we persist in times of adversity, there is sometimes not even a difference between keeping it going and doing nothing at all. We can adapt to everything, and the more practice we get, the more likely we'll do the work we love. Trying to master a new skill often results in setbacks; the rest will probably flow, though. Any obstacle can be overcome, if we have persistence. The truth rarely comes without talent. If there is no talent to speak of and the interest is missing, the search is definitely not over. Next, we have to address the mental slavery we're oppressing ourselves with. Millions of advertisements told us we have to be happy at all times. That there's no excuse for not being happy. This resulted in us wearing the mask of happiness on the outside, while feeling constantly irritated on the inside. However, people have many different emotions during the day. Some feelings connect to chains in particular directions and inhibit others. Some lead us in one direction only, and the third group are experienced on their own. We're also having mixed emotions at times. It can be strange to feel sad and simultaneously relieved at a funeral. Harsh conditions might trigger strong responses and cause anxiety and pain, whereas a sunny day creates feelings of relaxation and peace. We have no idea which thoughts will enter our mind in the next moments. They're happening without our conscious consent. Therefore, accepting whatever feeling or thought arises switches our experience from a reactive state to a peaceful one. We also need to ask the question what happiness is and how it feels, if we want to be able to identify it. Given there are many thousands of feelings during the day, one particular emotion cannot go on forever; it must fade rather quickly instead. To be happy doesn't mean to feel good all the time; it means to watch waves of emotions come and go. Happy people appreciate life for what it is and accept feelings as they come. There is nothing wrong with us if we are angry, worried, or scared—it's normal, since life is a constantly developing process, which can get difficult. An ongoing disconnection from life leads to confusion and suffering. Pushing down unpleasant feelings will never work. It causes a nagging mind and an unsatisfying existence. Having anxiety over the anxiety that might arise is unnecessary. Building layers of denial in order to maintain our mask makes it progressively complicated to peel the onion back to its natural state. A multilayered lie can even become our truth, if we're too invested in it. Waiting for inner experience to change is not the same as allowing everything as it is. If we stop trying to create better sensations, resting in our natural state becomes the norm, and we simply observe an ocean of concepts, thoughts, and emotions as they're created without judging them. Refusing to jump on a particular thought train prevents the chains from ruling in our heads. Feeling comfortable with what we do mustn't be confused with entitlement to feel happy all the time. By doing what comes naturally, we respect life for what it is and express ourselves as we are. Being alone is absolutely essential to differentiate between our nature and all the layers we integrated.

In the beginning, one of the most difficult feelings to endure is fear. It can be hard for people to recognize it as a necessary function, which developed out of the need to survive. If a tiger is chasing us, our bodies have to be ready and our minds must be sharp. Fear is not the enemy—it's an ally. An important part of us. When we're looking down from a height, we're a little hesitant at first, but then we usually get used to it and start to trust the experience more. Anxious people learned to be more afraid for many reasons but mostly since they hold onto a negative experience from the past, which changed their natural autonomic response. By a large majority, these people have exaggerated their negative notion of the future, although it'll not happen the way they've imagined. The emotion gets more and more overwhelming as story building progresses, and some of them won't even leave the house anymore. Angst beat them, and they've capitulated in the face of fear. As a result, their lives are empty of connection and vulnerable to alcohol or food addiction. If the story progressed this far, fear gets used as a means to keep reality out and illusions going. If it ceased to exist, other problems would come to the surface. Thus, people play a game of hide-and-seek, where anxiety interchanges with other issues until they're in need of drugs to calm their overemphasized reaction. Fear cannot prevent death, but it prevents life. It's a sensation inside a cavity. If we're displeased, we hope, and if we're pleased, we fear it's over soon. Acting from a place of stillness, we're able to deal with it in the moment instead of projecting nightmares onto the future, where we're not right now. If thoughts turn into obsessions, we attach meaning to them and the resulting distress triggers compulsive behavior. Rituals and avoidance patterns develop, and relief is often connected to odd coping mechanisms. The circle starts off again, if the thoughts come back or the fear-inducing idea is reemerging. Fear and OCD always go hand in hand. It doesn't matter how irrational a fear is, any chance it might happen causes obsessive things to occur.

While OCD can be surprisingly helpful in search for truth, it's more likely to destroy the life of the person. Oftentimes, there is no straightforward answer to fear, but most will reach a state of readiness at some point. When we are able to withstand the emotional storm and don't run away, we'll go right through it, and the feeling will disappear like a rabbit in a magician's hat. We all know the rabbit comes back, but we're aware of the trick and let go of excitement. It's an orientation toward the now and the assurance of a more peaceful death, since we had the courage to act fearlessly and survived the flood. Becoming a hero means to move forward regardless of how we feel. However, everything starts with us. We must love ourselves, before we can let go. And if we can't find love inside of us, we have to find something we are able to love. Even the smallest of things, a poem, a bird in the sky, or the food we eat. There is always something. The more we love and allow to be loved, the more freedom we will have. The more freedom we have, the more fulfillment we will find in our lives. This is called prosperity of the heart. We don't think much of ourselves as long as we aren't honest. But the truth cannot be used to fuel self-help addiction; it'll solely serve as the guideline in the pursuit of meaning. If we have a quiet moment, our mind will work in its default mode. If this mode is characterized by self-doubt or fear, uncertainty will nag us and we'll sometimes judge ourselves or others to make it go away. By allowing our thoughts and feelings as they are, we become aware of our idiosyncrasies, and negative self-talk might get eliminated through adjustments of our speech patterns and repeated feedback from others. Forgiving ourselves for all the things we have done and accepting ourselves exactly the way we are turns suffering into self-esteem. Treating ourselves with self-compassion and respect will result in a strong human being. Our rational mind should work together with the emotional mind to create a wise mind. Wise people take their emotions into account, since they're often more important, especially when it comes to gut feelings and the like. But they're also able to zoom out to get some perspective from their immediate intelligence.

Starting from the idea our thoughts and words are not us, we let wiser parts come forward to show us the way to authenticity. By being aware of these emotions, we'll feel ourselves out of conditioning and sense the emergence of our truth. Although conscious awareness must be primary, intelligent reasoning should be a close second. It may take a few months until the difference becomes clear, and it's not advisable to act out of the fog. When a wise idea has finally arrived and the laziness of using other people's truths is gone, we will have the courage to exist in the world with confidence. If things suck us in and grip our attention, they are asking for cultivation. The authentic guiding voice of the true self is never incorrect, but we may not be able to understand right away. Manifestation is a fluent process. It'll free our potential. Starting with the one thing that sparks our interest, and held up to our honesty, we built an intent and follow it like water a riverbed. Strict plans are not efficient in real life, since life is a free-running process, embedded in the circles of time. By witnessing how it changes, we can react to its demands and let go of the preference of the mind. Our ideas are not better or worse than other ideas; they are ours. Our attention dictates what we become, and our intention is what we create. By managing our focus instead of our time, we direct our energy more efficiently and achieve more, though pushing too hard may end in a failed transformation. By making sure every step is backed up by the right decision, we exercise the needed patience to succeed. We cannot design our future; we can only support its wisdom. Modesty results in compound effects and doubt is good. We simply keep moving forward and take in the scenery to process its implications. Intent has the outcome in mind by choosing the perspective of our destiny. It's existent before measurement, and it helps to overcome excessive calculations. Resilience keeps the threshold positive and integrity secures the truth. Only the next milestone is important, and everything else is too far away, except when it's not.

Adjustments have to be possible, and modest flexibility prevents doubling down on mistakes. Stupidity begins when we pretend to know all of the truth and follow a fixed path to the end, just to discover that we were wrong. To do the best we can in every situation results in zero regrets, and that's enough to keep confidence going. It's often surprising where these tangled roads lead, and it might get more interesting than we initially thought. What we always have to keep in mind is that attachment to outcome will destroy the joy of exploration. We will all experience loss at some point, so we should be prepared to let go of our preconceived narratives. If our instincts are aligned with our intelligence, the forces inside our head are tamed. When the competition of the tendencies are friendly, we can use it to thrive. Good and bad lose their meaning, if we're able to zoom out and sense the truth from afar. Following the tendencies means to trust our impulses and think of them as antennas of the life process. Focusing on sameness grays out the contrasts of the world. Working with the immediate senses is not applicable to understand the full scope of reality. Inquiring into life is done by forgetting the words to gain new perspectives of interpretation instead. Attaining the essence of our life, a unified perception of the truth unfolding in the moment, implies to us that it cannot be any other way. To be part of something doesn't change our innate truth; it only views us from a different perspective. Hierarchies of the mind cannot be helpful, since our way of thinking only results in the degradation of otherness. Using our minds can be helpful, however, to imagine outcomes, especially when they are negative. The difference between doubting our skills and learning from construction is the ability to collect experience of the future. But when time comes and life calls us to act, we mustn't hesitate or we might miss the opportunity. If we're waiting too long, we should address stagnation with discipline to prevent us from never feeling ready.

All of our positive perceptions come from setting the highest intend possible, because it makes suffering worth it. If the hope to be right is a recipe for failure, we should stop hoping and start dreaming instead. A better life becomes possible when we're ready to learn and extend our horizon. Every nuance of change in perspective can affect the whole story. The magical thinking of today is the science of the future. If we don't brag about our own truth and abstain from speaking ill of other truths, we'll benefit from them. Destiny is a step into an unknown universe, where education is enforcing our imagination by providing an environment for curiosity to flourish. But the education systems of today do the opposite in a lot of cases. Procedural and boring work needed to be done in the past, and for the capitalist to stay on top, they wanted workers who didn't dare to ask for dignity. Even better if they quietly accepted their slavery and pushed to improve their position in the system, because this cemented its relevance. The main attention was on following instructions and recalling information, and as a result, versatile human minds turned into machines. The reason for teaching wasn't at all obvious, and if people don't understand what things are for, they lose their meaning. Nobody has interest in meaningless facts, and that's the reason why school sucks to this day. The story of human knowledge may be quite thrilling and fascinating, but if learning is only about the memorization of things, it's easy to loathe. While higher education often encourages independent thinking more, it's still not as useful as it could be. It is possible to harness the creative capacity children have by truly quenching their thirst for knowledge. Thus, education has to change not only to account for the coming times, but also to help people find meaning and to stop the selfishness-story from developing. The recent emergence of platforms to grade the teachers are not very well received by the faculty, since it exposes their ineffectiveness. It shows that human beings are not numbers and that reducing them to hierarchical measurement feels degrading. What children need are teachers who pay attention to actual talent. The obsessive measurement taking place all over the Western world destroys all instincts for improvement and encourages selfish consumers instead of informed citizens. Some say authoritarianism stems from a lack of education, and that is partly true, since uneducated people can see through the lies. Well-informed people, capable of thought and careful consideration, are not wanted; they are feared. Funding isn't sufficient in many countries, and teachers face difficulties with already media-indoctrinated kids. If we learn that our chances are dependent on race, gender, money, power, fame, and stuff, we're getting ready to elbow our way through everything or we simply give up from the start. The privatized school system runs counter to that and increases the gap even more. Families took note, and now children are pushed to attend preschools, where they train their elbows and practice memorization already at an early age. All day schools are the norm in some places, since parents must work for families to survive. Most education systems in the West are derived from the Prussian model, after which first Germany taught their children to comply with strict discipline and do everything asked of them. While the German military of today has a disobedience rule, where soldiers are allowed insubordination if an order denies human dignity, the principles of teaching basically didn't change over the last 150 years. Although it was praised for making people literate and efficient, schools were at the same time responsible for generating wage slaves and low-aiming individuals, who worked in factories and fought in unnecessary wars. Basic schooling was free for all; however, it seems free often comes with a price as our modern times show as well. Indoctrination itself can be seen as the propaganda of the young, and it can't be avoided to some extent, since every interaction is a form of opinion forming. Some people blame the teachers for the useless youth, but if they only follow their own education, they can't be made responsible. A certain standardization of teacher education is necessary to keep the quality high, but the current system of so called "normal schools," which were formerly used to instill highly distorted values, never really got an update except for ending the violent beatings for badness.

Children were never really allowed to express themselves and, as a result, often didn't like going to school. A highly creative child is robbed of its vitality and curiosity to train endless hours in the rat race of education. The ability for self-control dictates performance and chances. Uniform value judgments of what good and bad mean are constantly emphasized by teachers, who themselves are standardized. There are exceptions of course; however, the majority permanently lives in the story-world, and even if they fight for meaningful education, they quickly bump into insurmountable walls. It might be a controversy to include religion in the curriculum, but if it's discarded, there has to be an alternative sensemaking process in place to make up for the lost option to acquire meaning in life. Private schools appear to be better organized and yield to superior education; the fact that only a tiny minority is able to afford them and the clearly unchanged interest of the rich easily explain the low funding and the overall premise of the system though. When children feel scared instead of being protected, they cannot find out who they are, because they're forced to fit into a regime of measurement and perfectly timed top performance. Perseverance and problem-solving abilities are crucial to succeed in life, but if they're not encouraged by an interest in the topic, they can't be properly learned. If state propaganda is constantly emphasized, children not only grow up with high expectations and ideas of ruthless competition, they're also damned to fail, because they'll not be able to view the them as part of us. The American dream for example, wasn't always exclusively about money; it was a dream where people are capable of attaining their highest potential to gain the recognition of others for what they are, regardless of circumstances of birth or position. Today, everyone is terrorizing themselves to attain peak performance on a few special days, which unavoidably affects a large part of our future.

While it is absolutely mandatory for kids to have an education, since it teaches many different ways of thinking, it also appears that people who are able lead a dignified life of their own are way better off than system slaves. If the past plays such a huge role in what people can do today, their true capabilities will not and cannot be discovered. If a system needs quotas to regulate for more equality, society is not organized by fairness, but ruled by power games instead. If skill, talent, and hard work were primary, rather than race, wealth, and other categories, a strong culture of specialists would emerge, who will be able to connect their knowledge in more ways, since the story wouldn't be of any importance. Human beings have to be creative to express themselves, but suppressing our love of beauty and connection not only produces scared children, it hinders the process of life and devastates them. Creativity and imagination are what bring forth the human race; however, if we don't stop to put our children in comfortable drawers inside the story-world, they will ask themselves all their lives who they actually are. Personality differences between sexes are at their highest in the most gender equal countries. As people get more freedom to express their truth, they are happy to do so. Applying this logic to other parts of society, a revolution of individuality would take place, because if opportunity would be totally equal, the call for equal outcomes wouldn't exist. A farmer is not a scientist, and people should be paid according to the value they produce. If we stop telling people they have to have a big house, expensive cars, and tons of stuff, there is no reason why they wouldn't be content with what they earn as long as it's fair and they aren't living a lie. Only in a culture where money, fame, and power are the most desirable things, people tend to be predominantly losers, who scream for a bigger part of the cake, although they're not willing to work for it, because they've learned that work is torture and school is boring and meaningless. The end goal of a society is to be a single organism, expressing itself through magnificent diversity and systemic levels of ability, interconnecting each other by necessity and love, while embracing fairness and competition to elevate the whole.

Education must be highly individual, and translating theoretical knowledge creatively onto the given field is the highest value anybody can produce. Specialization would be guided by truth, not dictated by money. The internet showed us how to carve out niches and specialize to serve a select crowd of people who are passionate about their occupation or are looking for a specific product to solve a problem. There will be more valuable occupations according to the translation performance; however, a carpenter simply dies if he has to sit in an office chair for days on end. We want to be helpful to each other, and therefore things would even out with time. When a certain size was reached, there would only be small holes in the distribution, which would close in due to the balancing capabilities of the system itself. The premise is the defining factor of every society, and if we go for something more truthful, since equilibrium is seldom and fluctuation necessary to develop further, we have the joy of watching the human race thrive in full agreement with the individual. Acceptance would be order and egotistic narratives chaos. It's somehow already happening, but the story is still much too strong for the truth to show itself. Chaos remains a factor in any narrative, but if people know how to harness its power to grow instead of purposefully destroying themselves, then competition is joyful chaos, not deadly suffering. The tests to distinguish if a child is allowed to attend higher education are based on prechosen topics, stiff memorization of facts and resulting value in regard to their usefulness as a worker in a highly selfish system. Creativity is not encouraged although it plays the biggest role in forming an intent for the future. If about a half of all the learned material can be successfully reproduced on specific days, requirements are reached and the student can progress to the next grade. Thus, if a child isn't interested in memorization and decides to do just enough, they will not be any smarter, and the complete picture is missed. Prioritizing quantity over mastery is what disheartens children and their interest.

In the standardization mania of the twentieth century, an irritating amount of legislation got passed to equal out any differences, but all that did was to feed the story. The No Child Left Behind Act, which is still in effect in the United States, was responsible for more privatization and less chances for everybody except the wealthy. Nationwide tests were employed to grade all students according to the same requirements. As a result, students learn like mad for these tests to get a chance for a better or more prestigious education in the future. It should be absolutely clear that the performance on a single test in a given day can't be sufficient to evaluate the capabilities of students, but their future depends on it. Even the military is using the tests to recruit candidates and sort out the aspirants who aren't intelligent enough. If a test seems so important for one's life, it's no wonder students started basing their self-worth on the test results. This causes a lot of stress and anxiety for parents and students alike. Mental health issues beginning at an early age are not the exception, and cheating has become a necessary evil for many. Some seem simply not smart enough to ace these tests. Intelligence tests are measuring the processing speed of the brain and the memorization capacities. Measuring creativity is not as easy, because the tests can't be standardized, if different people look at the results and the tests need to be completely different each time they're done. A creative solution to a problem is also more often wrong than not; thus, metrics are harder to come up with. Some people envisioned different intelligences and tried to create tests to prove their ideas, but most were not as promising as initially thought. People with higher intelligence usually do better on all tests that are currently conducted; the distribution of creativity is not taken into account, though. The correlation between grades and creativity is mostly nonexistent and some creative people might fail, although they possess skills no one else has. Everyone is different, and the possibility for rare, but valuable, talents is there.

What the future needs is not entirely predictable. In fact, when people try to predict the future, they simply follow an already established path to the end, because the outcome of new knowledge connections cannot be known. Some say that the majority of the money is most productive if it is in the hands of highly intelligent people, but they're equally unable to know what comes next. One also might argue the predictions of smart people are at least better, but innovations are not causal; they are exponential instead. Intelligence is a good metric for success, but it can't be the only one. Working hard is often as important as intelligence itself, since they are both correlated with life success. If expression of uniqueness would be encouraged, the outcomes would be more interesting and likely much more productive, since creative ideas are as important as functioning solutions. The metric system was designed to be a perfect measurement tool, but since physical bodies change over time, it was never as exact as people wished. The human condition is vast and tests are not sufficient to assess a person in its entirety. The American military is struggling to find young people who are apt for service, partly because of health reasons, but also due to the test results. Seventy-one percent of seventeen through twenty-four-year-olds do not qualify for military service. Is this due to the declining quality of people or are there other reasons? First, there are class differences. Higher income cities spent more on schools and provide better learning aids such as computers and other equipment. Teachers are paid better, and overall education is superior to other schools. Wealthy parents are also more likely to read to their children, which helps with vocabulary. Poverty causes a decline in IQ of about fourteen points on average, since poor people's brains are busy looking for food. A person who cannot plan for the future because they lack resources now is much less likely to pursue a more ambitioned goal in life. If people are labeled in a certain way, they'll turn it into a self-fulfilling prophecy and often suffer from a crooked self-image all their life.

Second, colleges are dependent on tests for consistency, and the college board provides numbers to sort out people right after application. They are both interested in keeping the system as it is, since that saves time and money. Students are obviously not their priority, and if the scores are not sufficient out of cultural reasons or language skills, some lose the opportunity to attend high quality courses. The third factor is intelligence. IQ appears to be genetically influenced by about fifty to seventy-five percent, whereas skin color plays no role. Maximizing inherited potential is up to environment, nutrition, lifestyle, learning resources, and parenting though. Good scores aren't correlated with better college performance. In fact, higher grades and lower scores surpassed higher scores and lower grades. While people with good scores do well in life, visionaries often dared to look into their interest instead of giving teachers what they wanted. Finding our passion for something is more important than scores. Comparing ourselves to others will forever be a problem, since there are always people who are smarter than us. Competition isn't helpful if it inspires people to cheat and feel insecure about themselves. If perfection is the status quo, natural development cannot take place. Threatening students to follow rules in order to generate wanted behavior feeds the story and results in uniformity and a lack of trust. If people and their talents aren't taken into account, they'll only care about numbers and themselves. Memories change and get less accurate the more often they're remembered. This makes memorization of facts even more meaningless. If we would start with the learners in mind and design the system from there, it would be much more successful and fun for the students. Mistakes will happen, but supporting people from the ground up would create the environment necessary to build a better future for all of us. The transition from traditionalism, which saw the world as having a basic order, to rational modernity, which resulted in a much more uncertain mindset started with the Protestant Reformation.

It shifted responsibility from god back to the people. When life was once predetermined and solely in god's hands, now the people began to impart meaning on their own, resulting in the idea that god's blessing came from financial success and the amassing of goods. In order to be saved, people didn't stop working when their needs were met. They kept laboring to accumulate as much wealth as possible. Individualism emerged, and capitalism found its way into people's heads. More and more bureaucracy was needed to organize the new system, and obeying to rules became essential. The regime divided labor in smaller chunks. It had strict regulations and a crystal clear hierarchy based on authority. But the rules could be changed at any time, and the people who created them needed to be different from the workers. They had to be charismatic and unique to earn their respect. What followed was an arms race to reach ever higher ranks in class, power, and status. Lower ranks cared for the repetitive and mostly meaningless work, and higher ranks governed society. It was important that all the people were treated with the same impersonality, and successful bureaucrats obeyed the rules to the letter. All citizens were the same before the rules; however, people are different since they have differing needs. A one-fits-all solution simply cannot be adequate. While lower classes have to keep up with a lot of frustration in dealing with stupid and irrelevant rules, higher classes fight mercilessly to avoid losing their status. Where is fairness, if power corrupts people? Who is damned to do meaningless work and who is qualified to create the rules? How do we choose the powerful? If ruthless competition was the way, we would enjoy ourselves. The human brain, for instance, was once thought to work by stimulus and response, but it more or less fires all the time. A majority of people are still using the model of the triune brain. Utilizing a hierarchy structure is easier after all. But the theory was proven wrong with the invention of molecular genetics with which the three-layer evolution model became obsolete.

The brain consists of all the same neurons throughout and it isn't superior to other brains. It just perfectly adapted to its environment and did so by predicting events in an uncertain world and not by following a set of predetermined rules. It constantly improves the previously learned routines for efficiency, and if it wasn't flexible, humans wouldn't have evolved this far. In childhood, when ninety percent of the brain development takes place, kids must play and explore the world around them. It's of importance to have save environments where they're able to express their creativity and have the ability to learn by controlling their play themselves. Interests have to be encouraged and ideas cherished. They need our full attention and support to progress in life, and effective communication is one of the most important things we can teach. They imitate us to learn and to make us happy, but if we hinder their natural curiosity and try to administer their behavior by forcing meaningless rules on them, they will turn out as stale as the bureaucracy we came to think of as so important to organize our progressively sick society.

To teach children about the world, we must begin by helping them understand the importance of creativity to overcome issues and create solutions for problems. The practical aspect of instruction has to be the most prominent feature of any school lesson, since procedures are important to follow proven recipes, but not as useful to gather a deeper understanding of the topic. To get things done, standards have to be followed; the creativity to know what to do, however, has to be first. Matching aptitudes with the curriculum and helping students produce their own ideas by guiding them through the process is crucial for development. Literature, music, and art in general are underrepresented, although the perception of beauty is a big part of what makes us human, and creativity couldn't be conveyed more effectively. Emotional stimuli result in comprehensive feedback of our brains and the more connections we make, the smarter we will become. Art tackles the essential questions like meaning, loneliness, and happiness, whereas rules only explain a fraction of a world we created ourselves.

Our institutions oppress us for no reason other than to uphold the story-world virtually nobody enjoys. The system became the oppressor, not the people who bear with its daily consequences. The rich and powerful will never step down, since the gamble of trusting a furiously sick society isn't worth it to them. They fooled themselves into thinking they're qualified to rule and enjoy a privileged life, which came from being born into the right family and having the luck to possess a fast processor from the start. Some people might rise from poverty to status, but it's not the norm. A long chain of events brought us into this world, and we may never know if it was necessary or not, but we have to make sure that upcoming generations do better. Much like in science, where wrong theories only die if their creators do, it will be the same with capitalism. Children need sensible education, since turning them into machines makes them miserable and ruthless. Honest narratives are far from linear. The imagination of the listener and the voice of the teller create links to make a narrative understandable within the creative frameworks of our mind. The education system of Finland is an example of how to do it right. During the first six years, children have no grades. There is a final test at the end of high school and it matters, but kids get enough time to find their passions. Teachers are screened heavily for their intentions, and only the best are allowed to teach. The calling for teaching and a love for children are required. They normally get tremendous autonomy within their responsibilities, and they're treated with respect and admiration. Contrary to normal schools, where teachers are prepared to line kids up into the hierarchy, their colleagues in Finland have environments to test new methods and ideas. They're not judged, but encouraged, and they're shown that connection and regard for individual learning needs are significant for development. Faculties are directly bound to research labs to ensure the knowledge isn't outdated and practical application is emphasized.

The highly successful Roman Legions knew this already, since they preferred recruits from the countryside. Soldiers from the cities weren't used to the machinery and unfit to deal with the implications of hardship. Romans viewed people from a whole-person perspective, and things like a sense of humor as well as good manners were taken into account. They adapted effectively in the case of defeat and grew stronger. What students in Finland get out of that comprehensive process is a lifelong appreciation for learning and a close sense of community. Their work ethic stems from an interest in progress. Schools do projects like book writing and experiment with storytelling to practice congruent skill sets, which are useful in everyday life and more likely to inspire children to find their truth. Homework doesn't exceed thirty minutes to allow the brain to process the teachings while the children relax. Most students only need a few minutes for it. This allows the question if that's enough to prepare students for a competitive world. The popular PISA study is often used as guideline for economic success, but the

World Economic Forum doesn't mention it as a criteria. Important traits like collaboration, creativity, and communication are not even tested. While the United States ranks low due to a lack of expectations and rising economic inequality, Finland frequently reaches the top ten. China, which dominated in 2018, expects students to work like machines, but are these marginal differences worth it? Is it maybe more desirable to grow human beings who are not only able to learn, but also to love? Although not everybody is capable of doing everything, we're all capable of doing the appropriate thing for us. As our interests evolve, we often doubt our abilities. We imagine ourselves as winners, but it appears we're not strong enough to make it. A thousand questions come up and we take endless thought trains to nowhere. Could we really be that if we would just believe it? Are we lying to ourselves? We want to avoid disappointment, but why do we protect ourselves from adventure? Quiet desperation and passivity is what kills us, not facing our fears. If life happens to us, instead of us making life happen, we waste our gifts and create a false story. By being conscious of our intents, we cherish the talents given to us. Some might believe to become a master we must possess talent before we even begin, but this isn't true.

While it's favorable to be better than the average beginner, it's up to deliberate practice if one is able to reach mastery in a field. Some sports may be less likely for some, but the majority of us are capable of fulfilling our dreams as long as they're guided by the truth. To feel strongly about an idea and the impetus to make it are more important than talent. The secret is to keep developing without falling back into comfortable routines. We should strive to steadily get better by constant repetition, increasing difficulty, and continuous feedback. It can be tough and may not always be enjoyable, but creating a meaningful life is not necessarily easy, since the reward is often correlated with energy spent. The world of quick fun causes us to live inside a loop of ever increasing stimulation, until we eventually act like an addict. To spend our energy wisely, we may want to embrace hardship, even if we're drowning in it. As we progress on this path, we will finally feel a progressive initiation into who we are. If we're eventually able to make our own rules and take responsibility for our actions, life will change and all the crushingly hard work pay off. The worst thing that can ever happen to us is to be successful at a life we hate, and by keeping that in mind, we'll never lose sight of our intentions. It's an accomplishment in itself to know the truth, but it isn't enough to know it alone. If we let circumstances hinder us, since we reached some success in the story-world, we're not any better than the people who stopped halfway. To balance rightful concerns and imagined self-doubt helps to know the next step. The best feeling connects usefulness with honesty. If we want to be proud, we must earn it by moving forward. By establishing our own thinking, we develop unique means of being in the world. A creative person is focused on inputs; an obedient person works for outputs. Creativity comes from maximized input, passion results from creativity, and stress is a sign of not being involved. Personal progress derives from advance in our interest.

It's not dependent on encouragement from outside, since the only fair judgment takes the person from yesterday into account. Learning from our mistakes takes humility, but it's essential to live according to our own standards. Distinguishing feedback from useless criticism and fighting negative thought patterns prevents cowardly behavior, because sensing a lie is impossible if we run from it. The feeling of being in the waiting room of life only emerges if we are too weak to look inside. However, by thinking about what we wish to avoid, we will eventually think about what we actually want. A repressive attitude toward the truth tries to limit the content of thought, since cowards are afraid to fail. They have no power over the world, because it has no meaning to approach change. Death is their inevitable truth, while everything else is not in their hands. Awareness is shifted to focus on trivialities, although they're as useless as everything else. If power is the ability to do whatever we want, true power is knowing how far we can go before it's too late. To be a doormat is hard, but blocking long-term success by emphasizing short-term limitations is a shame. The initial starting point might be lower; no change means no gain though. Narrowing experience prevents from tragic insights, but if we don't confront our demons and face them with honesty, we will never enjoy the benefits of looking the truth directly in the eye. Confronting limitation and fear will turn weakness into accomplishment if we fully engage in our craft. Depression is a problem, but we aren't the problem, we are the solution. Thinking about equipment, about what's needed to build the future, is the only way out of depression and into the realm possibility. Knowing the how is success' friend. The most creative people try everything and switch as often as they can to automatically generate ideas of significance. Multitasking one at a time, we find truth inside of chaos and pain. Self-starters have no process in the beginning; they create their routines themselves. By representing something larger, we meet resources inside that have the power to inspire others in the fight for freedom. Admitting vulnerability to harsh conditions around us, we open up our mind to solutions.

On the way out of depression, we'll meet flow. It makes practice worthwhile and hard work pleasurable. When everything comes together in a perfect moment of concentration on a completely obvious task, feedback is immediately available. The world vanishes into nothingness and the story comes to a halt. We have a feeling of total control over our task and lose ourselves. Time is just a moment. The moment of truth. The moment, we have found ourselves. To experience meaningful work, we create playful routines to dissolve the senses and imagine the world anew. We tilt our perception until we arrive at bliss. Bringing our attention to details in unison with the zoomed-out state of the observer, we engage in the adventure of life. Art is not the same as farming, but farming can be an art. Mundane work costs energy. Flow gets it back. A part of the environment cannot be in conflict with it. To find meaning is to become a master at being happy. Everyone has a baseline mood. It's the foundation of experience, and we go back to it as soon as the thing is over. If it's closer to the truth, it's content and relaxed, but if it's a blatant lie, it's agitated and nervous. The judgment of ourselves as being good or bad mainly manifests in childhood and is often transported by our parents. However, when we become an adult, the constant worrying about what people think paralyzes the ability to determine our self-worth. It not only dictates our life, it also destroys the will to live, since cowards are not able to find meaning. Other people tell them what to think and who they are, and as a result, they're existing inside a circle of stale unhappiness, until their soul confronts them with the urgent need for change. Work is only valuable if it's desirable on its own. The difference between slavery and the truth is that work is actually fun, if we dare to be honest. Money is important to be in control of our time, not the reason why we engage in an occupation. If people work for recognition, they're trapped in an unwinnable game, where the love of the craft is secondary and social status becomes their god. The desire to be recognized sabotages their lives, because not everybody can have a gold medal. Everyday life is unimportant and boring, since the greed for status wipes out the joy of doing the things they once loved.

It is not a shame to get a prize, quite the opposite, but the attachment to outcome should be avoided. We're gaining fulfillment by getting better; our development is a pleasure in itself though. As children, we must have an open environment to manifest our creativity. Many teachers and controlling parents disturb development by placing recognition before joy. We should be proud of our work, not for the prizes we have. Helicopters make us depressed, but if kids are allowed to play freely, they're practicing flow. The reason why people aren't able to change is often a tight coherence to patterns they've learned as a child. The common strategy to play it safe, even though it leads to suffering, is due to fear of lost continuity. Cowards are not only weak and refuse to investigate why, they're also envying others for having the courage to work on their shortcomings. They torment themself and seek revenge whenever they can, since others aren't allowed to make them feel this way. It's a displeasure in the advance of others, and it comes with a wish of possessing their belongings and sometimes even destroying their life out of their own malaise. Comparison shows them their inferiorities and turns caring people into enemies who have to suffer to satisfy their story. The envy of the masses became a political and economical tool to maintain control and oppress people. Technological progress made it possible to envy whoever is in focus of the media. Social platforms thrive out of attention addiction. The recipients of our envy were once dependent on the values of our tribe; now the whole world takes part in targeted efforts to sort people into worthless categories, which created the minds of the masses by repetition. Marketing firms, who manipulate with the help of psychological warfare, should be vary of their actions because they're creating a hostile and depressed world, but we all know they won't. The idealized few oftentimes aren't even interesting or worth listening to; they just happen to be famous. And if the envied status of the desired individual is unreachable, the feelings of inferiority will remain forever. Skills don't derive from envy, they emerge out of hard work.

By choosing the right role models, we gain mastery. Even if our heroes are already dead or too far away, there'll always be people who can serve as an example. If we prefer to live in the story-world and go for recognition and status, it's easy to find people who help us waste time. However, should we decide to change course for a more meaningful life, there is hardly a friend in sight. Blaming other people won't help. We must start our journey nonetheless. It might be hard to overcome the influence of the mob, and small-minded people may try to belittle our efforts. These people tend to create a personal story on why transformation isn't possible to make a case for worse opportunities, but by blaming life, they're losing the opportunity to find the truth and will die with the scar of failure on their face. As long as we keep moving forward in search for our truth, we will discover ourselves and write a new story. How long it takes is not important, and only the next step counts. Other people are different, and we won't empower them by making them more alike. The way to change the mind of other people or to win them over in the fight against false ideas is by example, not by going to war. The bittersweet plant is a climbing vine. It grows up trees and curls around branches until the whole bark of the host is covered. It robs the tree of sunlight and sometimes uproots it, because of its excessive weight. A predator of huge proportions indeed, it can kill whole forests with its overbordering growth. At some point, it commits suicide and doesn't even notice it, since there are no hosts left. It would do much better for itself if it would just let the tree live and grow only as much as it needs. When people try to remove it, they often forget to kill the root system, and as a result, the bittersweet clones and grows over everything. If they noticed it earlier, they would have a better chance of removing it by pulling out the roots right from the beginning. A very similar plant called the Virginia creeper is a much more pleasant guest in the forest.

It evolved with the host trees and doesn't mess with their photosynthetic capacity. Benefitting the host to benefit the whole is called synergy. It pays off for all parties, because the outcome is greater than what a single plant could have done on its own. Synergy occurs when all parties involved not only try to lift each other up but also desire a mutual outcome. It honors possibilities and strengthens relationships by valuing differences. Sameness is simply not as useful, and by compensating for each other's weaknesses, the synergists learn new things. The inner longing for change has to be characterized by open communication and mutual trust though. To be a part of the solution, we must consider the resources available. An effective system maximizes its output by directing focus appropriately. The parts only work for themselves if they don't understand what the others are doing. Thus, a productive prioritization is needed and a continuous flow of information must be provided. Keeping stress levels low intensifies focus; enjoyment supercharges it. An unpleasant job is different from a challenging activity, as it won't produce the results we have in mind. It leaves us in total uncertainty of future outcomes, and it's merely directed at short term pleasures instead of long term developments. Reconnecting to our bodies sharpens the ability to sense emotions and helps concentration. By asking questions about our states, how we feel, what our natural tendency demands from us, we enhance self-awareness. We're able to directly react to our gut feeling and use our mind to gain insights. When dealing with other people, we learn to live inside their heads for fleeting moments in order to view the world from their perspective. Controlling ourselves and fighting off temptations provides energy for future challenges. Patience keeps the mind quiet. Connecting through shared experience draws attention to solutions, and feelings resonate into mutual focus. Learning intensifies and creativity gets enhanced by generating new pathways to ever greater performances. The synergy of different minds enhances flow, embraces connection, and leads to an understanding of larger systems. To train focus, the mind must learn to come back again and again until long sessions feel effortless.

Connected systems can sense problems before they become apparent, and attention is exercised to alleviate them. A concentrated effort to simplify and balance large-scale solutions into immediate small-scale actions is the main idea. Discipline, deep connection, continuous focus, and self-awareness are fundamental to grow. We cannot know what we will accomplish if we aim at the highest goal possible with the belief we're able to make it. Every person started somewhere and instead of denying deficiencies, we have to work to master them. Failures are there to learn, and intelligence develops over time. Challenge should be embraced, and an unquenchable desire to grow is what we need to thrive. Growing works by letting go of safety, and becoming will always be superior to being. Concentrated effort is strength, only relying on talent foolish. Stopping with energy left in the tank prevents burnout and maintains momentum. Small, consistent daily progress ensures long-term evolution of skills and practices. Effective time management simply cuts everything out and starts adding. Every day we accomplished something is one cross on the calendar. The game is to never miss a day, and breaking the chain gets increasingly harder with every cross. Environment is a big factor in building and discarding habits. To encourage growth, new habits should be easily accessible. Wiping out bad ones works by preventing access. Neighborhoods, schools, friends, and spouses influence possibilities and grit. Choosing wisely where we live and with whom we spend our time has the power to radically transform our life. We'll always fall back into the systems we belong to, and our routines define the lowest form of activity. Providing as much value as we can helps our environment thrive and mirrors back to support us in times of need. The Japanese idea of favors works very well, since constant exchange of gifts leads to confusion whose turn it is. It provides stable bonds, but it also fosters attachment, which should be known but not completely avoided.

Resilient people get up after they failed, but powerful people get better by seeing the upsides of the fall. An intrinsic need for a perfectly functional healthy body resides in all of us. Training, fasting, and nutritious food is beneficial to stay in power and to maintain health. Our circadian rhythm serves as a guide for life routines. But life is short. Humans in the Western world mostly die at around eighty. All in all, we sleep for 8,000 days and work for 3,700. Household chores, including cooking and eating, 2,700 days. Commuting, 1150. That leaves around 5,000 for personal care, relaxation, and pleasure if we disregard all other activities. These numbers are obviously not exact, but the average adult, who retires at sixty-five has not much time to learn. Do we enjoy every moment of our life? Do we really taste the food we're eating? Do we spent unnecessary time hating the life we created? Do we focus on avoiding unpleasant emotions in fear of the truth? Is waiting for a better future the best strategy to move forward? Is running away the right solution? Is listening to losers the right way to get answers? When we feel water flow through our hands, the last contact is the first at the same time. Not only time is just a moment; our life is too. The continuous passage of time into the dream of yesterday shows us the fragility of existence and asks us to cherish the moment, while we take part in creating the future. Sacrificing the now to enjoy the fruits of tomorrow must be balanced with indulging the now and forgetting the self. Becoming finds meaning. Being is already there. The paradox of not needing to do anything to feel content is one of the blessings of isolation; however, it cannot be honest if we want to express our being to find meaning in our lives. Only after we've done something to enrich the experience of others have we truly fulfilled our duty to create more energy than we use. The pain of hard work is unbearable if there's no faith in the process, and if information is lacking, the great writings of mankind will inspire us to be more creative. A good book is painting a picture. It represents a truth of life and embeds it into words to throw it at us. The canvas consists of pages, and the emotions flow like water. It's in touch with the moment and mirrors a truth by enriching the view and adding perspective.

Our problems in life were always the same. Art is not about history; it's about experience. When time is scarce and the stakes are high, we frequently rush and forget to look around, but it's okay to be human. Having fun helps to digest information and zoning out relaxes us. We deserve to be loved, and we'll take some time to live. It's a balance of one after another, not both at once. Other people can be our greatest asset, but they also hinder our progress at times. By interacting with them to actualize our intentions or to gather feedback, we cannot avoid playing the social game. We are all actors on a stage, and the roles we play communicate our individual performance repertoire, which is derived from factors we often can't control. Age, occupation, and gender are all part of the greater picture of our identity. If we're sitting in a wheelchair for instance, this role may override all the others, since it's the most obvious. A new car can give an actor a neat look, but people won't be impressed if the role has a humpback. Sharing a role puts us in the same group with our peers and so the game starts. The umbrella role pins our status in society, and many people will use it to define how to treat us in the social hierarchy. Their perceptions create direct consequences in reality, and even if we refuse to perform, others will demand it from us by giving cues and adjusting treatment. People go great lengths to make interaction according to role assumptions smooth and effortless. To play their roles well, they exercise information management and a large part of their being remains in the dark until a third person joins the conversation and tears it apart. The mask they wear has to conform with the expectations of the people around them, and they will adopt new masks as they're created for them. The result is a divided person with a backstage and a frontstage identity. They prepare the roles in the back to later ace their performance on stage. That's why we're often surprised at how people behave as we get closer to them and the mask falls away.

The performance of their "best" self might be extensive and what seemed to be a nice person turns out to be a monster. Many roles are learned from our parents. They want to protect us from the mistakes they've made but fail to recognize we're not them. Great actors with a fixed set of assumptions will act according to the mask assigned to them. Our tribe presumes to know who we are and we accept and adopt the resulting masks. Sometimes, we fool people into thinking we are better than our current mask to lift our status. If two masks counteract each other, we're often confused and try to separate them from one another. Homosexual Christians are in constant conflict with themselves, given they want to follow the moral imaginations of the church. A triumphant success cannot look the same for all of us, so why do we accept fixed notions of it?

Our job in society is to ignore most of the sensory experiences the body produces, simply to hold up the illusion of a role we didn't even craft ourselves. If we don't know who we are, we will always play the roles assigned to us. The little person in our head operates the switches, and as a result, our life runs on autopilot, but if we want to be authentic, we have to embody ourselves. As long as the masks dominate our sense of self, we're at risk to become what others think of us. The longer we keep the stage play going, the harder it gets to divide the little person from the truth. While men are stamped by the notion of toxic masculinity, woman become expert liars to avoid giving in to sex. Peer pressure prevents the honest expression of their sexuality, because gossip might kill their reputation. Either they're too anxious to tell the truth or they ghost possible partners to save face. What starts with an honest interest often ends with the destruction of another person. Sensible individuals regularly feel responsible for their rejection. What is due to stupid moral ideas and difficult-to-remove masks quickly turns into unbelievable pain and suffering. A majority of people don't even know that their questionable actions can result in lifelong isolation for others. The belief in love gets diminished over many years, and the motivation to look for new partners is regularly exchanged with a lack of trust in people.

Utter disappointment and deeply buried ressentiments destroy the will to try again. This socio-cultural stage play of dishonesty is the reason for a lot of lonely, frustrated people. Technology made it possible to be completely isolated, and many openly decide to be alone. By being lonely, they're finally able to be themselves. When there is no other, there is no need to wear a mask. Although an immense amount of wisdom can derive from being alone, loneliness emerges out of involuntary isolation. A person familiar with themselves doesn't need anybody, but they choose to be with others, since a lonely life is not as beautiful. Participating in the healing of our scars and having the courage to try again is a heroic act, and if people finally dare to, they're absolutely entitled to be told the truth in order to be able to move on and find a person who cares for them. The behavior of today is the society of the future, and with the help of effortless information distribution, we got used to cowardly tactics in order to dodge rejection and pain. The relationship with our environment should play a role in our life, not dictate a life in which we play a role. The approval of others is nice to have, but it mustn't influence our self-worth. If our masks make it impossible to know who we're really talking to, we'll never be able to find the perfect fit. For some people, living alone is not even an option since they're still with their parents. Bleak financial outlooks and a hostile job market are good reasons to stay at home with Mom and Dad. However, by opting to live with them, we're making a big sacrifice. As long as we're there, we won't know how it feels to be a full member of society. The freedom to be treated as an adult is worth much more than some want to believe. A certain safety is needed to start something, but waiting too long for our real life to begin hinders development and makes us feeble. Loving parents will never send their child away. Adults have to go on their own. A good connection with the people who made us is important, but making the job market responsible for laziness and childish routines is not only wrong, it creates weak human beings.

For a young adult to be able to enjoy freedom, they have to move out and become the specialist they need to be. Parents have to let go at some point. True love knows when the time to part comes. Instead of wasting time and watching TV, young people must be able to state their worth. Why are our living rooms incomplete without a big flat screen TV? Hundreds of useless formats entertain us and, in return, ask us to buy stuff. Germany merely consists of lederhosen-people, yodeling a bunch a stupid words while drinking huge amounts of beer. They're all stupid, but Americans like to use clichés. Although it has become less of an issue, since people have become more enlightened these days, a general humming of Oktoberfest beer won't leave American heads soon. Germans only accept this hillbilly mask to make money from tourists, but it shows what happens if people mainly watch TV and don't experience actual reality. The living-room setup has become such a standard, nobody is asking why the couch gets always pointed toward the propaganda machine. It wants to tell us what to think and who to like. It keeps us in the story-world and makes us miserable, because we need more stuff. A few alpha males flatten everyone else to push opinions into our minds. In fact, nobody finds it particularly wrong to listen to these self-proclaimed thought leaders and their preconceived notions about the world. Someone eventually has to do the job of telling us what to think. It has always been this way, and people conform to everything, they say. This leads to ongoing conflict between peer groups who are united over their masks. Solidarity with our tribe will always be stronger than compassion toward other people, if we allow a small minority to use our roles against us. Solidarity leads to opposing peer groups, and conflict results in more solidarity. As long as the fiery hate burns, solidarity is high among peers, but if the source of conflict stops inviting more war, group cohesion decreases and solidarity with it. Alphas will try to defend their territory if we keep supporting them.

As a result, there's no beginning and no end. Just a positive feed-back loop. To enjoy entertainment to decompress from a long day at work is fine; being glued to bullshit is not. But why do people obey their leaders and how do they mark their status? Chimpanzees have two types of strategies to mark their status. One is aggression, and the other is grooming. A majority of apes usually prefer grooming over fighting, because it saves energy. Domination is a way to keep leadership if challenged; grooming consists of smart behaviors to create mutually beneficial relationships to others. However, are hierarchies necessary to cooperate successfully and to get things done? We've come a long way; and it should be possible to do without it by now. The modern leader is already much better than the old aggressive douchebag male, but a hierarchy of authority is simply not useful anymore. A good leader is able to self-reflect and cares for people by pursuing compromise. They aren't dependent on constant self-assurance through the use of force and don't use fear to dominate. Outstanding leaders get respect through vulnerability. People trust them out of shared experience where support is emphasized. They will go to war for their people, but when the war is finally over, they treat the other party with acceptance. While toxicity exists among men, being a great leader is the opposite of toxic; it's the courage to shoulder responsibility in spite of tough challenges. If the environment wasn't predominately hostile, these people would be more common, and a more peaceful way to work would be the result. Aggression is not a bad trait; it's only bad if people use it in the wrong way. Women have the power to destroy lives too. Manipulation and underhandedness can be an absolute horror if we're the recipient of it. While the notion of toxic masculinity seems to be the buzzword for feminists to defend themselves, they forget how devastating their own actions can be. Downplaying our violence and sexism is not the solution, but living in a hypersexualized society with hard working conditions turns some people into raging monsters. It's not an excuse; it's simply a causal chain from years of abuse to become an abuser themselves.

Men are suffering too. Refusing to see their problems and blaming them for being sexist, although they're constantly portrayed as beer slobs with sports addiction and misogynistic sex drives, is not the right way to help them get any better. To make things even worse, the supported picture of men who are rich, handsome, athletic, and successful will never be accessible for many of us. Balancing our sometimes aggressive will to thrive with being a capable and loving caregiver is possible; however, it would be much easier if circumstances were not as difficult. Life is often a challenge. Women regularly experience discrimination and violence, and their abilities are played down, but we have to ask ourselves how capitalism affects mutual treatment. There is no satisfying answer to this, but we must gradually erode it to find out. A lasting change of our society is only possible if the shift in perspective gets confirmed by outer circumstances. As long as the system goes on, we'll need leaders and we'll automatically encourage fights and suffering in order to grow to ever greater heights, which will eventually destroy our livelihood. The solution would be a diversification of competence. A system where nobody is above anyone. Power always corrupts, and we're not equipped to make perfectly sound decisions with our limited intelligence. Nature provides the blueprint for a better future. If we stop looking at two-year-olds to reinforce our story-world, we will be able to change our path and abide by the eternal structures who made us. If our actions are aligned with our environment, we're able to use our time for the things we love. Even apes understood this to an extent, since their alphas are not exclusively the strongest. A much more important feature is that they do almost all of the work. We should see these people as honorable members of society, because they're driving the human race forward. If the unnecessary fighting stops and they can finally focus on their work, it's hard to imagine what they will achieve. They would become carriers of knowledge and wisdom, someone to ask for advice. The weight on actual accomplishments could be much higher, since the source of progress is creativity instead of an ability to win wars.

Competition will not stop completely, though. Highly specialized teams will challenge each other to mark who is the most useful. Detachment of the exclusive need to win within a respectfully aggressive framework of forward-pushing intelligence. Working toward a better future is possible now, but we have to show that we can be leaders without having authority. Caring for others, helping them realize their potential, is available to everyone, as long as we don't go too far and overstep our abilities. Everyone benefits if we teach others with the simplest language possible, go back to learn about blind spots after, and repeat until we master the topic at hand. Analogy can be of great help to clear up questions, and by gathering perspectives, we gain insight into the process. Meeting people where they are to support building their intelligence improves motivation and trust. The courage to present our solutions might turn forced obedience into honest connections. The word conflict is rooted in Latin "con," which means "together" and "fligere," which means "to strike." It's a tool for creativity. To do good things, we must discipline ourselves. The story loses its power if we stop believing it. The person we were yesterday changes in a slow, incremental process to make up our thoughts and actions of the future. We're constantly rediscovering ourselves. The mind is an invention machine. It wants us to be safe inside a causal progression of reality, and we collectively decide what's acceptable in our world and who needs to alter their behavior in order to be a respected member of society. But if the past is gone and stories fade into nothingness, the old self is not influencing us anymore. While the Greeks preferred largish hips and round breasts, the woman of the Victorian era needed to be frail, pale, and weak. Tattoos once indicated gang associations; they are quite common these days, though. Deviance violates the standards of society, despises expectations, and disregards norms. We all dress and talk in a certain way, and people who don't conform to our stories aren't allowed to play the same game. We wonder what's wrong with them and why they refuse to be one of us. Some of them are considered crazy; others are closer to be regarded as criminals.

Although we might not know a person, we already judged them according to how they look, talk, or walk. What unites us is that we all want to survive and be with our loved ones, but the rest is up to weird trends and capitalist marketing fads. If people fail at the common notion of success, they'll often naturally deviate because there is no other way to make up for their imperfections. The poor deviate to meet their needs, and the wealthy do it to maintain power, but the consequences aren't the same, since money normalizes whatever they've done. However, deviance is necessary to develop new ways to be in the world and to forecast the future.

Although actors sometimes go through massive body modifications to prepare for performances, the average person would be considered a freak if they would attempt to do the same. Following fads may be harmful at times. During the Renaissance, when women used make up containing arsenic and mercury, heavy metal poisoning was quite common. Being late may prevent us from stupid mistakes and not conforming at all might keep us healthy. To differentiate between what's good for us and what's harmful, we need to know who we are and how our individual bodies work. Women seem to be worth more than men, since they're always evacuated first if the ship is sinking. Some cheat to avoid tickets by using their femininity. Deviance is only bad if we're labeling it that way. An actor might be a villain at first; however, the more we get to know them, the more we understand. Bad behavior seems to be unavoidable and adaptation lets us think differently. Breaking the law leads to punishment, though deviation from the norm is inevitable and very widespread. If we lose our families and can't survive on what we earn, we look for alternatives. Culturally defined goals may mark the perfect life during that period; deviance is the result of not being part of it, though. Women often use tactics to destroy their partner. They treat their wishes as unimportant. They prevent them from getting what they want only to hurt them, and they try to shame them by spreading misinformation.

While these can be called deviance, they're also a sign the woman lives inside the story-world and is looking for some kind of pointless revenge. The fear of being harmed eventually gets so intense that men will retreat from all relationships and drop out of society by rejecting norms and the widely promoted culturally accepted means to be successful. It's not entirely clear if women or men suffer more, but they're both regularly treated poorly. Men work the difficult, sometimes life-threatening jobs and often die earlier as a result. Women have to do sex work out of poverty or get sold into sex slavery at a young age. They're frequently suffering from severe trauma and will retreat from sexual relationships as well. Keeping one's dignity is hard enough in these circumstances; calling people out for not wanting to be part of society because of their problems is just wrong, however. The total control over a person is possible by continuously labeling them until they become the label they are given. Chauvinistic men, who have learned about sex mostly from porn, are often desperate for women and will try to reach their goal by any means. They lack the skills to attract a mate, and some never find someone, since they're simply too hideous. Sexual development begins in childhood. Experiences during rough-and-tumble play and other play routines are nonsexual ways of experiencing precursors to the preferences of the later adult. Attraction is partly due to the production of pheromones, which indicate if the partner is genetically compatible. While mental and physical systems work together to bring about the desire and means to have sex, many people will probably say they're more interested in the faculties of the mind. In men, sexuality is the way to channel aggression and frustration. Women tend to like being dominated. Both learn to identify mates based on certain cues, which either stem from our parents and society or get inherited for the survival of the species. Waist to chest ratio matters, and behavior influences arousal.

Men often miss the right context for when sexual arousal is appropriate, especially if they didn't have the opportunity to practice with their fathers. And when the adequate time is over, they're not able to learn it anymore. Rough-and-tumble plays help to regulate aggression, and if the father is less dominant, men don't learn how to control it. As a result, male adults are not able to respect boundaries and frequently behave like an unbelievably stupid moron. Apart from visual triggers, emotions are universal for arousal. Feeling threatened and safe at the same time often occurs in childhood, and we generalize these emotions by generating abstractions to aid sexual arousal during puberty. When the father plays hide-and-seek with his son and regularly goes too far, the boy will not be able to trust women later in life, and arousal mechanisms get confused with uncertainty and an obligation to please the woman in order to be loved. Whereas women oftentimes use previously agreed on routines to assure safety and trust, men try to make them uncomfortable by selectively disappointing expectations. The nice guys are less successful than their aggressive counterparts, since they're just not as arousing to woman. The attention-seeking tactics babies use to feel safe with their mothers include crying, mischievous behavior, and expected as well as forcefully demanded attention. Sometimes, they will also pretend to not care about it. While men need to securely have their egos broken, women must learn to deal with uncertainty and pain. Some babies find out that they're able to control their mothers by adopting assertive or offensive behaviors, which later become important concepts in intimate relationships and for relating to other people. All of the tactics and learned behaviors lead eventually to more or less sophisticated models of love relationships and general modes of being in the world. They are emphasized by positive feedback loops and frequently result in disappointment. When things happen to us time and time again, it's partly not our fault, but if we refuse to learn in order to change our relational patterns, we will experience the same disasters until we die. Also, a lot of people wrongfully think they are natural assholes, although they're looking for love in crooked ways.

Liking these people out of acceptance is obviously wrong, but hating them can't be the solution either. They deserve to learn and must be disciplined as soon as possible, before they're too old and refuse to change. A punisher mindset might be very successful in our society; crushing their egos is therefore seriously required. If women begin to understand these patterns in men, because they're chasing them like fierce dogs, they're often trying to do the work necessary and learn their part in the process. But that also means to practice all the horrible ways to destroy everyone else who is looking for an honest connection. Knowing these things is very important, since they're causing a lot of story-related stress; however, growing up takes time, as bad as it may sound. There are so many things out of our control that anyone who boasts about manipulating fate and the effortless creation of success by means of force and dedication hasn't learned enough yet. We must sit down and explore our own devices. To detect harmful patterns, to practice compassion; and to learn how to love. Mentally healthy children are the result of parents who aren't poor and ready for the job. By paying caregivers and educating them, we might make the future of humanity turn out much better than we might imagine. When spring is knocking on our door, humans tend to experience arousal states more frequently. Hormones sprout out of the system and a new cycle begins. The mind is often rich with fantasies, and we seek mates to calm our libido. As a result, people try to get to the point as fast as possible, disregarding the usual introduction period. Especially men seem to be affected by these hormonal roller coasters, but women are not far behind if at all. To escape from the real world, we're often fantasizing about trying our luck. The thrill of prompt sex even becomes a behavioral addiction for some. Since birth control is not a problem, the stakes are low, and a controlled sex life with rapidly changing partners is often the result. However, women who take the pill may choose different mates than the ones off it.

On the pill, woman prefer more masculine men, and woman off it prefer more intelligent and high-earning types. Divorce rates with masculine men are much higher and are often preceded by going off the pill. The large majority of women divorce their partner as soon as they want to have a child, because they get dissatisfied by their overly masculine appearance. Predator types therefore are wanted to procreate, and the others are preferred to start a family, but that's not how it works. Men will want to act more like a cool uncle, who comes and goes to their liking and brings presents before they leave again, but that's not possible either. So what can we do to solve the problem? Answer: allowing fantasies to happen. Enabling sexual fantasies not only helps the individual to catch up on childhood learning, it ensures they're also more capable of responsible behavior and of having grown-up relationships. To bring it all together, we could ask ourselves what would happen if we would cease using hormone-disrupting birth control pills. May there be a possibility the tyrants and despots of this world would be much less common? Would women be happier? Generalization is useless to predict the future, but it appears obvious that everyone would benefit. BDSM people are regularly attacked for their sexual practices. Psychiatrists try to treat them, as if they had a mental disorder, because their kinks disturb their everyday lives. But they're not alone. The others just don't allow themselves to make these fantasies a reality. If proper development couldn't take place, these thought patterns remain unsolved and hunt us until we allow them to be. Bosses who humiliate their employees out of pleasure know that it's wrong, but subordinates can't fight back, and the desires of their inner compass cannot be addressed. The fear of such activities overflowing into their lives is paralyzing, and crusty moral notions add to the uncertainty. A role exchange would alleviate their situation, though it's crazy to think about it. Violent suppression is often the result, because the thought alone is disgusting to them.

On the other end are softies and people-pleasers, who need to explore their aggression in order to deal with the assholes in their lives. A safe environment to allow these tendencies can be provided in BDSM settings, but it's not the only way. The humiliators could try Brazilian jujutsu and softies might look at weight lifting, full-contact sports, or drumming. By fantasizing about sex, we develop programs to act them out in the real world. While fantasy sparring may be a great way to collect experience with any situation we're afraid of, sexual thoughts centering around an immediate release of energy can be a lot more attractive. The interplay of letting go and holding on change interactional attachment patterns insofar as the partner hugs and kisses us, although we know it cannot go on forever. Adventurous sex has the ability to provide stronger arousal states by strengthening cooperation instead of coercion. It must take place in a trusting environment though. Missionary sex dominates the male by letting them do all the work; blow jobs dominate the woman for the same reason. Maybe that's why our women stop giving blow jobs after marriage. It appears to be the case for a lot of men, and it's mainly due to the entertainment we consume. People cannot have a grown-up relationship if the woman thinks it's about her. Women try to satisfy the subordinate sex dreams of men as long as marriage isn't gluing them together in debt and social constraints. The obligation to please the partner seems to be a tactic to convince men of a woman's trustworthiness, and it's used because predator types wouldn't stay otherwise. As soon as a baby is there, the woman is satiated with body contact anyway and the war is over, because couples are imprisoned by their offspring. The marriage is devastating for both parties in the end, since it's about power struggles in society, not about sharing a life. Any small habit can slowly turn into a reason for endless discussion. Men are often solely seen as breadwinners. Love becomes a means to compensate for insecurities the woman has and because she feels safe in an institution that grants her half of everything if it's over, she demands a myriad of useless stuff.

Society tells her how she has to look, act, and what stereotypes she must cultivate to keep the princess lifestyle she deserves. This causes a lot of fear, since she's constantly disguising herself in order to avoid rejection. The continuous fighting serves to keep the arousal alive, although it may be long gone. To deal with the soon-expected betrayal, she indulges in fantasies in which she avoids emotional harm by foreshadowing deceit. She unconsciously starts to manipulate information and is always looking for proof of her theories. Her spouse must be against her, and she is the victim of a heartless monster of a man. Trying to rationally explain to her that everything is okay isn't possible, because she is violently defending the truth she has manufactured. All the information in favor of the story is emphasized, while actual facts cannot reach her. Fairness, in her mind, only consists of things, which support her well-being alone. Even if the man wants to conform to her demands, she is trying to destroy him and ultimately the relationship. Absolutely obvious facts are turned around until she is right. She infinitely delays the moment of truth and gets angry, although she's cornered by valid counterarguments. Refusing to be honest eventually leads to the rejection she was expecting, and after a period of self-loathing and pain, she may or may not try again. To have the courage to accept the truth, even if it's not pleasant or convenient, could have saved her relationship, but she will cycle through these difficult emotions over and over regardless of who her partner might be. The mere possibility of a relationship is often more desirable than the relationship itself. Longing is love, because honesty hurts. Men frequently feel isolated, since they become a problem to be solved. Not only will she go through all his stuff to find out if he's cheating, she will also spy on him whenever possible. As a result, men are retreating oftentimes into drinking to fight the pain of being alone while being with someone at the same time. Sexual pleasures are far away and masturbation becomes their main sexual activity.

By watching porn, they look at women who are reinforcing the false picture their spouse tries to hold up. Whereas masturbation is a natural instinct people establish during childhood, hour long sessions with nonstop visual overstimulation only lead to a damaged reward system. Although it helps to relearn arousal patterns and releases sexual tension, the overall long-term effect is regularly negative, since addictive patterns get practiced and the benefits of being with a spouse cannot be experienced. It's generally healthier and much more satisfying to be with a partner because nature wanted to make procreation more desirable than practice. Almost all men experience some kind of immediate disinterest after masturbation, and woman benefit psychologically as well as sexually from being with a partner. Masturbation itself is not immoral or bad, nor is it damaging to the body, but sex with another human being is obviously better. Porn is not realistic, and it paints a wrong picture of how sex works with an actual partner. It may be tempting, it can be very harmful for a healthy sexual relationship, however. Men have a strong mating instinct, and just like a cat has the innate urge to eat birds, men will get even more aggressive if the option for sex is taken from them. By being curious for the truth and open minded, woman could stop men from leaving. Grounding assumptions in reality mustn't diminish self-worth. It's fundamental for a healthy relationship. Admitting mistakes is not weak but a sign of adulthood. What we're looking for is not longing; we want a lasting connection based on affection and love instead. Changing our intentions and showing who we are invites real love into our life. A sore heart has a tough time trusting again, but we have to be courageous. Collecting experience helps us to know what we want and who is out there, but focused individuals say no to distractions. Even a broken heart can build trust by quid pro quo. Sometimes it's better to entertain our feelings for a last time and keep the memories, since love and pity are not the same thing.

Having something to aim at is vital to get the wheel of self-discovery going. Trying to accomplish perfection from the start is a recipe for failure, however. The ideas we reaped from our voluntary solitude are critical first impressions of the truth. Following them may turn out as a dead end; the progression will build on the former skill set though. Inner strength cannot come forward if we let our emotions get in the way, because we think of all the things that could go wrong. Patterns of avoidance arise out of fear and a feeble mind. An intrinsic drive to move toward freedom combined with a courageous heart enables us to take the next step in spite of the pain that results from generating initial momentum. If we focus on purposeful behavior, our feelings will align with our intention and can be understood in context with the task. They're still there, but we're able to observe them without stopping on our path. Forcing ourselves to finish whatever we're doing trains our endurance. Embracing the thing we hate the most ensures its completion and overrides patterns of autonomic fight or flight responses. When the urge to quit is at its maximum and we're still able to stand tall, our outlook on life changes dramatically. Extreme stress and total exhaustion are indicators for reaching the point of no return. Quitting is an easy road to avoid challenging feelings; surviving utmost suffering and pain cement a powerful mind, though. The experience to know the right time to stop develops, if balancing between reason and taking the smallest step forward has become the norm. When reaching another block is its own reward, enduring pain turns into pleasure. Directing our aversion at our old self cuts through bad habits, and rewarding ourselves for reaching milestones makes the effort more worthwhile. Mastering limits doesn't mean we'll never feel anxiety or frustration again, it means acknowledging our limited existence to be able to face fears and live our truth. Purpose is not a man-made concept, it is our reason to live. To have the opportunity to work on ourselves is a blessing, since it only takes a single person to believe in someone.

If our past ideas generate their own positive feedback loop, we can too. The core of actualization is that the things around us can be transformative and even magical. We'll never know how far we might have come if we don't dare to pursue our highest potential. True satisfaction is witnessing our dreams fall into place, and it often happens when we have forgotten to meditate about them since we're absorbed by something else. Some people say there is more truth to the mask than we can find inside. However, our masks are gathering experiences, stories, and biases to support the narrative of our life, which we created to cultivate our shared reality in order to locate ourselves in a falsely constructed hierarchy. The brain is a decentralized network of ideas, controlled by a group of participants who are democratically voting for the truth. If all experiences in our world created the umbrella role, we have managed to convince enough nodes of the story's validity. All paths lead to one, often worthless idea we're basing our decisions on. Decentralization is normally used to prevent a single power from getting too big, since this is what tumors do, but repeating the same story over and over turns even the most diverse network into a source of immovable suffering. False happiness comes from upholding ideas we don't really want, which ultimately leaves us confused on why it doesn't feel right. It's so hard to let go because it worked in the past, even if it inflicted a lot of pain on us. Sometimes it helps to shake the snowball in order to forget these ideas; however, what we really should do is produce as many perspectives as possible. By first placing an innocent idea into the system, we ensure it doesn't get attacked too much and can survive even though it's surrounded by enemies, who feed on false causality. This invites more open-minded friends to join, and by supporting these friends, the threshold will slowly tilt toward the new paradigm, if we regularly talk, think, and act on them.

One change has the power to force the narrative to self-destruct, but in order to succeed, we need more points of view. Our desire for recognition frequently leads to the distribution of lies and the need for honoring supports rumors, which we almost never verify. What if we let the story collapse by dismissing our self-importance? Changing what we are able to change is all we can do; trying to change what we can't is insane, however. Our starting point will be lower. Doing the job well will push it higher and higher, though. Perfection is reached if we gave it everything we had so that there is no reason to feel like a failure. Quality is a habit, but nothing is lost if we've learned something. Info is what we need. As much as we can bear. Fully loading the brain to its utmost capacities. Blasting processor power to the absolute maximum. It doesn't matter how long it takes; the quantity of accessible ideas count. Even if we're struggling hard, the only way to recognize the patterns we look for is to have everything handy. Finding the end of the labyrinth results in comprehensive knowledge of the system and encircles possibilities for advancement of the current paradigm. A cul-de-sac is a blessing, because it kills off the amount of paths. Testing idea paths needs low autonomic arousal, since more of it inspires the brain to push for quick fixes. A high level of autonomic arousal is required to increase cognitive load, though. Drowsy states turn a branched-out tree of information into an ocean of possibility. It has no spatial boundaries, and everything has the same properties. The fourth dimension loses its meaning while the initial premise often dissolves under the weight of conflicting information. To swim freely without disregarding anything makes powerful creativity possible. The processor drain lessens, if we realize that stress and excitement can be felt at the same time. Thought is one after another, emotion is the sea. Perfect working functionality can only be accomplished by finding the right balance between arousal states. Every work is different, and people have varying starting points in life. Pushing toward our limits can be very stressful and might result in health issues over time.

This is only true, however, if we regard stress as a health hazard or fail to recognize our boundaries. To change the perception of stress, we first need to know what it does. Cognitive symptoms include memory problems, the inability to concentrate, and poor judgment. Emotional symptoms are feeling bad, depressed, overwhelmed, and angry among others. This causes dizziness, racing heart, and reduced sex drive and often leads to interrupted sleep and alcohol usage to lessen the impact. Retraining ourselves to regard stress as a tool instead of an enemy is essential to be successful with our intentions. Heart rate, body temperature, and muscle tension indicate the degree of fight or flight response in the body. It was initially designed to fend off inside and outside invaders in order to aid survival. Thus, it also has positive effects like improving memory, attention span, and immune response. On one end is collapse from a too-low heart rate; on the other is a panic attack that lasts for many minutes. We can think of stress responses in terms of threats or challenges. Threats usually result in fear; an interesting challenge has the power to motivate us. When people ask for safe spaces to avoid discrimination or harassment, they often look for environments in which their opinions are not getting challenged. Fearing to be marginalized results in dodging other points of view in order to prevent a feeling of inferiority. Humble people wouldn't do these things, since they're able to zoom out and realize that fear may turn into panic. By showing who they are, they're showing their willingness to learn. Even if it hurts. Fear isn't bad, only holding on to it turns a challenge into a threat. Going forward can feel dreadful, but it's also most rewarding, since it makes us joyful and the fear dissolves into nothing. Tough challenges are more bearable if we know why it's worth it. Once we're able to balance our responses, fear turns into pride. Our attitude about stress makes us fearful and tired, not stress itself. Changing it for the better will refine our ability to be optimistic and strong. To feel clear, alert, and ready to go, it's best to regard stress as useful. While bumping up the stress response is much easier than slowing it down, a few strategies can be helpful to get us in the right state.

Cold affusions are an advanced technique to push the immune response. Done right, they're very versatile and can be used for many things. Loud music and exercise also has the ability to get us going. Changing our breathing pattern is helpful in both directions though. As a rule of thumb, nose breathing is preferrable, and the diaphragm has to move down as we breathe in and up as we breathe out. Longer inhales and shorter exhales generate energy and boost heart rate; shorter inhales and longer exhales slow the system down. People who want to learn a more sophisticated version should look into pranayama, which is probably the best breathing technique out there. Another trick to calm down is called the physiological sigh, which can often be observed when people recover from crying. It consists of at least two quick inhales and a longer exhale. While it's not easy to bring down heart rate by physiological means, it is still possible, but there are mind-related strategies as well. The body and the mind are parts of a single system, but in between, there is a gap. Observing the stress pattern and not engaging in it needs practice, but it prevents us from freaking out. Longer exhales, combined with a compassionate mind, open up a world of calm and peace on the inside. It's the eye of the storm. Reactivity is diminished, and the more we train, the easier it is to deal with increasingly challenging states. Especially if a person is triggering us with contrasting ideas, we should always mind the gap. If we zoom out even more, it becomes clear that we're even able to observe our thoughts. The heart might be pounding, but observing a storm is much better than being blown away by it. Caring for others oftentimes creates resilience in times of adversity. High quality CBD oil has no serious side effects and brings heart rate and blood pressure down for up to twenty-four hours. Low confidence and low stress is not constructive. Low confidence and high stress makes us agitated and nervous. High confidence and high stress lets us explode. High confidence and balanced stress is perfect to perform optimally.

Besides changing perceptions and influencing the body, there are also other ways to condition our stress response. By determining deadlines, we are motivated to put in more work and if we hold ourselves accountable for our results, we'll archive more. Positive reinforcement is a cookie or a hug; negative reinforcement is the lack thereof. Setting realistic milestones prevents us from cutting corners; and reaching them should lead to something special. Hard work may be nerve racking, and multiple dead ends are frustrating; however, as long as we take regular breaks and look after ourselves, stress will help us succeed. Whereas success is the thing most of us want, we must be clear that individual success is about being better than we were yesterday. Balancing pleasure and pain assists us to stay motivated, and when we finally realize the joy of development lies in the here and now, we can stop projecting our happiness into the future. More and more people discover the power of being present, because it annihilates the pain of craving. To become the best version of ourselves, we need to make it automatic. For a severe addict, this may sound blasphemous, but it works. The temptation must be out of the question. Not messing with the topic grants us the freedom to do something else. We're just stopping it, since we're not fighting against it. The secret is to disregard the consequences and not weighing pros and cons. It has become second nature, since we simply can't do it any longer. We're not trying to stop it, because we're just not messing with it. It's over. Nothing is forever until it is. Giving up things in this way feels like losing something we need to live. As if we can't exist without it. The bond to an addiction is strong if it served us well, and it hurts to let it go just like that. But in reality, it didn't serve us in any way, it only filled the emptiness of our hearts, since we craved connection and contentment. An evolved human is perfectly rational with a slight tilt toward compassion. The leader of a meaningful life. But where do we go, if we decide to pursue loneliness in order to find the truth?

People will most likely stop understanding us or even try to keep us at their level. On one side, we want to explore who we are, whereas at the same time, we want to avoid becoming an outsider. Others often perceive us as rather odd if we're at work to uncover what's buried under our conditioning. And indeed, freedom causes differences to shine. A unique person is one who is courageous enough to deviate from the norm and committed enough to work on their deepest resentments and fears. The prize is a revolution of the mind, a metamorphosis from a follower to a responsible person. It's a privilege to grow up, not a nuisance. Being outside the system lets us see the potential of the present. An enthusiastic attitude toward unpopular things adds to a unique perspective. To put our mind to all the small details of a project not only shows our obsession and the fun it provides, it also helps us to assemble the future. If dreams become our reality, we have tried enough to know the truth. It's not a shame to use our hands to craft something beautiful and it's not superior to work exclusively with the mind. Slow progress prevents discrepancy and creates longevity. A craftsman knows the how, a planner zooms out, and a thinker asks why. They are all equally needed. When we discover the wonderful world of our interests, we joyfully immerse ourselves in order to master them. Finding a mentor is great, but not a prerequisite. To learn from our idols, we have to observe closely to get to the end of the labyrinth. Modeling is the false way to mastery; gathering information and learning about dead ends is. We want to be ourselves, but we're also respecting the priceless wisdom of the past and the knowledge of the present. Every person is different, and to serve people well, we need to make sure we're working according to our zoom level. A shoemaker is different from a street planner. A writer likes to work in a nice study. A carpenter enjoys working with wood. But all of them have unique feet. If the things we're creating are worth the price, when our life is in balance with who we are, when our desires fit with our honest imagination, a normal life is not as boring and simple as people might think.

It's, in fact, all we can ever ask for. Contrary to the reality of the story world, people may be content if they're living in the now and in alignment with the cycles of life. The word limitation represents a scarcity that only exists in the mind of the consumer, not in the creative mind of an explorer. People who embrace exploration will never be alone; they will be part of something greater instead. The fast production of our time is hyperefficient. It places profits before dignity, mass above quality, and money above all else. A normal worker, on the other hand, is worth nothing. Human capital is a term to show the lower classes what they are to the big corporations: disposable robots. This won't stop until we wipe the story out of existence. When the future rings and all the lowly paid jobs disappear, what are people supposed to do? Sit in front of their TVs while they wait for new products to arrive at the warehouses? New trends will be realized the day they come out. Tons of products will only exist for their novelty, not their usefulness. Things will work, since efficiency is king, but nothing will be truly beautiful. When all the countries are "developed" and the last folk is eradicated, the only thing left is to lie down and die, because there is no culture left. Where do we put our creativity to work? Where will our existence thrive? Nobody knows. But what we do know is that our hand is able to produce marvelous works of art. That diversity will make us stronger if we let it. That everyone has a right to live and to express who they are. Some might not be able to contribute in a big way, since they have the obligation to move slowly to a slightly better self, but the rest is free to explore the infinite depths of the human condition. Machinery is there to make creativity possible, not to measure our performance. Manuals may provide repetitive processes, but only humans can go beyond that. A computer doesn't know if a thing it created is useful, since machines miss the ability for creative abstraction. Creativity can't be measured; it's there to produce meaning and waves of happiness instead.

If people with diverse skillsets meet to serve the market by manufacturing individual handmade trousers, they would be useful and beautiful all at once. Can we put our individuality above all else to serve the greater good, without falling into the trap of selfishness? The endless challenge of improvement and growth doesn't oppose the moment; it enhances it carefully. The future will bring major changes. We'll have unbelievable amounts of data, and we need scientists who work with it. More and more data occupations are becoming available without a degree, since they're in demand right now. Solving problems using data doesn't have to be nasty business. It can actually help the world, if it's used with the right intention. Blockchain-enabled worldwide competition is a good one for example. The blockchain is able to verify data without the need for intermediaries. It's a decentralized system with which data can be trusted. Once inside the chain, data cannot be changed or destroyed, but it can be restricted for only a certain group to see or to protect private information. It would easily wipe out the mass surveillance culture of dubious workplaces, and it would turn insane quantitative targets into worker-controlled projects. The term artistic craftmanship is used in copyright legislation to protect all kinds of works. As long as we are conscious about our intention to produce a work of art and combine it with skill and aesthetics, many works can be called art. The huge world of handicrafts or older, more traditional crafts, which should be preserved for the future, are great ways for anyone to express themselves. Watchmaker, for instance, is an endangered craft many people appreciate. Some might wonder, since so many watch brands came up in recent time, but they're all basically cheaply produced low-quality mass products, made in China. What normally required an intensive design process, high quality materials, and meticulous quality control is now a bulk operation with individually stamped-on logos, where all the money is used for sneaky marketing tactics and bought reviews.

If our products are worth the money and made to the highest standards, marketing is only needed to inform the customer of their true properties, not to persuade them with lies. Congruent overlaps between tradition and modernity ensure familiarity in order to depart into the future. Conventionally approved means to work in society and the picture of the painfully successful life that comes with it cannot lead to a better world. We need new goals and new means to show our intention for connection and collaboration, and we cannot trust authorities, since they're trying to uphold the status quo. We're responsible for our reality and contribution. We need designers, craftsmen, farmers, chefs, helpers, teachers, and everyone else who is willing to make a rich world possible. We need many more worker-owned businesses apart from the already established ones, where quality and narrow competition create room for people to thrive. Where work is fun a lot of the time. Where we're allowed to explore possibilities to create our unique footprint. Where we can enjoy the fruits of our authenticity, not of our obedience. We're expressing a big part of our inner world through our work, and with practice and experimentation, we will be able to reach a permanent change of the story. Our story. The question is what story we're willing to believe in. A work of art declares our style, it shows who we are, and it results in timeless value. Reinterpreting tradition by mixing it with modern techniques makes fast innovation possible. We're all artists in some way, and we're here to express the meaning given to us. If our vision of the future enables us to feel inspired and free, the world will become a place we're not able to fully picture right now. Social evolution begins with every one of us. If we contribute in a meaningful way, there's no reason to keep a great idea to ourselves. Competition is needed, but if everyone has the same starting point, we'll evolve much faster. The best thinkers deserve their prizes; however, contribution becomes possible by encouraging fair achievement.

If competitive people need to know who's best, an effective way is to provide the same tools and means, but it's also not right to steal. Finding the middle way is important to move forward fairly. We need to know what the people want, who they are, and where they live. We need to talk to them about their situation and create products from their point of view. Our job is to improve them until they become unique. Beautiful products are often made with wealthy buyers in mind, but it doesn't have to be this way. Great design is not dependent on price, and reliable function stems from simplicity. A manual toothbrush is the same for everyone, since it fulfills a basic need. Even expensive brushes don't offer anything special. To make everyday products beautiful and expensive products available is the mission. By asking questions and slowly building our skills, we can start from where we are. Throwing infinite whys at certain problems might surprise us. Connecting emotion and functionality powers creativity. Gathering open-minded people with a similar intention gets the job done. Preferring locally sourced materials keeps cost down, and reusing the resources around us may provide a way to begin, if the money is missing. By consistently reevaluating what we're working on, we're actively avoiding bad choices. As our work gets more complicated, it often pays to radically change perspective and start from scratch to make everything better and more efficient. Beginning a new story is not easy, and changing the premise will take time; however, a trojan horse always finds a way to infiltrate. A silent rebellion begins with working inside the system. By providing goods and services as everyone else, we have the opportunity to influence the players and ultimately change the game, if enough of them are willing to see the benefits of change. As people spread out of the city when transportation ceases to be an issue any longer, we'll live in small communities again and diversity will be needed to assure microsocieties operate successfully.

There will be endless opportunities to learn and explore. To be apprentices to masters and to discover our possibilities. The standard way will become obsolete, and efficiency will have its place next to a compassionate heart. We don't need to wait for a long time to begin a new story, though. We're able to contribute right now, as long as we do it in a way we think is fair. If a complete city of seventy thousand people can get their services and goods for free because all of its inhabitants believe in it, we should take a closer look at why the Burning Man festival is gathering more and more visitors. While it's not the solution to our problems, it shows that change is possible, if we agree on a new shared reality. This is certainly a life worth thriving for, and although it seems far away, going back only two hundred years reveals the massive jump from a violent species to ever more subtle ways of competition, which is the path we're headed. Money is simply a belief system, and if we could stop judging everything by its price, we might start to appreciate life more. If we don't have enough money to live, we often get desperate and become more foolish. A lack of certainty prevents us from doing courageous things. Poor people cannot simply start investing, if they don't even have the means to eat. If we don't know whether we should laugh or cry, the situation is already out of hand. The act of laughing frees us from the burden of existence, even if it's only for a short period of time. Time seems to change the moment our perception changes. Although the past is always behind us and time only moves in one direction, it stops existing in states of immersion. It's part of every story, and we couldn't tell the tale of our life without it. There would be no tomorrow and no progression. But whereas time is essential to tell a story, it's just another perspective inside of it. The more perspectives there are, the more rich and thrilling the story can get. By living inside of it, immersed in the beauty of a piece of art, we can sense its worth. We never know where a painting or a piece of music will take us. Art brings people together because the feeling of losing ourselves creates a connection to the infinite richness of the universe. Nothing is missing when we laugh together.

Beauty is pleasing us without asking for anything. Once we experienced it, we carry it inside of our hearts, and we might never forget its importance to our story. Even if we don't get along with certain people, our emotions may unite us in the love for a creative idea that is taking our breath away. Dissolving our perception lets us swim in a fluent emotion, where many different states are possible at the same time. Artists look for consistency they sometimes don't understand themselves. Truth derives from a consistency we all believe in. Imperfections make us perfect for the story we have to tell. Existence not only tells a story, it also guides us through it. Waiting cannot tell a story. Certainty cannot tell a story. Weakness has no voice. Laughter shows our vulnerability. Embracing the beautiful idiocy of life enables us to laugh in its face during terrible times. Trying to control outcomes only hinders our ability to witness the truth. We cannot opt out of our life. We're the creators of our reality, even if we have no control over it. If we carry ourselves too seriously and cannot joke about our tragedy, we miss an immensely important perspective. When expected outcomes don't happen and we're lacking acceptance, we totally missed the punchline. Our own life is already enough reason to burst out in laughter, and we don't even need help from others to be a vulnerable idiot. Jokes may be on us or about us, against us or with us, but they are always funny. Everyone has the right to be laughed at equally. Bullies exist because they feel less alone and their life matters more when they've found a target to shoot their insecurities at. Laughing at them is not what they expected though. Enjoying a good joke with friends dissolves tensions and clears the spirit. It helps to make sense of the world, and it creates laughs out of suffering. Humor mirrors the horrors of society, and laughter alleviates the pain of hearing the truth. The impact of art belongs to us, as long as the intention of the creator is not revealed. Removing the mysticism behind our intention robs the adventure of life of its infinite meaning. The finite human mind is not capable of connecting every aspect into a congruent whole, unless the journey has come to an end.

Art has profound effects on the observer, if the experience is immersive, believable, and interesting. When people are shown parts of themselves that need attention, they're often able to change by virtue of being moved alone. If the intention is revealed and the meaning settled, the artwork becomes a commodity. People, who collectively agree on its meaning will want to buy and possess it, just so others admire them. They buy meaning to be a respected person, to show their wealth, and to keep their money moving. However, others simply enjoy the beauty of it and want it to embellish their living rooms. Artists deserve to make a living out of their work. A better solution to pay them would be a blockchain-enabled attention payment though. The possibility for a physical ownership should still be there, but the impact they create is a better indicator for success. People should be able to support the artists directly and without intermediaries, who will not be needed, since the distribution is immediate and in control of the creators. The solution to the poverty of artists lies in fairness. The enjoyment of an artwork depends on our sensemaking mechanisms. Electric signals get transmitted to the brain via the optic nerve, where they stimulate neural activity. Specific arousal patterns are responsible to represent color perception. Our brain filters bend and mend information to create representations of the experience within our story. To communicate what we see, we use language to tell others about our specific perceptions, which we previously agreed on. While the general idea of how colors look is virtually universal, people will always differ a bit about their representation of the exact color they're looking at. Development of these verbal representations follows a certain sequence in humans. At first, we're naming black and white, and then we find words for red, green, yellow, and blue. Some languages have only the first three; others have more. The succession doesn't always work this way, but it's common enough to serve as a general guideline. To name colors, we negotiate with others about our perceptions. But are we able to understand a color solely by the description given to us?

Assuming we know everything from detailed scientific papers and countless stories, would we be able to picture the exact same thing in our minds? How can a blind person represent the color red in their mind, if they've never seen it? They obviously can't. Experience itself can't be solely physical if awareness is needed for a congruent understanding to appear. The sum of the parts is not sufficient to gain knowledge of the world. A perfect reproduction of a bird might be able to fly, but will it be able to live? The recreation of complex life-forms is impossible without conscious experience. If languages are not capable of representing reality completely, there must be something else making up our experience of life. There exist quintessential limitations to what we can learn from materialist thinking, since feelings need consciousness. This difference is very important, because it shows that the framework of understanding is dependent on a basic assumption. If our view of the world is influenced by a collection of parts, which we believe represent reality, we will never know how it actually looks. The more representations we are able to hold at the same time, the more reality we will experience. When an experiment is reproducible, does that mean it conveys the ultimate truth? No, because the truth must take all perspectives into account. A system of two things is relatively easy to describe, since interactions can be controlled as far as measurement goes. Systems, which consist of three or more members, become infinitely complex rather quickly. A general paradigm to answer the most important questions can't be determined by a limited worldview. If two identical systems start to move, they will always end in the same place, but a tiny change in one of them has the force to disrupt the causality to an unbelievable extent. There is no way to picture reality without generalization. Thus, we will never be able to understand reality completely, but it's at least feasible to sense the meaning inside of it. If scientists think they have all the answers because a reproduction works, they've restricted other perspectives. Entertaining sensory interactions with our surroundings dissolves the thinking mind and opens the gate to understanding.

If we want to know the secrets of life, we must have a clear intention and an open heart. A deep knowledge can only arise if we're aware of our blind spots and allow them to vanish. Becoming aware of everything: colors, smells, tastes, and the multitude of other perceptions, we exchange our previous set of assumptions with the richness of experience. The analytical mind must be included, since we need it for a conclusive representation, but it's ultimately flawed and cannot extract meaning. The simplest explanation is the most difficult, and the mind of the child is the perfect starting point to transmit experience to others. When we're afraid and long for security, the ego wants to help us built confidence, but killing fear is futile. Our bodies try to make us aware of things our analytical mind cannot understand. Their magnetism can be very real, if we constantly get pulled into a certain direction. It's resonance that brings the mind back again and again. What interests us is often not even in our hands or cannot be explained rationally. Feeling great or anxious about a situation is a valid marker for good judgment. Simply listening to our gut is not the whole of it, but it gives us an idea of the workings of our awareness. Clarity and fogginess indicate further ways to find out what to focus on. Allowing our indescribably complex sensemaking mechanism to bring about the necessary changes prevents us from getting sick. Observing what affects us and where our anxious feelings come from guides us to the source of our misery. Having the courage to look it in the eye resolves its power over us and lets the fear evaporate into nothingness. Dreams have many different functions, but if we treat them in perspective to our current experiences, we can extract hints to what they might mean. Believing a certain story for a time is useful to move forward; not allowing life to change by holding on is irresponsible. Emotional sensemaking can be much more effective than thought; however, it isn't always right. Rationally thinking about our problems simplifies complicated issues to graspable chunks and helps to achieve reality. Sometimes, we must stop, think, listen, regroup, and come back to a problem to actually know how to fix it.

Since people cannot be put into categories of fixed characteristics, we can only fairly interact with them by respecting the present moment first and the perceptions and facts after. As long as the initial judgment is leaned toward the positive, we have the option to disregard the story and truly listen to the person. There is music that only unfolds over time and cannot be understood otherwise. Really understanding people is a task of a lifetime, and even then the end cannot be reached. Good and bad lose their meaning in the face of complexity. Admitting unawareness of the truth is the first step to actually finding it. If the truth cannot be verified completely, it's hard to judge people by the limited understanding we have. Disbelief and certainty both need proof to be entirely correct. When children are raised in a naive way, they often can't help but to find themselves in a false story. Transmission is unavoidable, and nature combined with nurture make their self into the individual standing in front of us. There must be a belief to begin with, or else we can't move in the world. If we cannot get misconduct out of our head, we might have missed the teaching. People can change, and although it's understandable to close down in certain situations, almost everyone deserves the benefit of the doubt and a second chance. Thinking about payback only corrupts our reasoning. We should negotiate with ourselves when to let go or when it's worth it to investigate further. Talking with friends and family might provide more perspectives. Feedback frees us from circular reasoning and being stuck. Thinking can become an addiction, and endless "what if" questions don't add anything meaningful. Former experiences must be taken into account; however, the past is over and the future is not yet here. The expectations and beliefs we hold toward another person influence our actions. They're impacting the self-perception of the person and cause their actions toward us to change. Our beliefs will be gradually positively reinforced until we're able to completely let go of our perception, since we've successfully built a feedback loop. When we go out in the woods, there are a lot of crooked trees that haven't gotten enough light.

Accepting them without judgment honors the forest and acknowledges imperfection without hurting others. An individual consists of endlessly nested social organisms with complex layers, which all live inside of a fluid continuum. Biological and physical systems are basically the same, except they're spread out differently. The word "true" comes from Old English "treow," which means "good faith" and "trust," but also "tree." A word may tell an entire story, and the older the word, the richer it is. True means "factually correct and faithful to reality," but the earliest correspondence is linked with the uprightness of a tree. Trees are among the oldest organisms on earth. Some believe that Pando in Utah could be one million years old. Planting a tree supports all other beings around it by nourishing the soil through mycorrhizal networks and increased water retention. Time and space are concepts to describe the truth.

Circumstances are bound to time and space. Uniting all perspectives into a concordant story is the last answer. Our emergent reality only cares for where the story goes in the frame of its unlimited possibilities. The truth expresses itself through us and with everything we will imagine. Great art has no ulterior motives; it just is. By seeing the beauty of existence, we experience a solution to the deepest questions. Why is there something rather than nothing? Why not kill ourselves and stop all this miserable suffering? Why do anything if the sad story of our life is all there is? Why work hard if there is no prize at the end of the tunnel? Radical acceptance shields us from losing our mind. An answer to these questions might be a craving for experience, an evaporating drop of adventure on a warm stone in the middle of the night. Beauty is all around us if we dare to see it. Balance is the initial state, but it must always be disturbed to keep the narrative going. Our perception might lead to happiness or pain; the next tendency is coming nonetheless, though. After infinite iterations, it's all the same to the observer. The universe needs the other, a means to differentiate one thing from another. There can be no perspectives if everything must be equal. Nothing would exist! Maybe it's an illusion we cannot grasp. A projection we cannot understand.

Knowledge has only one dimension; knowing to know has two; knowing to know what we know is the third. But it gets impractical if we want to describe further abstractions. This is where feelings start. Time is not a thought, it's a perception. A nice dinner in a beautiful space has no worth until we taste the food and enjoy the surroundings. Our experience will make sense if we create a unique perspective. Our accomplishments will become outdated someday, but we helped other people, who will come after us. If we build our life on reputation, we'll suffer tremendously if we find out we were wrong. One of the hardest truths for the ego is that it doesn't matter. We should never forget this is our life and we want to look further instead of settling. If there's even the slightest possibility for things to get better, it would be stupid to end everything too early. We cannot know if a death wish is inspired by a stupid story and should try everything to find the truth first. Although other people might be suffering much more than us, a comparison is not possible since we live in our own reality. Therefore, we cannot diminish our suffering by contrasting, only by thorough investigation. A plot twist sometimes emerges out of nothing, and maybe that's what we always wanted but never wished for. We should consider each new problem by itself and whether worrying about it will make a real difference. By changing our perspective, we change our story, but true freedom is the absence of any story. By throwing it out like a pair of old shoes, we're able to free up energy to discover ourselves anew. Regardless of how much effort we invested to create our story, it's most likely still false. Using all our senses is where freedom begins. Experiencing actual reality is often hard, but thinking about it isn't the same as living with it. To exist without thinking is possible, but accepting the numbness caused by the fear of allowing certain emotions robs us of all possibility. Others cannot be in charge of our life, and fulfillment can only come if we dare to go all the way. Freedom requires us to think for ourselves. It'll make us uncomfortable, and it needs responsibility. When we take control of our life, we often don't know where to start, but a long journey always begins with the first step.

We'll learn to grow our skills and to live perfectly aligned with our truth. Constant growth may be exhausting, but frequent breaks help us to relax, and regular reevaluations will keep us engaged. Freedom allows us to trust people who deserve it. Finding the truth gives us the opportunity to move with confidence in the world. Controlling our beliefs will get much harder and our livelihood will come from a work we love. When everything was chaos and only a tiny point of life existed, another point came into existence to create the first dimension. In the second dimension, we're only able to perceive 2D things. Everything has a length and a width, but no depth. Seeing 3D things would mean to see something getting bigger and smaller again until it vanishes. The third dimension is our everyday experience. It has length, width, and height. The fourth dimension is time, and observed from the fifth dimension, it looks like we're inside of a snake, which starts at birth and ends with death. Thus, in the third dimension, we can't see the progression of our existence, only the state we are in now. Zooming farther out, the fourth dimension turns into a timeline of the universe until it ends, and time travel would be possible from the sixth dimension. Jumping to the sixth dimension turns the fifth into all possible causality chains, if all the chains had the same conditions as they started. A 3D space that would contain all possible futures. The seventh dimension grants us an overview of all initial conditions. Alternate timelines with different starting conditions would cause infinite infinity, though, and we can view them from the eighth. The nineth dimension contains all histories, starting conditions, and laws of physics, and the tenth covers everything we can imagine. It contains all possible everything. That allows for a bold closing. We are all one!

AFTERWORD

THANK YOU FOR READING *Not Really*. I hope you've found something of value in this book. It would mean a lot to me, if I inspired you to go out and enrich the world with your unique perspective. As I'm writing this, there are many questions popping up in my mind. Wouldn't it be great to establish another way of looking at the world? Wouldn't everyone benefit if we'd be able to unite in diversity? What if we all stopped believing in false stories? Homogenous groups will always hold prejudices, but the more diversity exists, the harder it will be to find allies who are willing to fight.

If you want to tell me something or have a question, you can contact me via my website.

Stefaneberhard.com/Contact

If you are interested in upcoming books or simply want to stay in touch, you can follow my mailinglist.

Stefaneberhard.com/Mailinglist

It's quite remarkable how little we actually know if we only look from one perspective. Please take the time to review my book at the store you bought it from. I'm very curious to know what you think and it would help spread the word. Thanks again for going on this journey with me.

Much love,
Stefan

Made in the USA
Monee, IL
10 May 2025